LIORA BLAKE

First Step Forward

POCKET BOOKS

New York   London   Toronto   Sydney   New Delhi

Pocket Books
An Imprint of Simon & Schuster, Inc.
1230 Avenue of the Americas
New York, NY 10020

First Pocket Books paperback edition December 2016

POCKET and colophon are registered trademarks of Simon & Schuster, Inc.

For information about special discounts for bulk purchases, please contact Simon & Schuster Special Sales at 1-866-506-1949 or business@simonandschuster.com.

The Simon & Schuster Speakers Bureau can bring authors to your live event. For more information or to book an event, contact the Simon & Schuster Speakers Bureau at 1-866-248-3049 or visit our website at www.simonspeakers.com.

Interior design by Bryden Spevak

Manufactured in the United States of America

10 9 8 7 6 5 4 3 2 1

ISBN 978-1-5011-5511-6
ISBN 978-1-5011-5512-3 (ebook)

First Step Forward

= 1 =

(Cooper Lowry)

There are two types of hits you take in pro football: the kind you see coming and the kind you don't. And after eight years in the game, given the choice, I would take a surprise hit every time. Why? Because thousands of hits later, I've learned that the rag-doll effect will be to my advantage. If I see that human freight train coming, I will tense up; it's only human nature. When I do, that hit will sing through every nerve ending, every joint, even the smallest bones in my toes.

Five minutes ago, that's exactly what happened—I had a front-row seat to my own impending pile-up and ended up taking the *wrong* kind of hit. So hard that I felt compelled to check and see if any of my teeth were knocked loose before trying to stand up. Once I'd determined that all my pearly whites were still intact, I jogged over to the sidelines and tried to appear unfazed.

My eyes stay fixed on the field, that lush green expanse surrounded by everything I've ever wanted. A full stadium, a jersey with my last name on the back, and a fourth-quarter clock ticking down to a win. We're in the red zone, and my last catch got us there. Unfortunately, getting there also involved a strong safety known as "Stinger" bulldozing my ass to the ground. The nickname? It suits him. I ended up looking like a Slinky gone haywire in midair and hit the ground in a pile.

"Lowry. Over here, kid. We gotta do this."

When Hunt snaps his fingers in front of my face, I tilt my head and give him my best *don't worry, doc* expression. A team trainer is either your best friend or your worst enemy, depending on what you need. Trainers have the good stuff: the pain meds, the sleeping pills, and the sideline syringe that keeps you in the game. They also deftly ignore your bullshit, refuse to believe that *don't worry* smile, and with one signature, they can have you on the sidelines in a suit and tie instead of a uniform.

"What month is it, Lowry?"

"October."

"What day of the week is it?"

"Sunday."

"Who scored last?"

A grin slips on my face. "Us. Me, specifically."

Hunt shakes his head and grins back. At the end of the third quarter, I caught a wide-open pass and sauntered into the end zone like a king. That put us up by fourteen points and now, with less than a minute on the clock, it's nearly guaranteed we'll leave the field with a win.

But nothing in this world is a sure thing. I don't care how close a victory feels or looks; shit happens. Guys fumble. Lightning strikes. A naked nut job parachutes onto the field. Zombies storm the stadium. Live television and pro sports mean anything goes, so there are no assurances that all four couldn't happen at the same damn time.

My eyes dart back to the field—on the lookout for those pesky zombies—and Hunt gives my arm a thump with his tablet.

"Jesus Christ, Lowry. You aren't going to miss anything; it's in the bag. Let's finish this thing."

He refrains from grabbing the face mask on my helmet and giving it a jerk until I pay attention, because under the scrutiny of the league's mandatory concussion protocols, that sort of shit is a thing of the past. These days, after a rough hit, instead of a whack to the back of the head and a command to shake it off, we end up on the sidelines answering inane questions about how we feel and standing on one leg like a flamingo to show we won't fall over, all just to prove our brains aren't entirely scrambled.

I tip my chin down and paste on an earnest expression.

"Hunt, just give me this. The last few seconds. Then you can ask me every stupid question you need to. I won't even threaten your life when you point that annoying little light in my eyes."

Giving up with a sigh, Hunt tucks his tablet under his arm and flops down on the bench, knowing it's easier to give in on this one. Leaning back, he puts his hands on top of his head, clasping his fingers together, and tries to relax.

If I'm not on the field and in the middle of it all, savoring the last few minutes of a game is my favorite time. Always has been, because when I was a kid, my first coach told us those were the seconds that mattered. In those moments, he said, we would understand the truth about success, failure, and teamwork. In my eight-year-old mind, everything he said was already the gospel, so I believed every word.

When the clock hits zero, the crowd noise surges—seventy thousand half-drunk people in the Rocky Mountain altitude who don't give a shit about anything but us right now. Our win, their win—in this city, no one can tell the difference.

Hunt stands again and cocks his head in my direction, silently asking if we can get this over with now. With a single nod from me, he's back on task, asking me to repeat words back to him, recite a series of numbers, and stand still for his inspection. When we get to the part where I have to lift one foot off the ground, a twitch in my knee nearly sets me off balance.

But I've done this all before. I know how to answer the questions and command my body to do what it should. You don't survive eight years playing pro ball without learning the right answers.

"Scale of one to six. Zero means none present. Six means severe. Head pain?"

"Zero."

Lie. The pain brewing at the base of my skull, where the occipital nerve meets my spine, feels like it might snap into a hundred sharp shards of glass if I turn my head too far to one side.

"Dizziness?"

"One."

Lie. It's more like a five, but I never answer zero to everything. It's more believable that way.

"Blurred vision?"

"Zero."

Lie. There are fuzzy little bright white stars passing in front of my eyes, and if I blink for too long, they multiply.

Hunt scribbles on his clipboard, and then signs the bottom of the page.

"You know what to do, right? No aspirin, no liquor. Go home and take it easy."

"Yup."

We both know I'm lying.

In the locker room, I attempt to look as whipped as possible. Feigning complete exhaustion keeps the media at bay a bit, leaving only the bravest and most foolhardy of them to step near my locker. A swan dive to the ground like the one I executed earlier means that the broadcasters spent the entire time-out saying things like "hope he's OK" and "that was quite a hit." All while showing the same clip on a loop for amusement and ratings.

But that's what makes the show, doesn't it? Watching a guy like me, who, if I'm on my game, is the idiot carrying the ball downfield with a target on his back. Depending on whose side you're on, you're either hoping I make it or hoping one of those three-hundred-pound guys tackles me to the turf.

When I hit the ground tonight, it felt like it always does: heavy, unforgiving, and crushing. Then everything went silent in my head. Those seconds, when you can't figure out where you are, what your middle name is, or why the sky looks so shimmery, are scary as fuck. Because suddenly your body isn't your own, which is the strangest sensation. When I was playing high school ball in West Texas, I used to wonder if those moments were like what happens right before you die. Eventually, after years of coaches and trainers shaking me sane again, I stopped worrying about it.

The ruse of exhaustion almost works. I'm already halfway down the hall when Bodie Carmichael from Channel Eight steps right into my path and sticks a mic in my face. I actually groan out loud. He does the usual, slicks back his greasy hair and smirks, before launching in.

"Hell of a hit, Coop. How are you feeling?"

The impulse to give him the antagonistic sound bite he wants rushes through me.

How am I feeling? Well, shit, Bodie . . . I feel like a dude named Stinger just made me his bitch. Like I just swallowed my own balls, then gnawed on them for a while before trying to reattach them with a dull knitting needle.

Bodie would love it, the viewers would love it, and it would make the perfect epilogue to tonight's sportscast highlight reel. But the team media director? Would she love that answer? Not so much. I take a labored breath and respond more appropriately.

"I'm good. Glad we put this one to bed. That's all that matters."

I refuse to linger long enough to offer Bodie the chance at a follow-up question. Even the exchange of a courtesy nod that acknowledges the precarious balance between athletes and reporters feels like more than I can handle, so I step back and continue down the tunnel. That's all he's getting from me tonight. Hell, it's probably the same as any other night, but with my head throbbing in waves, it feels more justified than ever.

On a forgiving day, the media refers to me as quiet, taciturn, or reserved. Every other day, they just say I'm a prick. There's truth in both.

═══════

Attempting to celebrate our win at a downtown bar was a shitty idea. I knew it was, but we just sent the opposing team home to the West Coast with another loss under their belts and a few more guys on injured reserve. And that kind of performance is what football-crazy cities love, trouncing their longtime rivals in a blazingly glorious beat-down. We don't pay for drinks at bars most nights anyway, but tonight, whatever we want, it's there. Alcohol. Women. Accolades. Ass kissing. Take your pick.

I thought one drink would be fine. But I overlooked how effectively liquor hits the bloodstream after adrenaline fades and your dehydrated body starts to wane. It has a mainline effect you can't elude, even when you try to chase the whiskey with twice as much water, hoping to drown out the whooshing sound in your head of your own blood rushing through your veins.

Which is why, when the cute coed standing in front of me—whose name I can't remember—tries to hand me another whiskey sour, I wave her off. That headache I lied about is everywhere now, radiating from each hair on my head.

Darci? Sandi? It's definitely something with an *i* at the end, I know that much. Giving blondie here my complete focus would be a nice diversion, but my head is screaming and my teeth are starting to hurt.

"Sugar."

That will have to work for now. A bland endearment that also manages to call up what's left of my Texas accent. When I say it, though, I realize exactly how much of a prick I sound like. Names are always better. But descending into lame platitudes is only to save face from the fact that I now think there might be two of her standing there. Maybe more. And I can't remember any of their names.

"I'm good on the drinks. You take that one."

She smiles and takes a sip, looking up through her eyelashes at me. *Fuck.* Not sure if I'm crossing my own eyes or what, but three of her is definitely too many. If Hunt were here, he would cross his arms and shake his head before dragging me out of this noisy bar to drop my stupid self into the nearest bed. Taking a play from that book, I'm going to take myself out of here.

I casually slap the bar top in a move that signals my intentions and lean toward her so she is sure to hear me.

"I'm gonna have to call this one early. I got rocked today."

Giving a small pout face, she lets her blue eyes go wide, then narrow. She's annoyed but covers it quickly. Very, very well done, Darci-Mandi-Sandi.

Once she rights her expression completely, she draws her hand to rest against my chest and proceeds to purr.

"Poor baby. I saw it. Do you need someone to look after you tonight?"

When we walked in tonight, it was obvious that she was a jersey chaser. I watched her scope us out, taking a complete and nearly instantaneous inventory of each of our faces, then pause as she determined who had the best game, the biggest contract, and the least number of ex-wives. With two touchdowns today, a five-year contract so good it made the news when I signed it, and zero ex-wives, I won.

But now I'm bailing on her, so her only option is to put this little act into overdrive. Wild guess that she doesn't really want to take care of me. I might puke if the pain gets worse and I'm thinking a scalding-hot bath full of Epsom salts isn't exactly the sexy vignette she had in mind for a night with *the* Cooper Lowry, number eighty-two wide receiver on an NFL team poised for a playoff run that already has Vegas bookmakers working overtime. The poor girl probably doesn't know how she'll make up the lost time if I leave, since every other starter in the room is already drowning in women and alcohol.

Scanning the bar, I whistle at one of the practice team guys and wave him over. The kid is eager and willing and fit—what more could she want? He's got a jersey just like the rest of us. If everyone's honest, that's all she's interested in anyway.

"This is Derek. Third-round draft pick last year, sweetheart."

Baiting the hook for Derek is almost too easy. She scans him from head to toe, then turns on her charm, complete with her hands on his biceps and her hip pressing into his thigh. She doesn't even say good-bye when I let my highball glass slide across the bar behind her.

Despite having grown up on a few hundred acres of ranch land and missing the respite of that, living in downtown Denver does have its advantages. Primarily, it means I can walk nearly everywhere I want to go. From my loft, it's two hundred yards to my favorite coffeehouse; another two hundred beyond that is the best burger in town. Our practice facility is less than a mile north and the stadium is two miles due south. Unless I'm desperate to get out of the city, away from the buildings, noise, and fans, I can easily leave my truck parked for weeks at a time.

Some imagine that Colorado is still cowboys and Indians, but these days it's mostly hipsters and weekend warrior triathletes. Between the track bikes zipping along down by the Platte River and the miles of groomed urban trails, this city is becoming a place made for everything but your car. So much so that when people drive, it's usually badly. Very badly, very rudely, a brake-check away from road rage. People think Texas is no-holds-barred when it comes to attitude, but a Coloradan behind the wheel puts the *wild* in the West.

I thought that leaving the sweaty bar, with its weird lights and loud guitar rock anthems blaring in the background, might clear my head, but it's freezing out, which does nothing but make my skull go from throbbing to screeching. The puffs of warm air leaving my mouth hang in front of me, and the distraction of it lingering there nearly topples me into the street. Stopping on the sidewalk, I shove my hands into my pockets and try to refocus my vision properly.

The traffic light nearest to where I stand cycles from red to green and I hear an audible click as it does. Which is not a good sign. Because a sudden case of supersonic hearing usually lasts approximately twenty minutes, and then I'm on my knees, holding my skull in my hands and wondering if this is how an ax feels landing on your head. The rebound effect of a tough hit can go on for days, tricking you into moments of peace for a bit, then walloping you like a baseball bat to the face.

The only thing that might help is filling my giant, football player–sized bathtub with a gritty layer of slowly dissolving Epsom salts and water that's hot enough to turn my skin cherry red. If only my nights were full of the endless debauchery expected from a guy with my job. But my body has made debauchery less practical, while my outlook on life has made even the idea of it less tempting over the years.

Veering across the street, I drag open the door to a twenty-four-hour pharmacy to grab an extra bag of salts, just to be safe. When I get home, I probably won't leave again until it's time for Tuesday's practice. As long as there is a fridge full of food and enough batteries for the remote controls, I'm good to hunker down until then.

The place is empty, as it should be at nearly midnight

on a bitterly cold Sunday night. The clerk at the counter looks up from the five-inch-thick textbook he's reading and gives me a half-smile. I give him half of that in return.

Slipping down a far aisle, I stretch my hands out to draw against the edge of a shelf, enjoying the bit of stability. At the end of the shelf, I can see what I want. An enormous, glorious bag of salts. When I arrive there, I realize with new clarity that the bag is on the bottom shelf, and I will need to bend over to get it. Who in the fuck puts Epsom salts on a bottom shelf? The only sad souls who need them are old people and guys like me. Neither category is capable of reaching down that far without collapsing or shedding a few tears. I brace my hands on the uppermost shelves, close my eyes, and hang my head.

"Mother*fucker*."

A complex calculation takes place in my head at this point, a slightly drunken multiplication of the moves required to dip and grab what I need, while simultaneously trying to avoid blacking out. Just when I've put all the pieces together and visualized them in my head, a voice breaks my concentration.

"Excuse me. Are you OK?"

It's a woman's voice, soft but clear, laced with apprehension. Of course. It would have to be a woman seeing me like this. All I can manage in response is a grunt.

Her voice lowers and I can sense her moving down the aisle toward me.

"Do you need some help?"

"Yes. Shit, yes, I need some help."

When she gets within a foot of me, I can smell her; she's covered in the scent of something coconutty. It quickly becomes the best damn thing I've experienced tonight and in reaction, I suck in a heavy inhale through my nose. She probably thinks I'm completely insane, but I just need this tropical breeze–scented woman to hand me a bag of salts, and we can both be on our way. She can head back to the beach, or heaven, or wherever she came from. I point down at the low shelf.

"I need a bag of Epsom salts. If I bend down to get them, I might never get back up. I just need the salts, please. I'll give you anything if you just hand me a mother-fucking bag of them. Anything."

Then she laughs, a gentle laugh, absent of judgment or cruelty, and she clearly isn't laughing *at* me because the sound of it is more pitiful. I slowly draw my eyes open just as she starts to duck under my arm, dragging her scent along the way. All I can see is the top of her head, a pile of wildly messy, light auburn waves in a sloppy bun, a red bandana wrapped around to secure the longer pieces back from her face. She's twisted her way between me and the shelving, on her knees and leaning toward the bottom shelf.

Then she looks up to face me—from between my god-dam legs—while pointing at the shelves.

"Big bag or small?"

Christ. It's possible I've developed a brain tumor in the last few hours, because she's fucking gorgeous. Pretty tan skin, hazel eyes, and full pink lips. In the right side of her nose is a tiny gold hoop piercing. She's wearing men's pajamas—not the kind that girls normally wear, pink and covered in kittens or some crap. No, these are throwback-style, oversized, old-man's pj's in navy blue.

When she tilts her head back and lifts her arm to point more directly, just shoot me now, because I get a clear view of some very nice, very naked cleavage. The kind of cleavage I might normally endeavor to spend a great deal of time exploring. I shut my eyes and groan, hoping that not being able to see any more of her skin will somehow make this more manageable.

"Big bag. The biggest one down there."

I hear her shift forward and another waft of the coconut whatever-she's-wearing rises. When I open my eyes again, she's dragging a bag off the shelf and then slips out from her perch on the floor in a graceful squat-hop over my planted foot.

Good job, asshole. Just stand here while this woman saves you from yourself, and don't even bother trying to do the decent thing and move out of the way while she drags a bag off the floor for you.

The raised-right, polite version of me—who takes full appreciation of fine-smelling, pretty-cleavage-possessing, helpful women—has been replaced with the supreme dickwad version of myself. I normally reserve that guy for the media and people who test my patience. But right now, no matter how gorgeous this woman is, I'm just a guy who can't muster much beyond a grunt because his job sometimes involves being a human punching bag.

Once I orient my limbs properly, I turn and shove away from the security of the shelves. Miss Hawaiian Tropic thrusts the bag toward me and tilts her head incrementally, taking inventory, likely trying to determine exactly what kind of a jerk I am.

"This won't help with a hangover—you know that, right? It's probably dangerous to soak when you're drunk anyway."

Blinking, I crease my forehead tightly. "I'm not drunk; I'm in pain. Rough day at work."

She nods slowly and narrows her eyes.

"You should add some lemongrass oil to the water. It's good for detoxifying impurities and soothing inflammation."

Raising her index finger toward the ceiling to stop me from going anywhere, as if that were even a possibility, she shuffles off down the aisle and peers around. Craning her head down a few random rows, she disappears for a second and then pops up again, her soft-looking waves moving slightly with every step.

Returning, she hands me a small bottle. "Shake a few drops in after you get the tub full."

My eyes drop to the unreasonably tiny print on the bottle. Before I can make out any of the words, I notice her feet. Shoeless, but clad in a pair of thick, ugly, oatmeal-gray ragg wool socks.

"Are you not wearing any *shoes*?"

She looks down and lets out another gentle laugh.

"Yeah. That. Nope, no shoes. No worries, though— I don't think I stepped on any big-city syringes or anything. I just crossed the street from the hotel; that's all."

She points across the street to a downtown hotel, and

I trace my gaze over her face again as she looks away, that tiny gold hoop dangling from her perfect little nose. Combined with the bandana wrapped around her messy hair, it's decidedly a hippie-tastic look, but fuck me if it doesn't look completely hot on this girl.

When she drops her arm and faces me, the pain threatening to shred my skull in two hits a crescendo, because her pretty lips drop open a few inches as she stares for a moment, then starts to babble. As she speaks, her eyes don't leave mine and no particular expression covers her face; she simply blathers on and proceeds to devour me with her eyes.

"They wanted seven dollars for the bottled water in my room. Seven dollars, can you believe that? It's appalling. Seven dollars for twelve ounces of water they poured from a municipal tap and bottled in non-biodegradable plastic loaded with BPAs and f-toxins. But the tap water in that hotel tastes like radiation and fluoride conspiracies. I figured I could at least pay slightly less for the privilege of poisoning the earth and everyone on it. Lesser of certain evils or whatever."

Nodding, I wait for her to break this staring game, because I'm planning to enjoy it as long as I can. Until she gives in or a blood vessel breaks loose in my brain, I'm just going to stand right here and enjoy the view.

Eventually, she mumbles something about landfills and going to hell, then slips past me and makes her way to a refrigerated case at the back of the store. Once she arrives at the counter to pay, I sidle up and drop my bag of salts next to her bottle.

"Let me buy this evil, guilt-ridden bottle of water for you. As a thank-you for your help."

Her eyes drop and don't meet mine again. Not even when she mumbles a protest, then a thank-you. I watch her toddle across a four-lane street, jaywalking in those wool socks, then slip through the revolving door of the hotel.

Just a few buildings down the street, I stumble through the entrance of my warehouse loft building and jab at the elevator call button until the creaky beast finally appears. *Charming authenticity*, my ass. Tonight I'm convinced the developers of this warehouse conversion kept the prewar-era elevator in place because they're cheap bastards.

Once inside my loft, I fill the tub and shake five drops of that oil into the water. Stripping my clothes off and letting them land in a pile, I slip into the heated water and sit there as long as possible, until my limbs feel manageably heavy and my mind promises sleep without pain.

= 2 =

(Whitney Reed)

I'm definitely *not* imagining things.

The loan officer is actually checking out my chest and my legs, and probably has plans to inspect my rear view when he finally ushers me from his office. While I sit here and try my hardest to sound professional, yet enthusiastically passionate about my orchard, he's staring at my cleavage. The whole thing is beyond pathetic, but the fact that I've considered how to best use his gross inventory of my assets—and not the kind on my business proposal's balance sheet—to my advantage is even worse.

I sat there and tracked his gaze for a good ten minutes after I arrived, drifting from my legs and up over my chest repeatedly as he asked me questions that had very little to do with my business. Where was I from? (Washington State. A little town built by a sawmill baron and now kept afloat by people who would hate to admit to its un-green beginnings.) How did I spend my time when I wasn't working? (I scoffed internally, but claimed an interest in cooking and reading, the sort of half-hearted answers that seemed appropriate for half-hearted questions.) Was I living out there all alone? (This one was tricky. Saying yes meant the smarmy bank officer with my address might put his car's GPS to use. "Alone but never lonely" was my glib answer).

I showed up here, dressed in a loose purple batik skirt that hit just above the knee and a scoop-neck white eyelet blouse, determined to look effortlessly bohemian while wowing him with my business acumen and playing to what I hoped was his compassionate nature. Yet all it seems I've managed to do is wow him with my minimally exposed cleavage and my gams. Both of which are just fine as gams and cleavage go, but what I really need is for him to admire the reports and data I've compiled in the three-ring binder I just handed him. Without that, I won't secure the re-fi I need to save my struggling orchard and home. Short of that or a Mother Earth miracle, I'll be homeless by the New Year.

Just when I thought I had found a home, a place where the dirt beneath my feet was mine, I'm on the path to losing it all. And to make it even worse, my fate rests in the hands of a kid with ink on a business degree that hasn't even had a chance to dry yet.

"Your revenue forecasting is very aggressive, Miss Reed."

He flips pages as he speaks, so quickly I can only assume he is skimming without reading a word. Perhaps the graphs were all he needed to see, the straight-line trajectory I used to forecast the next five years and that would turn my tiny apple farm from sinking ship to smooth sailing. It's all there, the black and the white of my story.

Every thin dime it would take to save my future is noted and footnoted, despite the way Mr. Campbell continues to flick each sheet like a toddler with a picture book.

"Aggressive? Maybe. But I think you can see that between the marketplace's desire for organic, locally harvested fruits and the moderate yield expansion design I'm using, it isn't overly optimistic."

Yes. That's the way I rehearsed this role. *Go me,* with all the confident answers. At that moment, I was a seasoned pro instead of merely a grief-stunted woman who left her hometown three years ago and drove until she found a place that seemed idyllic enough to get lost in.

Mr. Campbell slaps the binder shut and tosses it on his expensive desk. It lands with a flat thud, and I fix on that spot for a moment, curtailing the instinct to launch myself toward it and swipe the precious evidence of my failing business into my arms. Campbell leans back in his high-backed leather chair and runs a hand over his jaw. Another perusal of my chest follows.

If only this year hadn't been so chock-full of meteorological misfortunes. First, there was the frost. One lone night in April when just a few hours of below-freezing temps killed off nearly ninety percent of the tender blooms on my trees. Then came the damp, wet weeks that followed, which only served to stymie pollination and eventually kept some fruit from setting the way it should.

Then it hailed. A last gasp of late summer storm that within fifteen minutes put more fruit on the ground than was left on the trees. Once the hailstorm ended, I walked the tree rows and did the only thing I could. I started to gather the heavily bruised and gouged fruit off the ground, dragged it all into the house, and spent the next four days making apple butter. Waste not, want not, I thought . . . at least it was *something* I could sell.

Unfortunately, what people really want is whole fruit, bags and boxes of apples they can load into the back of their Subaru and use to create their own masterpieces at home. Apple butter is a novelty at best, one that takes time, sugar, lemons, jars, lids, bands, and labels to make—not exactly a profit powerhouse.

Mother Nature and her grumpy attitude was all it took. My business is too young and tenuous to withstand even one bad season, plus I had already blown through the savings I'd accumulated over the winter from the temp jobs I took on, just trying to keep myself—and my trees—properly fed and nurtured.

Now it's mid-October, when I should be smack dab in the middle of harvest, running ragged from hitting every market I can; instead I'm three months behind on my loan and formally in foreclosure. While a sale date hasn't been set yet, I know I have four months at best to see if I can find someone, somewhere, to take a chance on me.

Moving his hands to the top of his head, Campbell begins to rock back and forth in his chair.

"Here's the thing, Whitney . . . Can I call you Whitney?"

I nod my head and give him a small smile. One side of his mouth turns up in a knowing smirk, nearly convinced in his own mind that I might crawl across his desk any minute now and drop my insatiable self in his lap.

"Excellent. So, as I was saying, Whitney . . . three years ago, you bought a ten-acre farm with a dilapidated house, no water rights, and three hundred apple trees, half of which were so diseased and neglected they had to be removed. You paid cash outright for this behemoth of an orchard, and then proceeded to take out a business loan to keep the operation afloat, using the property as collateral. Now, here you are, with your existing loan in foreclosure, looking for a way out." He pauses and flips open my intricately prepared binder. "And this year, you've shown just two thousand dollars in sales. Can you see my hesitance here, Whitney?"

I lean back into my chair and do my best to stay strong. I promised myself all the way up here that I wouldn't lose hope, that I'd do whatever it took to persevere.

Straightening my spine, I grip the chair's armrests tightly.

"I understand, Mr. Campbell, I do. But my business plan *is* sound and there's tremendous market demand out there. I'm not just looking for a way out. What I need is a bank that can look beyond my situation, see all the untapped potential that's there, and help me find a way to restructure the debt so it's more manageable."

"My loan committee isn't interested in untapped potential. If I take this to them, all they will see is an orchard with no revenue to speak of, owned by a woman who's already ninety days behind on her current loan." Sighing, he leans forward and shoves the binder my way. "I wish I had a different answer for you, Whit. I wish there was a way we could start a relationship here—trust me, I do."

OK. That's it.

Final. Straw.

In the span of three minutes, he went from "Miss Reed" to "Whitney" to "Whit." If I stay another five minutes, he will have the word *honey* on the tip of his forked tongue. Then he alluded to starting a relationship with me, complete with a licking of his lips that signified his definition of a relationship would likely include me purring in his ear about how we might come to a creative compromise.

This is now, officially, a wasted trip. I drove three hundred miles, over Kenosha Pass in fifteen-degree weather, in a truck with an intermittently operating heater and no defroster. Then I dropped a few hundred dollars on a hotel room so small that the bathroom door wouldn't even open fully before whacking the side of the bathtub. I spent thirty-seven dollars on a room-service club sandwich for dinner and fifteen dollars on blueberry pancakes for breakfast. And they didn't even have the decency to give me more than one pat of butter for the pancakes. Who uses only one pat of butter on pancakes? No one.

Standing up, I tuck my sacred binder into the crook of one arm and reach across the desk to shake Campbell's hand, drawing the folder up to cover my chest as I do. His hand is clammy. *And* he gives a cold fish of a handshake. I strengthen my grip to prompt him, but he gives nothing back. He's just a kid with a bad handshake.

And I'm just a woman out of options.

───

When I lurch out the doors of the bank, my dress-up kitten heels clicking across the concrete, I walk determinedly until I round a corner out of sight. Once the bank and Campbell are sufficiently behind me, I find the side of a building and lean back with my head tipped up to see the sliver of sky visible between skyscrapers.

With the overwhelming size of those buildings looming around me, things feel impossibly bleak. Instead of *if*, it's only *when*. When I lose my little farm, when they come to collect everything that no longer belongs to me, I'll have nothing to hold on to except the realization that I squandered every dollar that my father's untimely death left me with. I'll be adrift. Again.

———

Back inside the shoe box–sized hotel room, I strip off the batik skirt and ball it up, shoving it into one corner of my suitcase, leaving on the black leggings I wore underneath. The kitten heels are tossed in favor of a pair of wool socks and chore boots. The white eyelet blouse comes off to reveal a white cami. I slip on a zip-up hoodie, and when I put my whiskey quartz necklace back on, the negativity of Campbell and failure dissipates. I press my palm to the crystal, hard enough that the rough edges of it nip at the skin of my chest, and take a deep breath. If my father could see me right now, he would shake his head, call me a hippie, and proclaim he loved me anyway.

Once my body feels like my own again, I zip my suitcase shut, taking a last look around the room to make sure I haven't forgotten anything. Satisfied that all my meager belongings will return with me, I drop two dollars on the bureau for housekeeping, wishing it could be more, and go to throw open the heavy hotel room door, tossing my suitcase out into the hallway with a swift thud. It bounces awkwardly and before it tips on its side, a hotel uniform–clad man is reaching out to grab it. Behind me, the door shuts with a loud click and I leap forward, trying to save my own bag. We stumble against each other and when he steps back, he looks entirely flustered for a moment, before regaining his composure and straightening his tie.

"Ms. Reed?"

I manage to right my suitcase and find my balance so neither of us will topple over.

"Yes?"

"Ma'am, your credit card was declined this morning. We tried to call you earlier, but we need you to settle your bill before checking out."

Shame rises up, because beyond the problem of my loan, money remains an ever-present monkey on my back. Every month, I gather my bills and stare out at my little apple saplings, then sit down with a piece of scratch paper and a pencil trying to get the numbers to add up the way I wish they would. It's a precarious balancing act, sometimes stretching the propane bill to next month while catching up the car insurance this month, all in an effort to find a few extra dollars. If only I had fancy handbags or a nice car to show for it; instead I have rusted farm implements, fertilizers, and pruning shears.

At the front desk, a pert little woman with a platinum-blonde pixie cut takes mercy on me, running my card four more times in successively lesser amounts until it finally clears. I dig into my wallet and fish out a fifty I keep tucked away—my "for emergencies" stash—then hand it over to settle up what my credit card wouldn't cover. I try not to whimper when she gives me only jingling change in return.

The valet disappears to retrieve my truck from the hotel's secured underground parking and under the canopy of the entrance, I sit down on the top of my rolling suitcase and watch the city traffic as it passes by.

It's chilly out, so the crisp air easily seeps through my zip-up hoodie and leggings. My real jacket is in the truck, tucked behind the seat along with a box of bone meal and various well-used pairs of work gloves. Perhaps if I manifest a vision that I'm a traveler in a faraway land of tropical temperatures, I might stave off the cold in my mind.

Closing my eyes, I summon up the sight of it all: white sand burning the soles of my feet, a broad-brimmed hat that does nothing to quell the relentless sunshine, and a companion of the male variety with sweat beading up in all the right places.

The delusion works for a few minutes, until a blaring car horn ruins it all. Across the street, standing on the edge of the sidewalk, a guy in loose track shorts and a hoodie pauses to adjust his iPod earbuds. After a quick scan of his frame, I decide he might be the ideal specimen to share all that relentless sunshine I just imagined with. His hood is up, covering an already knit hat–clad head, and when his gaze darts across the street to gauge traffic, he catches my stare.

The expression on his face, sullen and irritated, is unexpectedly familiar. If it isn't surly salt guy from last night, it's his evil twin. Or maybe his good twin. Because the guy in the drugstore was just as moody, dour, and brooding, with a dash of miserably ill thrown into the mix.

If he hadn't been built like a modern-day Roman god, with short but shaggy dark blond hair, I wouldn't have remembered him in such acute detail. Plus, when he fixed his blue eyes on me, full of glowering and focused attention, I nearly offered to take him home and put him in the salt bath myself. He looked so pained, so desperate for something tender and comforting, I wanted to bake him a cake and rub his shoulders until that seemingly permanent furrow in his brow finally lessened.

Before I can look away, my truck appears and blocks the view, announcing its arrival with rough-sounding exhaust and a motor that sputters so loudly it's vaguely embarrassing. Sighing, I slip around to the back and twist open the rear glass on the truck topper to drop my suitcase into the bed, amidst the short ladder and various bushel bins that crowd the space. The decision to buy this truck, reliable but small, for cash was a good one, simply because it has a shell. I might end up sleeping in it soon.

"Hey."

Gah. He might sound slightly less tortured this morning, but surly salt guy's voice is every bit as husky as it was last night. If I said it didn't resonate down to my gold toe rings, I would be lying. I let the back glass thwack shut and twist the handles on both sides, securing it for the drive. Turning, I place my hand to the crystal pendant again and give a slight tilt of my head.

"Hey there, salt guy."

His eyes are clearer this morning, and with the exception of the dark circles underneath, he looks like his night hadn't ended up all bad. Probably had a house full of cake-baking, shoulder-rubbing women at his disposal.

"You look better this morning."

He nods, sharp eyes flickering to where my hand lies on my chest. I drop it in reaction and watch his gaze soften.

"And you look a lot less like an elderly gentleman escaped from a retirement home. Not that those pj's and wool socks weren't all kinds of bizarrely sexy last night, but that might have been my impending migraine talking. Apologies if I was a complete asshole."

I take note of the word *sexy* immediately and despite knowing that what I should do is call him out on it, demand his offer of an apology, instead my heart proceeds to flutter. Freaking *flutter*.

After Campbell, I should have had enough of men and their pointed comments and roving eyeballs. My chest should be tightening, and my hands should be clenching up into little annoyed fists. Unfortunately, surly salt guy and his unreasonably pretty eyes only inspire a full-body sensation of feminine triumph—while also prompting my pulse to thud harder in my neck.

"Not a complete asshole. The first word I heard you say was *motherfucker*. Then after that, *motherfucking*. But you bought my bottled water, so my karmic scorecard remains clean on that transaction. Even-steven."

I slip around him and make my way to the driver door, where the valet kid waits with my keys in his hand. The exchange would dictate a tip, a problem compounded by the sudden awareness that I'll need to fuel up at some point on the way home and I'm most definitely broke. Might have to stop by a pawnshop on the way out of town; surely a short ladder might get me enough cash to make it home. I lean into the truck and flip down my sun visor to unearth a five-dollar bill stuffed underneath a stack of business cards tucked there. As I hand it to the kid, he relinquishes my keys. Salt guy follows and comes to a stop next to my car door.

"What's your name?"

Before I can stammer out something evasive or glib, I blurt out my name. My whole name. First, middle, and last.

"Whitney Willow Reed."

He raises his eyebrows before thrusting his hand forward, prompting for a handshake. And I, Whitney Willow Reed, do nothing but look down at his hand with confusion. From behind us, a loud bellow comes from across the sidewalk, in a manly kind of catcall.

"COOOOOP! YOU KICKED ASS LAST NIGHT!"

Still holding his hand out to me, he lifts his other arm up and casually gives a two-finger wave in the direction of the bellower.

"I'm Cooper Lowry. Cooper *Marcus* Lowry, if that matters."

I take his hand, finally, and shake it flimsily. Salt guy, Cooper Marcus Lowry, has some seriously strong hands. No soft Campbell-esque cold fish here. I grip stronger in reaction. Then I realize I'm now shaking too aggressively, up and down in a wide path, and for far longer than appropriate.

Dropping our hands awkwardly, Cooper steps back and takes a glance at my truck.

"Headed home?" I nod and turn to slip my keys into the ignition. "Where's home, Whitney?"

"Hotchkiss. On the Western Slope."

Cooper studies me for a moment, eyes narrowing as he does. He was adding me up, trying to fit the pieces together. If he only knew. I'm like a puzzle composed of mostly corners, missing all those critical links that belong in between.

"Long drive. What does a girl like you do in a town like Hotchkiss?"

There is a momentary desire to wail and shout *nothing*. I do nothing, I am nothing, and I'm going home to nothing. No prospects, a sad end of harvest, and a cold, empty house. Instead, I turn and lean into the truck, rummaging around on the passenger side to pull out a half-pint mason jar.

"This." I hand him a jar of my apple butter and he twists it side to side to read the label, then hands it back. I toss it on my driver's seat without turning away.

"Delaney Creek Orchards? You work there?"

"I own it."

"You own an orchard? Impressive."

His compliment actually brings about the sensation of needing a good, long, slobbering cry about losing the only significant thing I've ever done to the front of my mind. But impressive? Hardly.

"Don't be impressed. It's only ten acres, with a bunch of struggling apple trees, a handful of pear trees that yielded a grand total of twenty pears this year, and a house so drafty I have to layer a wool cardigan over those pj's just to stay warm enough at night. And double up on the socks sometimes."

He nods thoughtfully, and I immediately want to bake him another cake. But up close, in the daylight, it doesn't appear that much cake crosses Cooper's lips. Those lips, the ones he now proceeds to purse the smallest bit, couldn't have seen much but clean living and lean protein for the last few years because if I couldn't surmise accurately about the contours of his body last night, I absolutely can now.

Under that hoodie is likely nothing but ridges and abs for days. And the legs, gracious . . . the legs. Quads and calves, hamstrings and whatever those muscles are that are adjacent to your shins—they're all there, plus a few others I definitely couldn't name, in every inch of their bulky, toned, well-worked glory.

My gaze settles on his legs and fixes there long enough for him notice, because he proceeds to flex his calves with only a minuscule lift of his heels. Too much power there, too much strength, too much masculinity for any one body to manage. Especially for my out-of-practice body to handle. The sight reminds me of the obvious: that I need to cease this silly semi-flirtation with a stranger, get in my truck, and go home. I have far, far bigger problems. The kind I need to focus on with a clear head.

Before I can make my goodbyes and wish him well as he skips off to run a marathon or whatever that body of his is primed to do, Cooper's face contorts and he squeezes his eyes shut. Then he pinches the bridge of his nose and groans.

"You OK?"

"Throbbing headache. Comes and goes. Mostly if I'm doing something crazy—like, you know, trying to stand upright."

He drops his hand and takes a deep breath, then opens his eyes again. When he does, those eyes are unbearably gentle, every bit of his broody charisma giving way to something infinitely simpler. In a move that contradicts my recent internal reprimand to get in my truck and screech away, I reach out and take his left hand in both of mine. He doesn't seem shocked—likely because Cooper is probably unnervingly accustomed to strange women touching him—but he narrows his eyes and lets them drift between our interlocked hands and my face.

"Relax your fingers."

He unclenches his fingers and lets the tips graze against my open palms. I take two fingers and begin to press firmly against the meaty part of his hand, between his index finger and thumb. When he flinches, I press harder. Then his face goes slack and he closes his eyes.

"I have no idea what in the fuck you're doing right now, but if you could just stay permanently attached to me like this for the foreseeable future, that would be awesome." Cooper lets out a long sigh, and his chest seems to slowly deflate as he does. "What the hell is that?"

"It's just acupressure. This one works for me if I have sinus pain, but you can also just do the tips of your fingers for headaches. Just press like this when you have pain."

Cooper's eyes stay closed. "I'm guessing it won't feel as good if I'm doing it and not you."

I let out a small chuckle, moving my hands to press on the end of each of his fingers. When I start to reach for his other hand, I remember that we're blocking the hotel drive. But the area remains nearly empty, save for a little boy standing about ten feet away, who is staring at us, shyly, with his hands clasped behind his back. Just behind him, I spy a couple, gently prompting the boy to move closer.

Cooper realizes I'm now only holding his hand limply, because he opens his eyes and then tracks my stare over his shoulder. When he does, he drops my hands and turns toward the boy, dropping down to a crouch.

"Hey, buddy."

The kid immediately turns into a pile of mush, gush, and grins, outpaced only by those of his parents, his mom even doing a strange silent clapping thing while she bounces on the balls of her feet. The little boy pulls his hands out from behind him and thrusts forward a black marker. Cooper waves him closer and takes the pen.

"Alright, buddy, what's your name?"

"Sean."

"What do you want me to sign, Sean?"

Every bit of surliness is gone from Cooper—not a trace in his voice, his body language, or his words. The little boy looks to his parents for an answer and they mock whisper to him, "*Your shirt, honey. Have him sign the back.*"

He turns and stands stock-still while Cooper signs the back, just over the boy's tiny shoulder, before recapping the marker and handing it back to the boy's mother. After an awkwardly enthusiastic round of handshakes, they scuttle off and Cooper returns to my side.

I raise an eyebrow and cock my head.

"Pray tell, Cooper Marcus Lowry, what is it *you* do for a living? I'm guessing whatever it is, it's way more impressive than owning a ramshackle excuse for an orchard in southwestern Colorado."

Cooper shrugs. "I play football."

"For a real job? As in professionally? Not like, my buddies and I have a rec league and we roll around on some grass and act like we're in a beer commercial? When in fact what you really do is manage an office supply store?"

A sharp snort tears from Cooper's mouth and he scrubs his hand over his face.

"No, it's totally legit. I mean, I've been in a beer commercial or two, but I get paid to play ball for real."

Wacky. That's what this is, straight-up, bad-trip weird. I just spent a handful of minutes slobbering over and hand-rubbing a guy who plays for . . . I don't even know. The name of our football team escapes me, if I ever knew it at all. Only occasionally does the topic of football come up in Hotchkiss, and only when I'm at the co-op. Even then, I'm not a part of the conversation; it only takes place in my orbit, between the men buying chicken feed and bovine antibiotics. Evidently, I should have been paying more attention.

"Sorry, I'm sure I should have known that and properly addressed you by shouting your uniform number while waving a foam finger or whatever. I don't even own a TV, so I'm not exactly caught up on the local sports scene."

Cooper locks his eyes on mine and steps closer until he can put one hand on the top of my opened truck door and the other against the roof, effectively trapping me in a two-foot space where his body is crowding mine in an unexpectedly pleasant way. He tips his gaze to look at me.

"I'm glad. Not about you not owning a TV; that's just weird. But I like that you didn't know who I am. Explains a lot."

He smells like sweat and possibly—*lemons*? Then I remember the lemongrass oil. My mind immediately takes a very direct and unruly path to Cooper soaking in a tub. Naked, obviously. And grumpy. There is also the possibility that my fleeting fantasy includes him groaning and grunting a bit, huskily and unsatisfied.

Perhaps my pupils flare or I actually drool, because he steps back and makes as if he's leaving.

"One more thing, Whitney. It's a favor, I guess. A personal request."

I draw my hand up to set it on the armrest of my door panel and try not to dig my fingernails into it too hard.

"Sure. Shoot."

He points into my truck. "Can I have that apple butter? That's a serious throwback for me. I haven't had decent apple butter since my grandma died."

My shoulders release on a laugh and I crane into the truck to retrieve the mason jar. When I turn back, I catch the last moments of his eyes tracing my form. It never matters, does it? Here stood an apparently well-known guy who probably had his pick of women, but he still couldn't help checking out my goods. It must be genetics or some evolutionary instinct. Even if I wanted to chalk it up to more, it surely wasn't.

Cooper saunters off across the hotel drive with an athlete's gait, purposeful and flawless, while holding the mason jar in the air.

"I'm an apple butter snob, so this shit better be good. Otherwise, I'll bring my complaints directly to your door, Whitney Willow Reed!"

My truck door is halfway shut, my hand on the keys to fire the engine. All I can do is laugh. And, perhaps, pray that my apple butter absolutely sucked.

= 3 =

(Cooper)

The blonde ending up in my bed last night was Whitney's fault. Really, it was. There wasn't a single other reasonable explanation as to why I let a girl who would *not shut up* come home with me.

This rationale will make sense to only forty-nine percent of the population. Because a woman, no matter how hot she is for one specific man she can't have, will not take another replacement home with her just to take the edge off. Women don't think like that. But with men, our decision-making skills are often driven by irrational dick-based instincts. It's stupid. We know it, you know it, but there's the truth of it.

When I left Whitney standing under the covered entrance of the hotel, I walked straight back to my loft, set the apple butter on the kitchen counter, and considered how to deal with the inconvenient semi she'd inspired. Because as I suspected from my momentary glimpse of her cleavage, it seems that under those awful pj's, Whitney was hiding an amazing body.

Firm everything, but with curves exactly where they belong. A combo that can be elusive around these parts. In Colorado, where everyone is climbing fourteeners and knocking out ultramarathons, it's surprisingly hard to find a girl whose body is tight while still holding on to a few curves. Because the seriously active types around here can lose the good stuff when they train so hard.

I don't want a woman with a six-pack. I want her belly toned but soft, I want her ass firm but full, with plenty up top to keep me occupied, and I want some hips to hold on to. Ones that don't include hip bones threatening to cut me open if I have her under me. In short, I want her to look and feel and move like a woman. And Whitney is nothing but perfectly toned, perfectly rounded, and all woman.

Let's not even touch the topic of her eyes, or her hair, or her lips. Definitely not that cute little nose ring. Or how good it felt when she rubbed my hand in hers. The hand thing is what did it. When she started, it just felt nice, but then it made my head stop hurting, which left space to consider how good her hands would feel rubbing and stroking other things.

I went home with all of that swimming around in my brain. Frankly, I can be just as dumb of a jock as the next guy, and I'm not bright enough to make better decisions when my dick is involved in a fantasy about a girl who lives on the other side of the state and appears to have her own things going on. A ten-minute conversation was all it took to know Whitney is not the type who would aspire to be some football player's girlfriend, sitting in the stands and cheering, or playing pretend besties with the other WAGs.

Women fall into two distinct categories in my reality: jersey chasers and non–jersey chasers. Staying away from jersey chasers is best because they're never worth the drama. Pick the wrong one, on the wrong night, and the next thing you know, a picture of you sprawled out naked and sleeping in bed goes viral. Likely captioned with something you definitely don't want your mom to read.

But I was tense. Fucking tense and horny and pissed that someone like Whitney lives in the middle of nowhere instead of *here*. I tried running a few miles to see if that might help. I tried playing video games that involved a lot of things getting blown up. Nothing worked, and I had only a few dwindling options left for distraction. Finally, I called up a few guys and we made our way to a bar crawling with an after-work crowd, hoping that even if I only nursed a club soda, I might still find a little relief.

Callie, the blonde who talked nonstop for five straight hours, was sitting on a barstool surrounded by guys in cheap just-out-of-college suits, waving her hands around and laughing at her own story. She saw me no less than five minutes after we walked in and proceeded to begin the age-old routine of seducing a man from across the bar.

Hair flipping. Minimal, possibly inadvertent, eye contact. Seductive drink sipping. Lingering, possibly intentional, eye contact. Precisely timed crossing and uncrossing of legs while wearing a short skirt. Followed by obviously intentional, *come over here and talk to me* eye contact.

Once I played my part and wandered over there, I got the rest of the act.

The laugh-and-touch-my-forearm thing. The whisper-in-my-ear thing. Eventually, the rub-a-hand-up-and-down-my-thigh thing.

I saw it, understood the game, and went with it. Have I mentioned that she talked a lot? About sports and work and clothes and her friends and her family and her new kitten and the car accident she was in and, for the love of Christ, she talked about nail polish for a good twenty minutes.

Once we got going she talked dirty, but it was a poor showing. I'm all for a girl who lets me know, in explicit detail, exactly what she wants or how she likes it, but at a certain point, I just wanted her to be quiet for a while. So much that we went a second round because I thought I might lull her into a silent stupor if she came hard enough. It worked, but I still hated myself for trying to make a nice girl into the image of another woman. All I could do was pray that whoever is up there and calling the shots might overlook this night when it comes time to decide if I'm spending the afterlife behind the pearly gates or shoveling more coal into the fiery pits of hell.

When my alarm clock goes off, I sneak out of the sheets to hit the shower and do my best to keep quiet, because Callie is still sleeping in said stupor and I'd love to keep it that way until I've at least had some coffee.

As the hot water pours down over me, every limb starts to relax. This relaxed state leads to thinking about the woman I wish were tucked in my sheets right now. A sidestep from that leads to the obvious. Me, hard—and not in the best of situations to do anything worthwhile about it. I end up standing there almost helplessly and will myself to make it go away. Because if I wander out to Callie with this thing, she will think it's about her, which it isn't, and it would be rude to pretend otherwise.

When I towel off and go into the bedroom, the sheets are rumpled but empty. My heart kicks up a notch at the possibility that she skedaddled and saved us both from a lame good-bye scene. I throw on a pair of warm-up pants and my hoodie, while giving myself a silent lecture for being a dick, deciding the punishment will be to juice up a green smoothie, which I despise, and glug it down on my way to practice.

Rounding the corner into the kitchen, the sight I find squashes my hope for a smooth getaway. Because there's Callie, still here and wearing my T-shirt.

First off, I think we should reserve the whole wearing-a-guy's-T-shirt-in-the-morning move for two people who are starting something. You know, the girl you took to dinner, the girl you texted flirting, funny things to, the girl you don't want to leave right away because you really want to strip that shirt off her and screw her in the kitchen until you're both late for work.

There's a second problem, though. Which is that Callie found Whitney's apple butter and now she's standing in my kitchen slurping up a spoonful of it. I watch her devour a heaping mouthful and lick the spoon clean. Then, *please no*, she does it again.

So. Much. Worse.

The woman is double-dipping into my apple butter.

I understand exactly how irrational this sounds, given that my mouth and her mouth did far more intimate things than double-dipping last night. But this is different. I had plans for that apple butter.

As lame as it sounds, I was saving it. Yesterday, when I set the jar on the counter, I was picturing it on some thick multigrain bread from the bakery down the street, toasted up with a bunch of butter. Swirled on top of the plain Greek yogurt the team nutritionists want me to eat even though it tastes like feet. Spread on a toasted waffle when I'm too beat to do anything else before dropping into bed.

"This stuff is *soooo* good." Callie licks the spoon in what seems to be an attempt to look seductive. "Where did you get it?"

"It was a gift. Kind of," I answer flatly.

Her spoon clatters into the sink and she sets the lid back on, tightening the band over the top of it. Then she shoves it absentmindedly across the counter, where it bumps into the backsplash. I try not to growl or curse or drag her gently by the arm and show her the door. Taking a deep breath helps. Barely.

"I've got to get to practice. I need you to get dressed and head out."

Her face falls, and then I really feel like shit. This is why I don't do this. This is why I've kept it in my pants for the most part these last few years. I'm short-tempered, I say a shit ton of things I shouldn't, and I don't do disappointment well, especially with women. When Callie smooths down my shirt, then tugs on the hem like she's awkwardly trying to cover herself, I take a step forward and run my hand across her hip.

"Hey." She takes a cautious peek up at me. "Thank you for last night, Callie. But I'm not good for anything more here. I've got a long few months coming and I'm not exactly good at dividing my focus during season. OK?"

Everything I just said is true, which means I can give Callie a conciliatory grin and hope she doesn't want or need more than that, because I'm practically worthless for anything off the field. It works, because she smiles and goes to get dressed. All that matters is that she didn't cry. No tears means a win given the context, and I'll always take a win no matter how it comes.

October in Colorado is a crapshoot when it comes to weather. From bitter-cold mornings to afternoons full of balmy sunshine, you never know what's to come. Today happens to be so cold that the disgusting green smoothie I concocted starts turning slushy by the time I gag down the last swallow and hit the front doors of our team headquarters. Once inside, I take a swig of water from the cooler in the hallway, just to clear out the last of the awful taste in my mouth.

"Uh-oh. Somebody's drinking a green juice. She wear you out that bad?"

I turn and give a glare to the smart-ass teammate of mine who enjoys my misery, in any form, far too much. Aaron Bolden is two hundred and fifty pounds of muscle and technical brilliance, but most days I think he's also a good hundred pounds of mouth.

Aaron is an outside linebacker who knows exactly how to x-ray an offense to find the inevitable hole that exposes their weakness, even when they didn't know it existed. Despite occasionally wishing we weren't teammates and then he wouldn't know me as well as he does, I can't tell you how thankful I am for never having to line up across from him, even with all the bullshit he throws my way.

He's also the only guy who's been here in Denver as long as I have. Other than Aaron, it's been a carousel of new faces and egos to fill the rest of the line, so over time, he became my other half on the team—a work wife, if there is such a thing in football.

Still, he has a certifiable motor mouth and, unlike so many others, he isn't the least bit hesitant to point it in my direction. Especially since he was witness to my performance at the bar last night, right up until Callie started rubbing my thigh, at which point Aaron claimed an emergency text from his wife and bailed with a smirk on his face.

I crumple the tiny paper cup from the water cooler and shake my head in his direction.

"I'm fine. The juice was punishment, not replenishment. The only thing she wore out was my hearing."

Aaron lets out a huge laugh. "What? Chatty Cathy didn't have an off switch?"

"Not that I could find. And I looked. Trust me."

A hard slap lands on my shoulder.

"Had to see that coming, dude. I told Kendra the whole story when I got home and she bitched at me that I should have run interference. Like your dubious taste in bedmates is *my* fault somehow. Also, she claims to have found the 'perfect' woman for you."

"Fuck. *Again?*"

Aaron's wife has few enduring passions in her life. Her twin boys, Aaron, her sisters, Justin Timberlake, White Castle burgers, and finding me a wife. Unfortunately, her instincts when it comes to sourcing my true love are usually way off base.

"Some charity maven she met planning an early education fund-raiser. Which means the woman is probably alimony rich, but has a decent rack thanks to a set of expensive implants, and spends most of her time complaining about being bored because she's essentially unemployed. So unless you've decided that's your type, beware of all invitations to our home in the near future. Any supposed barbeque get-togethers are merely love traps—remember that."

I groan. Aaron shrugs but grins. Because underneath any bro-code alliance we have, he's married to the woman who set a love trap that he happily fell into and he has no interest in untangling himself from it.

"Too bad. I do like her potato salad."

Aaron saunters off toward our team conference room, where we'll spend the next three hours watching game film.

"Horseradish mayo and those fancy little gherkins. That's her secret."

Everything is just fine until we hit the field in the afternoon. Sauntering out to the green turf, my head feels clearer than it has in days. There is less pain, less haze threatening to dim my vision or knock my legs out from underneath me.

When the drills start, though, all the pain comes rushing back in dense, relentless waves. The aches, the nausea, the sensation of clammy sweat on my face, the feeling that my limbs don't belong to me anymore. Hunt has been watching me all day with an unnerving constancy. If I stumble or hesitate, he makes a note on his clipboard. A few times, he huddled up with offensive coaching staff and they stood there watching me, focusing on my every move. Under their scrutiny and the way my body won't get on board, I feel a little like an uncoordinated chubby dog in a tutu out here, putting on a pitiful show for the judges.

In this world, a flash of hesitation on a practice drill lands a question mark next to your name on the performance notes. A tick of inaccuracy in your hands can lead to a conversation with Coach about whether you make the field on Sunday. When these things happen, it means you have to buck up ten times harder than yesterday to keep your job. This game, the reality of being a pro, is a ceaseless merry-go-round of fiascos and victories. In between each one, you have to hold your breath and dig deep, calling on each scrap of bootstrapping tenacity you possess.

Pressure is a given, but every day and every practice is like a job interview; most people don't understand that.

It isn't only about game day or even a season; it's a relentless audition for your dream. The only damn one I've ever known.

Two hours in, I drop three passes in succession. Wide-open, here-it-comes, land-in-your-lap passes. We're running the pro football equivalent of tossing the ball around in a city park with your friends, one-on-one, to build timing and drive consistency between passers and receivers. All you have to do is focus on reading the pass before you reach for it.

In the air, every ball has its own unique qualities, defined by the quarterback and his style combined with the conditions. Dry air turns the ball slicker, a quarterback with a longer extension means a higher arc that slows the ball, and it's my job to figure it all out in the span of seconds. But when my mind won't pitch in and my body won't stay on task, I can't complete the simplest of tasks. After those three passes land on the field and bounce away from my hands, I hear the whistle, and Hunt shouting my name.

Back in the training room, Hunt runs through the same tests we did Sunday on the sidelines. The use of a foam board intensifies the tests, designed specifically to throw me off balance if possible, and it works. I'm a spectacular mess of clumsy and weak appendages. By the time we stop and Hunt runs through the questionnaire about dizziness, sleep patterns, and foggy memory problems, I think I might pass out for real. I've never been so grateful for a folding chair in my life.

There is a final question, the one I always answer *yes* to.

There is no other answer. Ever. When the day comes that I consider answering *no*, I will gladly walk away, because the fire and love for this game will have gone dark.

"Do you consider yourself fit to play football?"

I stare Hunt down and nod my head. "Yes."

Hunt's eyes darken a bit, and then he shoves the medical clearance questionnaire across the table to me with a pen. I already know where to sign. Scrawling my name where it belongs, on the line that states I don't want to be anywhere else but on the field Sunday, I shove it back to him.

"You have a concussion, Lowry. Mild enough, but mark my words, kid, if you lie to me again on the sidelines, I will have you on IR so fast your stupid head will spin. I can't do my job if you lie to me."

"I took a hit. That's part of *my* job, Hunt. We don't need to make it a big deal. I'll be fine by Friday afternoon and I intend to be on the team plane to Phoenix."

Hunt sighs and starts to shove his papers into a black binder, then slaps it shut so his hand lands on the front with a thud.

"Go home. You're out until Friday. Come by that morning and we'll decide then. Take the next two days and do nothing. I mean *nothing*. No girls, no booze, no clubs, no lifting, no running. I don't even want you watching TV or playing those idiotic video games. Sleep as much as you can, take up bird-watching, but that's it."

"Sounds like a slow form of torture. I'm not good with being lazy; you know that. If I end up taking a sledge-hammer to the walls in my loft, that shit will be on you, Hunt."

Standing up to leave, Hunt looks old all of a sudden, weary of telling a bunch of overgrown boys to behave and take care of themselves. Slipping the binder and his clipboard into a messenger bag, he pulls it over his shoulder.

"Someday, years from now, Lowry, I want you standing on a porch with a pretty girl at your side and a bunch of towheaded kids running around making you nuts. If you don't take this shit seriously, if you keep lying to save your season instead of your goddam body, that won't happen. You'll be raging at things no one else can see or drinking yourself into an early grave because you can't think straight. Alone. Don't choose the game over everything else. There has to be more than this game, kid."

I want to take off on a tear out of the room, but he starts for the door before I can. Leaving me sitting there like a fool, hating the unforgiving mirror he just held up to my life, confronted with the reality that there isn't anything more than the game for me. Since I was eight years old, this has been everything.

Hunt slows his gait and then stops in the doorway without turning to face me.

"Get out of town, Lowry. Find a change of scenery and enjoy it for the next forty-eight hours. Go somewhere football is the last thing on your mind. Shit, we live in Colorado. People come here to get lost all the damn time."

At home, I toss my bag in the hallway and slump into the couch cushions. I want to erupt with anxious energy and restless anger at something, anything. A bag, a blocking dummy, at nothing but the silence in my living room. I can't even watch TV. Can't do anything but stare at the walls until they close in on me.

Before it takes me down, I jump off the couch and head into the kitchen. Maybe if I eat something it will take the edge off the hunger to drive my fist through the wall, effectively smothering one hunger by feeding another. Leaning against the counter with a bowl of quinoa and grilled chicken in my hands, I catch a glimpse of Whitney's apple butter jar, sitting right where Callie left it after she tossed it aside. That sight rouses an idea.

Maybe I will get out of town. You know where I've heard is nice? The Western Slope. I can take I-70 straight out of downtown, and before you know it, I'll be in Glenwood Springs.

Then Carbondale.

Then Paonia.

Then maybe a little town called Hotchkiss.

I hear they've got fruit orchards full of apples and peaches and pears down there. The Gunnison River runs through every mile, with rainbow trout and browns aplenty in the cold, clear water. A tranquil, relaxing lifestyle where a guy might get lost for a couple of days.

I bet some people don't even own TVs.

= 4 =

(Whitney)

Mountain roads are perfect for thinking. Every long, lazy curve means your thoughts can follow that same path, nearly on autopilot, while your subconscious works away on whatever problem is at hand. Today, while I'm downshifting to coast the descent of a high mountain pass, inspiration strikes.

While I don't own much when it comes to orchard equipment, my Polaris UTV has to be worth something. Not enough to deal with my loan, but enough to stay on top of basic living expenses for a while. With this season nearly over, I should be able to go without it—at least until I've managed to implement the winning Powerball strategy I also devised during my time on the road. All odd numbers, a combination of my father's birthdate and my own. Lucky or not, the numbers mean something, so I figure a karmic multiplier could benefit otherwise hopeless odds.

When I hit the edge of town, I veer into the Hotchkiss

Co-op parking lot before I have a chance to change my mind. If you want to sell anything farm or ranch related, this is the place to make that known. Because instead of craigslist, I plan to use a far more reliable sales approach. *Garrettslist.* As in, Garrett Strickland. Full-time country guy extraordinaire and the Hotchkiss Co-op's main employee.

When I pull the front door open, a familiar scent of seed, fertilizers, and dirt immediately surrounds me. Within seconds of stepping inside, I'm greeted the usual way.

"Johnny Appleseed! Have you come to your senses yet? If you marry me, I'd be able to reach all the high limbs for you. Our kids would be perfect, you know. My redneck charm and good looks are a genetic blessing I'd be happy to pair up with your gorgeous DNA."

Garrett proceeds to flop forward onto the countertop just adjacent to the cash register, resting on his forearms and drumming his chafed and well-used hands on the dirty, junk-strewn laminate. Despite my fatigue, his goofball proclamation hits just the right note. Even if Garrett is twentysomething, too young for me, and I feel nothing but sisterly toward him, his easygoing charm always brings a grin to my face.

If you live here and don't know Garrett, you're likely blind, or deaf, or perhaps been confined to your home undergoing some sort of exorcism. He's a hometown boy who can do no wrong and looks like he just stumbled out of a Cabela's advertisement. Or got lost on his way to a music video shoot for Florida Georgia Line, where he'll likely be shirtless and standing atop a hay bale. Because while he's lanky and tall, the sturdy biceps and taut abs that sometimes appear when he loads bags of fertilizer into my truck bed make it clear that he's also built like some redneck version of a male model.

He's usually sporting a sweat-stained Browning Buckmark ball cap paired with slightly grubby jeans and a shirt that always has camo on it somewhere. And the second he gives you one of his five-thousand-watt grins, women want to kiss him and men want to drink beer with him. Or go hunting. Possibly shoot sporting clays. Maybe just be his wingman while a passel of blonde girls in short-shorts giggle their way over to find a spot next to him on the dropped tailgate of his old Ford truck.

I shuffle toward him and rest my hips against my side of the counter.

"You know, someday you're going to lay that flirt on the right girl. She'll crawl right over this countertop and the next thing you know, you'll be tied down in all the right ways."

Garrett widens his eyes. "You think? I sure as shit hope so. Every day I come in here, just waiting for some gorgeous girl to walk through that door and launch herself at me."

He looks away slightly, mock wistfulness at play. "She'll be wearing cutoffs with a pair of Justin's. And one of those shirts with the thing that goes—" He makes a gesture toward his neck, circling it.

I laugh. "A halter top?"

His face lights up. "*Yes.* One of those. Maybe with an over-and-under slung on her shoulder. And, like, some feathery angel wings or something. Just so it will be easy for me to identify that she's my fantasy girl come true."

Another grin from Garrett before he slaps his hands on the counter and pushes himself upright.

"So what's up? It seems you didn't come here to ask for my hand in marriage. You need some more alfalfa seed? Or you gonna keep the yarrow as a cover crop? If so, you'll have to keep ordering that online. Can't imagine we're going to stock it."

My shoulders slump and I mimic his previous posture, arms supporting me on the counter.

"I need to sell my Polaris."

"Yeah? You ready now, or is this something you're just thinking about? Gonna be a tough winter for you without it."

I groan. "Don't remind me. But, yes, I'm ready now. I have to be."

Garrett doesn't press for more, he simply grabs a pen from amidst the stacks of mail, catalogs, and assorted papers littering the space and asks for the specifics on my UTV. Perhaps it's out of courtesy—or maybe it's because he's a kid who knows exactly how losing everything feels.

Valedictorian of his class and an all-state wrestler, Garrett's the kind of golden boy who is truly golden, without artifice or bullshit. After graduation, he made his way up to Fort Collins on a full-ride scholarship to study ag sciences. But three and a half years into finishing his degree, his dad collapsed in the field during harvest season. Garrett came home to what he thought would be his farm, only to discover there was too much debt and not enough cash to be able to keep the land that had been in his family for generations, all of it sold at a fire sale before the head-stone was placed on his dad's grave. Now he works here, and even when he should be nothing but bitter, he rarely seems less than perfectly content with life as it is.

So, Garrett Strickland already understands—without me uttering a word.

═══════

Thirty-six hours later, Garrett and the rural grapevine are enough to land a sale. I mistakenly assumed that holding a wad of cash in my hand would make it easier to see Kenny Euland pulling out of my driveway with my Polaris loaded in the back of his Ford F-350, destined for work on his cattle ranch a few miles down the road. I want to feel relieved. Instead, I feel defeated. Too many setbacks in too many days have left me hollowed out and exhausted.

Kenny was nice enough about the whole thing. No dickering about the price, no questions about why I was selling it. Instead, he simply inspected the tires and took a quick gander at the undercarriage, then dug out his wallet to produce three thousand dollars. I signed the back of the title and we shook hands as his teenage son, Tanner, fired up the UTV and eased onto the ramp extending from the dropped tailgate.

The entire transaction took less time than my meeting with Campbell at the bank—but this time, I came away with actual cash. All I can do now is pray that the tepid temperatures hold as long as possible, because if winter comes calling too soon, the cost of propane to heat the house will be too much.

Until then, I need to *make* something. Create instead of collapse. I press my whiskey quartz necklace to my chest and decide it's time for chutney.

———

Chopping up pears in my kitchen, I'm hoping the pathetic harvest of Harrow Sweets I yielded this year will be enough to finish the chutney recipe I want to try. The pears are just a touch beyond ripe for eating out of hand, but still firm enough to hold up in a recipe that demands a bit of texture. I taste a few pieces and despite getting only a single crate of fruit this year, I find the pears' flavor is perfectly balanced.

Months ago, I would have taken this moment and thought: *Next year. Next year will be even better. Next year will make all the work worth it.* Instead, I know that I should savor these, because I may never have the privilege of this again, the unique experience of holding fruit I tended to and grew. Someone else's fruit may be in my hands and it might taste just fine—great, even. But it won't be mine.

I toss the last of the chopped pears into a heavy cast-iron pot along with the others. In go a few cups of raisins, then a heap of sugar. After that, it's a squeeze of lemon and a shake of allspice, with a splash of cider vinegar to brighten the mix. Just a touch of savory to make it a true chutney: crushed garlic cloves, some diced onion, and mustard seed.

The pot is nearly overflowing, but simmer it all down, down, down and soon enough, I'll have the bittersweet results of my final harvest.

———

Three years ago, when I drove into Hotchkiss on my way to anywhere, I was so exhausted from traveling for days on end, I drove off the side of the road and straight into what is now my orchard.

Just two months out from losing my father, with a check in my pocket for over a hundred thousand dollars, I had nowhere to call home. Then I literally knocked down the faded "FOR SALE" sign that sat next to the driveway. There were overgrown bushes, grasses, and thickets everywhere, but I could still see the house from the road. A small farmhouse nearly obscured by wild hedges, white clapboard so faded it looked gray, and a wide porch with spindly posts that listed in too many directions to be structurally sound. I looked about for evidence of Boo Radley, but had no luck.

When I crept onto the property and stepped on the porch, it felt right. I looked out upon the tree rows and for the first time in months, my feet seemed rooted to something real and my heart didn't feel two beats away from deflating. It seemed I needed to live here if Boo didn't.

Similar to all the other impulsive and foolish decisions I'd already made in my life, this one followed suit. I righted the sign so I could jot down the real estate agent's name and number. The next day, I wandered into her office and she vocally questioned my sanity, taking a long look at the remaining dreads in my hair and the loose maxi dress I had on.

The old Richardson orchard? Are you nuts? That place isn't suited for a girl like you.

She was probably right.

But logic wasn't my jam right then. I had spent two summers in high school working at a local orchard and loved it, so in my mind, that place *was* suited for a girl like me. I figured that my heart would do most of the work and I'd fill in the gaps by checking out some books on orchard management from the library. Ignorance was my ally and my enabler—which is a hell of a combination. Looking back, I was living off the propulsion of grief and the way it pushes one moment into the next without allowing you time to breathe, let alone think, through a sound decision.

When my dad died in a freak welding accident at his manufacturing job, I was on the road traveling with a gourmet root beer concessionaire, which was the latest of my wanderlust work endeavors. Within days of arriving home, a lawyer representing my dad's employer already wanted to talk to me about a settlement. Money was the last thing I cared about as we sat on the porch of my father's trailer house, the same place he'd rented for the last twenty years, the same tiny metal box I grew up in. And without him there, I knew I could never think of it as home again.

All his greasy Harley parts were still strewn about the space we called a yard, and hundreds of hot rod magazines were stacked in the living room, on shag carpet we should have replaced decades ago. Despite the trailer park, Harley, and hot rods—all of which shouted *tough guy*—my dad loved in a way most people never can. He loved my mother until the moment she left, then gave her up to another man with nothing but sadness. Never anger, never spite.

He loved me in the same wholehearted way, and never wavered, even when I disappeared right after graduation, only to show up on his doorstep months later, in the rain, crying because the boy I loved left me behind at a truck stop without even saying good-bye. Jack Reed just opened the door wider and stepped aside to let me in.

Even when I threatened to change my name to Rainforest (in support of saving them, obviously) he just laughed so hard he choked a little, then patted my head and asked if I honestly expected to find a real man to take care of me properly with a name like that.

Good men, the ones you can count on to hold you up when it matters, won't go there. I'm sorry, they won't. If you want another idiot like that communist you dated, the one who insisted we call him 'Elm,' go ahead and change your name. But if you want more than that someday, then Whitney will do just fine.

I kept my name. Still looking for that real man.

The curse of an old house is in its inefficiency, as evidenced by the state of my kitchen right now. One batch of chutney on the stove and a water-bath canner heating up next to it and the small room has turned unbearably, blazingly hot.

The jars are sterilizing and the chutney has cooked down just right. And the smell is wonderfully spicy and bright in the air, but still sweet. I give the concoction a peek and start to stir. Just as I get the sides scraped down, the rumble of a truck approaching crunches on the gravel driveway outside.

A sharp knock sounds at the door—two raps—and my poor heart does a leap. A quick prayer that it isn't Kenny Euland back with my UTV, demanding a refund. I have that cash spent twice over in my head by now.

I continue stirring, but call out over my shoulder, "It's open! I'm in the kitchen!"

The screen door creaks. Followed by the whoomp of the front door coming open with a slight shove, releasing the poorly fit thing where it always sticks against the door jamb. Then nothing but near silence. Kenny would have hollered something back. The shift and swish of fabric is all I can hear for a moment.

"Do you make a habit of just hollering 'it's open' to anybody that knocks on your door? Because I could have been an escaped convict from the super-max looking to take a hostage."

I allow myself a second to process a hazy recollection of that voice, the gravelly tone, before the memory of its owner comes into sharp focus. When a bubble of chutney jumps the pot edge and lands like fire on the tender skin of my forearm, I know this isn't a dream, because I can feel the burning sting there. I turn slowly, curious to see if I'm about to have my day unexpectedly turned inside out.

Cooper Marcus Lowry is standing in my kitchen, wearing a puffy vest coat over a thermal shirt, faded jeans, and the silliest-looking socks on his shoeless feet. The socks are bright red and covered in some garish kind of Texas lone star design. He takes a survey of the room and in the seconds that pass while he does, I consider a few things about the scene.

First, he looks annoyed. Exasperated. While I already suspect this to be his default expression, it's unclear what currently has him so sourpussed.

Second, he looks just as good as he did two days ago—no, he actually looks better, because despite the annoyed facial expression, he looks less pained than before.

Last, in acknowledgment of his even better good-lookingness, I remember that I can't claim the same.

Because I'm currently wearing a pair of decade-old denim overalls.

Overalls.

Not exactly what I would have chosen to put on if I had known a grumpy, delicious, better-looking-than-before football player was planning to stop by. Overalls aren't exactly boy bait; even I know that. Especially when these are not sexy-slouchy overalls. Rather, these are baggy-frumpy, perfect-for-grizzled-rancher-type overalls.

Earlier, I had my zip-up sweatshirt on over these wildly attractive overalls, but in the time since I started to work on my chutney, the heat of the kitchen forced me to toss it off and onto the vintage Formica table in my kitchen. Therefore, I now get the privilege of standing here in overalls and a tank top.

For fun, let's add in the fact that I'm also not wearing a bra. And I'm not exactly the kind of girl who is built to go braless in polite company. Also, my hair is piled up in a knot on my head, secured by a lone chopstick, leaving the back of my sweaty neck and the terrible yin-yang tattoo there fully exposed. Even better.

When Cooper finally looks directly at me, I vaguely want to throw a pear at his head to teach him a lesson about surprising women in their homes when he should know that he's so damn good-looking they might rather die than be seen like this.

His expression remains flat. "Seriously. You shouldn't do that. Just invite anyone in. You don't know who's out there."

I take a quick glance at my chutney and realize I have to turn the heat off or risk scorching the entire batch. Reaching down, I switch off the knob and gawk into the safety of the bubbling pot.

"I try to assume the best of humanity. Also, I'm a little tied to the stove right now." A grunt from Cooper, followed by the sound of buttons snapping open on his vest.

He removes it and drapes it over the back of a mismatched chair next to my kitchen table, then sidles over and stands just behind me so he can peer over my shoulder. And since he's a few heads taller than I am, the stance means he can likely see right down the gaping front of my dowdy overalls.

"Jam?"

"No, it's chutney."

I move forward a half step, while consciously demanding that my nipples do nothing overt in response to his nearness, because, hell, he smells good. Not like sweat and lemons as he did before, but good nonetheless. Some kind of handsome athlete–scented pheromones, I suppose.

He pushes up the sleeves on his thermal shirt and moves over to peek into the water bath, where the sterilized jars are simmering.

"These ready? You want me to pull them out?"

Jesus. Talk about leaping right over the obvious bizarroness of this scene. Kudos to him for ignoring any normal instinct to explain why he is even here in the first place.

I take a moment to assess the wacky turn of events of my day.

Sell UTV. Fondle cash in my pocket and consider utter failure of my life. Make chutney from the world's worst-ever pear harvest. Have a man who smells good show up unexpectedly. Offer him a view of certain body parts I wasn't planning on any man seeing in the near future. Because *overalls.*

Once the inventory is complete, in every bit of its cringe-worthy glory, I decide there isn't much to do but go with it for a bit. I'm pretty sure he isn't a serial killer and there isn't anything particularly bad about a hot guy standing in your kitchen and offering his help.

"Do you know a lot about canning, Cooper? Pardon my surprise, but I find that just a teensy bit unbelievable."

He's already off and washing his hands at the sink, before coming back to start pulling out one jar at a time, careful to tip all the water out. He sets the first one on a clean dish towel I had previously placed on the counter.

No preamble, just a shrug.

"I'm the youngest of four boys and I was a surprise. I showed up six years after the others, so when I was little, I ended up stuck with Grandma while they were out doing cool stuff in the summer. She was always putting things up and I was her helper. I think I could remember the process in my sleep if I had to. Sterilize, fill, wipe the rim, place the lid, set the band, and in they go. I was usually rewarded with an Otter Pop while the jars processed, but I'm not sure if you have any of those in your freezer."

Stepping back, he makes room for me to start to fill the jars. Silence as I do. Well, if he isn't going to address the obvious, I am.

"What are you doing here, Cooper?"

He wipes the rim on the first jar and keeps his eyes fixed on the counter, waiting for me to finish the next one.

"I needed more apple butter. Took a drive and here I am." Taking a quick glance my way, he tilts his head. "Your website sucks, by the way. You're making it really hard for people to find you."

"Oh my God. Are you joking right now?" I heft the pot down to the counter so I can scrape the last of the chutney to one side, just enough to dollop into a small bowl for sampling once it cools.

"You show up here out of the blue and act like it's totally normal to jump in as my little chutney helper, despite the fact that we're basically strangers to each other. You bitch about my hospitable nature when I don't have my front door locked properly. *And* you're insulting my website. No apple butter for you."

My breathless, slightly annoyed delivery elicits a chuckle from him but nothing else. Sigh. This guy and a simple explanation. Like pulling teeth, I tell you.

"Now try again. What are you doing here? My apple

butter isn't *that* good. So taking a five-hour drive to get some more sounds a little nutty."

I place the lids on as Cooper threads a band over each.

"What hurts is I didn't even get to try the apple butter. It got . . . contaminated."

His lip turns up in a little snarl as my stomach bottoms out. I'm extraordinarily cautious with my canning, so any contamination references are not good.

"What? Was something wrong with it? Was the lid sealed? What did it look like when you opened it? Shit. I'm sorry you got a funky one."

"Calm down. It was fine. Or, 'soooo gooood,' as I was told."

He drawls out the words and adds a loll of his head for effect. It becomes obvious that Cooper is imitating a woman with his mocking tone, and that the woman he's mocking was probably somewhere private enough to sample the apple butter I sent home with him. The twist of my belly at that image is entirely unjustified, so I bite the inside of my cheek to stave it off.

"Ah. A woman got to it first. This gal have a name?"

His entire body tightens up and every bit of agitation there shouts that I've poked into a space of his world that he'd prefer I didn't. I lower the jars into the water-bath canner again, setting the timer on the stove for thirty minutes. Cooper sets the lid on the pot with a touch more effort than necessary and it makes a sharp clanging noise when he does.

"Of course she has a name. The point is that I need more apple butter because she double-dipped in the jar you gave me before I even had a taste. And I needed to get out of town because my team trainer likes screwing with me when I don't need it. I'm in a bad mood because I haven't slept well in three days and my head feels like it's twice its usual size. How the fuck has your day been?"

When I turn to face him, I consider telling him to fuck right off because my day—scratch that, my *year*—hasn't been all cavorting puppies and double rainbows, either.

But the look on his face is pure tension and heat, like he's considering the idea that if we just dropped to the floor and went at it, that might make things better for a while. My belly does a swift gallop at the sight and I'm sure my responding expression is clear. That I wholeheartedly agree. All we need to do is flip a coin to see who's going to be on top.

When Cooper's jaw tics a fraction, it reinforces both eagerness and hesitation on my part. It's obvious that Cooper Lowry could be the best kind of distraction there is. All that moody strength bottled up with a touch of angsty oomph, and you likely have a bottle rocket just begging for a lit match. Just so happens I have matches in a kitchen drawer that's only two steps away. Shove past the duct tape, random twist ties, and scraps of yarn littering that same drawer and voilà, we could waste an afternoon the right way.

I don't need to know more about his problems, or care what the apple butter double-dipper woman's name is. He doesn't need to know I'm facing financial ruin and may end up sleeping in my truck a few months from now. The reality here is that nothing beyond this room is relevant between us. We can stand here and shoot the shit, make chutney, and pretend that our real lives are on pause.

Unless we decide to do something else. Like have really sweaty, awesome, mind-blowing sex.

I take a deep breath and let it out slowly.

"My day's been just about as sucky as yours. Right up until a grumpy lout knocked on my door. Then things started to look up."

Cooper raises his brows. Even better, I get a tiny twist of his lips into what some might call a smirk. That's good enough for me. Because all that matters right now is we're two bad-mood bears with no place else to be.

= 5 =

(Cooper)

"My day's been just about as sucky as yours. Right up until a grumpy lout knocked on my door. Then things started to look up."

A wave of endorphins roar through my nervous system when a flicker of invitation lights in Whitney's eyes, and all of my vital organs begin working double-time just to keep up with the rush.

Thank God for my shit luck with a fly rod.

When I left Denver at six o'clock this morning, I told myself I was simply doing what Hunt said to do by getting out of town and searching for a change of scenery, one that included a little fall fishing. I packed a bag, put my fly rod and gear in the truck, and set the GPS for Paonia. *Not* Hotchkiss. Because the nine miles between those two towns seemed like sufficient proof that I wasn't driving halfway across the state for other, less sound reasons.

Maybe if the fishing had been good I would have stuck to the plan. Maybe if the rainbows were leaping out of the Gunnison River to greet me, that would have been distraction enough. But a cold snap last weekend meant the fish wouldn't take to anything I tried, so nothing, I mean *nothing*, was happening. I gave up after a couple of hours and reeled in.

Before my waders were off, I had already rationalized this side trip to Hotchkiss by claiming it was about the apple butter. Whitney had an orchard and a business, after all. I was just a prospective customer interested in patronizing said business.

Sure. Apple butter. Not the least bit nutso to use a condiment as legit reasoning.

Now I'm standing in her kitchen and she's looking at me like I'm covered in honey and she's a brown bear with a wicked sweet tooth. I can't decide if that look means she wants to deck me or ride me. Maybe she can't decide, either.

In the short time I've been here, I've managed to insult her business acumen, bark about her letting strangers in—hello, irony—and bite her head off when she needled around about my nameless apple butter contaminator. I'm lucky she *hasn't* decked me yet. Maybe I should have brought a doctor's note. Hunt could have written something up to explain my current state.

Please excuse Lowry from any random instances of stupidity or the inability to explain why he might show up at a stranger's house, claiming he needed a condiment replenished. He has a concussion. Also, he's an impatient asshole ninety-five percent of the time and this only makes it worse. Most important, please do not somehow manage to make a pair of overalls so strangely hot, he might consider dragging said overall wearer to the kitchen floor so he can kiss and nip the bare skin of her neck for an hour—or ten. He's not supposed to do anything but bird-watch and sleep, so tackling you to the floor for said neck nuzzling is not an option.

What we've learned today is that I should not be without a plan. Ever. I've built an entire career—fuck, my entire life—on a self-imposed regimen of routine. Shove a stick into the spokes of that routine and I'm off the rails before you know it.

Whitney steps around me to rummage in a cupboard. Once she moves out of my sight line, I close my eyes for a beat before stalking over to her kitchen table, dragging out a chair, and slumping into it.

"You want some tea?"

Up on her tippy-toes, Whitney stretches to reach into the dark recesses of a cabinet that's jammed to the gills with stuff. If she isn't careful, a pile of crap is going to topple out and onto the floor. She twists to pat around in the back of the cupboard and when she does, the side of her body comes into view. Her tank top rides up, exposing a swath of bare skin on her torso—golden and smooth—tapering to the space where her baggy overalls hang low enough to offer a peek of the lacy aqua-colored trim on her panties.

Immediately, I close my eyes. *Do not even think about more here, Lowry. Do not tumble down this enticing rabbit hole to consider the specifics of that lace trim.*

But it's already too late. Just that tease of lace drives all kinds of possibilities to the forefront of my mind. Is she wearing something tame? Like those little boy shorts that women seem to love these days? Or maybe something hotter, a style that barely covers the essentials?

Goddammit. Stop. She's offering you tea and you're think-ing about her underwear. I give my head a shake and squeeze one hand into a fist.

"Tea. Sure. Just nothing with caffeine."

She tosses one of the boxes back into the cupboard and it falls on its side to lie atop all the other junk in there. A nudge with her forearm closes the door. The urge to quick-step over to that cupboard and fix that unholy mess, or at least put the damn box right side up, rises inside me.

Before I can follow through on that thought, she bends over to light one of the stove burners, and the sight of her ass turned in my direction is distracting enough to tame the irrational need to clean up the cupboard. Because I'm sure if I went over there and started in on an unrequested honey-do to organize her kitchen, that would only do more to confirm the crazy.

The stove clicks to life, followed by a hiss of the gas seep-ing up to set the flame. With lime-green enamel and white accents, the stove appears to be decades old, the kind of relic that most people would have gotten rid of years ago.

Adding to the vintage vibe, figurines of those creepy cherub-faced Hummel kids my great-aunt loved so much, along with a bunch of tacky decorative collector plates, line a high shelf that spans the radius of the kitchen—all covered in years of grease and dust. A quick survey of the rest of the house reveals that Whitney obviously has a thing for retro in all forms.

The living room alone looks plucked from a soundstage for *Mad Men*. A low-slung sofa and love seat in burnt-orange velvet fill most of the space, with a boomerang-shaped coffee table placed in the middle. A few ornate, gaudy gold table lamps sit on tables covered with yellowing doilies. In a different house, perhaps a mid-century modern renovation, this would be hopelessly hip. But here, the look is all grandma. As in *don't put your feet on the coffee table, you're sitting too close to the television,* and *turn down that music before you go deaf.*

A comment about her home décor is brimming on my lips when my phone rings. I slouch down to pull it out of my pocket and Hunt's name flashes on the display. While taking a side-glance at Whitney, I bring the phone up to my ear.

"I've got to take this."

She gives a blasé shrug of her shoulders and then sweeps her hand out toward me in a *have at it* gesture.

I utter one word when I take the call. "Hunt."

One word from him in response. "Lowry."

In a battle of stubborn wills, Hunt and I might manage to drive each other to the brink merely with our mutual ability to say as little as possible whenever we choose. Sometimes I want to just shake his hand and congratulate him on being a worthy nonverbal sparring opponent. Other times, I just want to put him in a headlock until he sputters the word *mercy* and gives in.

Silence for a moment. Hunt sighs loudly.

"You know why I'm calling, so just give me the update. I didn't dial you up to listen to your mouth breathing in my ear. Three questions: How are you, where are you, what are you doing?" Another sigh that ends with a snort. "Speak, Lowry."

"I'm fine. I'm out of town."

"What are you doing? And be more specific about what 'out of town' means. Because if you say Vegas or Cancún, I'm going to lose it."

"Hotchkiss, on the Western Slope. Doing a little bird-watching, just like you told me to."

There's enough ambiguity and possible condescension in the bird-watching reference to spark Whitney's interest and as the teakettle starts to whistle, she shuts off the burner while also managing to shoot a withering look my way.

I tilt the phone down incrementally and speak in her direction.

"I didn't even mean it that way—relax. I'm bound to say something else truly offensive at some point, so you should save any outraged expressions for when I do."

A laugh erupts from her and once she's let it all out, she shakes her head, turning back to pour hot water into the two mugs she's set on the countertop. The mugs are thick-handled jadeite, in a minty-green color that evokes luncheonettes and coffee shops—back when *coffee shop* meant blue plates and bottomless cups, not overpriced frozen concoctions that pack more calories than actual coffee.

"Who the hell is that?" Hunt barks into the phone, then manages to lower his voice a notch and speak measuredly. "Pretty sure I said 'no girls,' Lowry. Women, as a general rule, are not relaxing. They're work and trouble and fun. None of those things are on the menu for you right now."

A mug appears in front of me, placed there by a delicate hand with those soft fingers I remember too well. Her nails are unpolished and trimmed relatively short, but nothing about that reads as unfeminine, merely natural and unfussy.

"Calm down. We made pear chutney together. Now we're drinking hot tea. The kind without caffeine."

"I call bullshit. Is she wearing clothes? Because the only way what you just said might be true is if she also happens to be naked."

I look up and take an inventory of Whitney where she sits in a chair opposite me, tugging on the sides of her tank top so that it covers her properly, then pulls her legs up to press against her chest. Once she's comfortable, she locks her gaze on me.

"Nope. She's definitely not naked. Unfortunately."

Despite the glare that accompanied her interpretation of *bird-watching*, this time—when my words are anything but subtle—I don't find myself on the receiving end of a scowl or a swift kick to the balls. Instead, Whitney's widened eyes focus on mine, soft and heated, even when there is still surprise evident in how her mouth has dropped open a bit. Hunt proceeds to grouse on, mostly about me making brainless fucking decisions. When he finishes by hollering my name way louder than necessary, I snap my focus back to him and lower my voice.

"Look, I did what you asked. I'm following all of your rules and I have this under control. I'll see you on Friday."

My phone thuds to the tabletop after we exchange curt good-byes and I end the call, tossing it facedown. I thread my index finger through the small handle opening and lift it up to take a small sip, all while carefully avoiding Whitney's stare.

When the tea hits my taste buds, I want to flop my jaw open and let the vile liquid just dribble back into the mug. I don't even like tea particularly—with the exception of authentic sweet tea from back home—but this is beyond bad. Worse than the musty, weak herbal tea that I was expecting. It tastes like someone dropped my nana's potpourri into a teakettle, then strained it through a fine sieve of red clay. I take a labored swallow and put the mug back down. Whitney lets out a snort.

"Are you even capable of insincerity? You know, the polite kind most people use to get through basic social interactions? Or do you always show all your cards? Because you couldn't look any closer to spitting that out right now."

I shake my head and let my tongue roll out of my mouth for effect. "Not really. Bullshit isn't my thing. What is this? It tastes like dirt and air freshener."

Another laugh, but muffled because she's just swallowed a mouthful of the liquid torture.

"It's a rooibos blend. I can make you something else."

Waving my hand in the air, I brush off the offer and not so subtly shove the mug farther away from me on the table. The room gets quiet, all except the ticktock of a clock. Finally, Whitney breaks the silence.

"I'm guessing if I asked what that phone call was all about, you'd say 'nothing.' Right?"

With her knees still tucked up to her chest, feet crossed at the ankles, and one hand toying with the handle on her own mug, Whitney focuses her eyes on my chest.

I take the opportunity to look at her more intently, even if it's only for a few moments. Hoping that in these stolen seconds, when I take a good look, I'll see the same gorgeous girl I did in Denver. If not, if all I see is someone unremarkable, I'll be disappointed, no doubt. Superficial or not, I want to see a woman worth driving five hours for, no matter how insane that sounds.

Sunlight through one small window above the kitchen sink shows everything. The same slightly tan skin, flushed a bit from the heat thrown off by a pot of chutney and a boiling teakettle. The same sexy mess of wavy hair pulled up haphazardly with a few tendrils escaping from the sides. A slim, graceful neck that begs for a few nips of my teeth, just hard enough to leave faint marks, proof I've been there. That's all I need to see. Whitney couldn't be unremarkable if she tried.

I clear my throat and wait for her gaze to find mine before answering her question.

"Probably."

"That's what I thought. Moving on, then."

Jesus, how long has it been since someone took an answer of mine at face value? I've spent too many years enduring a litany of follow-up questions—from coaches and sportscasters, trainers and agents—that I almost don't know how to react when Whitney says nothing else.

She takes another sip of her tea and peers at me from over the rim of her mug, with nothing but an easy expression covering her face. Tension starts to release inside me, unraveling from every rib bone and tendon that lines my chest cavity, leaving behind enough space that I can breathe deeply for the first time in days.

Hunt told me to get lost somewhere. Lost never felt so good.

= 6 =

(Whitney)

Silence stretches around us for at least five minutes. Five long, self-conscious minutes that mimic the itchy feeling of a first date gone awry.

Cooper busies his gaze, gawking about at every countertop, shelf, and knickknack there is in my kitchen. He eventually turns and looks over his shoulder into my living room. At what, I don't know. I live here, so taking inventory of my hand-me-down furniture and the shabby cabinetry isn't exactly a new, or pleasurable, endeavor.

The only new vista in my world is sitting across from me, dwarfing my kitchen chair with his big body. Despite having stood next to him and had the shadow of his frame right behind me, Cooper looks unmanageably large right now. So much so that staring for too long leaves me feeling a little dazed. But, still, I focus for as long as I can. Because Cooper Lowry is *definitely* worth looking at—grumpy attitude, curt conversation, and all.

He has this strong jawline, a tired description I never particularly understood until now. Apparently, a strong jawline is considered attractive because on the right guy, it can inspire a series of delicious images. Including one where your cheeks and lips become a little chafed from rubbing across the few days' worth of very manly scruff that covers his face, his jaw set in a seemingly perpetual clench as you do, while you venture to figure out how to relax him properly.

"You give tours?"

I was still pondering the merits of the aforementioned jawline, so I didn't notice Cooper turn his attention my way. The fog clears only enough for me to recognize that he's talking, but I don't have a clue what he just said. I look up at the space above his head, practically at the ceiling, to save face.

"What?"

"Tours." He pauses, then lowers his voice to match the deliberate delivery of his next words. "Do you give tours?"

Tours? What is he babbling about? I was busy touring the contours of his face with my distractible mind and the only thing I might offer up at this moment is a tour of my lips against his scruff.

All of which has to become obvious when I respond, because my voice comes out husky and breathy.

"Tours of what?"

The combination of my cable-after-dark voice and the way my eyes are unfocusedly glassy turns Cooper's expression both surprised and smug. Then he actually widens his stance in the chair, slouching down incrementally and letting his legs open slightly more.

The whole move has an inviting arrogance to it. As if

he's making room for me, ensuring that when I inevitably leap onto his lap I'll have a nice, wide, solid place to land. Which suddenly seems like a very bad thing, a ridiculous notion best left in fantasyland, because I probably can't handle all of *that*.

Every other man I've ever been with has been half of what Cooper is. We're talking stereotypical hippie types: militant environmentalists who aren't afraid of a hunger strike, fanatical vegans who sometimes just forget to eat, and guys who happily make their homes in remote yurts that are only accessible by snowshoe—every one of them skinny and lanky, more bone than brawn. Weightlifting, or football, or whatever crazy tree trunk–tossing work-out it is that has shaped Cooper's body, are all things that would be virtually impossible for my exes.

When Cooper looks directly at me and shifts his posture again, putting all the categorically male areas of his body center-frame, I'm positive. He's too much. Just too damn much for my decidedly girly insides and my muddled brain to take.

"Tours of the orchard. This is a business, right? I came here for some apple butter, after all. Be nice to see how it's produced."

Oh. Yes. The orchard, of course. My failing little enterprise, the one I had the pleasure of claiming amnesiac ignorance of during the last hour or so since Cooper bumbled his way into my kitchen. The discouraging parts of my life descend in a downpour at his request. Because no matter how kissable his jawline is, that's not enough to make reality go away.

I sit up straighter in my chair and blink twice to clear away the last of my indulgent daydreaming.

"You would officially be the first person to take a tour of my orchard. So don't get carried away asking a bunch of questions or wanting to know where the gift shop is."

"No gift shop? That sucks. I'm big on commemorative T-shirts. I was hoping for one with some pun about plucking ripe fruit or handling bad apples. Maybe something about Eve and biting into her apple, shit like that."

When I laugh, Cooper actually smiles. A full-on, gorgeous smile. None of the half-grins and lip twitches he's previously offered. And it's a hundred times more potent than his jawline, his scruff, or his enticing manspreading. Pretty sure a girl might expire from just trying to get Cooper to smile like that as often as possible.

"There is a root cellar where I store the apple butter I've canned." I stand up and move to grab my hoodie off the tabletop. "If you want, we can pretend it's a gift shop. I'll act like I'm opening it up special, just for you. You know, the VIP kind of treatment I'm sure you're used to."

Behind me, he gives a soft chuckle, and I have to stop myself from turning around to see if the smile is there again. I force my feet to keep moving toward the front door, where I pull on my boots. Next to my set are Cooper's, a pair of broken-in Danners with fraying laces—shoes I would more likely assume belonged to one of the many oil company fracking guys who live and work in the valley these days than a pro football player. Even one who also happens to know a decent amount about proper canning procedures.

Cooper's feet appear in my sight line, those garish Texas-themed socks on display, and I stifle a laugh.

"Nice socks, by the way."

"Don't hate. My mom gave me these socks. It's a Texas thing. We're compelled to put the lone star emblem on anything we can. Pot holders, can koozies, hats, bedding, towels, underwear, socks, you name it."

"Do you own all of those things you just listed? With the Texas thing on there?"

He looks away for a moment and thinks. "All except the can koozie. I'm a bottle guy. No need; it would just be a waste."

"Sure. Because the other stuff isn't a waste at all. Everyone needs a pot holder with that emblazoned on there."

"Not everyone. Just people from Texas." Cooper goes to lace up his boots and cranes his head to survey the living room again. "Your house is nice. I like these old farmhouses with the big front porches. And the décor is . . ."

He falters a bit and his brow line does a series of odd contortions. Immediately, I can tell he's summoning up an attempt at a bogus nicety as he gathers his thoughts.

"*Interesting*," he finally adds.

It's hard to decide if the fact that he sucks at giving bullshit is a good thing or not. On one hand, who doesn't like a guy that seems practically incapable of lying? On the other, sometimes we women depend on those artfully finessed answers that smart men provide when we ask loaded questions about delicate things. Topics that include our bodies, our emotional states, and the hierarchy of our importance in their lives. A guy who can't fib his way through that stuff without looking physically tortured could be tough to keep around.

My expression turns entirely earnest. "I know, right? I have mad, awesome, bitchin' style, don't I?"

I wait for his reaction, with a better view now, because he's standing upright and waiting for me to finish lacing up my shoes.

Another round of weird face acrobatics ensues before he nearly chokes on one word. "Yes."

Dropping onto my rear end and letting my knees come up toward my chest, I give in to a jaded-sounding chuckle and drop my head lazily into my palms.

"Promise you won't try to feed me a line ever again. It's so painful to watch when you try to do that."

I sigh and look up at him. "Nearly all of the stuff in this house was here when I bought it. An old lady lived here before and she was the kind of woman who put plastic covers on the furniture, so everything was in great condition. Her family was happy to include it in the sale and I didn't move here with a ton of household stuff, so it worked out. So my style is actually more *scavenger* and *opportunist* than anything."

He lets out a pent-up exhale and extends his arm my way, offering his hand to help me up off the floor.

"Thank God. Vintage is one thing, but all those Hummel figurines and the Norman Rockwell plates on the walls are too fucking much. I don't care how gorgeous you are, if you honestly collected all that crap yourself, it would have killed it for me. No amount of hotness could outweigh that kind of crazy."

I take his hand but duck my face at the same time, hiding my reaction to hearing the flatteries buried in his not–particularly suave pronouncement. We step outside where the weather has turned significantly colder since this morning. The swell of fresh, cool air is a blessing because it quickly returns my cheeks to their normal color.

Dense moisture hovers about and low clouds have settled in the distance, all sure signs that snow is coming. And when it hits, that will mean this season is officially over. I used to welcome the first frost—Mother Nature's way of providing a reason to rest—but this year, I'd love it to hold off for a few more weeks.

When I look across the wide dirt driveway, where rows of trees fan out toward the horizon, my land looks almost new to me. For so long, I've worked this orchard with my eyes focused only on what was directly in front of me. Looking for the first spring buds, thinning small fruit, cursing at the evidence of codling moth worms on my fruit. I rarely looked up to see beyond those tiny things and now that I do, I realize that losing this place would hurt in so many ways. The regret alone might kill me, not to mention the sucker punch that would come with trying to figure out how to start over.

After my dad died, I took care of settling his limited estate and once that was done, the instinct to wander was as strong as it always has been. Except this time I was running away from the unpredictability that I usually drove headfirst *toward*, because his death meant I was suddenly without the soft place to land that I'd always counted on. This orchard, this land, is where I found my grown-up self

and left behind the girl who used to think that a permanent address should only come with a headstone. Whether
it was grief or simple maturity, I don't know—but I do
know that I'd give anything to have another shot at making this work.

"This place is amazing."

Cooper's body nearly presses to the back of mine when
he speaks and every one of my senses registers the inti-
macy. Between us, there is the scent of spiced sweetness,
the pear chutney that permeates our clothes, masked only
by the coconut oil I slather on my skin and whatever it is
that Cooper rolls around in to make him smell so nice.
AstroTurf? Sweat? Other football players?

Each of us lets out a slow exhale and the chilly air means
I can see the evidence in front of me, a reminder of how
near his face is to mine. Close enough for hijinks. Close
enough to turn this tour into something more interesting
and satisfying.

Before I can attempt some utterly feminine move that
might make this concept clear to him, he's walking away,
toward the orchard rows. He turns to look over his shoulder, while pointing ahead of him.

"This way?"

Fine. A tour. He seems dead set on the damn thing.
Maybe, despite his talk about my being unfortunately *not
naked* and tossing the words *gorgeous* and *hotness* around,
he isn't into the idea of our just giving up our clothes
and going carnal on each other. Maybe he's just one of
those guys who likes getting a woman worked up, even
when they have no interest in having anything stroked

other than their egos. A shame, really. I may not be able to handle him, but I've also never shied away from a new adventure.

Cooper continues forward at a slow gait, with his head up, his eyes focused straight ahead, and his shoulders back—a posture that looks so comfortable on him, I'd be surprised if he ever takes on a task in any other way. We come to a stop at the end of a row and I reach up to trim a spindly low-hanging limb on one of the Braeburn trees, using a small set of hand shears from my pocket. The leaves have started to drop, making any unproductive branches like this one more obvious.

"You should get a goat." Cooper waves his hand toward the ground around his feet.

"Why would I want or need a goat?"

Cooper points to the space between the trees, where a soft thatch of yarrow is growing.

"Keeps the weeds down. I read this article about it. Goats would eat this stuff and you wouldn't have to mow it."

"That's a cover crop." I move closer and slide a hand over one of the tallest spots on the plant. "Yarrow is good for attracting the right kind of bugs. Ladybugs and lacewings love it—they're good bugs. And *they* love eating aphids and mites—bad bugs that want to get on my fruit."

"Yarrow." Cooper repeats the word as if he's committing it to some important part of his brain, filing it away for later use. "I'm guessing you're doing the organic thing, then, right?"

"The organic 'thing'? Sounds like some big-oil-Texas-boy judgment in there with the way you say it. But, yes, I am doing the organic thing."

Moving to another tree, I hand-thin a few more branches and toss them on the ground. "I'm nowhere near certified, but I'm keeping everything organic and biodynamic."

"Biodynamic." Again, he rolls the word around, thoughtfully. He looks over to me. "I'm not a big-oil Texas boy, just so you know. I'm a cattle-ranch kind of Texas boy. But I definitely picked up on the judgment in what *you* said."

"Some sort of enormous feedlot operation? That would explain the way you said 'organic thing.' It would also explain that truck of yours, parked in my driveway. That shiny beast shouts big *something*."

Cooper gives a mocking, withering lift of his brows and I realize how much it sounds like I'm about to chain myself to one of these trees, naked, while chanting ELF slogans at him. I mumble a vague apology but it sounds half-hearted to my own ears, so I try again. Louder and clearer, to make it stick. Cooper traces one of his hands over the yarrow, threading it through his open fingers.

"Not an enormous feedlot operation. Try a sixth-generation family-run cattle ranch. But even a bunch of farm boys who like their trucks big and shiny understand about keeping things greener. We're not some pack of idiots running around claiming climate change is a myth. So I wasn't judging. I was asking."

He pauses, and I clip another branch off with a sharp snap of my shears. Cooper steps closer and leans in to inspect the cut mark.

"In the spirit of not making more blind assumptions about each other, maybe you could explain why in the hell you keep cutting off those perfectly good tree limbs?"

I gather a handful of the twigs up and break them down into small sections.

"I'm thinning a few unproductive limbs. The curse of being a fruit farmer is that you can't walk down a tree row without seeing something that needs to be done." I hold up one of the twigs. "These little sections I'll use to graft—"

The words *next year* are nearly out of my mouth before I remember how unlikely that may be. I shove the twigs into the front center pocket on my overalls and cast my eyes over Cooper's shoulder.

"—I'll use them to graft. At some point."

The little pieces are tall enough that the tips are only an inch or two away from the bare skin exposed on my chest, above the neckline of my tank top. When I shift my focus to Cooper again, he's watching me, assessing my expression. His forehead creases for a moment, and then he steps near enough to reach for one of the grafting twigs. When he does, his thumb grazes just above the placket of my overalls and my skin immediately becomes a strange mix of frigid and scorching.

He notes my reaction, the way I don't pull away or flinch. His next touch feels wildly intentional, thumb skating lazily until his stroke meets the upper valley between my breasts. I take a deep inhale and hold it for a few beats. That move drives all the needy, hot-cold parts of my flesh closer to his touch. If I hold my breath much longer, I'm bound to get light-headed, but the second I release that in-evitable exhale, Cooper will be incrementally farther away and I'm not quite ready for that—just a few more seconds should do it, long enough for me to properly savor every moment of his fingers exploring my skin.

Screw it—maybe if I pass out, he'll have to perform some sort of first aid. With his mouth. Or his hands, all ten fingers doing whatever it takes to revive me. All I know is that, somehow, in the last two minutes we went from launching barbs—*You're a hippie! Yeah, well, you're a big-oil earth killer!*—to . . . hell, I don't know what to call it . . . just *this*.

My body demands that I breathe, so I give in and let out a painfully slow exhale. Cooper plucks out one of the twigs.

"Grafting is where you take and push one piece into the other, right? Even if they're from totally different trees, even if it makes no sense. But if you make sure they stay joined up for long enough, let them work into each other, eventually they come together."

He inspects the little piece of wood before looking to me, the same heated and frustrated expression on his face as when he first arrived. I nod slowly. If he weren't looking at me like that, I would laugh hysterically, because he's managed to turn fruit grafting talk into a vaguely dirty topic and I can't tell if it's on purpose or not. I should be rolling my eyes, scoffing, or generally telling him to give up this corny attempt to eroticize the act of shunting two twigs together.

Unfortunately, his gaze has started to drift down the

front of my body in a measured inspection, and any instinct I had to mock is long gone. Then he starts to roll the little nub of wood between his thumb and middle finger, with a gentle dexterity that makes my mouth go dry.

His obscene handling of the twig stops and he places it back in my pocket. This time his touch feels like it's everywhere, even if he's only lightly tracing the center of my chest before dragging his fingers slowly across my collarbone.

"Now. What about that gift shop? I'm ready to buy up some souvenirs."

= 7 =

(Whitney)

In the root cellar, a large building set on the north side of my property, the clean dirt smell inside is almost refreshing. Heavy fieldstones cover the outside and the rear portion is set back into a large berm of earth, keeping the inside cool and dry. The space is bigger than a typical root cellar, with tall shelves lining each of the walls, and the top ones are high enough that I can reach them only with a stepladder. The few remaining crates of late-season apples are stacked along one shelf, mostly an heirloom called Hubbardston Nonesuch—little beauties that most people haven't heard of, but inevitably fall in love with.

Cooper strolls around and peeks in the crates, hands shoved in his pockets, but doesn't touch anything.

"Try one." I point to one of the crates.

"You sure?"

"I do grow them for people to eat."

He reaches in and plucks one out, a tiny Nonesuch

with multi-toned red skin that hints at its long history—heirloom fruit that looks appropriately artisan, untouched by the manufactured perfection of Big Ag seed science. After a quick turn of it in his hand and a swipe across his jeans to polish the skin clean, when he bites into it, I automatically swell up with excitement. It's silly, but I love this moment. The first bite someone takes, the sound of how crisp it is, the way I can almost taste it along with him. It's pride and delight, all wrapped up in someone else's taste buds. In this case, we have the added bonus that it's Cooper's mouth on my fruit. That mouth, my fruit.

When he mumbles through a mouthful, the whole scene gets even better.

"That's awesome." He pulls the fruit back from his mouth, staring at the space he just bit into with the coolest kind of awe on his normally pouty face. Another bite. Another mumbling. "Seriously. Fucking. Good."

The small size means he's done in five bites and when he looks slightly disappointed that he's finished, now holding just a well-bitten core in his hand, I consider stalking over there and kissing him. For a whole host of reasons, but mostly because it's nice to remember why I put so much into this now sinking ship of a life. Maybe I didn't go into it with the best plan, maybe I threw myself almost blindly into this, but I gave it my whole heart. However this ends, I'll have that as a takeaway.

I drag an empty milk crate over from one dark corner of the room and set it in front of the shelves where jars of canned apple butter are stored. When I step up and reach out to the top shelf, the height forces me to one foot, on tiptoe. The precarious stance means most of my body weight tips to one side and I didn't quite set my feet in the center of the crate, so it jumps a little and I have to grab the edge of the shelf to balance myself. I'm far too familiar with this hazardous dance, but I never seem to remember that the crate is a tipsy perch.

This time, I don't particularly need the shelf, because before I've really grabbed on, I spy Cooper tossing his apple core onto one of the low shelves, then latching his hands on my hips, firmly.

"Get down."

I wave him away once I have my balance, twisting my midsection a bit to indicate that I don't need his hands there anymore. "I got it. I do this all the time."

"That doesn't make it a good idea."

He wraps one sturdy arm entirely around my waist and proceeds to swing my body off the milk crate, placing me back on the ground. I feign dusting off my overalls—of imaginary cooties or dirt, perhaps a few strong-man-hands-induced tingles.

"Grabby, much? I'm not a football you can just toss around at your leisure."

"I wasn't tossing you around. Just tell me what you were trying to reach for. I'll get it."

I point to the uppermost shelves. "Your precious apple butter is in those boxes."

When he steps like a sure-footed mountain goat onto the crate and easily pulls a box down, I decide this is a perfectly fine turn of events. Strong jawline, yes, but Cooper from this angle is also a damn fine sight. He steps down just as effortlessly and stands there with the box in his hands, looking down into the contents.

"These? They don't have those labels on them."

"I know. All those boxes up there are like that. I just got a new shipment of labels, but I haven't dragged these inside yet to put them on."

He looks down at the box in his hands, and then back up at the others. "I'll carry them in for you. All of the boxes on the top shelf?"

"No, no. Just grab as many jars as you want to take home and set that box there. I'll deal with the rest later. I've got a fall farmers' market in Grand Junction this weekend, so I'll make some time to get this handled before then."

"*Or*," Cooper shrugs, "I could help you now. I'm here, and I've got the time and the arms to heft them inside for you."

"No, it's fine. I don't need your help—"

Words are useless, apparently. He's already walking away, ducking down a bit to clear the low doorway of the root cellar, calling back over his shoulder.

"In the kitchen? On the table?"

I let my shoulders sag. Stubborn man. Nice, yes. Hot and helpful, also yes. But so, so stubborn. I don't even bother answering. Pretty sure he'll just do what the hell he wants, anyway.

Ten boxes later, Cooper strolls up onto the front porch and deftly uses just one finger to pull open the rickety screen door before stomping into the house to unload the last box. I've lingered behind to shut and latch the root cellar door, just as a faded red Ford truck with a lift kit rumbles into the driveway, a little faster than advisable, loud exhaust growling exaggeratedly in its wake. Tanner Euland rolls to a stop right beside to the enormous black Dodge that Cooper parked next to my truck, and gives me a wave before getting out.

"I hope your dad didn't change his mind and send you to negotiate a refund on my Polaris, Tanner."

Tanner unfolds his large frame—he's both tall and bulky, the way I'm sure his dad was at that age, before too many years of beer got ahold of the bulk—from the driver side and laughs.

"No, ma'am."

I absolutely adore that he calls me *ma'am*. Mostly because there isn't the least bit of condescension in his tone; he isn't some smart-mouthed kid who sounds smarmy when he says it. Just evidence of the honest, rural, homegrown manners knocked into his brain since he was a toddler. Reaching into the truck bed, Tanner pulls out a pair of hickory-handled loppers.

"We found a couple of things in the bed box that belong to you. Dad asked me to drop them off on the way to practice."

"Oh, Jesus. Thank you." I take the loppers and breathe a heavy sigh. These are my best pair, sharp and curved just right for efficient pruning.

Tanner moves to the passenger side of his truck, pulls open the door, and leans in. I follow and take up a spot just behind him, peeking around his frame, because it suddenly feels like Christmas, even if I'm just getting my own stuff back.

The screen door to my house slams shut and Cooper heads our way, just as Tanner's head pops up from where he was rummaging around near the floorboard of his truck, now waving a small-toothed saw in the air.

"This, too."

I clap my hands together. Cooper sidles up next to me, a slight grimace on his face, taking in the lopper, the teen boy with his back to us who is waving a saw in the air, and my delight at all of it. Tanner turns and when he sees Cooper, it's déjà vu of the boy at the hotel.

The kid's face goes slack. His mouth flops open. And then he drops the saw on the ground and it just misses our feet.

Tanner mumbles a half-whisper. "Holy shit."

Cooper gives a grin that's mostly just the twitch of one side of his mouth going up, followed by a chin nudge in Tanner's direction.

"Hey."

Nothing but a choked sound from Tanner. That and a set of googly, crazy eyes.

I poke Cooper in the side with my elbow and he looks down at me, brow furrowed.

"Say something."

"I did say something. I said 'hey.' "

Another poke to his ribs. He responds with a low, short growl. "I'm getting there. But the kid just dropped a sharp, shiny-looking saw on the ground, a little too close to all of our toes. I want him to get right for a second, first. I've done this before, you know?"

Finally, Tanner manages to breathe again and Cooper bends down to pick up the errant saw, handing it my way, where it's safely in the hands of someone indifferent—well, relatively so—to the presence of this pro football player.

Cooper extends his hand to Tanner. "I'm Cooper."

Tanner blinks. "I know."

Poor kid. He's normally much more composed than this, well spoken without being an annoying know-it-all, and ceaselessly polite. Kenny brags on his son whenever possible, so I already know that Tanner is a national honor society member, finalist for a Boettcher scholarship this year, and he speaks Spanish fluently. The boy knows a whole lot of words in not just one, but two languages, and yet he can't seem to find any of them right now.

"Cooper, this is Tanner Euland."

I set the saw and the lopper aside on the ground between my feet before giving Tanner a gentle tap on the arm to reacquaint him with reality. His hand shoots out immediately and grasps on to Cooper's, shaking it enthusiastically.

Cooper takes the hand jostling in stride, finally pulling back, without making the scene even more awkward. "Good to meet you, Tanner. You live around here?"

Something melts across Tanner's features then, the look of a kid who just realized that Cooper Lowry is actually standing in front of him, being completely open and perfectly nice. That revelation restores his ability to speak, and Tanner manages to explain that he lives down the road.

"Oh!" I extend both of my arms and grab each of them by a bicep. "You guys totally have something in common."

They both look at me as if I've suddenly taken on the role of an extremely odd matchmaker. One who is simply bursting with excitement about the amazing commonality I'm about to reveal.

I give Tanner's arm a squeeze. "Tanner's family has a cattle ranch." I offer the same grip to Cooper's very defined and pronounced bicep. "And Cooper grew up on a cattle ranch."

I waggle my brows. They both just stare, giving blank looks that convey their continued confusion at my announcement.

"What? You both have cattle ranching in common. I'm just saying, it's something you both know about."

Again, nothing but two vacantly perplexed faces pointed my direction. I consider walking away and letting this play out sans my unappreciated conversation starters, but Cooper takes and pats my hand with one of his until I drop my grip on each of them, letting my arms swing awkwardly by my sides. Then he captures my free hand, lacing our fingers together. Tanner's eyes drop immediately and mine follow, both of us gaping at the unexpected display.

If this teenage interloper weren't here as witness, I'd ask Cooper what this is all about. I'd bring our linked hands up until they were directly in his sight line, then jiggle them for effect and demand an explanation. Instead, I stand there and fixate on the way our hands fit together, joined in perfect proportions, his grip strong, but still comfortable. And the way his hand warms my previously cold fingers only adds to the surprising Goldilocks just-rightness of the whole thing.

"I think we have other stuff in common, too." Cooper glances into Tanner's truck, where a gym bag and a set of football pads take up most of the bench seat. "You headed to practice?"

Tanner's soft face turns bright and he arches his back a bit, the move a subconscious sort of strut. He's headed to the gym for practice, he says, then casually throws in that they have a big game on Friday. Cooper responds just as informally about his own game on Sunday, somehow answering this seventeen-year-old kid's game talk with his own, as if the two are same-same.

When the conversation takes off from there, I realize I'm doomed. Hopelessly doomed to never keep up with this discussion of run-heavy offensives, shotgun something-I-don't-understand, zone-blocking gobbledygook, and no-huddle hokey-pokey.

Cooper finally drops my hand for a moment, working to explain a concept by using his arms to gesture widely. Watching his body language come alive when he does, it becomes clear that this—football, the game, his team, all of it—it's who Cooper Lowry is. Authentically, at the core, and rooted in every part of his body.

Cooper pauses, then crosses his arms over his chest, tilting his head toward Tanner.

"You hunt, right? Waterfowl? Or shoot trap?" Tanner nods in response.

"OK, then think of it that way. When you shoot ducks or clays, you swing *through* the target, you don't stop the gun. That's how you have to think about being a receiver. Because the number of times a ball sails right into your hands, when you're standing on the field just waiting for it, are basically nil. Doesn't happen. So don't let the ball come to you; figure out how to go get the damn thing."

That little speech, the tone of his voice, the way his rhetoric was bone-deep without posturing, makes my heart swell a bit. Even if we were just wasting a day together— for reasons neither of us could probably explain—reducing Cooper to a series of clichés was incredibly shortsighted on my part.

I let my eyes find the dirt in front of me and focus my gaze there, considering all the ways I may have underestimated the guy standing next to me.

Cooper takes up my hand in his again and squeezes. "Sorry. We're ignoring you. I got on my soapbox there a little bit."

His apology makes everything worse, compounded by the fact that when I look up, his face is more animated than it has been all day. I give a loose shake of my head.

"Not sure I could offer much to the conversation. Throw the ball, catch the ball, don't drop the ball. That's all I got."

I get a laugh from both of them, the kind that might accompany a head patting if I were a toddler. I let it slide, only because I set myself up for it a bit, jabbering about like the Hollywood caricature of a woman who knows nothing about football. If I had lip gloss in my pocket, now would be the time the script calls for me to reapply it, daintily yet haughtily.

"Crap." Tanner looks at his phone and then shoves it back in his pocket. "I'm so late for practice. Coach will never believe me when I tell him why, which means I'm gonna run suicides for a while."

Cooper makes a face. "Shit, sorry. Suicides are the worst."

A resigned dude expression passes between them as Tanner sticks his hand out.

"I can't believe I met you. I can't believe you're *here*."

I'd take offense at the way he emphasized the last word—coupled with a glance my way—but come on, who wouldn't agree with him? Even I agree with him.

Cooper shrugs nonchalantly, signaling that he can't quite believe he's here, either. Then he tilts his head.

"You guys always play on Friday nights? Every other week at home?" An enthusiastic nod from Tanner. "Well, if I make it down here again, maybe I'll come by and check out a game."

You'd swear that Cooper just alluded to buying the kid a pony, conjuring up a genie in a bottle for him, and hiring a stripper, because I've never seen a teenage boy look closer to a strange mix of crying and squeeing before. Fortunately, he resists both urges. He also manages to back out of my driveway without damaging anything, while staring at Cooper the entire time.

It's early evening now; the remaining light is dusky and receding quickly toward the mountains. I'm suddenly exhausted. Playing tour guide and trying to keep up with all the wacky events of my day means my shoulders are starting to sag heavily and my feet ache.

"I guess I should go, too." Cooper looks as fatigued as I feel, but he pauses, hesitating.

"It's getting late. Let me get that apple butter so you can head out." I turn to trot inside, but Cooper tugs the sleeve of my hoodie to stop me.

"I already stole a couple of jars and put them in my truck when I brought the boxes in. How much do I owe you?"

The near darkness means I can't see much of his face, shadows mostly, but his hand slips down from the grip on my sleeve and latches on to mine again. The move feels less orchestrated now, more natural than it did in front of Tanner. I let his hand tangle in with mine and give a playful tug to our entwined fingers.

"Just take them. Consider it compensation for all your help today. Moving those boxes and being my little chutney helper. Plus, I'm pretty sure you made Tanner's entire year. Thank you for being so kind to him—he's a good kid."

"He's just me, fifteen years ago." Cooper raises his free hand to tuck an errant strand of my hair behind my ear, and it feels like the perfect setup for him to do something more.

Because it's just the two of us here. Standing in the dark, holding hands, and letting the shadows keep whatever this is under wraps. But he doesn't. All he does is thank me for everything and release my hand gently, before walking away to his truck. I head inside without turning back.

I strip off my boots just inside the front the door, then flip the living room and kitchen lights off as I walk to my bedroom. My hoodie lands on the floor, my overalls are unbuckled and kicked into a heap, and my tank top is replaced by the men's pajamas I wear to sleep. Just the top, though, leaving the bottoms at the foot of my bed because the house feels too stuffy.

Then I proceed to perform a dramatic belly-flop face-plant onto the bed, giving up a groan that is the voice of so many things. Excitement mixed with exasperation. A foolish sort of giddy confusion. And just to muddle up the mix, an achy dissatisfaction starts to hum through my body, through every limb, across every inch of my skin.

A sensation I haven't felt in years, so foreign now that I'd almost forgotten how it feels. Want. That's what this is. Just restless, pouty, frustrating *want*.

= 8 =

(Cooper)

I drop my forehead against the steering wheel in my truck. Then thump it a few times for good measure, because concussion or not, I need the jostling to reset my sanity. If I don't clear my head, I'm probably going to do something stupid, like flip a mental bird at Hunt's instructions, grab my bag, and go pound on Whitney's door until she lets me in.

After I'm inside, there won't be any talking. No needling at the differences between us, no more lingering looks that tease and tempt without going anywhere. If I make it inside that house again, my hands are going to strip her of all those terrible clothes until I can finally look at her properly. Once I've visually mapped the sight of her naked body enough to commit every inch to memory, we still won't need to talk. Even if she is funny and sharp, smart and fascinating, we can save the chatter for later. Until after I'm satisfied, she's spent, and we're both pleased with how the day ended up.

And there it is. The heavy ache in my dick that's persisted most of the day, clouding my judgment and generally making a nuisance of itself. I thunk my head to the hard plastic again and the corresponding dull pain prompts a realization.

My head hasn't hurt all day. Not even a tiny twinge of the pain that's plagued me since Sunday. Nothing. Either Whitney is the perfect prescription or this place is so remote it's healing, I don't know which—but my brain likes the relief.

Just like Hunt instructed, I found a place to get lost in, and it worked. Up until Tanner arrived, I barely thought about football. Even when he and I started talking, I still wasn't fighting the sticky fear that rises up when I think about my concussion. Because Tanner was a rear window to my past, to the safe harbor of high school, where the relentless pressure that comes with being a pro is nonexistent. If I'd only understood then how amazing it was to worry more about getting laid than scoring anywhere else.

All that misty-eyed reflection may also explain my adolescent descent into hand-holding with Whitney. When I did it, she looked at me like I was certifiable, and I took it as a blessing that she didn't yank her hand away. In the moment, I was just trying to keep her somehow tethered to that spot, because she was babbling about cattle ranching and when we didn't *ohmygod* at the revelation, it looked like she was about to walk away.

And I didn't want her to. I wanted her right there next to me, as close as possible. If she had walked away, I would have followed her like an overgrown duckling or something, with a seventeen-year-old kid as witness to the entire pathetic scene.

My head begins to ache, just sitting here, but part of the problem is that I'm starving and exhausted. I need food and sleep. Unfortunately, as with all of my other actions today, I didn't plan ahead when it came to the important details of spending the night away from home. Fortunately, I have a GPS and a glove box full of Clif bars.

Leaning over, I flip open the glove compartment and pluck out a bar, tear the wrapper open with my teeth, and take a bite while giving the key a half-turn in the ignition so the GPS lights up. I poke around until the navi system lets me search for lodging in Hotchkiss, Colorado.

No Results flashes across the display, and Carmen, the name I anointed the GPS voice with, repeats the same, while oh-so-gently asking me to retry my request. She asked nicely, like she always does, so I double-check my spelling and hit the search button again.

No results. I take another bite of my bar and think. When I drove through town, I didn't see much. A stream of quaint, old-timey storefronts that didn't make much of an impression, with the exception of a barbeque joint that seemed to span an entire block. What I don't remember seeing is a motel of any sort. *No results* might be the truth.

Taking a deep breath, I glance toward the jars of apple butter on my passenger seat. I grab one and twist the band off, then pry the lid until it unseals. I take what's left of the

Clif bar and drag it through the apple butter, scooping up as much as I can manage, and toss the concoction in my mouth. A few bites are all it takes. I let out a satisfied but defeated grunt.

That settles it—Whitney's damn near perfect. Because even though I'd never tell my grandma, this shit is better than hers. As if I weren't already having trouble convincing my dick and my brain to get the hell out of here, this only adds to the list of reasons I want to figure out a way to stay. I look up toward Whitney's house, where the lights in the living room have gone dark, but the window on the far left side has a faint glow. I'm guessing that's her bedroom. And she's probably still awake.

If I go up to that front door, though, I need to stay strong. Politely compliment the apple butter and ask if she knows about a motel nearby. That's it. As much as I want to do more, live out every filthy daydream I tried to tamp down today, I can't. My body can't. My head can't. The last thing I need to do is make my concussion worse by tossing Whitney across the closest available flat surface and going at it until the sun comes up. Because explaining to Hunt that my worsened lack of coordination is the result of an all-night fuck-fest wouldn't be pretty.

But every success I've earned and accomplishment I've garnered has come from the same source. *Me*. My will-power. My determination. My self-fucking-control.

Therefore, I can absolutely walk up there, knock on the door, look Whitney in the face, and keep my eyes fixed on hers while I ask a question. It's that simple.

All I have to do is keep my dick out of the equation.

I sit in the truck for a few more minutes, until I've tethered all my resolve into a tightly held ball inside my chest. I do this before a game, and it works there, so the same theory should apply here. Stay focused while I get in and get out.

Ah, shit, but not *in*-in. Great. That little mantra doesn't work here. Now all I can think about is getting in. And then out. And then in again. Repeat, repeat, repeat—*fuck*.

The dome light kicks on when I shove the truck door open so hard it nearly springs the hinges. I purposefully leave the keys in the ignition, thinking that if I do, it might be another deterrent. On second thought, maybe I should stay in the truck—with the doors locked and the motor running—and honk the horn until she stomps out here. Then I can crack the window just enough to ask where the nearest fine lodgings are.

But she's five foot nothing and a hundred-something pounds of organic farming hippie girl, after all. So, suck it up, Lowry.

The screen door creaks when I pull it open, then lay three loud raps against the wooden frame.

I swear, if she hollers "it's open" this time, I will lose my mind. And not in a fun, wild sex way, either. More of a scolding and snarling, *don't you understand how pissed I'll be if something happens to you* kind of way. She's saved from the lecture when the porch light comes on and I see her peek out the front window to assess the situation. Her eyebrows rise in surprise, and then descend into a furrow.

The front door swings open. And Whitney is standing there, dressed—or rather, undressed—in a way that prompts a pitiful plea to every patron saint of poor judgment there is. God help me, I need all the strength I can get. I really, really do.

"Did you leave and come back? Or have you been sitting out there for the last half an hour? I'm sure that fancy truck of yours has a butter-soft leather interior and a finely tuned German sound system, but still. Weird."

Here's the problem: she's talking and waiting for me to say something, but I've already broken one of the rules I laid out earlier. The one about looking her in the face and keeping my eyes where they belong. What I didn't factor in when making this rule was the possibility that she wouldn't be wearing any *pants*.

The old-man pj's are back, but they're only fifty percent of the ensemble. The top is present and accounted for, although I'd swear that a few extra buttons at the top are undone, but the bottoms are nowhere to be found.

Whitney's legs are smooth, honey-toned, and bare, all the way up to just above her knees. It's possible I'm drooling. I'm positive that my jaw is slack enough to catch a few flies. My hands twitch at my sides and I decide to latch them on to the door frame as a fail-safe measure. Maybe if I just stop looking at the leg part—especially the glimpse of inner thigh where her stance means I could slip my hands between her knees and then stroke slowly upward—maybe if I shift my attention away from that space, I can get through this.

With every bit of determination I can muster, I drag

my gaze downward. Probably a bit more leisurely than I should, but her perfectly tapered calves become just another snag in my sight line. Pretty little ankles, too. Who knew that a pair of petite ankles, one of them ensconced with a delicate henna-inspired tattoo, could look so good?

Keep your eyes moving, Lowry. Feet. That's all you have to get to, her goddam feet, the least intriguing part of a woman's body and the most likely safe zone you have right now.

I continue my laborious visual trek.

Fuck. Me.

Would it be too much to ask for just one part of her body to be a neutral space for me to look at? Apparently, yes, it would be, because she has this cute little gold toe ring on her right foot and I suddenly want to kiss that tiny spot.

This, coming from a guy who absolutely does not have a foot fetish of any sort. As long as a woman keeps her little piggies properly pedicured so that I don't mistake her feet for my own, that is where my interest ends. The occasional foot massage? Sure. Only for making her feel good, though—not to get me going.

But that glint of delicate gold is the embodiment of Whitney's soft-focus sexiness, the raw but gorgeous way she doesn't have to force it, because it's always there.

The last resort is for me to close my eyes. Tamp my damn eyelids shut and force them to stay that way.

"Is there a motel around here?"

My voice sounds like I smoke a pack a day and enjoy

it. Gravel on a growl, the rasp of a man who can't quite manage a normal breathing cycle.

"What? A motel?"

Whitney comes closer; I can hear her moving, the creak of a floorboard as she does, and I open my eyes before I can remind myself to keep them closed. Her legs have shifted, the ball of one foot now perched on the top of her other foot. A small gust of cold air runs through the doorway at that moment and gooseflesh erupts on her bare skin. I drop my hands from the door frame reflexively, letting them swing at my sides.

I want to reach forward and *fix* that. First, warm her skin, and then become the proper reason her skin is responding that way. By slamming the door shut behind us and letting my fingers re-create what the cold air caused.

Whitney lowers her voice. "Are you telling me you don't have a place to stay tonight?"

I take a deep breath. "This was a spur-of-the-moment trip. I didn't make a reservation anywhere and Carmen keeps telling me the same thing. 'No results, no results, no results.' I just need to know where the nearest motel is."

"Who the hell is Carmen? Do you have a girl stashed in your truck? Because if she's been out there all day, I swear, I'll bring her inside to stay the night and leave you out in the cold."

"Jesus. No. I don't have a woman stashed in my truck. Carmen is the name I gave the GPS voice. I entered *Hotchkiss* in the navi system looking for a place to stay, and Carmen seems to think there isn't anything around here."

Whitney giggles, actually fucking giggles, and I manage

to stop looking at her legs and feet long enough to find her face. When I do, she cants her head a bit.

"I do know of one place that might take you in."

My shoulders slump in relief. Now we're getting somewhere. Because I just want to find more food, then a bed to collapse on. I give her a tired, imploring expression, hoping she can see how beat I am.

She lazily sweeps one arm up and out, gesturing to the space around her. "Chez Whitney."

My body turns tense, preparing to share the four hundred reasons that is not a good idea. She notes the shift and gently pats the side of my face with her hand.

"Go get your stuff, Cooper. You're too tired to drive."

I try not to lean into her hand but don't quite succeed. When she doesn't pull away, but presses down a bit more and lets her pinkie sweep a tiny path across my jawline, all I can do is yield to what feels good. Whitney. Her touch. This place. And the way those things have managed to make everything better.

When she drops her hand, I let out a measured exhale and shuffle back to my truck, grabbing the keys out of the ignition and then my duffel bag from the backseat. Inside the house, I drop the bag on Don Draper's orange velvet couch in the living room. Whitney gives the front door a shove with the flat of her palms to close it and turns the flimsy lock on the handle.

"Any chance that Chez Whitney has a room-service menu?"

"Not an extensive one."

"I'm not picky. Just hungry."

She releases her auburn mane from the chopstick that's been holding it up in a bun all day.

"There's a big bowl of kale–wheat berry salad in the fridge and some leftover braised chicken in there, too. A decent loaf of sourdough on the counter next to the stove. Just poke around and eat whatever you like."

She runs her fingers through her hair and the bottom hem on her pj's rises up as she lifts her arms. "If you don't mind, I'm going to grab a quick shower while you eat."

I nod and turn away quickly, both because of the extra skin she just flashed and because the kitchen is *this* way. At this point, it's debatable which base craving I'm fighting worse, food or fucking.

Whitney slips out of the room and I yank open the refrigerator door. A stainless steel bowl is on the top shelf, about half-full of the salad she mentioned. I take it and the adjacent platter of chicken out to place on the counter. Pulling plastic wrap off both, I strip the meat off two pieces of chicken and toss it on top of the kale salad, taking a quick glance around for the bread loaf. But when I spy it, in all its white sourdough glory, all I can picture is Carolyn, our team nutritionist, shaking her head at me. Whole grains or no grains, she always says.

The shower turns on with a squeak and a groan that emphasizes exactly how ancient the plumbing of this old farmhouse is. I work hard at not imagining Whitney stripping down as I rummage through the drawers for a fork. Fork in hand, I take a heaping bite of the salad and exhale heavily. It's good, thankfully. Real food in her house, the clean kind I need, is another plus for tonight, since an organic fruit farmer isn't going to Lean Cuisine her way through life.

"Cooper?"

Whitney's voice emerges over the sound of the shower. I freeze and look up, half hoping she'll be standing in there naked and half praying she won't. She doesn't appear, so around a mouthful of salad, I call back.

"Yeah?"

"Do me a favor, will you?"

If her "favor" involves shower gel or a loofah, I'm bound to see if I can shove the rest of this meal in my mouth at once and scramble in there to help.

"A little bowl of that chutney we made is in the fridge. Try it and tell me what you think. First, try it on its own. Then pair it with the goat cheese that's on the bottom shelf. I think it's better that way, but I'd like another opinion."

Shower gel and a loofah would have been nice, but more food works, too. Still clutching my precious bowl of salad, I source the chutney and goat cheese before sitting down at the table. Five minutes later, my fork clangs against the bottom of the stainless steel bowl as I scrape up the last bite. A quick wash of the bowl in the sink—no dishwasher that I can see—and I grab a couple of other pieces of silverware for my second course.

The first spoonful of chutney hits my mouth and while it's not bad, it's also sickeningly sweet. The sweetness overwhelms everything, even the flavor of what I think might be some damn good pears. Does she really want to know what I think? At this point, she has to know I'm incapable of lying with any finesse; she's called me on it more than once, so she had to understand what she was getting into when she asked. I take another dollop up and slice off just enough goat cheese to top it.

Just as I lift the spoon and open up to eat it, Whitney appears in the doorway with her pj top on again, the bottoms still MIA, scrunching her wet hair with a towel.

"And?"

I can smell her from here, soap-scented and clean with a bonus layer of that coconut scent I'm already starting to identify with her. When I give my assessment of the chutney, there's a dual meaning to my words, because with her standing there half-dressed and edible-looking, both Whitney and the chutney have one very specific trait in common.

"Sweet."

She nods. "I know, right? Too sweet. That's all you can taste."

With a quick chin nudge toward the spoon I'm holding, she prompts me to give it a try. When I eat it this way, I understand what she's saying about the goat cheese— the tangy bite in its flavor cuts through the overpowering sugar. I nod a few times so she knows that this works.

She twists her body to one side so she can continue to work her hair with the towel. "I guess my recipe needs a little work."

I lick the spoon clean. "I'm sure your next batch will be better. The pear flavor is killer, though, so a few more crates of those and you can play around with it."

The hand holding the towel she's been using goes stiff

for a moment, then slack, as she drops her arm. Her expression changes just as quickly, becoming weary and broken, unlike anything I've seen from her. What I said to cause that, I don't know.

I do know that I hate it. My mind starts to reel through the last few minutes, searching for the words that I shouldn't have said and trying to figure out how to fix it. Before I can, she disappears, claiming something about her hair getting frizzy. Leaving me behind—and one pushy decision away from stalking in there after her.

———

Ten minutes later, her hair dryer finally shuts off. I've flopped onto the couch, pulled off my boots, and started to consider how best to recline my six-foot-three frame without the assistance of a contortionist.

She slips into the room and leans against a far wall.

"I'm exhausted." She rolls her shoulders to loosen them. "Sleep?"

"Absolutely." I arrange the decades-old throw pillows together, trying to assemble a pile that might best mimic a real bed pillow.

Whitney snorts. "Oh, come on. You are not sleeping on that couch."

"It's fine. I'm good here."

She waves her hand toward me, in a beckoning gesture. I shake my head and grip my hands into fists that I set on my thighs. I give her a firm look, which she ignores. Her next move is to give an impish little tilt of her head in the direction of the bedroom.

"Whitney," I say, slowly and quietly, obvious warning in my voice.

Turning on her heel, she saunters off, a languid amble that matches the tone of her response. "Cooper."

She doesn't have to say anything else because—let's be fucking real here—we both know I'm going in there.

= 9 =

(Cooper)

In Whitney's bedroom, the space feels claustrophobic. Between my keyed-up state and the actual small dimensions of the room, a nervy energy permeates the air.

A dark, hulking, ornately carved bureau is pushed against one wall and a matching dressing table is along the opposite wall, both of them crowding the space. A queen bed sits in the middle and it's the only thing that doesn't look ten decades old; it's just a box spring and mattress set on a flimsy metal frame, covered by a light blue comforter—the kind of setup your parents send you off to college with, cheap and basic. Let's hope that the stark contrast between this economy bed and the rest of the furniture means we aren't sleeping on the dead old lady's bed.

Whitney is sitting cross-legged in the middle of the bed, facing me, her hands clasped loosely as she toys with her fingers. The sight of her there, looking just the smallest bit nervous but still self-assured, adds to the sensation that the walls are slowly collapsing the room in on us. Closer and closer, until we inevitably land on top of each other.

I make it to the edge of the bed and stop. She draws back the comforter on one side of the bed, a wordless encouragement for me to take that spot. I take a deep breath.

"I can't sleep in my clothes."

"OK."

"I won't be able to sleep."

"OK." Whitney stretches her arms out behind her and leans back, lazily. "Naked? Is that what you're driving at?"

When her expression becomes a playful mix of goading and hopeful, my entire body turns toward high alert.

"Not naked. Just boxers."

She nods and continues to sit there, waiting for the show, it seems. My heart lurches into my throat because I suddenly feel like it's my first day on the job as a male stripper and I've just realized I'm going to suck at this job. Even if I spend every Sunday on national television, this display, in front of this woman, is entirely nerve-racking. If we were going at it, stripping and tugging and wrestling each other's clothes off, I'd be in my comfort zone. But Whitney's scrutiny, the odd self-consciousness it brings on, is new to me.

She wets her lips with a dart and sweep of her tongue. Instinct takes over, and I yank the button on my jeans open, pull the zipper down, and manage to tug my socks off at the same time that I shuck the jeans. I latch on to the back of my shirt, grasping the neckline to pull it off.

Then it's just me, standing here in my dark gray boxer briefs, waiting for what's next. All I can think about is this line from a movie my high school girlfriend insisted we watch on repeat.

I'm also just a girl, standing in front of a boy, asking him to love her.

Fucking Hugh Grant movies. They're like the earworms of romantic comedies. I'm stuck in place, half-hard, and all I can think is: *I'm just a boy, standing in front of a girl, asking her to do something, anything, to make his cock stop hurting.*

Seriously. Fuck off, Hugh Grant.

I suck in a deep breath and hold it for a moment. Whitney lazes her head to one side as she runs her gaze over me.

"Huh." Her brow furrows, perplexed.

That's not the reaction I usually get when I strip down. I mean, let's be honest, I work out *for a living*. I consume thirty-five hundred quality, clean, lean calories a day and have eight percent body fat. I've made the pages of the *ESPN The Magazine*'s Body Issue three times. I'm definitely not a couch potato and Whitney sounding disappointed isn't the response I was hoping for.

She rights her head and rises up on her knees, then starts toward me, shuffling forward until she's at the edge of the bed and resting back on her heels.

One of her hands starts to trace a meandering pattern across my abs, using just the pads of her fingers. My cock reacts, going thick and heavy, until I'm fully erect so quickly it's embarrassing. She has to have noticed, unless she somehow happens to be hopelessly farsighted—but I'm guessing there's not much luck of that. Probably looked like some lame nature documentary, those time-lapse sequences of flowers and caterpillars growing to full size in five seconds.

Her fingers dip low enough to tick the top edge of my boxers and if she isn't careful, she's going to end up sweeping across the tip of my dick, because I'm nearly escaping the upper band. She stops tracing and looks up, then taps a spot in the center of my stomach with her index finger.

"I was convinced that when you took your shirt off, I'd find a little blue thundercloud with raindrops," she taps again, "right here."

I let out a grunt. "What the hell are you talking about?"

"Like Grumpy Bear. The grouchy Care Bear." She sighs and presses her open hand to my stomach. "I guess these abs will have to do."

My pelvis tips forward, almost unconsciously, because I want her to start using her fingers again.

"I'm not always grouchy."

Probably doesn't help my argument that my tone is closer to a snarl than necessary. Her hand barely moves, heating the spot where she's letting her palm rest.

She laughs softly. "Of course not. Sometimes you're a little ray of sunshine, I bet."

I push my hips out again and ball my hands into fists at my sides. She begins grazing each individual ab, using both hands and all her fingers now, snaking a lazy trail to what currently feels like the center of the entire fricking universe.

"Tell me one thing that makes you happy, Cooper. Turns you inside out from liking it so much. Always makes you smile like a little kid. And you can't say football—that's too eas—"

I grab her hands, because she just mentioned football and she's a hairsbreadth away from my cock and I have to stop her before she closes the gap. Should have slept in my goddam truck. I knew this would happen, that the two of us in this house together would lead to wandering hands—but the restless, greedy parts of my mind wanted it too much to let rational reasoning win out.

But on Friday, I have to show up at team headquarters and prove to Hunt that I'm ready. I need a decent night's sleep and a safe drive home tomorrow. Anything that might derail those objectives is off the table. Right now, no matter how much I want her, the big picture of my career takes priority.

Whitney takes a long breath in and I realize that her body has gone rigid, so edgy that I can feel the tension radiating from her hands. She's nervous or scared, I can't tell which, but if I don't explain myself, I'm bound to make it worse.

"I have a concussion," I blurt out, a hell of a lot louder than the acoustics of this tiny room require.

Her hands flex in mine for a moment, then go so limp that I have to tighten my grip to keep ahold of her.

"Excuse me?"

She moves to pull away and I let her go, even when I hate the way she creeps back just enough that it's clear she wants more space between us and all I want is less of it. I push out a short, gusting breath.

"A guy named Stinger knocked me on my ass in Sunday's game and I ended up with a concussion from it. That call I got earlier was my team trainer, checking in. He told me to get out of town and take it easy because if I don't get some rest and prove that my stupid brain is healed, I'll have to sit out the next game."

Whitney's body slumps and her mouth drops open like she's not sure what to say. I have to add one more piece of information, just in case she thinks taking it "easy" is my way of setting up a slow round of sex, all lovemaking style with a light jazz soundtrack to suit, a little Kenny G to set the right mood.

"So, I can't—I can't do anything . . . vigorous."

That sounded stupid. *Vigorous.* Straightforward probably would have been a better approach.

Look, you can clearly see that my dick is so hard I could fell one of your apple trees with it. I want you. But I think that you and I aren't going to be very good at keeping it mellow and gentle. We're bound to break some furniture, bruise each other in some amazing ways, and turn my concussion into a full-blown aneurysm. Can't risk it. Please put some pants on. I'll just go sleep in the root cellar.

"I can't fucking believe you." Whitney drops the weakest, most pathetic punch ever, to my stomach.

"What don't you understand about 'I have a concussion'? Then you go and punch me?"

"Exactly. You should have said something about that— oh, I don't know—eight flipping hours ago! Instead, you spend all this time giving me a bunch of hot, smoldering looks while manspreading your way around my house, and I'm thinking there's going to be some wocka-wocka action between us. But the whole time you knew nothing could happen." She lands another gnat-like swing. "Which makes you a tease, Cooper Lowry."

She gives a side-glance at nothing in particular, merely a moment for her to regroup, it seems, because she starts in again.

"And I let you carry in a bunch of heavy boxes when you shouldn't be doing anything vigorous. We walked around in the cold for an hour, a teenage boy was *this close* to injuring you with a wily handsaw, you didn't eat anything but an apple until an hour ago, and I don't think I saw you drink any water today. Now you're probably dehydrated, and that's just peachy for a head injury. You're a bullheaded, stupid pain in the ass."

She has to take a deep breath to recover. I wait for her to calm down, lest I risk another pitiful punch from her.

"You done?"

"No. Who is this 'Stinger' person? I'm pretty sure I hate him. I'll give *him* a concussion."

Her expression is the best combination of pissed off, indignant, sad, and worried. Even if I'm still hard and doing this might make it worse, I just want to lie on top of her and see if I can get her entire body wrapped up in mine, close enough to hold her in a full-body bear grip. Because hating on Stinger is her gut-check reaction to my revelation, not caring if I can't play, not worrying that the pro ball player standing in front of her is on the receding edge of his career. I'm not a meal ticket or a bankroll; I'm not my contract or my jersey. She just thinks I'm a pain in the ass. God, she's fucking fantastic.

"I'm not a big fan of him, either. But I love that you're getting all wound up to defend my honor. Good thing the big bruise he left on my back is almost gone."

She scrunches up her face and leaps off the bed to inspect my back. A gasp is followed by a snarl, when she finds the remaining evidence of where Stinger's knee nearly burst my appendix. Then her hands are on my ass, but not in a particularly good way, because she's primarily just shoving on me. I lurch forward a bit, taken off guard for a second, but find my balance enough to shoot a look over my shoulder.

"If you aren't in that bed, under the covers with your eyes closed, in the next five seconds, Cooper, I'm going to put you there."

I let out a huge laugh. "I'd love to see you try."

"Five, four, three . . ." She stops when I pull back the top sheet and slip under the covers. Hands on her hips, she gives a short nod. "Good boy."

That shit would normally find her flat on her back, me on top and wrestling her hands above her head so I can prove that I'm no boy. I settle for reaching out and grabbing a fistful of her pj top and giving it a yank. She half-stumbles onto the mattress and lands in an awkward straddle over me.

Her face is right next to mine and I can tell that her top is shoved up enough to leave her uncovered in the best places. I put both of my hands to work, one snaked up through her hair to rest at her neck, the other sliding across her hip until I've got my fingers tucked under the top edge of her panties.

Whitney's eyes flare and she starts to make a noise that sounds like she's about to protest us doing anything *vigorous*. But we can do this right, we're both adults and capable of setting limits, so I give a little squeeze of my hand at her neck to quiet whatever she was about to say.

"I want to kiss you, Whitney. Because if I don't at least do that, I'm going to lie here awake all night. But we can't let it get out of control. Like I said, nothing vigorous."

"Good luck with that," she whispers.

I grin, then pull her in, as tenderly as I possibly can. Her lips part, the best invitation there is, but she's also moving her hips in anticipation of more, so I have to wrap my arm around her waist. Because those hips of hers pushing down to meet my unsatisfied cock is a short road to letting this get out of hand. Our mouths meet, and she's nothing but softness and heat against me, opened up just enough to let my tongue tease her across her lower lip. I give in to a low grunt and sink in.

She's moaning softly and every taste between us is wet enough to keep our mouths moving across each other's without turning sloppy, her hair is falling down around both our heads, and that scent of coconut is everywhere. Whitney puts the brakes on first, curving her body up like a cat so that our lips are barely touching. Then she lands a faint, tiny little peck on my cheek, a move that apparently means we're done here.

She rolls off me without a word, shuffles under the covers, and leans over to switch off the table lamp. I curl onto my side and reach for her, one of my hands to her hip. She shimmies her body back and nestles into the space that suddenly feels crafted with her contours in mind. An ass that fits perfectly against my dick, legs so petite I could easily throw one of my own over hers and keep her anchored down.

She pulls my hand into hers, tucks them both under the sweet softness of her breasts. Immediately, I know that I'll sleep easily tonight, restful and almost satisfied.

"Fireworks."

Whitney turns a bit in my grasp. "What?"

"You asked what makes me happy, something that makes me smile." I burrow my face into her hair for a second and breathe in. "I'm a total sucker for fireworks displays. The big ones, like Fourth of July."

She lets out a tiny sigh. "That's *such* a good answer."

When my eyes open, it's evident that I slept longer than I should have. Sunlight is pouring in through the window above Whitney's bed and landing squarely on our tangled-up bodies. I'm on my back and she's half on top of me, her head resting on my chest and one arm thrown across my torso. We must have been like this for a while, because the places where our bare skin meets up are starting to feel a little sticky from the heat.

I reach down with one arm and pad around on the carpet for my jeans, doing my best not to jostle Whitney too much, and fish around for my phone in one of the back pockets.

Nine o'clock. This is good and bad. Good, because that means I slept for a solid ten hours last night. Bad, because a little quick math reveals that with a five-hour drive ahead of me, I won't make it home until mid-afternoon. And that's if all the I-70 traffic gods are working in my favor, an unlikely scenario given that it's early ski season and the interstate will likely be a clogged nightmare of SUVs, tourists, and morons.

The phone drops out of my hand and thuds on top of my jeans. I look up at the ceiling and try to muster the energy, the motivation, to move. Whitney wiggles a little, a drowsy stretch that means she's on the verge of waking up but could just as easily fall back into a deep sleep, and all I want to do is stay put. Her hand starts to rub across my chest, dipping low and coming to a stop when her fingertips crest the edge of my boxers.

That becomes my cue. Ten hours of sleep still isn't enough to risk anything more here. I gently try to move her arm off me, but she takes over and sweeps downward to pull away. Unfortunately, this draws her hand directly over where physiology makes it clear I'm a guy and it's morning. I actually have to grit my teeth at the painfully good, completely cruel, sensation.

She turns away, curls up, and does the cutest little fidgeting thing with her head into the pillow, until she seems to settle into sleep again. I pull on my clothes and walk quietly out to the living room. A glance out the front window reveals a light dusting of snow on the ground and frost covering my truck windows, which means I should go out there and start it up. Even when the only thing I want to do is crawl back in bed, curl up next to Hawaiian Tropic, and sleep another ten hours.

When I head back inside, I have to give the front door a shove to get it open. Whitney is standing in the middle of the living room, looking beautifully sleep-tousled but uneasy.

"Promise me you weren't planning to leave without saying good-bye."

I screw up my face, pushing the door shut behind me. "I just needed to start my truck. It's a diesel and the temps dropped last night, so it has to warm up."

She twists the bottom hem on her pj's with her fingers and doesn't look my way. *What the hell?* I'm not a fan of this version of Whitney: the uncomfortable, eye-contact-avoiding woman who thinks I'm a callous dickhead who would strip for her, kiss her, let her rub all over me, and then slither out like a snake.

"Jesus, Whit. I might not be the world's most sensitive guy, but I was barely able to drag myself away from you this morning. If I didn't have a job that takes priority right now, I wouldn't have even gotten out of your bed. I sure as fuck wouldn't pull some shitty disappearing act without saying good-bye."

"Good." She looks up and I get it now. She needs some reassurance here, because at the core of it, last night reeks of a hookup—just without the sex.

"In fact, my good-bye scene was pretty involved."

I get a tiny twitch of her lips, one side lilting up in relief. I take a step forward.

"You were going to be in some position that made it easy for my hands to end up on your bare skin, and you were going to do that little squirming around thing that makes it hard to think straight. I was going to spend a good amount of time kissing and sucking on your neck and stuff. How do you feel about hickeys? Not big, ugly, purple middle-school-dance-make-out things, just a couple of little marks down low. In places only you and I know about."

Her face lights up and before I understand exactly what's happening, she's across the room and crawling on me like I'm a goddam tree. I manage to keep my balance, bend my knees a little to get ahold of her, and then I'm on board with the plan.

I grip both hands under her and when she gets her legs properly wrapped around my waist, I start to kiss the hell out of her. I suddenly love the fact that this house is so small, because all I have to do is take a few steps and there's a wall. A sturdy surface to back her up against, using that leverage to work my mouth down over her jaw, her neck, her collarbone, as deep as I can until I have to boost her up a little. She yelps when I haul her entire body up, far enough to get my face right between her tits, to kiss the swells that are exposed and bite a little spot, because I want her to look down tomorrow and see that mark, think of this moment when she does.

She rolls her hips forward and I have to lean back a bit, fighting the irrational urge to blow off everything else, stay here, and drag her back to bed. When we finally look at each other, she's wild-eyed and that makes it even harder to let go, but my truck putters in the background, a noisy reminder of my long drive home. I drop her down.

She rights her shirt and looks over my shoulder.

"Are you hungry? I don't want you driving on an empty stomach."

Ducking around me, she scampers into the kitchen and then I'm standing there looking at the wall, dazed and wondering if my face buried between her tits was a mirage or a true event. She disappeared so quickly that my short-term memory has turned hazy in the wake of her bolting away.

A bunch of things rattle in the kitchen—a drawer opening and closing, a cupboard door thudding shut. I turn around and she's standing in the space between the kitchen and living room, holding a banana in one hand and a jar of peanut butter in the other.

"Here. Peanut butter has protein and bananas are potassium-rich. Both good for you."

Christ, she's trying to take care of me. Normally when this happens—a woman starts to demonstrate any nurturing tendencies—I get itchy. Like, all-over, skin-crawling itchy. Because I already have a mom; she lives in Texas. And I can take care of myself just fine. I cook, I clean, I do my own laundry, I even iron my own dress shirts. I've never needed or wanted a woman for any of those tired domestic reasons.

But nothing's itchy right now. Whitney is pointing a banana at me like it's a cowboy pistol, waving it around a little and shaking the peanut butter jar to match. Slowly, I make my way over to her and take the banana.

"The peanut butter can stay. Plenty of Clif bars in the truck for protein." Her arm drops and I kiss her forehead. "But I appreciate the thought."

She's standing on the porch when I drive away, wrapping her arms around her waist to keep the cold air at bay. I shake my head, waving my hand toward the front door of her house, hoping she'll do what I asked her to do three times already—go back in the house where it's warm. All she does is wave back, shooing me away with a half-smile on her face.

And she claims I'm the stubborn one.

= 10 =

(Whitney)

I hate the mailman.

I'm sure he's a perfectly nice fellow. He's always wearing a safari hat as he roars down my county road in a seventies-era Jeep CJ7 that has only a US POSTAL DELIVERY magnetic decal on the door to identify it as such. The safari hat is almost costume looking, a pith style, with a hard plastic brim at the front and a leather cord dangling from the chin to act as a strap, just in case his rural mail delivery route turns adventurous. His well-kept, short gray beard indicates he someone's granddad and I'd guess that he has a detail-oriented hobby of some sort. Like building histor-ically authentic model airplanes, collecting obscure British stamps, or carving intricate art out of tree stumps.

The problem is that he's always leaving bad stuff in my mailbox. Mostly, it's bills I can't pay. Sometimes I get a fun catalog or an enticing store circular that appears promising, right up until I remember that buying any-thing fun isn't an option. I never find greeting cards from a long-lost cousin or checks payable to me for large sums of money.

Maybe today will be different, though. Maybe Cooper drove straight home and penned a love letter to me. I try to picture him crouched over a piece of fine stationery, chewing on the end of a pen while considering the best way to elucidate the memories of his time here. Or, perhaps, wax poetic about hickeys and a newly acquired appreciation of rooibos tea.

Impossible. Cooper might be oddly romantic—in a blunt, cantankerous way—but I suspect that love letters aren't his forte.

So, today, as the mailman speeds away from my box, I prepare myself for the usual. I wave; he waves. I consider keeping on my way, headed out the driveway to a farmers' market in Grand Junction, without stopping to see what unpleasantness he's delivered. But delaying my fate won't change a thing, so I heave my truck into park and walk the few gangplank-like steps to my mailbox.

When I pull the front open, a bright white envelope is on top, and its heft hints that I won't like the contents. I spot the return address and my heart sinks. It's the name of the bank, but in care of a very swanky-sounding attorney's office. Five partners: Hall, Haverstock, Smith, Kole, & Cartwright, LLC.

Five partners is overkill, I think. Three is more than enough. Enough to take on someone like me, at least. I rip open the envelope. When the first few inches of the letter come into view, my already sunken heart manages to tumble again.

NOTICE OF SALE DATE

Dear Ms. Reed:
RE: Delaney Creek Orchards
     79562 County Road 56
     Hotchkiss, CO 81419

Pursuant to the mortgage agreement
and Colorado Property Code
51.0025.79, the above referenced
property will be sold at public
auction to the highest bidder on
JANUARY 10th at 10:00 AM. Location:
Outside steps of the DELTA COUNTY
COURTHOUSE, in DELTA, COLORADO.

Shit.

I've done enough research to know what I have in my hands: the final nail in my apple-stuffed coffin. If my situation felt desperate before, the addition of a real sale date means it now feels dire. Any hope of persuading the existing bank to restructure the terms or approve a payment plan to get caught up on the past-due amount is off the table. My only option is to find a new bank, one that employs an ever-benevolent loan officer who believes in championing the underdog and likes taking chances.

Crumpling the letter up into a ball and tossing it out the window as I drive might feel good, but wouldn't be terribly constructive. Instead, I need to get my keister to

Grand Junction, sell some product, and keep trying. Between now and January tenth, I would apply for every loan that exists and turn over every new stone along the way.

I know they might win in the end, and I may not find a way out, but I'll be damned if I'm going down without knowing that I kept at it until the sheriff showed up to get the keys.

═══════

The Mesa County fall harvest market is held inside a new expo hall at the county fairgrounds. Unlike the regular market held on Saturdays during the summer, this event is centered around the hardiest veggies of the season, those that survive a light frost and are pantry friendly: squashes and onions, potatoes and hardened-off garlic, bags of dried beans and Pennsylvania Dutch Butter popcorn. For me, it's a great time to sell the few crates of storage apples I managed to salvage this year and find homes for all those jars of apple butter.

This is the first of two harvest markets held each year. The second will take place a month from now, on the Saturday after Thanksgiving, in hopes of capitalizing on everyone's spendthrift mood just before Christmas. The only drawback is that it's a marathon event, nearly ten hours with setup and takedown of my booth, twelve hours if you count travel time. By the time the crowd finally starts to thin out, it's nearly four thirty, and the giant cinnamon bun I splurged on this morning has long since metabolized.

On the upside, I won't have much to haul back out

to the truck. All the apples are gone and after the cost of the booth and fuel, I'll still head home with five hundred dollars in my pocket, which counts as a success, even if it won't fix the bigger problem of my loan.

Gathering up all the silly marketing materials I once thought were so important, I stack them neatly into cardboard boxes tucked under my display table.

I have it all: refrigerator magnets with my logo on them, a roll of little apple stickers I thought would be cute for kids, even a gallon-sized bag full of bright red golf balls. The golf balls aren't my fault—I ordered red ballpoint pens and the company sent golf balls. Sometimes I fib and tell customers that they're apple-scented, just so their presence doesn't appear entirely random. The power of suggestion means that people automatically take a sniff, and then offer a delighted sound to indicate how much they enjoy the, in fact, nonexistent scent.

"I've been looking everywhere for you."

I wrangle my upper half out from under the folding table where I was trying to fit the baggie of golf balls into the remaining space in a box. Justin Clarke of Chinampas Farms extends a long-abused Tupperware container my way, tipping it down so I can peer in.

"Beet chip?"

Justin's shoulder-length blond hair is pulled back in a ponytail, topped off with a snap-back hat that has the logo of a global seed conglomerate (one with a name rarely uttered aloud because no one wants to risk a possible Beetlejuice phenomenon) with a big red X through it. A hemp cord is around his neck, with a cannabis leaf charm dangling from the center. There are a few tiny green flecks of metallic paint on the charm, just faded enough to mimic the color of his eyes.

If Justin ever does something wild enough to have a biopic made about his life, all they'll have to do is find Chris Hemsworth, douse him in patchouli, force him to lose about fifty pounds of muscle mass, and stick him in a pair of carpenter pants. Shoo-in for the part. Between Justin's good looks, his earnest love of this life, and his ability to roast up the best beet chips I've ever tasted, he's the veritable rock star of this farmers' market. I've watched gaggles of women circle his booth unnecessarily, like fresh-faced vultures in North Face jackets.

"I bet you have no idea how enticing the offer of beet chips could be to an exhausted apple farmer, do you? Because I could do one of two things right now. Propose marriage or knock you over the head and abscond with your beet chips. I'm that hungry."

Justin rattles the plastic container and laughs. "I choose option A. I have kale chips in my truck. Can't wait to hear what you might do to get your hands on some of those."

I gather up a handful of the beet chips and admire the rainbow of colors in my hand. Chioggias with their distinctive candy stripes, the rich red of Detroit Darks, and beautiful butterscotch discs of Golden goodness.

Speaking around a mouthful, I point to the Tupperware. "Your beets?" He nods and I take another handful. "Why were you looking for me?"

"Why wouldn't I be? No particular reason, other than the obvious. You're the best-looking apple farmer here."

"You just want my apple butter." I slide two of the pint jars his way while snagging another handful of chips.

Justin gathers up the jars and tucks them into the crook of one arm. "How'd you do today?"

"Good. And I couldn't afford otherwise, so I'm glad."

"That bad?" I give a blasé shrug of my shoulders to answer without having to say anything more aloud. He narrows his eyes. "How's next year looking?"

I nearly answer with every depressing descriptor that comes to mind. *Nonexistent. Impossible. Long-gone memory.* But I find a word that sounds far less melodramatic.

"Fuzzy."

Justin sets the jars down on the table and pulls his phone out of his back pocket, poking around until he finds whatever he's looking for, then digs a mini steno pad out of a cargo pocket.

"This is a new slow money program based in Boulder. Check it out—you might find some resources through them."

Slow money. I hadn't actually thought of exploring that option, but I'd heard enough about the concept to know it might be a perfect solution. The slow money movement was all about supporting local food systems, grounded in the idea of connecting investors to the organic farmers and food producers in the places where they live. These were people who believed heartily in lending money to bee-keepers, goat farmers, and wild fermented food makers. Maybe even an organic apple farmer who needed a second chance.

He tears out the sheet from his notepad and hands it

my way. "You headed home right away? If not, we could grab dinner somewhere. A couple of Mesa State girls I met swear by a Thai joint over on the east side of town."

I pause. Two weeks ago, I might have considered his offer. Pondered what could happen over dinner—or after.

Justin's farm is set on twenty acres of gorgeous land in Fruita. He's certified organic and found a way to thrive through drought conditions, hailstorms, and the expansion of a natural gas pipeline that claimed eminent domain on a good one hundred feet of his south property line. We made out once, after a Saturday market, in the heat of July. We were halfway through a growler of local beer he kept iced in the Yeti sitting in the back of his truck and—well, he looks like a skinny Chris Hemsworth, so, *hello*.

But that was BC.

Before Cooper. Before a guy who seemed so wrong for me showed up in my kitchen and somehow ended up in my bed a few hours later. Before he kissed me, spooned me, and marked my skin in places I haven't stopped staring at for the last two weeks.

When those delicate marks started to fade, I missed the sight of them. Which is why it's easy to give Justin a hug and send him on his way, with instructions to get those Mesa State girls to buy *him* dinner.

Because Cooper said he'd call and he did. He called just as he was getting ready to board the team plane to Phoenix, and I could hear how relieved he was at being healthy enough to play. He thanked me for letting him stay at Chez Whitney. Then he lowered his voice and asked if I had marks on my breasts, and told me he wanted to put more on my skin, in even more interesting places.

I could barely breathe, let alone respond. I wanted more so intensely that it was mind-numbing. And under the weight of my real life, numb sounds damn appealing.

━━━

Across the street from the expo hall is a big-box store, one I've managed to avoid for years, refusing to play part in their world domination by way of plaguing the world with too much plastic junk. Unfortunately, I need a few things best purchased at a place like that, rather than paying three times as much at the local Hotchkiss grocer. Toothpaste and toilet paper, dish soap and the jars of coconut oil I use for moisturizer. With a fat stack of cash in my bag, I may even splurge a little. Whitening toothpaste, here I come.

A fifteen-minute walk through the store and my cart is already half-full, so I make a beeline for the registers. Halfway there, I stride past the shoe section and a few displays of clothing, where I find myself unexpectedly slowing to a stop.

Here, the so-called lingerie department is less about frills and lace, more about flannel and fleece. But a few more seductive ensembles are jumbled together on a sale rack, hangers twisted every which way and delicate straps flopping about in a mess of tangled fabric. At the very front of the rack, I zero in on a cherry-red slip of sorts—essentially see-through because of the lace, it's definitely sexy and the exact opposite of what I currently sleep in.

The tags show that it's my size and it's on sale, marked down to a measly twenty-two dollars.

I try to picture myself wearing this. Conjuring up the idea is hard, and the first image that comes to mind isn't of me . . . instead, it's Cooper. His face, his hands, his body. All of him, entirely focused on me.

I'm guessing that Cooper is a lingerie guy. Lots of men are. But he's probably seen a hundred different iterations of this look, on women who wear ludicrously expensive ensembles to bed every night, purchased from places other than a big-box store. So, if I buy this, it needs to be for me. For the times when I'm tired of seeing myself in multiple layers and my skin demands something softer.

I toss it in the cart. Who cares if I'll only wander around my empty house in it, wearing wool socks to stay warm enough? Who cares if I shouldn't blow twenty-two bucks on a scrap of cheap lace likely constructed with a one-time-use-only design in mind? We all need to see ourselves in a new light sometimes.

= 11 =

(Cooper)

Boarding the team plane after a hard-fought overtime win probably isn't what most people would expect. I'm guessing fans think that it's like some party cruise in the air, despite the fact that we're essentially on a business trip—with our bosses sitting at the front of the plane to observe any hijinks.

Instead of a frat kegger on steroids, it's more akin to an incredibly well-orchestrated preschool pageant. Assigned seats; a flight crew of patient folks who know our names and finicky preferences and feed us every half hour. On the way home, the flight attendants even pass out warm cookies and ice-cold milk. After that, naptime is inevitable for most of us.

Eight years in and my assigned seats—plural, because we each get two—are at the very back of the plane, a sign of seniority. An ice pack is already waiting for me, to treat the mild hamstring strain that cropped up during the third quarter. Even though my head feels nearly back to normal after last week's win in Phoenix, another part of my body has predictably started to break down. I've worked hard to stay lean as I age, trying to ask as little of my joints as possible, but the reality is I can't bulldoze my way through every play like I did when I was years younger and oblivious to the way injuries add up over time.

I settle in, pull my headphones and iPod out, then check my phone again. A voicemail from my mom and a text from each of my brothers, but that's it. Looking up from the display, I scan the rest of the plane. Most of the guys have boarded now and nearly all of them are face-first in their phones, either texting or talking, and I'd guess that on the other end of most of those phones is a woman. Wives, girlfriends, fiancées, exes that aren't really exes, the hookup of the week, or some random girl from a bar who left an impression.

I've always had a routine for my time in the air, all based on how the game went. A loss means I cue up a perfectly curated set of songs that provides a soundtrack to analyze every error on the field. Shinedown's "It All Adds Up" is the first track, NEEDTOBREATHE's "Keep Your Eyes Open" smack dab in the middle, and Gary Clark Jr. with "The Healing" at the end. By the time we land, I've visualized the appropriate correction for each screw-up and I'm able to move on.

A win is easier. I reward myself with an audiobook through my headphones—even the serious military history stories and political biographies that I prefer are a great way to zone out. No matter what, I've rarely given my phone a second look once I've settled into my seat.

Today, watching all these other fools grinning and laughing away, for the first time, I want the same thing. Even now, I'm leaving my phone faceup on the extra seat, trying to determine if glaring at that spot hard enough will miraculously conjure the stupid thing to life, with Whitney on the other end of the line.

"Why so glum, chum?" Aaron ends the call he was on and looks across the aisle, sporting the perpetual half-smile he travels through life with.

"Nothing."

"Not buying it. You look pissier than usual. And you're doing stuff with your phone instead of donning your headphones and pretending like everyone else doesn't exist."

I shake my head and look out the window. Shifting the ice pack under my thigh, I wince when the muscle seizes up at the adjustment.

Screw this. I'll be damned if I'm going to just sit here and mope. There's probably enough time to call her, so I grab my phone. But just when I find Whitney's number and get ready to hit the call button, I pause. Maybe I shouldn't call.

No.

Wait. Definitely, yes.

Maybe if I call she'll think I'm overbearing, which I am, but we already talked for a while yesterday—just like every other day that's passed since I left her house. So, maybe if I don't call today, she'll wonder why.

Christ, this is insane. I might like Whitney, but I sure as hell don't love feeling this stupid. Time to man up and find my balls.

Taking a deep breath, I press the call button.

"Hello?"

I try to draw out my agitation when she answers, wrestle that feeling around, to stay frustrated as a matter of male pride. If only her voice didn't fascinate my dick so much, I might succeed. Instead, just her saying hello means that every damn organ in my body perks up to say hello back.

"Hey, it's Cooper."

"Hi." She gives the word a long roll off her tongue, and any remaining bits of irritation dissolve. "Did you win?"

I smile and take a look out the window again. "Yeah, we did."

"Are you in one piece? No guys named Stinger that I need to rough up?"

"Nah. My hammie is giving me fits, but that's because I'm old. You don't need to be my enforcer this go-round."

Twisting in my seat, I notice that a large dude—one who needs to get a life—is all ears on my conversation. Aaron has his elbow propped on his seat arm, chin propped on his fist, unabashedly eavesdropping. He smirks and raises his brows. I flip him the middle finger and turn back toward the window.

"I'm headed home and I didn't know what you were up to this week, so maybe . . ." I start to fumble over the words, hesitating until Whitney makes a humming sound to encourage me. "I wanted to know if you might have time to come to Denver. Stay with me for a couple of nights."

She doesn't respond right away. I start to fill the quiet with details.

"We have part of tomorrow and all day Tuesday off,

and a late start on Wednesday. I'd come to you, but with the drive, we'd barely get any time together. I thought your schedule might be a little lighter this time of year. I know you have things going on and this is short notice, but I just . . ."

Aaron continues to gawk, hanging on every word and stockpiling God knows how much mockery as he waits. Another twist of my body closer to the window, but I refuse to cup my hand over the phone. If he hears me, and gives me shit for every syllable, so be it. I'm used to it anyway.

"I want to see you, Whitney. But I'm in the middle of the season and that means my free time is almost non-existent." I pause and force myself to wait for her to say something. When she does, it takes only a few words for me to pick up on the lightness in her voice.

"Well, lucky for us, I have something I need to check out up in Boulder." She takes a slow inhale, as if she's already anticipating what's bound to come next when we see each other again. "I'll need your address."

The flight attendants start to make their way down the aisle, reminding everyone to start powering down.

"I'll text it to you, along with the codes for the garage and elevator."

"Oh, hell. Don't do that. I'll never get there."

"What? Why?"

"This is a landline. If you try to text me, those messages will end up somewhere in the digital ether."

"Don't you have a cell?"

Whitney snorts. "I do. But it's on a pay-as-you-go plan

and adding more minutes is at the bottom of my financial priority list right now. I prefer to eat and heat the house."

Shit. Money. A basic life thing that I haven't had to worry about in a long time. Sometimes I forget that money—or a lack of it—is top of mind for most people, especially when their living comes from the land. I watched my family worry through season after season of uncertainty, but neglected to remember how that same insecurity is part of Whitney's reality. All those worn-out clothes and the beater of a truck in her driveway merely seemed like part of her hippie girl persona, but I overlooked how that also probably meant she wasn't flush with cash.

My favorite flight attendant stops in the aisle and points to my phone, wordlessly implying it's time to wrap up my call. I give her my most earnest but silent plea for another quick minute by widening my eyes. She rolls her eyes and holds up two fingers, disappearing to the rear cabin, buying me a couple of minutes to tell Whitney that I'll call her back when I land, give her all the info then. The instant I toss my phone onto the seat, Aaron starts in.

"*Whitney*, huh? What did she use in her love trap? I can't imagine what kind of bait works best on Cooper Lowry. Honey doesn't work, I'm sure." He taps an index finger against his mouth, looking up to the cabin ceiling as he does. "Maybe Kendra will have some ideas. She's going to have a field day with this."

"I can't emphasize this enough, Bolden." I use both middle fingers this time, but I'm grinning. "Fuck. Off."

Mid-morning on Monday, when I sprint out of our abbreviated practice, Aaron is standing in the main doorway out of the building, blocking my way—cheerfully, and on purpose. I try to dodge around him, but he blocks me with a dropped shoulder to the center of my chest. I try to shake him off by pretending to throw an uppercut to his jaw. He grabs my fist and laughs. The only choice I have left is to step back a few paces and glare, breathing heavily through my nostrils.

"Kendra wants to meet her."

"No."

"*I* want to meet her."

"No."

"Why? What's wrong with her? Two heads? Nine ears? Missing her front teeth? She's interested in you, which means her judgment is suspect, but I hang out with your surly ass, so it would be hypocritical of me to count that as a failure."

"She's perfect. *You're* the problem. Kendra isn't a problem per se, but she's still Kendra, and this is a new thing. I don't need your wife's particular brand of inquisition to scare her off. We both know I can do that on my own."

Aaron tilts his head and studies my expression for a moment. When he registers that I'm serious, he steps aside and pushes the door open, giving a sweep of his arm to indicate I'm free to go.

I barely make it halfway down the front sidewalk before he's hollering.

"I can't promise that my wife won't just show up at your place unannounced! The woman has her own mind, so keep your lights off and the doors locked!"

Whitney said she would be in Boulder by the early afternoon but didn't say when she would head toward Denver, which left me to wait.

And wait.

Every minute that ticks by tests the patience I don't possess. I don't like waiting. I like routines. Expected outcomes. Schedules and disciplined habits. Boring? Yes. Do I care? No.

Not having a plan makes me jumpy. But this entire situation is my own personal unscaled mountain. Inviting a woman to my place for a few nights with every intention of trying to make sure she likes it enough to do it again? Brand-new territory.

The last time I put this much effort into getting a woman's attention, I was a kid and so was she. Senior prom with Abagail Pruitt. A limo I couldn't afford, a hotel room I really couldn't afford, a rental tux that didn't fit very well, and a box of condoms that I didn't need because she drank too much cheap wine in the limo and passed out. That was my last foray into wooing, so I'm a little rusty. Too many years of singular focus on my career and perfectly contented domestic solitude make it a little hard to jump back in without pulling a muscle or two.

Plus, there was no warm-up. Whitney was a surprise, showing up without warning, without any intention on my part. I wasn't looking for anyone. I certainly wasn't looking for *her*. In a million years, I never would have conjured up an image of Whitney when considering the kind of woman who might be perfect for me.

All of this explains why I'm now standing in the coffee and tea aisle at Whole Foods—my third trip of the day—trying to decipher the best choice among the copious varieties of herbal tea on display. I think back to the crap Whitney served when I was in her kitchen. The name escapes my mind, even if the flavor is still on my tongue.

The bigger matter at hand is that I came back to the grocery store for the third time, just to get tea, just in case she might want some. Five boxes later, I circle around to get an extra bag of steel-cut oats to have on hand for breakfast. Then I toss in some wheat berries because I know she eats those. I double back through the store for goat cheese, another known. I also decide to get some wine. But does she like red or white? Maybe I should get some steak for dinner instead of the salmon I bought earlier. Does she eat red meat? Was the braised chicken in her refrigerator a fluke and most of the time she's a vegetarian?

Christ, I need a drink, or a neck rub, or something— because I'm fucking wrecked and my wooing muscles are starting to ache already.

= 12 =

(Cooper)

Back at home, I put away the groceries and then change the sheets on my bed. After that, I spend another twenty minutes debating what to wear, and as I flick through the hangers in my closet, it's clear I've officially said sayonara to any testosterone-based dignity I once had.

After I've selected the right T-shirt and jeans, I put the vase of sunflowers I bought on the coffee table, but only after I cut the stems and rearrange them four times. I keep a clean place, so there isn't any need for a speed round of housekeeping, but I triple-check to ensure there aren't any grubby practice clothes hiding anywhere. I might be used to the persistent funky odor from all my sweaty gear, but Whitney won't be.

I check my watch. Six o'clock. I'll give it ten more minutes and then I'm turning on the Xbox. If I don't distract my head and my hands, I'm going to end up doing something suspect. Like rewiring an electrical panel or alphabetizing my pantry goods.

A faint knock at the door is enough to inspire a panicky tremor in my chest, until I'm just standing there with a pounding heart and the sudden inability to move.

Not acceptable. I have to get my shit together. Now.

I pull open the door and Whitney's there, looking a little harried and wearing a loose dress that hits just above the knee. The soft-looking fabric is covered in a busy maroon pattern that kind of hurts my eyes, and she has what I'm guessing are black tights on underneath. And all I can think about is how she looks great and I'm glad she's finally here—and if those are tights, as opposed to thigh-highs, how the fuck am I going to get them off without the scene turning fumbling and comedic?

Whitney tugs off a crocheted black scarf from around her neck, then points her index finger straight down at the floor.

"You live above a cupcake bakery."

I nod and step back so she can come inside. The door swings shut behind me and from the back, the dress is slightly shorter, so I can tell that those are definitely tights because they're too thick to be anything else. Tights can be cute, but they're sometimes a bitch to get off a woman's body. Especially when it's a first run and you're trying to keep your moves smooth and awesome so she doesn't think you're a total idiot. Later, when you really know each other and a hundred stupid things have occurred in bed, it's easier to laugh about the way she has to shimmy and tug her own way out of any complicated ensembles.

She stops in the middle of the room with her back to me, points to the large plate-glass windows that face the street, and then cranes her head over one shoulder to look my way.

"You live above a cupcake bakery, there's a craft distillery across the street, a gourmet burger joint next door to that, followed by a very provocative-looking lingerie shop, a hookah lounge, and a chocolatier. This loft is the epicenter in a hub of vice and sin. How is it that you aren't four hundred pounds and half-blotto all the time?"

A quick turn and she takes an inventory of my loft, up and down, side to side.

"Wow, this place is amazing. Is that the original brick? The elevator has to be the original—it sounds like it might plummet to the ground, but in a good way. And these floors. Beetle kill? The blue tint gives it away, but it's—"

Holy fuck. She's a hurricane of words. Her body isn't moving, but all that nonstop talk makes her vibrate with nervous energy. Please, please, don't let her be a sleeper version of Callie. I don't want to discover that during the time I spent with her in Hotchkiss, she was on a sedative of some sort and this is the real Whitney. That would be worse than discovering she's . . . I don't know . . . a die-hard Chiefs fan. Married. Really a pod person.

She pushes on by announcing that the fireplace is nice. Is it wood or gas? She likes the barn slider doors. Have I ever eaten at the taqueria on the corner? She splurged on a tea from the Dushanbe Teahouse while she was in Boulder. It's called Dragon Eyes. She thinks it's good but a little bitter when it cools off.

I give her *my* best dragon eyes, which means I widen them and tilt my chin down, hoping she'll take a breath, remember that I'm still standing here, and notice how I'm waiting for her to be quiet.

"Whitney."

She gets in another few lines. Something about how hard it was to find the entrance to my parking garage, all the one-way streets, that she wasn't sure if she should park next to my truck or in front of it. I try again. Lifting my hands up in front of me, palms out, in a universal *hold the fuck up for a second* gesture.

"Whit." She stops. *Thank you, God.* I step forward cautiously and she starts to inhale and exhale slowly but deeply, her shoulders rising on every pass. I'm near enough to reach out and press both hands to her face, grasping her jaw gently in my palms. "Hi."

A small laugh before she blinks a few times. "Hi."

"Nervous?"

No hedging, no waffling; she just sighs. "Yes."

"Good. I'm glad it isn't just me."

"You don't seem nervous." Her lips purse into a slight pout.

"I'm using my laser-like game-day focus to appear unfazed. But two things happened before you got here that will illustrate how messed up I am over this."

She widens her eyes with a grin. As I point to the coffee table, where the vase of sunflowers sits in the center, she tracks the motion with a quick glance and gives a *so what* expression.

"I arranged those sunflowers in that vase four times. I bought them for you, even though I didn't know if you like flowers, or if you're allergic, or if you would rail on me about the idea of killing an innocent plant purely for aesthetic purposes. Then I spent twenty minutes trying to arrange them properly. Secondly, I actually had this thought when I got home: *I have no idea what to wear.* After much debate, I settled on this T-shirt. Because it brings out the color in my eyes."

I bat my eyelashes for effect and Whitney sputters out a surrendering laugh, complete with her entire body relaxing. She tips forward so her forehead rests against my chest.

"Why is this so weird?"

I try not to say something too heavy, too much for the moment. For two people who barely know each other, it's obvious that neither of us seems particularly used to feeling this way. Yet we both seem to be laying a shit ton of expectation on whatever this is. I slip one hand into her hair, find the back of her neck, and let it rest there.

"Because we want it to work? I think that's why. If we didn't both want this, we wouldn't be trying so hard."

───────

Dinner helps. Wine helps.

Whitney likes white wine, not red. I like the way she starts to turn soft-edged and her words become languid after I offer her a second glass. When she gets about halfway through that pour, she's unabashed about taking a good, long look at the guy sitting across from her, all while she toys with the amber necklace she's wearing and fingers her collarbone like she wants him to remember where he marked her before.

Other things I learned during dinner: She hasn't been

a vegetarian for seven years and even then, she wasn't particularly fanatical about it. Sunflowers are definitely in her top ten when it comes to flowers, and the only things she's allergic to are cats. Because of that, she really wants a cat, which she'd name Kemp, after a term her hot rod–fanatic father often used.

Whitney asks about my family and is appropriately awed and horrified at a few choice anecdotes about my brothers. And I barely tapped the well on that topic, because a household with four boys is rife with the disgusting, the bloody, and the idiotic.

She wants to know about playing ball, but she doesn't ask the easy questions. Most people want to know where I played in college or try to get me to tell them which guys on the team aren't making the cut. They want gossip about big names and the inside track on strategy for their fantasy football crap. But Whitney doesn't know any big names; she claims ignorance, and it's obvious that she's being honest.

Instead, she asks if I like using my body this way, or if I ever wished for a different life. She wants to talk about how it feels when a guy like Stinger gets a hit on you. Whether winning is always satisfying. I don't know how to answer half of what she asks, because the questions aren't anything like the media-day merry-go-round that I'm used to fielding.

I'm still trying to figure out how to explain the significance of draft day when my phone rings for the sixth time since we sat down to eat. I left it on the catchall table I have next to the front door but the ringer is turned up, so it's impossible to pretend we don't hear it.

"Your phone rings a lot." She takes the final swig of

wine from her glass. "Don't feel like you have to ignore it—I won't mind."

"It doesn't normally ring this much."

"Even more reason for you to check it. Maybe someone's trying to get ahold of you. What if it's some other girl and she wants to see you, but you don't answer and then she just decides to surprise you? Comes over here dressed as a lusty milkmaid, or just in a trench coat or something. Talk about awkward."

The ringing stops. I send a sharp look her way. "Don't say stuff like that."

She twists the stem of the empty wineglass around in her fingers. "Like what?"

Standing up, I pluck the wineglass out of her loose grip and then bend down so that my face is right in front of hers.

"About other women. There aren't any other women. No milkmaids, no trench coats. Unless we're talking about any interesting clothing options you have stashed in your overnight bag."

Her face goes slack. The wine is doing its best to keep her features honest. Gathering a few more dishes, I drop them off in the kitchen and go investigate my phone. I scroll through the missed calls and they're all from my agent. He hasn't left any voicemails, but that isn't unusual. Austin Nichols isn't known for his patience, which is why we get along and why he's a damn good agent. Nevertheless, we've barely started negotiations and if he's getting antsy this early on, that isn't good. I stride back to Whitney and shake my phone in her direction.

"All of them were my agent calling. Do you mind? New contract negotiations just started."

"Go for it. Tell him I said that the contract should include some kind of clause about a restraining order on Stinger."

━━━━━━

An hour later, I step back inside from the terrace and with the exception of a dim light coming from the bedroom, the loft is dark. It seems Whitney found the bedroom on her own and kept herself occupied while I established myself as the shittiest host of all time. Despite my leaving her alone for that long, she didn't once peek out to check on me, and certainly didn't stomp out to the terrace and sigh theatrically to get my attention as some women might have.

A blessing, because Austin was calling for good reason. Aside from the usual knackering about salary guarantees and options, it seems that my team—the organization I've dutifully given the past eight years to—has decided I'm damaged goods. Because when your new contract includes a split clause, it's a sure sign that behind closed doors, they've determined that you're headed to the pro athlete version of a remainder pile, where careers go to wither and flame out.

With a split contract, if I end up on injured reserve, the team can cut my weekly salary in half. Fine. The money isn't the issue; I have plenty of money. Enough to live out the rest of my life without another earned dime, so from my side, this is about everything *but* money. Austin is confident we can get them to dump it, that I shouldn't panic because this is routine for guys my age. The only problem is I'll always know it was there. Even if we sign a final contract without it, every time I limp off the field or Hunt studies my gait, that doubt—their hesitation at my value—will eat me up inside.

I head into the kitchen because my mouth is dry and I need a glass of water. When I flip on the light, the kitchen is spotless. All the dishes are clean and Whitney set everything to dry in a drainer. A quick peek in the fridge reveals that she put all the leftovers away in plastic storage containers and even rearranged the shelves so that the quarter-full wine bottle would fit without listing to one side. I let the door shut softly.

Drawing open a high cupboard door, I go up on my toes to grab a glass and my hamstring reacts, taut and tight under the stretch. Christ, I can't even *hydrate* without a reminder that I'm suddenly playing on borrowed time. I fill and then drain the glass in a few gulps, set it in the sink, and take a deep breath.

Normally, I'm a goddam expert at compartmentalizing, honed by my career and the way you learn to play through anything that gets in your way. Pain. Fractured bones. Torn ligaments. But tonight, I'm not sure how to put all of this aside, even when Whitney is here and all I wanted an hour ago was to treat her right until it felt like the perfect moment to stop talking and start touching.

"Cooper?"

My head falls forward at the sound of her gentle voice drifting through my otherwise silent loft. I run a hand through my hair and attempt to get my head together. She doesn't need to take on my bullshit. No matter how much I think she might be a perfect sounding board for all my fucked-up emotions on this topic, we're not there yet. Nowhere near the place where you can stand in front of someone, holding an enormous pile of woe-is-me, and ask that person to help you figure out how to cope with it.

I shut the light off in the kitchen and make my way to the bedroom. Whitney is tucked into my bed, slumped down in a pile of pillows she's arranged, reading a book.

My bed is huge, a custom-ordered beast that remains the only thing I don't regret about hiring an interior designer when I moved in here. When this showed up, a dark walnut platform bed with a leather headboard and a generously oversized mattress, after just one night I decided it was worth every penny.

Amidst the pillows and the goose down–filled duvet that's covering her, plus the sheer size of the bed, Whitney looks tiny. Her eyes slant over to me and she puts one finger between the pages of her book to hold her spot, then shimmies up out of the pillow nest.

When she does, the duvet cover slips down and suddenly, all I can see is red.

As in, red lace.

And where there isn't red lace, there's skin. Bare, beautiful skin exposed to the space where Whitney's breasts are straining the flimsy-looking material and her nipples are nearly peeking over the low neckline.

Between the surprise at seeing her in something other than the navy-blue pajama top I'm familiar with and the tensions fueled by my talk with Austin, I don't think before I speak.

"What are you *wearing*?"

A split second is all it takes to realize how those words came out all wrong. I sounded horrified, pissed off, and almost repulsed. Which I'm definitely not. Whitney immediately starts to flush, the skin on her neck and cheeks going as red as the lace, and she tugs up the bedcovers.

Fuck. This beautiful woman, normally so comfortable with herself, is shielding her body from my view, and that shit is my fault. My head starts to throb, not from the concussion this time, just the strain of my brain working overtime to find a way to fix this.

I like lingerie just fine. Yes, it's pretty, sexy, sometimes downright wickedly hot, and it puts all the best parts of a woman's body on display. Breasts up, ass out, easy access and all that. But the best thing about a woman wearing it—in *your* bed—is that it means you're getting laid. She's already decided that for you and so you have to work at fucking it up. Of course, leave it to me to do exactly that.

Before I know it, she's scurrying out of the bed, trying to make a getaway to the only room within scampering distance, the master bath. Where I'm worried she might decide to make a run for it, even if she has to use the window and a fire escape.

God, now I really can't think, because that little red lace number barely covers down to her ass and it's so sheer that I can see everything. The curve of her hips to her waist, the arch of her back, and the slopes between her thighs. The damn thing is flimsy, with only two delicate little straps to hold it up, and I'm certainly not going to let her make it into the other room, because all of my angst from earlier has evaporated. My only problem now is how to cut her off at the pass, convince her to let me explain away my stupidity, and hopefully twist those straps between my fingers to see how little effort is required to tear them in two.

She's a quick thing, though. Up on her toes, she's hastily padding across the carpet silently, like a little fawn. Unfortunately for Bambi here, I've got long legs.

Whitney makes it to the bathroom doorway just as I block the entryway with my body, throwing both arms out to grip the frame with my hands.

"Where are you running off to?"

No response from her. She closes her eyes and screws up her face into a grimace, a wretched-looking one, the kind that means she might start crying. Both arms come up and cross to cover herself.

My entire chest starts to ache at the sight and I want to touch her, make this better in whatever way I can. But she's on guard, keeping her stance closed off. I drop my arms from the door jamb, hoping that if I relax my posture, she'll do the same.

"What I said came out wrong. I was surprised, that's all."

Her head dips and she rolls her shoulders. I lean closer. Near enough to let my lips skim her temple, holding there until I hear her breath hitch.

"Is this for me?"

She finally opens her eyes and shakes her head, but I don't buy it. The way her gaze doesn't quite meet mine, the way her eyes track across the rest of the room just to keep from looking directly at me, she's deflecting. I try again.

"No? Damn. Because I wanted you to say it was."

All her tension visibly starts to unravel. Her gaze testing mine, checking my face for any signs of bullshit. I let my eyes travel down the length of her body and because she's so close, most of what I can see is her tits. Even though I've had an up-close look at that cleavage, and buried my face deeply enough to lick and suck marks there, this sight line means I can see the true, complete shape of her. Perfect handfuls that beg for attention, and just . . . hell, there's so much there, I could spend days getting to know every inch. Later. When I've proven how much this means to me, I'll take my time and enjoy mapping that part of her.

I drag my eyes back up and know immediately that she saw how intently I was eating up the sight, because she's less apprehensive now. Like she finally understands exactly how much I want her.

Time to drive that point home. Wrapping one finger around a delicate strap, I twist it tightly and pull downward, emphasizing how easily I might tear it clean away.

"I wanted you to say that you saw this sexy scrap of lace in a store somewhere and thought of me. That you wanted me to see you wearing this. That you knew it would make me hard, how I'd want to fuck you the second I saw you in it."

Whitney lets out an unsteady, excited noise, a cross between a moan and a tiny wail. I have to stop myself from taking that little sound as a green flag, her eager permission to rip this slip off without a word of warning.

"I bought it for *me*." Her eyes meet mine, no wavering now, just the hottest fucking kind of confidence I've ever seen. A peek of her tongue to her upper lip. "But I wanted you to like it."

From those words and the way her expression quickly turns open and vulnerable, I feel like I may have managed to dig my way out. My hands go to her hips and I urge her back from the doorway, until she bumps into the edge of the low dresser that sits against the wall.

"I love it. Not just like it, I love it. Your body is . . ." My hands start to move, taking inventory of her shape along the way, up to grasp her waist, then up again to skim her breasts, until I settle them at the base of her neck. "Fuck, Whitney. This body is everything I want. *You* are everything I want."

Her mouth meets mine before I can tell her any more. Open and heated, no tentative lead-in, just further proof that kissing Whitney is better than anything I've ever experienced. Better than my first kiss, better than any wild, hot woman I've had for one rowdy night without wanting more.

We're both primed enough to dive right in, but even so, when her hands come to my jeans and fumble around, I shove my hips forward to block her. She startles a bit and her hands freeze. I stroke my thumbs across the slopes of her neck, gently, until her gaze meets mine.

"Give me the lead here for a second, OK? I want to make you feel good."

Whitney gives up a little huff. "You *are* making me feel good. Aside from how you opened up the conversation when you came in here, I already feel really good. Is there more? Because I'm not sure I'm strong enough for more; I might pass out." Her eyes flicker upward for a moment. "But in a good way, I guess."

A grin creeps across my face. God, this woman. So many kick-ass traits wrapped up in one sweet little package. Sexy and funny, honest and clever—and stacked like there's no tomorrow. Everything I want, right here, and she's actually asking if there's more. Silly, silly woman.

One of my hands leaves her neck and tangles up in her hair, cradling the side of her head as I move my mouth toward her ear.

"Yes. There's definitely more." Whitney lets out a breathless, whispered curse. "Just let me give it to you."

My other hand goes to work, moving slowly down her neck until her breast is in my grasp. I cup her for a moment, savoring the weight and the feel of her flesh under my palm. When I stroke her nipple and then pull it between my fingers to toy the bud into a hard peak, her hands drop away from the waist of my jeans and grip the edge of the bureau.

I watch her, taking in all the ways she's showing what turns her inside out. The way her mouth drops open and her chest rises, the tilt of her head to show she's dissolving into the sensation as her hips twist toward me in tight little jerks. Fingers tracing with a featherlight touch, my hand drifts to her thigh, pausing only to take in her expression and make certain she's still with me. When I glide my hand between her legs, the hot, wet slip of skin I find waiting for me is my answer. She's definitely with me.

It's amazing how quickly your attention can shift in a moment like this. A few minutes ago, I was obsessing over my contract and my career. Now, all I care about is giving Whitney what she needs. Her body, pressing and moving tentatively, experimenting with her own response to my hands, has become the only thing that matters.

Whitney's breath turns labored as I use two fingers to slick the wetness already there into more. She's warm and ready, so I concentrate my movements, circling to keep the pressure exactly where she needs and wants it. Now would be the moment I'd usually slide a couple of fingers inside, working her with a few perfectly angled thrusts of my hand. But I decide to keep them right where they are, because my cock has called dibs on the first stroke inside her, and for now, I'm dead set on rubbing her pussy just like this, until I work out how to feel her come from just that touch.

Her head falls forward to rest on my shoulder and when she lets out a frustrated sigh, I nearly change my plan. I take my hand that's still in her hair and use it to urge her closer to me.

"Whit, just press your pussy against my hand and show me what you like. All I want is to feel you coming all over my fingers."

I slow the circle of my fingers, begging her with that teasing touch to let go. She opens her legs a few inches and I add a little more pressure, encouraging her to keep going.

"Fuck, yes. You know what to do. God, you're so wet and warm right now. I can't fucking wait to feel all that on my dick."

Her pussy grinds directly onto my hand for one demanding circle of her hips and my world compresses to that space, not an inch more or less. Whitney relinquishes every hesitation she was holding on to, and I can feel her body closing in on release as her movements become less fluid, greedier. And suddenly, I'm holding my breath, wondering what this amazing woman will be like when she comes.

If anyone asked us to accurately describe our own orgasms, we probably couldn't, because we're pulled too far under to know how we sound or move. Maybe we go taut, but think we're thrashing and wild. Maybe we think we're loud, when we're actually nearly silent. With Whitney, when she goes off, it's so much to take in, and all I want to do is soak up every wild bit. She's lost, riding it out—completely, entirely, through to the last ebb. And the way she wrings and holds on until she's sure she's taken it all? That's the best part.

I wait for her to open her eyes, then let my hand slip from between her legs and suck her taste from my fingers. Her mouth drops open and her eyes fix on my mouth.

"Watching you come is the hottest thing I've ever seen. Fucking *ever*." All I get in response is her breathing heavily. "You take it all on, so hard, the whole thing. I love that."

Whitney releases the death grip she has on the side of the dresser and rests her trembling hands on my shoulders. Hazy amusement dances in her eyes.

"So many things make sense now."

I kiss her. Just because, just to be closer to her. "Like what?"

"I looked you up to make sure you aren't married or currently on trial for a heinous crime of some sort and when I stumbled onto articles about your contract, I thought there was a typo. I mean, sixty million dollars to catch a football? No one has hands that valuable. But I get it now. If I had sixty million on me, I'd hand it all over. Just toss it at you and make it rain."

She laughs, light and satisfied. A twitch of dread rises inside me and I have to remind myself that she doesn't know about Austin's call. All she's saying is that she likes the way I just touched her—she isn't talking about money as if it's anything but an anecdote, or hinting that if there weren't another fat contract coming, she would think less of me. But doubt continues to creep in before I can tamp it down properly. I pull back a little and focus on her face.

"Is that a problem for you? The money?"

She tilts her head, frowning slightly. "A problem? For me? No. I was just trying to make a joke. And reference your ability to deliver an orgasm with those hands so proficiently. Well, one hand, actually. Even more impressive."

Her answer soothes the prickle of anxiety. Then she presses her lips to my chest, kissing a sensitive spot just below my collarbone, and it's enough to put me back on track. I lean forward and brush my lips to her temple.

"You ready to see what I can do with both hands? My mouth? My cock? Say yes, because I'm so fucking hard right now it's painful."

"Yes. I was worried you might be a tease again." She goes for my jeans and gets the top button undone, then freezes. "Wait. Is your head OK? Are you cleared for vigorous stuff?"

I shove up the bottom hem of her lace thingy and then lift her entire body, dropping her onto the top of the bureau.

"I'm fine. The only head that hurts right now"—finishing the work on my jeans, I pull them open and push down my boxers enough to set my cock free, sliding a cupped palm over the tip—"is this one."

Whitney leans back to rest against the wall, takes in the sight of me giving myself a long, slow tug, and lets her smooth legs fall open in invitation.

Even though I shouldn't, risking that I'll lose all sanity and just push in unprotected, I step forward enough to slick myself between her legs, then lean in to kiss her. We kiss so hard, so wild, that it feels like we're already fucking, rubbing against each other while my cock nudges across her soft skin. A few more of those strokes before I find the strength to pull back, drawing my hands down her body and giving a little squeeze to the soft flesh at the tops of her thighs.

"Condom. Stay right here."

Her eyes fall closed. "Hurry."

Cute. Her issuing an instruction to hurry, like I was planning to drag my feet. I grab a condom from my nightstand and roll it on in record time, and when I get back to her, she looks entirely set for a ride. Shimmied forward on the dresser with her legs spread even wider.

But seeing her this way, so gorgeous and ready, I suddenly want to savor the sight for a second before I push inside. To relish this, the way I want her so intently. Even if it's also scary as hell.

My voice goes hoarse. "I don't think I've ever wanted anyone like this. So much."

I didn't even mean to say it aloud. Whitney doesn't press for me to explain, just leans forward to take me in hand, giving a leisurely pull from base to tip. Even through the latex, it's incredible, and when she comes close enough that her mouth is just inches from mine, my heart stops for a few beats.

Voice lowered, she leans even closer.

"If you want me, Cooper, I'm right here. All you have to do is come get me."

Ah, Christ.

Fuck it.

Fuck waiting. Fuck savoring. Fuck relishing.

One rough yank and I've got her right on the edge of the dresser, off balance so she has to grab my shoulders. I press the tip to her opening and try not to pound right in on the first stroke. She's still crazy wet and slick, but when I push forward, her body doesn't immediately yield and we both feel it. Whitney whimpers.

"Lean back." She does, but not enough. I put my hands to the dresser, my arms just behind her to form a cage. "More. I won't let you fall."

When she does, I guide myself toward her again, gently teasing her opening. The head slips in and just that nearly drives me to take, take, take. I keep one hand pressed at her back and use the other to grip the base of my cock, all to prevent myself from grabbing her hips and ramming the rest of the way home. Because she's still not there yet. Her warm, tight body wants to challenge mine, and I need to be patient. But, hell, if we don't figure this out in the next ten fucking seconds, I might die right here, just from wanting.

"Open up your legs a little wider. I swear it will be so good—I just need you to trust me."

Her body eases on a deliberate exhale, head to toe. After that, I slide in easily. A few experimental thrusts at the pace I'm desperate for quickly become too much, but slowing things down doesn't particularly help because it seems Whitney *really* likes that tempo. Arching her back, moaning, moving her body with every beat, from her hips to her shoulders.

The lace of her slip falls and covers the space where we're joined, ruining the vantage point from where I could see every stroke and watch the way I'm moving inside her. Keeping one arm wrapped around her so she won't lose her balance, I use the other to yank up on the lace.

"Take this off. I love it, but I want to see you."

Without pause, she pulls it off, revealing the entire span of her gorgeous, honey-kissed skin. I lean down and capture a nipple in my mouth, sucking until it's so hard, I know it aches for me. When I release the hard peak with a loud pop, she immediately starts tugging on my shirt, and I understand what she wants before she has to say more. My shirt hits the floor just as Whitney shoves her hands inside the back of my boxers.

"Take the rest off. I want to see you, too."

I let out a low growl, wishing I could give her what she

wants while still trying to ignore the orgasm that's building at the base of my spine.

"Later. I can't strip down unless I pull out, and that can't happen. Pretty sure it would kill me."

I'm entirely serious but she laughs, and her hands grasp my ass harder, digging her nails in a little. That impatient move surges my hips forward, into rough thrusts that rattle the furniture. Whitney isn't giving any sign that it's too much, so I keep going. Hard, then harder still. I can't register anything but her and my own drive toward release. The building could catch fire, a tornado could whip through my loft, a pipe could burst and flood the room—none of it would matter; I'd still keep fucking this woman into oblivion.

Pressing closer, my body grinds against hers and when she starts to come, she turns rowdy. Louder. Chasing that feeling with a frenzied focus that forces her to grasp around for better purchase until she whacks a picture frame on the dresser, sending it to the unforgiving concrete floors in my bedroom, where the glass shatters.

"Oh, crap, sorry." She stiffens, trying to keep her movements less rambunctious. "Sorry, sorry, I didn't mean to—"

I grunt and tighten my grip on her. "Just a picture of my idiot brothers. Don't worry about it."

She pants out a chuckle that lasts only a few seconds. Then something shifts; her body somehow feels even more willing, silently asking me to take more of her.

A few encouragements to match, the dirty kind—Whitney begging me to keep going, telling me how good this is, pleading with me not to stop. The best kind of words from a woman, filthy and hot, nearly begging me to fuck her sideways, while still being entirely real.

A series of very complimentary words about my cock become all I can take. Two hard, jerky thrusts and my orgasm barrels forward in a long wave. By the time the sensation starts to fade, I can't quite feel my toes. Hell. *That* hasn't happened before.

Whitney slumps to the wall, and I follow, my body tipping to fall against hers. I summon just enough strength to kiss her neck, taste the salt on her skin. She twists her fingers through my hair, gently, and the tenderness in that touch puts me one breath away from collapsing.

I wasn't quite expecting this. Great sex, sure. I knew it would be, but the intensity, the spectacle of it all, is more than I planned on. Even now, we're still working over the last embers. Moving against each other, determined to take every bit, refusing to give until we're sure that's all there is.

=13=

(Whitney)

As it turns out, Cooper's loft *is* the epicenter in a hub of vice and sin. His bed? The axis point, the nucleus, the *hotbed*.

I'd blame it on Cooper himself, but despite being essential to all the debauchery, he was also capable of rising at six this morning and disappearing for a while to work out. Then he came back and made a very responsible breakfast for us: steel-cut oats with flaxseeds, topped with agave, walnuts, and sliced fruit. I stayed in bed while he did all of this, trying to decide if I could spend the rest of my ever-loving life tangled up in these exceptionally soft sheets.

When he invited me here, I was quickly able to deduce that the two of us, left uninterrupted and alone, would likely end up here. "Here" being his bed—which happens to be an enormous piece of furniture, topped with a marshmallow cloud–like mattress and a plush goose down–filled duvet. And if he's in it? No hope for a gal. Just give up and stay put.

Still, combining this trip with a stop at the offices of the slow money venture that Justin mentioned meant I was thinking with my brains, not merely my decidedly biased lady hormones. Unfortunately, the *slow* money part is just as the name suggests. With a backlog of applications and an exhaustive vetting process, I left their offices thinking they might have been my answer—about six months ago.

After I explained my predicament to a kind-faced representative, she was sympathetic but couldn't offer anything more than an assurance that they would do their best to expedite my completed application. I left Boulder in a defeated funk. Only when I merged onto the interstate toward downtown Denver did the funk start to fade, merely because a few days with Cooper sounded like a pretty effective way to escape my financial realities for a bit.

I vaguely recalled the moment in my kitchen when I admitted to myself that Cooper was probably too much for me. But my body had decided it did not care if he was more than my brain or my heart could handle, just so long as he was the one doing the handling. And right up until I parked my workhorse Toyota next to his shiny Dodge, I was convinced that I would be able to keep it together, go up there, and knock on his door. Then Cooper would be right there. Would he look the same as he did when he left my place a few weeks ago? Good God, would he look even better?

Impossible. I was sure there would be no justice in that; the world would be a foolish, unreasonable, far too tempting place if he did.

This morning, wonderfully cocooned in his bed and sore in the best of ways, I realize how wrong I was. The world *is* a foolish, unreasonable, far too tempting place.

━━━

Here's an interesting discovery: Cooper is all about the touching. And not just the kind that leads to clothes coming off. He's an absentminded toucher, from his fingers resting gently at your elbow when you cross the street to his arm pressed flush to yours when you take the elevator downstairs. His hands will inevitably make a home against your ass whenever the mood strikes him. This mood strikes him *a lot*.

Which is why he's currently waiting at the counter in the gourmet grocer we've stopped into—alone. I didn't feel comfortable with the way his arm and hand placements were trending toward inappropriate. Not to say that I didn't *like* it. I like a lot of things he does with his hands; that doesn't mean he should do them in public.

I make my way over to an adjacent wall display where a host of artisanal goods are for sale, abandoning him to wait as they finish assembling a perfectly curated picnic lunch for us. The always unpredictable Colorado weather has imparted a spring-like day, full of sunshine and temps in the sixties. Cooper suggested we leave the loft for a bit, take in some fresh air, and try to keep our hands to ourselves. You would think that since this was his idea, he'd do better with the hand thing.

My eye catches a pint jar of pickled asparagus on the shelf and I admire the packaging. The branding is spot-on, sharp and chic, while still looking appropriately artisan. Next to the asparagus are pickled beets from the same company, so I pull a jar down to read the back label, curious whether the company is local.

Just as I read that the beets were sourced from Justin's farm, Cooper appears behind me, slipping his free arm around my waist, high enough that his fingers rest under my breast. He pushes his arm up a bit more, until his hand is cupping the full underside, and because I'm wearing an ivory-colored tunic top in a thin fabric that drapes loosely, it's impossible for him to miss the way certain parts of my body react to that touch. Cooper's response? To run his errant thumb, slowly and directly, over my already taut nipple.

Christ. I should tell him to knock it off. Twist away until our postures are more dignified and less lusty. And I will. Any second now.

"You want some of those? I vote no, because beets are a terrible childhood memory for me, but if you want them, grab 'em so we can go. I'm hungry."

Another discovery about Cooper is that he eats a lot. Big quantities, all the time, and he routinely announces that he's hungry. How he survived at my place with only an apple as fuel for most of the day, I don't know.

I finish reading the label and hold up the jar so he can see it better. "I know these beets."

"Personally? Like you and the beets are friends?"

"No, the beets are from my friend Justin's farm in Fruita. He has the best beets." I place the jar back on the shelf and use my hand to form a cup, mimicking the shape of a beet at its peak. "They're just the right size, always perfectly sweet, and so good. He's always good about sharing them with me."

Cooper grunts. "Can't say I love how you talk about your buddy Justin's beets. Sounds a little dirty. I hope he's some old farmer, with a bunch of ear hair and arthritis."

I give up a scoff. Cooper's grip tightens around my waist and his hips flex forward to meet my lower back. I'd guess that describing Justin as the featherweight boxer version of Chris Hemsworth wouldn't be well received, so I sigh and twist away, patting his hand.

"We have Justin to thank for my coming up here. He told me about a slow money venture based out of Boulder that's focused on investing in local food sheds. I needed to check out their application process, see what the odds are on getting a loan approved."

Cooper furrows up his brow. "You need a loan?"

I nod and start toward the registers. "Yes."

I don't expound or elucidate, despite sensing that Cooper has turned his ears on and is waiting for me to do exactly that. He doesn't need to know more and I'm not up for sharing. Honestly, one of the best parts about the last eighteen hours has been putting my problems on the back burner, and I'd like to keep it that way.

We take our place in the checkout line and I can feel Cooper growing tense behind me, his body so close to mine that his fixed stare is practically boring a hole in the top of my head. The line ticks forward. Cooper taps my shoulder. I gather up my resolve and take a long inhale, because *here we go.*

He lowers his voice a notch. "Why do you need a loan? Are you in trouble? Tell me how much you nee—"

I cut him off before he can even finish that sentence. "No."

He starts in again, trying to whisper, as if that helps. We're surrounded by people, all within the marginal radius of personal space as dictated by grocery store lines everywhere.

Translation: too damn close to be discussing my personal finances.

I repeat myself, slower this time. Firmly and unequivocally. "No."

Maybe it's because my jaw goes taut, or maybe it's because I refuse to make eye contact with him, training my gaze straight ahead. But Cooper's body releases a sigh, labored and slow, evidence of him working hard to stay quiet.

Cooper isn't flexible. Strong, yes. He also has the endurance of a safari animal, or the Energizer Bunny, but manlier. He's very coordinated, has great balance, and can do more than one thing at once. Lots of things. So *many* things at once.

But Cooper trying to eat during a picnic, while sitting awkwardly on a stadium blanket, is like watching the Tin Man do yoga. Long limbs that don't quite hinge enough, knees and elbows that won't stay put when what he wants is just beyond his reach. Must be all those muscles.

Once we've finished eating, I stretch my legs out, fold

up the sweatshirt he brought along, and place it on my lap, giving it a pat to prompt him. Poor guy needs a flat surface and encouragement to stretch out. Cooper immediately rolls down, head in my lap, and lets his eyes close. I lean back onto outstretched arms and spy a group of guys across the park, setting up a small area for disc golf.

"I want to talk about the loan you need."

I groan aloud. The sunshine and food made me sleepy, in a good way. Now the sixty million–dollar man is going to ruin that.

"No."

One eye opens and he shades the sun from his face by propping one hand to his forehead. "Why not? Maybe I could help you. I don't understand why this is a problem."

"Because it's squicky."

"Squicky? Is that a real word?"

"Squicky is the feeling I get when I have sex with a guy and the next morning, he's trying to give me a large sum of money. Squicky."

Cooper rolls slightly to one side, making it so he doesn't have to shield his face.

"But if it's a loan, it would be different. It wouldn't be squicky."

More of the absentminded touching commences. He toys with the lower areas on my shirt, letting one finger slip under the bottom hem, grazing the skin on my belly. That doesn't help me think, so I still his hand.

"If I had sex with a guy from the bank and then he gave me a loan, wouldn't that seem squicky?"

His expression hardens. "We're not talking about you

sleeping with another guy. I don't want to talk about that, at all, in any context. We're talking about you needing a loan and me being in a position to finance it."

He's such a brick wall, mentally and physically. Despite his being the touchy-feely, thoughtful, sexy, fun Cooper for the majority of my time here, it seems the stubborn Cooper was still hiding just under the surface. A low grumble rises from his chest when he realizes that I've effectively closed the conversation by going silent. For nearly thirty seconds, he does nothing but twist the hem on my shirt and gnaw on his upper lip with his bottom teeth.

Finally, he stops abusing the hem and simply gives a tug on my shirt, aiming to get my attention.

"So what's your plan, then?"

When I look down, his eyes have gone soft. I shift my gaze back to the guys playing disc golf. If I continue to look at Cooper, I'll end up saying too much. When I do, he might somehow convince me to take him up on his offer.

And even the thought of that is just ridiculous. He's a pro football player and I'm an organic fruit farmer. He probably voted for Bush. Twice. That alone seems reason enough to prove why the two of us can't be more than short-lived and unsustainable.

But, let's say I take his money. Desperation takes over and Cooper opens up his checkbook, as I sign off on a loan to repay him. We play for a while, sleep together until the inevitable happens. In the best-case scenario, we flame out, finish up, and part ways as friends. Every month I'll write out a payment to him, tuck it an envelope, and drop it in the mail. For years. Until, eventually, he has a full life. A new address, a Mrs. Lowry by his side, some kids with eyes like Cooper's and wild mops of light blond hair to match. Maybe I'll get Christmas cards from them.

With *photos*.

I'll hate it. Hate *her*, especially. The elusive, someday Mrs. Cooper Lowry. Because she'll know the sound he makes just before he comes. A sharp growl that disintegrates into a satisfied groan. She'll love the silence between that moment and his mouth finding some part of her skin. A kiss to her shoulder, the small of her back, the inside of her wrist. The way he can fuck her so hard, so fiercely, that she can't do a thing but take the pleasure until somehow, he manages to cover her entire body with his so gently it turns her insides to fairy dust.

Nope. Not happening. I'd like to exist under the myth that I'm the only one who knows about the near-orgasm sounds and the fairy dust–inducing way Cooper puts his powerful body on top of mine. It's too weird, too depressing, to think otherwise.

I take a deep breath and keep my eyes up.

"I bought that place with money I got from losing my dad. He died at work when the tank blew up on his welder. Totally random, but the company paid out a settlement and I used it to buy my orchard. To make a long story short, I ended up leveraging the property to keep the operation afloat and then this year I lost too much fruit to frost and a hailstorm, and missed a few payments. I'm on borrowed time at this point."

I allow myself one quick glance down at Cooper. The

same soft eyes are there, but worry has settled into the fine lines around them.

"So my plan is to keep looking for a loan. A *real* loan. You and I barely know each other, and muddling up whatever this is with a loan has 'worst idea ever' written all over it. Even though losing my orchard would be like losing my dad all over again, I have to do this the right way. I'm on my own with this one."

Cooper doesn't say anything. He simply takes one of my hands and puts it to his chest, his own two hands on top. His shirt is warm from the sun. His chest is full and I can feel him breathing. Just the weight of him holding my one hand in place is enough to steady me, keep my heart where it belongs, instead of crumbling into a few hundred regret-filled pieces.

My dad would have liked Cooper. *"A good man,"* he'd say. *"The kind you can count on to hold you up when it matters."*

"You look cute eating that."

Cooper takes a peek my way as I try to figure out what he's up to.

After lunch, we stopped at the cupcake store that is part of the ground-level retail shops below his loft. We're barely out the shop door before I've peeled back the cupcake wrapper and taken a large bite. I could have waited until we got back upstairs to eat the cupcake he bought me, I suppose. But it's likely that I may need my hands free once we're behind closed doors again. I'm planning ahead, just to be safe.

First, though, I need to determine why he's proclaiming that I look "cute" shoving a cupcake into my mouth. Not possible. Maybe if you're five years old, sure. But a grown woman craning her jaw open as far as it will go and shoving a raspberry buttercream–frosted concoction into her mouth while walking down the sidewalk isn't cute. I take another bite but stop to chew it properly, giving Cooper a narrow-eyed glance as I do.

Cooper proceeds to deliver his next line with possibly the world's worst attempt at sounding nonchalant. He looks like a hot PE teacher who just got his first shot on-stage in a local dinner theater production of *Our Town* or something. Stilted words, delivered way too loudly, and with jerky hand gestures to boot.

"Oh, look." Cooper points across the street at a sleek, big-name electronics store. "I want to go over there for a second."

He's obviously trying to keep his face neutral, but it's doing that wacky contortion thing that he can't control.

Worst liar/actor ever.

I take a quick lick of my lips to ensure no frosting gets away and give him a nod. "Go for it. Can I have your keys to head upstairs?"

"You should come with me."

Oh, oh, oh. Whatever his plan is, the snare trap lies inside that shiny store full of high-priced laptops and cell phones. I take another bite of my cupcake. Cooper shoves his hands into his pockets, eyes flitting around aimlessly for a second, before yanking his hands back out and crossing his arms over his chest.

I finish my bite slowly, for funsies, because I want him to stand there looking uncomfortable and twitchy for a bit longer. Once I've had my fill, I give in.

"We could stand here and finish out this poorly acted scene where you pretend that you don't have a scheme of some sort, or you can just tell me what's up."

Cooper shoves his hands back into his pants pockets and widens his stance. The effect is both hot and intimidating, although I think he's going for resigned and long-suffering.

"I would like for us to go in there so I can get you a cell phone. I'll add the line to my account and pay for everything."

Huh. Wasn't expecting that. Interesting. Maybe a little suspect.

"Why?" The last bite of cupcake disappears into my mouth and I toss the wrapper in a nearby trash can.

"I want to be able to get in touch with you. Call you, text you. I don't like the idea of you being without a cell, either. That truck you drive around in isn't exactly brand-new."

"Sounds a little squicky. Like you want to put a leash on me, but via a cell phone."

Cooper rolls his eyes, shakes his head, and sighs. A trifecta of exasperation. I should be offended, but watching him try to rein in any further irritation is somewhat entertaining.

"Stop saying that word. I'm not trying to put a leash on you. I just want to be able to talk to you."

"You do talk to me. On my landline. I'll need a better reason than that."

He thrusts one hand up in the air, palm out. "You know what? Fuck it. Forget I mentioned it."

Cooper's long legs manage to get him halfway to the front door of his building before I can catch up. I grab his shirtsleeve and get him to stop, but he doesn't turn to face me.

I give a gentle tug on his shirt and bump my hips into his. "Hey. Don't get pissed. Tell me what the real reason is."

His gaze tracks over my shoulder for a moment, before his shoulders sag and he sighs.

"When we're on the team plane, the other guys are always face-first in their phones before we take off. Either talking or texting their girls, wives, whoever. Usually, I'm listening to my iPod or trying to sleep. I never had anyone that I wanted to be on the phone with."

He pauses until I grasp the subtext of his last sentence. Realization dawns and when I nod my head slowly, he continues.

"What if I want to text you something? Something I can't say on the phone, when there's a bunch of my asshole teammates around?"

I grin and raise my brows. "Like what?"

"I don't know. Private stuff."

He's awkward now. Which is interesting, because he's usually very up-front. Very up-front and very filthy, perfectly so. I guess I get to be the brazen one for now. Mentally, I rub my hands together deviously. Awkward Cooper going up against Brazen Whitney. I like it.

"Are you going to send me dirty pictures? Like of . . ." I waggle my finger downward and widen my eyes.

"I am not sending you any dick pics."

"Why not? What if I want you to?"

"Because I'm not an idiot. If you want my dick, you'll just have to come get it."

Challenge lights in his eyes. Troublesome and enticing, it seems Awkward Cooper has exited stage left. My lips feel suddenly unattended and needy, so I trace my tongue across the upper one and watch Cooper track the motion with his eyes.

"OK."

He doesn't move his gaze. "OK to what?"

"OK, I want to come get it. OK, you can get me a phone."

The words sound nearly trancelike, because I'm staring at his mouth, the way his jaw slackens and his own tongue peeks out to touch his upper lip. My eyes start to glaze over as I consider exactly how I want to *get it*. One side of Cooper's mouth hooks up lazily.

"Good." He grabs my hand, and with a rough tug, we're walking. Him quick-stepping and me stumbling along behind him, trying to keep up. "We'll come back down in a while and get the phone. Later."

= 14 =

(Whitney)

The next day, Cooper is awake again at six a.m. He's like a little human alarm clock or walking day planner, because it's clear he abides by a relatively strict schedule.

Up at six a.m., a protein shake at eight, food every two hours after that, but nothing after seven p.m. Consistent water intake, a complex array of supplements, and a full eight hours of sleep a night. While he didn't spell any of this out, I picked up on the routine pretty quickly. Apparently having such valuable hands, and a body to match, is a full-time job.

So, I know what time it is when he nudges his face into the crook of my neck and starts to nuzzle a series of kisses there. It's six a.m. On the freaking dot, I'd wager.

I'm lying on my back, head flopped to one side, positioned perfectly for what he's up to. One of Cooper's arms is across my belly, with one leg also thrown across my body, his thigh set squarely atop my hips. I had no idea how good all that mass could feel, those limbs pinning my body to his bed, diminutive under his size. There isn't a thing domineering about it—instead the posture feels protective, a giant manly refuge that's warm and sheltering. I'd happily take up residence here if a tornado or some other natural disaster required we take cover. Better than any musty storm cellar or basement, that's for sure.

When he starts to pull the covers back, though, things become more interesting. The slow drag of my T-shirt being pushed up, exposing my belly and breasts. His mouth traversing all those spaces, down to my waistline, down again to my thighs. A demanding but gentle shove on both legs to move them open as his lips skim up the inside of one leg. I shimmy down a bit, get ready for what's coming next: Cooper on top of me with his whole body, rubbing and stroking and teasing until he decides it's time for a condom.

Things start to go off script when he rustles around in the sheets, getting more comfortable with his face between my legs. Then he settles in, biting the flesh on my upper thighs before leaning in to put one long drag of his tongue across my opening.

Uh-oh. I start to squirm a little, edging back from that touch. He notes the shift and summarily misinterprets it as a needy squirm, and he rewards the action by burying his face deep, taking a mouthful and giving a low, lurid groan. I try again, but he wraps his arms around my legs and grips them in place forcefully. My body likes the aggression, heartbeat kicking up in the right way, but this still isn't going to end the way either of us wants it to.

"Cooper," I whisper, grabbing a handful of his hair.

Again, these things too easily seem like encouragements. He responds with a grunt, more pressure of his tongue. "Cooper, stop. Come up here."

His head pops up. "What's wrong?"

Jesus, he looks drunk. And combined with how he's breathing a little jaggedly, his mouth shiny, it's the most amazing sight. It's a good look on him. If only that were enough.

"That," I wiggle my fingers toward where he's taken up camp, "doesn't work on me."

Eyes wide, he shakes his head. "Excuse me?"

Blah, this sucks. I'd take a long harvest day with cockleburs in my shoes over this anytime. But in addition to Cooper's regimented schedule, I think his football career accounts for another personality trait. Cooper is *really* competitive. As evidenced by the way he groused and groaned through some video game he was playing last night, he likes to win. He doesn't much take to the idea of losing, even to a computerized opponent. Anything he can't surmount puts him in a bad mood. In this case, he's going to want to win at giving me an orgasm with his mouth and he's going to end up disappointed. I let out a gusting exhale and look at the ceiling.

"I can't orgasm that way; I've never been able to. It feels good, but it doesn't get me there. So if you try, you're going to be upset when it doesn't happen. I've already figured out how competitive you are. Your mouth squaring off against my vagina isn't a good matchup."

A cough from him, the strangled sound of disbelief and surprise.

"First off, your pussy and I are on the same team. I'm team captain and that amazing place between your legs is MVP. And, if you hadn't noticed, we play really well together."

I start to laugh because what he's saying is sweet and silly, but his expression is complete seriousness. He crawls up my body until his face is right in front of mine.

"Just because you've had trouble before isn't a reason to throw in the towel on this. All we have to do is try some things, figure out what you need." He takes and gently sweeps a few tendrils of hair from my forehead, tucking the wayward pieces behind my ear. "I'll stay put until it happens, so you don't have to feel pressured about being quick or anything. I won't give up."

"You're assuming it's because guys don't try. But I don't think that's it. I mean, Elm, he would practically make a day of it. He was very attentive in bed and—"

One of Cooper's palms appears inches from my face. He slowly lowers his eyelids.

"I'm begging you not to tell me anything more about other guys. I hate thinking about anyone else touching you. But are you saying that your reference point for this experience is a dude named *Elm*? Is that his real name?"

"Not his given name. I think it was Brian. I don't remember, but he changed it to Elm."

"Enough said. I'm sorry, but a guy named Elm isn't going to be able to eat pussy properly. Just isn't possible."

I sigh and run my hands through my hair. We can talk this topic to death and it won't change anything. "Let's just drop it, OK?"

Cooper rises to rest back on his heels between my legs. He runs his hands over my thighs tenderly, then leans forward incrementally so his hands can keep moving upward, coming to a stop at my rib cage. My back arches so slightly he probably doesn't notice, but I feel the unconscious shift of my body tilting toward his touch. Cooper gently sweeps his thumbs across the skin just under my breasts but doesn't move. I cast a wary glance at him and his mouth curves up on one side.

"You don't need to look at me like that. I'd never push you on something like this. Just promise me that you'll think about letting me try at some point." Cooper draws his hands back down, resting them on my inner thighs, and takes a long look at the space in between. "But I can still play down here, right? Like, for foreplay and stuff? I'd hate to think that taste was all I'm ever going to get."

My entire body heats, from my cheeks down to my kneecaps. I nod and croak out an agreement. He puts a soft kiss to the spot where my belly meets my hip bone, eyes locked on mine while he does.

"Right now, I'll go get a shower. Then I'll make you some breakfast."

═══

I try to go back to sleep. Convinced that if I shut my eyes, I won't fixate on how talented Cooper is. Especially with sex stuff. He's quite gifted in that area. My eyes close, but every moment of him demonstrating that talent on my body in the last few days flashes through my mind on a loop. I try to think of other things. Puppies and sunshine. The calming effect of waves crashing on a beach.

Cooper infiltrates every image, though. Carousing with the puppies while shirtless. Letting the sunshine heat his (obviously) shirtless skin. Emerging from one of those crashing waves. Shirtless.

Gah. None of this is helping.

He's competitive, I remind myself. *He's impatient. Occasionally grouchy.* Shirtless or not, all those traits add up to a guy who won't take failure graciously.

The shower shuts off after a few minutes. Water rushes in the sink as he brushes his teeth.

Hmm. Minty fresh.

He strides back into the room, tugging on a pair of boxer briefs. "Oatmeal?"

"I changed my mind." Draping a hand over my eyes, I wait.

A dresser drawer opens and he rummages though it for a second, then I can feel him sitting down on the edge of the bed.

"What, you want a scramble or something? I have some spinach and portabellas. We could go crazy and add some turkey bacon, too."

"No. About the other thing."

All movement at the end of the bed ceases. I refuse to uncover my eyes just yet, not until this uncomfortable silence dissipates. Maybe if I recite the alphabet backward, that will provide just enough distraction from the mortification of waiting this out.

Z, Y, X, W, V, T . . .

Just as I realize I've skipped over the letter *U*—so critical to my currently *unbearable* state of being—my legs are abruptly yanked upon. Cooper's hands latch on to my ankles, pulling me down to the end of the bed. I let out a sharp squeal and attempt to fasten my hands to the rumpled bedcovers, grasping for purchase where I can.

Cooper continues to grip my legs and grins when I meet his gaze. Oh, that grin, it's trouble. In a good way. He ticks up one eyebrow.

"Changed your mind, did you? Tell me more."

"I want you to."

"Want me to *what*?"

I groan. "I want you to perform oral sex on me."

He drops my legs without warning and they bounce on the bed. His face screws up. "Fuck no. Absolutely not."

This guy and his truth-telling. If I weren't trying to avoid flushing entirely scarlet, I'd kick him in a very precious part of his body. I might miss out on any further good times, but he deserves it, so I'll make the sacrifice.

Before I can punish him, he's dropping to his knees, pushing my legs up until they're pressed against my chest while he clutches the back of my thighs in his hands, hard.

"Will I eat you out? Yes. Lick your pussy? Absolutely. But I will never, ever 'perform oral sex' on you. This isn't junior high health class. Just say what you really want. For me to go down on you and be the first guy to feel you coming on his face."

All I manage to get out is a moan, because his face lands between my legs, taking inventory with easy teases at first, testing for a reaction. He starts in a little more, circling with his tongue, letting his lips cover the space I'm pushing closer to his mouth because this already feels more promising than it ever has. Then he stops, releases his grip, and my already weak legs flop to the bed. When his head pops up, I actually grunt.

"Just so you know, I might be competitive, but I'm also comfortable with feedback. People have been evaluating my performance since I was a kid. Telling me to run faster or go harder, how to hit a pattern differently and lower my center of gravity. So you just need to tell me what's working and what isn't. I don't necessarily need you to say it with words—just let me know somehow. I'll make the correction."

My eyes drift closed. I try to make my head stop throbbing, a sensation brought on the second he started talking. I take a deep breath.

"Here's your first correction. Stop talking."

He *is* good with correction. No discernable pause, just him back where he belongs. My head stops throbbing, only for me to have that same sensation start in down below. The same intense pulse, but entirely better when it's between my legs.

Ah, Elm never did *that*. Cooper slips his hand up and uses two fingers to bracket my clit as he sweeps the tip of his tongue softly to that spot, the pressure of his fingers adding a new kind of intensity I've never experienced. I shift so that my knees are bent and I can press the soles of my feet to the bed for a little leverage. Cooper draws his hand away and sneaks lower, those thick fingers then teasing my opening, encouraging me to push closer as his mouth works just above. I nudge my hips up and every twist from there becomes another correction, positive reinforcement he somehow incorporates into his next move. When I whisper one word—*please*—he slides two fingers inside, so fluidly I lose my breath at the fullness.

The pressure is perfect, triggering a familiar sensation, the one I want to break the surface. But I try not to think about the endgame. I focus on my body, on Cooper, keeping my eyes closed while picturing him in my mind, and . . . oh, hell. *Yes. Like that.* I let a quiet whimper out, my body asking for more of whatever that was he just did with his lips, and he hears every nonverbal syllable.

I lift my hips up into a bridge pose, thinking that will bring us closer together, but it does something else entirely. Entirely fucking spectacular. His fingers crook to accommodate the angle, and then he's stroking that spot—the place where unicorns are real and orgasms become cracktastic versions of the norm.

A low, strangled moan rises from my throat. Cooper uses his other arm to hold my hips up, thrusts his fingers harder, and it takes only a few of those short, intense strokes for all of my senses to go haywire. Staying quiet is impossible, because it's the first time I've felt my climax go off like a bomb—swifter, mightier, headier.

Cooper waits it out, through every second of the trembling and quaking, before winding me down gently. He slips his arm out from under my hips and brings my body to rest in a heap on the bed. I can't see much beyond the stars dancing in front of my eyes but manage to force my gaze downward, where Cooper is resting back on his heels, looking nearly as staggered as I feel.

When I unexpectedly giggle—because that was *awesome*—the look on his face turns smug, evidence that he's appallingly proud of himself. Probably be for the best if he didn't try this particular trick again too soon. The self-satisfied vibe he's putting out means his head won't fit between my legs.

I flop a hand helplessly about in the air, flicking my fingers in his direction.

"Go ahead. You did what I thought was impossible, so feel free to pound your fists against your chest, Tarzan."

Cooper stands, shaking his head languidly. "It's like you don't know me at all."

He hauls down his boxers. His cock springs out, hard and thick, pointing my way like a damn divining rod.

"My chest is the last thing I'm interested in pounding right now."

Oh. *Oh.* When I scoot back a little farther onto the bed, he smacks the palm of his hand against my outer thigh. Another swat and I realize what he wants. Note to self: *If Cooper swats your hip like that, it means turn over, because he has a plan. A plan involving you with your ass in the air.* I'll try to remember that.

When he leans over me to reach his nightstand, his cock nudges between my legs and we both groan at the flush contact between our bodies. Cooper yanks the drawer open, snatches a condom out, then hastily rises to rip open the wrapper with his teeth and curses when I push my body back toward what I want. Waiting is torture, even for those few moments. But then he's there, seated deep with one push. I've never felt so deprived and simultaneously sated before. It was merely seconds we lost to be safe, and though my lust-hazed brain hated the pause, once I had him again, just that stifled the rest.

He takes one slow thrust, then stills.

"Holy fuck, it's a good thing I love my job."

I drop my face to the mattress and try to figure out why he's talking about football. *Now*, of all times. Currently, I have a one-track mind and football certainly isn't on it.

"Really?" I say. "You're honestly thinking about football right now? God, what does a woman have to do to keep your attention?"

"That's my point. In a few hours I'll be at practice and it's possible all my attention will still be right here, where I can't get enough." Cooper starts to move, my hips firmly in his grip. "If I didn't love my job so much, I'd see if I could make a career out of tasting you and fucking you. You'd hate me because I'd never let you out of my sight. Or put clothes on."

Only Cooper could make such a boorish speech sound somehow charming. One of his hands reaches out and takes up my arm, gently twisting it behind my back, where he can wrap my forearm in his strong grip. His other hand falls to the bed, and the position gives him all the power, all of me, to do whatever he chooses with. And I couldn't care less.

════

The phone Cooper bought for me is a shiny, pretty thing. Rose gold and sleek, but oddly demanding. Ever since we brought it home, it's needed something. A charge on the battery, setup on the Wi-Fi connection, downloading this and that. The ancient slider phone I'm used to never required this much devotion. Even now, my digital newborn is chirping for attention.

I take a quick peek at the phone's face and toss it aside. Cooper can deal with it. His idea, so he can coddle it. Tossing my clothes into my bag, I congratulate myself on finding the motivation to leave Cooper's big bed. Because despite knowing I have to leave soon, with real life calling to both of us, leaving his bed is hard. Nearly impossible. Nothing but good things happen in that bed.

I look at it longingly.

Good-bye, bed. I'll miss you.

My red lace ensemble is the last piece of clothing to land in my bag. Striding into the main room, I carry my bag in one hand and the phone in the other.

"Two things. One, this phone you insisted on tethering me with wants to update some iOS thingy. Should I tell it to do that? Also, are those oats ready? Because I'm hungry after all the spectacular orgasms that transpired this morning. So many dazzling sex acts before breakfast leaves me depleted, like those fasting workouts you were trying to explain over dinner last night."

When I look up, there are three faces staring back at me. Two more than I'd planned on, obviously.

"Hello there, people I don't know." I shoot a look Cooper's way. "People I didn't know were *here*."

The two new faces continue to peek in from the hallway, while also jostling their way into the loft. The woman elbows in front of the man; no matter, he still has a clear view because he's easily a couple of heads taller that she is. They both get eyes on me and start to grin, politely but goofily. Cooper does not follow suit. He merely groans and lolls his head back theatrically.

"Why are you guys here? I'm pretty sure I was clear about how this"—he waves a hand among all of us—"shouldn't happen."

The man takes a glance Cooper's way and shrugs. "Just figured I'd come pick you up for practice. We could walk together. Hold hands and catch up. I haven't seen you in a few days and it just feels like a lifetime, sunshine."

"With your wife along for the ride? I'm not in grade school, so I don't need a crossing guard or a chaperone. You two already have kids and I'm not one of them."

The woman takes a playful swipe at Cooper's shoulder without even looking at him. She must be used to knuckling him into behaving properly, because she doesn't miss and Cooper doesn't flinch. The man reaches around her and extends his hand toward me.

"You must be Whitney. I'm the best friend, Aaron Bolden. This is my wife, Kendra."

Cooper crosses his arms over his chest and draws in a resigned breath. I reach for Aaron's hand and have to steady myself when he latches on. Big guy, even bigger handshake. Cooper leans toward me and speaks in a stage whisper.

"Don't listen to him. He's not my best friend, he's a menace."

Kendra proceeds to inspect me, in the efficient and unforgiving way only women can. Her gaze lingers on my nose ring. Then her eyes scan the rest of my form, gathering all the other data she needs from my outfit. A black long-sleeved henley over black jeans, both faded to a near gunmetal shade, the jeans rolled up to show off a pair of decade-old duck boots. She's clad in white skinny jeans with a casual but silky-looking halter top, a cropped blazer in light gray, and heels to match. A large, expensive-looking handbag is in the crook of one arm.

But her inspection isn't entirely unfriendly. Her eyes aren't critical, they're cautious. The turn of her mouth doesn't read as a sneer, merely her taking stock to determine if I meet her standards. She cocks her head.

"Cooper is the next best thing to Aaron, in my opinion. I love him like he's my own. I'm not big on the people I love getting hurt. Do you get me?"

I pull my head back a bit and furrow my brow. Cooper grumbles a series of expletives as Aaron's jaw drops, hanging playfully agape. I blink and try to decide how best to respond. Unflinching honesty makes it easier to know where you stand, I guess.

"I get you just fine. And I'm pretty keen on him, too. Did you hear what I said when I came out here? The words *spectacular* and *dazzling* were used. When he's not being stubborn or grumpy, it's hard not to acknowledge his awesomeness."

Aaron starts to howl, a loud, boisterous sound that echoes down the hallway. Cooper wraps his arms around my waist and presses his forehead to the back of my head, relaxing enough to put a kiss to the crown. Kendra allows a slow smile to replace her previously pursed mouth. Her gaze cuts to Cooper.

"Thank God. I can finally cross this off my to-do list. She's fabulous." Kendra exhales and smiles, letting Aaron drape an arm over her shoulder as he nods in agreement.

That indulgent display, for Cooper and each other, forces me to acknowledge how big Cooper's world is. He has so much. A big career, a big family, big love from friends who truly know him and want to protect him anyway. The surly and controlled parts of who he is aren't off-putting when you know the rest of him, too. The honest, thoughtful, passionate, steady traits can easily smooth over those moments when he speaks before he thinks.

I think over my own life in contrast. No family to speak of. Plenty of acquaintances in Hotchkiss, but no one like this. The sort of folks who show up at your door whether you like it or not, because they refuse to let you shut them out. Before this moment, I didn't realize how lonely my life had become. Not painfully so, because it was a slow burn, a quiet turn toward solitude that I hadn't noticed until now.

When I leave here, Cooper's world will continue on this way. Abundant and blessed, big beyond measure. I'll go home and do all I can to save my little piece of the world—all on my own.

= 15 =

(Cooper)

"**B**olden said you met a girl."

It's a good thing I'm facedown on the massage table. That way Hunt can't see me roll my eyes. He's flipping pages on his clipboard, documenting the state of my assorted injuries and evaluating each of my other minor aches, those little time bombs that have yet to implode. Operative word being *yet*.

When the team massage therapist, Mikel, presses harder on my hamstring and drags his fist across the length of the muscle, discomfort ripples through my entire leg. Despite how much it hurts, pain is a gray scale, a measure of how bad I want to play versus how much my injury will allow. For now, my hamstring remains a manageable nuisance.

Another stroke of Mikel's knuckles to the outside of my leg, the most painful area, and my leg twitches. He notes the reaction and, to my relief, dials back the pressure just enough that I don't need to hold my breath anymore.

Mikel is built like one of our offensive linemen and he

has an Eastern European accent so thick it's nearly impossible to understand what he's saying, but he doesn't say much anyway. Before Mikel, our massage therapist was a retired French Canadian power lifter named Jacques. Before that, it was Sven the Swedish lumberjack. All huge guys with various accents and very little to say. Despite how hard we've campaigned Hunt to make this experience a little more enjoyable, we always end up with some version of Mikel—never a Michelle, Jacqueline, or Svetlana, with soft, dexterous hands and a subtle, but still sexy, accent.

"Bolden said she was different. But the right kind of different. I have no idea what that means. A jersey chaser with potential?"

Through the opening in the face cradle, I let out a grunt. "You and Bolden need to stop talking about me. Gossiping like two women over martinis. But, no, she's definitely not a jersey chaser, with potential or otherwise."

Mikel prompts me to turn over and when I do, Hunt has his clipboard clasped to his chest, observing as Mikel bends my leg in toward my abs, gauging my range of motion. Hunt's eyes don't shift as he speaks.

"Tell me about her. I'm curious, gotta admit."

It seems my massage therapy session is quickly devolving into a psychotherapy session. Mikel presses my bent leg as far as he can until my body resists, which means it doesn't go far. To distract myself from the tension, I think about how spectacularly bendy Whitney's legs are, and words start to tumble out.

"She's cool. Not a jersey chaser. She's actually totally clueless about any of this." I throw my arms wide to gesture at the training room, Hunt, me, Mikel—all of it.

"We're nothing alike. She's patient and funny and takes most stuff in stride, and enjoys pointing out how I'm none of those things. She owns an organic fruit orchard down southwest and looks exactly like you might expect an organic farmer to look. In a hot way. Nose ring, no makeup, but great skin, and a perfect body under super-casual clothes. Drives a beater Toyota and doesn't hesitate to make it known how much she hates my fossil fuel–consuming Dodge."

Hunt continues to jot a few things down in his notes, but there's an amused expression on his face. He's been married for thirty years and from what I can tell, happily. His wife is a pixie-tiny woman who smiles a lot, so much that I can't imagine how a cantankerous guy like Hunt managed to keep her for so long. But it's obvious he loves her, and more important, after all those years and raising three girls together, I'm pretty sure he still genuinely *likes* her—thinks she's beautiful, loves to see her smile, and wants to keep her happy.

I get that now. The way a woman can be so goddam likable and gorgeous, you just want to try to be less of a jerk than you usually are and do whatever it takes to keep her happy. That's all. OK, maybe I want to keep her naked, too. But *happily* naked.

Before I can remind myself to shut it, I keep talking.

"We're definitely hot for each other, so we've got that for now, I guess. Not sure if we can be more. Two people so different might have a tough time making something last." I shrug.

Hunt flips his papers, then pats an open hand to my shoulder as he turns to walk away.

"I don't know, kid. I think it sounds like you just described the beginning of a hell of a love story."

═══════

Seattle.

You couldn't pay me to live here. It's rainy and dreary, and the humidity that comes with it is hell on my joints. They can keep their coffee; I'll take the three hundred–plus days of sunshine that Colorado has to offer. So, with my joints screaming and a Monday-night game against a team that's hard to beat, this road trip won't be over soon enough to suit me.

We spent the afternoon on their practice field and finished out our day with the standard media circus. After a shower and dinner, I'm settled in bed and looking forward to the brightest spot in my day. Calling Whitney. It's a routine now: in the couple of weeks since she left Denver, I've dialed her up every night just before we both go to sleep.

She answers with a smile in her voice and the sound has the same effect it always does. A grin across my face, followed by my dick perking up to greet her. Whitney immediately asks about practice today, how I'm feeling about the game, so I don't get the opportunity to indulge the one part of my anatomy that doesn't care about football. Twenty minutes later, I realize that I've talked her ear off, analyzing this team and their defense to my captive—and likely bored stupid—audience.

"Sorry. I'm rambling. It's just that we can't move the ball very effectively and that drives me nuts."

"It's fine. But I honestly don't understand how you guys can know all of this stuff about the other team and not be able to work around it. You said they do this 4–3 thing with the gaps. Can't you just fill the gaps with other guys or something? More bodies would, like, neutralize what they're doing, right?"

The question is both naïve and adorable, but more important, it's obvious she was listening this whole time, through every rambling speech and sidetracked commentary of mine. I always assumed that a woman who knew nothing about the game would be impossible to have in my life for longer than one night because adding subtitles to everything I say would get tedious quickly. But even when she doesn't understand, Whitney doesn't need subtitles; she just listens harder. And I definitely want her for more than one night.

"Do you know how much I wish you were here with me right now?"

The truth of how much I miss her is hard to ignore after blurting out something like that. Inside, I wince. No matter how much I want her, or miss her, it's no damn excuse for sounding that needy.

She laughs softly. "Wow. My question must be really dumb if that's your response."

I tell her it isn't dumb but can't say anything else. If I try to say more, I'll end up babbling about all the things that are bearing down on me right now: my contract negotiations stalling out, the way my entire body hurts, the pressure that comes with a good season. It's just over halfway through regular season and we're sitting pretty in the standings, but staying on top is harder in some ways than clawing your way out of a losing streak.

On the road especially, everything is working against you. The lack of time and sleep, combined with constant change and stress. My body wants a release and my heart wants some respite—unfortunately, my brain knows the cure for both is more than a thousand miles away.

Her voice lowers. "You want me in your hotel room or what? You want to show me around Pike Place Market? Buy me a salmon?"

My heartbeat slows when I register the provocation in her voice and my first thought is the obvious. That I want to fuck her straight into the mattress for a few long, sweaty hours. Maybe that isn't the best answer. I close my eyes and try to think of something less cock-centric to say.

But I can't, because she's breathing softly into the phone and that means I'm picturing her kneeling between my legs, making the same sounds as her mouth hovers right where I want it. That image makes my dick so hard, and so quickly, that it pisses me off.

All the quality time I'm spending with my right hand these days is making me more edgy, instead of less so. I've never been one of those guys who routinely jacks off; something about too much time spent that way feels a little pathetic. Either I found someone to take home or I did something more productive. Got in a workout, finished a project, fixed a meal. These days, I'm worried I'll end up with carpal tunnel if I'm not careful, and I don't need another injury, especially one that's depressingly self-inflicted.

Whitney says my name, quietly, checking to see if I'm still here. I sigh and run a hand through my hair. "I'd love to have you in my hotel room, but that would never happen."

"Why?"

"Because they treat us like we're at church camp. No women in our rooms—no exceptions."

"Not even wives?"

I snort. "It doesn't matter. Once we're back at the hotel, we're on lockdown. Dinner, a shower, we can order one in-room movie on the team's dime, and then lights-out."

"But there can be relaxing benefits to a little alone time with someone. Might help you sleep and show up to the game with a clear head. Don't they know that?"

Great. She's alluding to sex and extolling the benefits of an orgasm. No hope for my cock now. I let one hand slide down and draw the heel of my hand across the front of my boxers.

"I'm sure they do. But they probably figure it's far less complicated to just let us order porn with our free movie. Keep it simple."

"Do you?"

Now she wants to chat about whether I use my movie for family-friendly options or some less so? *Fuck it.* I give up and take myself in hand and use a firm grip to stroke the entire length, exactly the way I like it. After a few passes, I let my fist come to work slowly over the head. A drop of pre-cum immediately beads up and I use it to slick over the underside. A low groan tumbles out when I focus pressure and friction on that spot. Whitney draws in a little gasp, because, yup, she's figured out exactly what I'm doing.

"Sometimes. But not these days."

"Why?" she asks.

Her voice is cautious, tempered by what sounds like nervousness. Why, I don't know. She has to know that *she's* why. Because Whitney is slowly becoming my default, for everything from the carnal to the comforting.

"My dick likes you best. He likes it when I picture you, think about how good you feel, how fucking wet you get. We don't need anything else."

She doesn't give any indication that she's offended. Instead, she lets out the hottest damn appreciative noise. A moan mixed with a murmur, the sound of savoring something she likes, and it's enough to drive me right to the edge. I try to hold back by squeezing down almost painfully, staving off the climax I'm not ready for, because I want this to last a little longer. Then Whitney slays whatever control I thought I had with three whispered words.

"Are you close?"

I can't answer her, because I'm not close, I'm there. Spilling into my hand at the sound of her voice, until I'm wrecked from coming so hard that my heart is threatening to thump out of my chest.

And if I'm not careful, the damn thing is going to thump its way right into Whitney's hands.

———

The first plays of any game are the best. No other feeling in the world can mimic this one, because you take the field with only a hyperconscious state of awareness that sharpens every movement into hi-def and melds the cacophony of sounds around you into nothing but a low, muffled rumble. I'm loose and serene for those moments. Zen? Maybe. Football is my meditation—without it, I'm half the person I should be.

We bulldoze our way through to the second quarter, leading by fourteen. Coach calls a play that will put me in position and when I line up, I try to clear my mind of everything else, because if this goes the way it should, I'll be waiting for a wide-open bomb. But waiting is the death of instinct, and catching a ball is best done by reflex. Nothing but white noise and muscle memory to guide you.

I run my route, but the ball doesn't quite make it. It comes up just short, and desperation means I'm suddenly trying to outwit an inanimate object, along with the hulk of a cornerback who wants to hand me my ass.

I take a long leap, feel my fingers touch the ball. *You can catch this one*, my mind shouts. *Lean forward, stretch every limb out, and grab it. Then plant one foot, just enough to pivot your body the direction you want to go.*

Lies. All of it. The propaganda of hope, ego, and stupidity.

Instead, when my knee goes, I'm convinced the sound

is loud enough to be deafening. But what I actually hear is for my ears alone. It's the sound of my reality imploding. Because talk all you want about concussions; most of us don't give a shit. But my knees? Fuck up my knees and you kill my career.

No one will remember this but me. The acute, painful, spirit-breaking moments that pass while I wait for Hunt, splayed out at the eight-yard line with my left leg pointing the wrong direction, my mind consciously cataloging every tiny thing that's happening. Because if this is the last time I'm ever on the field, I want to remember every single second.

Fans think that game days define a career, that those moments make us who we are. But, for us—the players—there's no difference.

In October or July, on a Tuesday morning or a Sunday afternoon, it doesn't change a thing. We're pro ball players no matter what. Every day, until your body or your heart can't give another yard.

=16=

(Cooper)

Thanksgiving is typically my favorite holiday. With the exception of those years when I've had a game, I'm usually at home with my family and we're the embodiment of every cliché that goes along with the holiday. So much food we can't possibly eat it all, but we damn sure try. A television blaring in the background all day long, Macy's parade in the morning and football the rest of the day. Loud voices, bad jokes at each other's expense, a kids' table crowded with my nieces and nephews. Picking at the leftovers while my mom tries to put them away and squeezing in a nap before pie.

But this year, I'm a week out from a knee injury that feels fatal and I can't handle the idea of going home. Even dealing with the orthopedic surgeon who examined my knee became a test in keeping my fists to myself.

"You have a grade-two MCL injury, which is not good. But you managed to avoid concurrent ACL or PCL damage, so, you know, . . . yay for you."

I wanted to drag him across the desk by his purple paisley tie.

So even though my family would do everything they could to distract me or make me feel better, I told my mom I had to beg off coming home because of physical therapy appointments. It was a half-truth at best, but what I needed this year was something else. Some*one* else. Which is not to say that I don't recognize how lying to my mom will likely land me in a special part of hell. The privilege of raising four boys has already paid her primarily in heartache and worry, instead of gold and accolades as it should.

Whitney knows about my knee; she checked the game report online and called me right afterward. I was on the bus, headed for the team plane, and had just taken another syringe-full of who knows what from Hunt. It numbed the worst of the pain, so I couldn't give a fuck less what it was.

Whitney asked if I was OK. I told her my knee was blown.

She paused, and then tried again.

"I asked about you, *not your knee, Cooper. Are* you *OK?"*

If I hadn't been on the team bus, with Hunt bent over my leg and rubbing the injection site to take away the sting, I might have told her the truth. That no, I wasn't OK. And I wanted her so badly I didn't even know how to deal with it.

Standing on my terrace, I flop down into a deck chair and prop my aching leg up on the patio railing while I dial Whitney's number. My knee brace digs into the flesh at the top of my calf, so I prop my phone between my ear and shoulder, give the contraption a little twist, and wait.

She answers with my name. Not *hello*, not *hey*, just my name—soft and sweet, exactly what I need to hear.

"How do you feel about Thanksgiving?"

She makes a harrumphing noise. "I think it's a holiday that honors gluttony, sloth, xenophobia, and the overconsumption of material things by bookending the day with Black Friday. All of it justified by the ruse that we're supposedly practicing gratitude and the whole thing is somehow patriotic."

I groan. I should have spent a little more time relishing the way she said my name before opening myself up to one of her hippie tirades.

"I happen to love Thanksgiving."

"This does not surprise me in the least. You're a white kid who plays football, born and bred in Texas—this holiday has Cooper Lowry written all over it. But what's your point?"

From my vantage point on the deck, car horns blare, people call out to each other, and the light rail rumbles past. All this noise means that if I don't find a way to decompress, I'm going to lose my mind. What I need more than anything is Whitney. Her easy way, her honesty, her body. Here's hoping that she'll take me in for a few days; otherwise I'm bound to end up on Aaron and Kendra's doorstep, holding a casserole dish of mashed potatoes and misery.

"If you aren't doing anything, I was thinking about coming down to your place so we could spend the holiday together. I'll make dinner, all the traditional stuff, but you can feel free to point out all the injustices associated with cranberry sauce or whatever. You up for that?"

She doesn't immediately answer and my heart lurches into my throat. *"Give me this,"* I want to say. *"I might be a worthless mess right now, but please, just give me this."*

"Are you sure?" She chooses her next words carefully. "Your family would probably be good for you right now. Wouldn't it be nice to have them around for support? You should be wherever you'll find some peace, with people you can trust. You need that, Cooper."

I wait for her to finish, hoping my voice won't betray me.

"Exactly. Now let's talk pie. Are you a pecan pie or pumpkin pie kind of girl?"

= 17 =

(Whitney)

Some might argue that I should have done more to encourage Cooper to go home for Thanksgiving. They might be right.

Maybe I should have sent him home to his mother, who is probably the kind of woman who bakes the world's best cookies, makes a proper bed with hospital corners, and knows everything about assorted injuries—from cuts and scrapes to broken bones and hearts. All I have to offer is a nearly empty first aid kit in the bathroom, one dust-covered bottle of peroxide, and a variety of essential oils with medicinal properties. That's a complete inventory of my nursemaid tools.

But I'm selfish, it seems. He wanted to be here and I wanted the same. Thanksgiving or not, good idea or not, I didn't care enough about doing the "right" thing to tell him no.

Also, he's bringing pie.

Cooper's truck pulls into the driveway, announced by the rumble of that powerful diesel engine. Despite thinking that a truck doesn't need to be that loud, I have to remind myself not to run out onto the porch, to keep my wits intact, and I issue instructions to my fluttery belly that I'm going to count to ten before I saunter out there to greet him.

Ten seconds feels like an hour. I take a deep breath. At some point, I'm bound to stop feeling this way. I hope so, because this has to be bad for my nervous system, all the heart palpitations and shortness of breath.

When I let the storm door thwack shut behind me, Cooper is still in his truck, glaring at something on the dash display. The engine finally shuts off and the driver door swings open. His left leg comes into view, encased in a complicated Frankenstein-looking knee brace over the black track pants he's wearing. No ACE-brand bandages for pro football players, I guess. I'm pretty sure this isn't a situation where my arnica oil is going to be of any use.

Once he manages to extract the rest of his body from the truck, he looks up and sees me. Relief covers his face—a tired, beaten-down, head-hurting kind of relief. And, if I'm even one tiny part of granting him that, I'm good with it.

Cooper doesn't move, just looks my way, waiting. When I raise one hand and give a small wave, he smiles and more relief spreads across his features.

To hell with it. I waited the ten seconds, didn't run onto the driveway like a loon, or squeal. I've earned the right to hop down off the porch and scamper my way over there. He's dressed for the cold snap that hit the state last night, clad in a heavy coat layered over a hooded sweatshirt, the hood up and a beanie underneath that. I lurch to a stop in front of him and falter.

Last night, I crawled under my cold bedsheets and counted the number of hours until he would be here. Now that he is, I can't figure out what to do first.

Cooper decides for me. His warm hands press to my face, cupping my cold cheeks.

"Jesus, Whit. I had no idea I was capable of missing someone like this. Come here."

His mouth hovers above mine and I have to lean up to get what I want. One faltering kiss follows. We pause, trying to determine what just happened, to decide if we've already lost something between us. But when he slants his mouth over mine, giving it another go, doubt disappears and we're back to what we had. His tongue flicking against mine, between playful nips to my lower lip. My hands are everywhere, across his chest, starting to snake up his layers of clothing, until suddenly I'm off balance, swaying in place.

Cooper pulls back and rights my body when he sees the way I'm wobbling. The universe is clearly imbalanced in his favor, because that is the only explanation for why a guy with a knee injury can stay upright, while his touch tests the bounds of my equilibrium.

His eyes light with wry amusement and he cocks one eyebrow. "Don't fall down. One of us being busted up is enough."

Inside, he helps put away the groceries he brought along and inspects the turkey I traded a box of apple butter for, from a heritage breed farmer down the road. I'm determined that if we're going to play to Thanksgiving tradition, I'm still not going to Butterball my way through it. Cooper might inspire me to do a lot of things, but sitting down to a meal of tasteless, hormone-fed, saline solution–plumped meat isn't one of them.

He leans heavily on the refrigerator door before letting it close softly. Turning away from the countertop where I set the two—*two!*—pies he brought with him, I catch the last moments of his face screwing up in discomfort. I rest against the counter with one hip and prop my hand on the other.

"Short of some miracle act of flexibility, which I know you don't possess, I'm guessing you haven't elevated your knee since you got in the truck. Go sit down and put your leg up. I'll get you some ice."

Cooper shakes his head and scowls at the opposite wall. "I'm fine."

I sigh and try to determine the best approach for this situation. I'm hoping he isn't going to be an enormous lout the entire time he's here. Maybe the team doctors sent some pain medication with him. I'd gladly poke him with a syringe full of good-night juice if he keeps it up.

"Cooper, I'm not trying to baby you. I'm not interested in mothering you. But if you think I'm going to watch you suffer for no good reason, when a damn ice pack might alleviate some discomfort, let me assure you, I won't. So suck it up, go sit down, and elevate your leg."

Grumble, grumble. He goes and sits down. Grumble, grumble some more.

I fill a plastic bag with ice, then whack it with a rolling pin to break down the cubes into smaller pieces, wrapping a clean dish towel around the bag. Cooper has landed on the couch, reclined in a pouty slump, with his bum leg up on the coffee table. He stretches forward to take the bag from me, but I send a glare in his direction until his hands retreat. His leg isn't up high enough, so I prop two pillows under his foot before placing the bag of ice.

Cooper waves his hands toward the mess on my coffee table, where piles of paper litter the top, with my laptop in the center of the disarray and a pocket calculator resting to one side of the keyboard.

"Project?"

Three new letters arrived from the bank's foreclosure attorneys in the last few weeks, all reiterations on a general theme of *no joke, we're coming to take your shit*. As if I were unclear about the lovely state of my affairs. The letters are scattered on the keyboard, and I don't much care for Cooper to see the details of my impending failures, so I slap the laptop shut.

No miracle phone calls from the folks at the Boulder slow money outfit, either, so I've been researching other community lending organizations, emailing a few more loan officers at big banks, and reading up on every last-resort alternative that exists.

"Still trying to get financing. The Boulder thing hasn't panned out, so I'm investigating other options."

I shimmy up next to Cooper, one arm propped on the

back of the couch. He squints a little, purses his lips. *Oh, boy.* He's trying not to say something. Failing to hide his frustration, as usual. I raise my brows.

"You're clearly not investigating all your options."

"Yes, I am. I'm looking into all the non-squicky options available to me."

His head flops back to the couch. "You say I'm stubborn, but you're worse. I mean, who else in your position would just tell me to go to hell, when they—"

I cut him off by raising my palm and closing my eyes. He pauses. I lower my hand and he starts in again. "Just tell me how much you need. It can't be that much. You can't possibly need millions—"

My hand is apparently quite powerful, because just my palm being thrust forward quiets him again. I keep my hand up until I've said what I need to say.

"I'm not sure why you don't want to hear me when I say this. No. Not *maybe*, or *convince me*. No."

"I don't want to hear it because you're being shortsighted. Let's talk about this. I'm here for a few days; we'll talk through what you need and come up with a game plan."

"OK, sounds great. After we talk about my financial failures, do you want to talk about your knee? Or your contract? Because we can. I'm sure you'd love that."

His face darkens. I lock my eyes on his and refuse to waver. *Glare all you want, Lowry.* We continue staring, giving each other hard looks until I find myself focusing too much on his mouth. Then he's leaning toward me, placing a hand at the back of my neck, and groaning into an open-mouthed kiss that effectively ends our scowling duel.

Cooper traces his lips down my jawline, then nuzzles his face deeply into my neck, so much that my hair covers his face. He inhales and then releases it slowly, defeated.

"I don't want to fight about this. I want to help you, Hawaiian Tropic. You said you don't want to baby or mother me. Good. I'm not trying to play Prince Charming to your Cinderella, either. But watching you struggle isn't OK with me. If I told you to suck it up and let me help, would you?"

"Nope. There's a huge difference between getting someone an ice pack and writing a check for a large sum of money. But more important, did you just call me *Hawaiian Tropic*?"

He grins, a sheepish little tilt of his mouth, before setting his gaze to mine.

"You smell coconutty all the time. That first night in the drugstore, I noticed it right away, even though my head hurt like hell. I'm guessing it's some sort of fancy lotion or something, but it makes me think of suntan oil."

I shake my head. "It's not anything fancy. The opposite of fancy, actually. I buy coconut oil by the vat and use it everywhere."

Cooper tips his head to one side and blinks. "Everywhere?"

That—the way Cooper manages to turn a simple word or phrase into the promise of more—will never get old. Two open hands to his chest and I push him back, righting him on the couch until I can carefully straddle him. Once I do, he grabs my hips and gives a push. I lock my quads and glance down at his legs.

"Are you sure? I don't want to hurt you."

Cooper growls and pushes down again, until I settle my weight watchfully. Even so, the ice pack falls off his leg and rattles to the floor. I cast a glance over my shoulder and make to retrieve it. Cooper stops me.

"Leave it." I start to ask him again if he's sure, but he cuts me off. "I'm *fine*. If I'm not fine, I'll tell you, but until then I need you to stop asking."

Without pause, he yanks my shirt up and off. A quick tug on my bra cup until his tongue finds my nipple, which pebbles to a peak almost instantly. His palm cups my flesh and every touch is as good as I remember. I can feel him, already hard under the thin fabric of his pants, and when I start to work my body over that spot, Cooper nudges his hips up to meet my movements.

"Fuck, this is what got me through the last few weeks being away from you. I came so hard every time I thought about you this way, rubbing your pussy against me. My fingers, my face, my cock. Couldn't stop thinking about it."

I grind down harder and Cooper encourages every roll of my hips, using his hands to guide my movements. I draw my core across the length of him, urgent and rough, seeking more pressure. Cooper lets out a sharp grunt and stills beneath me.

"Hold on. One second, I just need to . . ."

I realize he's been holding his breath and that grunt was actually a harsh exhale. He tries to slouch down so my weight is farther from his knee brace. I lift my body and once he's in position, he swats my hip to prompt me. I stay put, rest my hands on his shoulders, and give a resigned sigh.

"This is a bad idea."

Cooper smacks my thigh again. "No, it's not a bad idea. This is a *good* idea."

He tugs on my hips, but because I'm holding his shoulders and engaging every muscle in my body, I don't move. I shake my head, eyes closed.

"Whitney, get down here. I already said, if I can't do something, I'll tell you. You've lost your mind if you think we're going to be able to stay off each other while I'm here, just because of my knee."

When his hands slip around to the front of my leggings, his fingers hooking the fabric at the waist and rolling it down enough to skim the skin just inches from where my body aches, I nearly crumple. The hinges of his knee brace creak quietly when he leans forward to kiss my belly. After that, all I can hear is the squeaky reminder of why I need to take care of him, if he can't be trusted to do it on his own.

I pull his hands away, but his mouth remains pressed to the skin of my belly. His wary eyes flicker upward just as I move backward and slip off him, finding the floor between his legs.

"I have a better idea."

He curses and grumbles under his breath. Looking up, I draw my hands across his thighs.

"Honestly, that isn't the sound I wanted to hear you make when I landed here," I say.

"Yeah, well, this isn't how I wanted you to end up there." His head tips back to face the ceiling.

"Why?"

My hands come to lie across his length, still over the

fabric, but despite that barrier I'd swear he grows harder at the contact. Maybe it's a leap to think that an orgasm can solve anything of significance, but I want to try. Fix his world for as long as it takes to forget the rest.

"The last thing I want is some pity blow job because you think I can't take care of you properly. I can."

I grasp the waist of his pants. He might be objecting with words, but he lifts his hips anyway, pressing up with his arms so I can tug down and set him free. He exhales sharply as I take him in hand and when I take a slow pull from base to tip, he actually shudders. Cooper Lowry— all that mass, all that power—just shuddered under my touch. Nothing could be better.

"There is no such thing as a pity blow job. Doesn't exist. Women might do this for a million reasons, but pity isn't one of them."

Leaning closer, I rub my thumb over the tip. "Maybe while we were apart, I was thinking about how I hadn't had you this way yet. How crazy it would feel to have a guy like you at my mercy."

Cooper's head jerks up off the back of the couch. He captures my face in his hands and stills my movements.

"I've been at your fucking mercy since we met."

His expression is entirely serious. No joking around, no bullshit. I turn my face enough to kiss one of his palms.

"Does that bother you?"

His gaze roams my face, moving one thumb across my mouth, the tip just breaching my lips. I suck gently, giving him a preview of what my mouth can offer once he releases me, letting my tongue slip softly across the end of his thumb. He draws his hands up, threading his fingers through my hair.

"Not nearly as much as I would have thought. I think I like it."

Good answer. I bend down and his hands drop from my hair. He's tired and sad and feeling less than his usual demanding self, so I take him in without toying. All the way on the first stroke, and he groans loudly when my hand comes into play. Just as I find a steady rhythm we both seem to like, he gently pushes on my shoulders to shift his body away. I look up to find his eyes hooded and heavy, hands balled into tight fists set atop his thighs.

"Tell me how far you want this to go. I'm already hanging by a thread here, so you should tell me now if you expect a shoulder tap or something."

I nearly laugh, letting him slip from my mouth while keeping my hand in position and roaming. Up and down, lingering over the head, circling.

"Such a gentleman all of a sudden." Another pass with my hand, but with a firmer grip. His jaw clenches. "No need. You have one responsibility right now, and that's to relax enough to let me do this. That, and maybe grab my hair a little."

Cooper's jaw slackens and his entire body seems to sag in relief.

"Fuck it. Pity me—I don't care. I'll do whatever you want. Relax, tug on your hair, anything. I've been away from you for weeks and nothing I did would take the edge off. Just don't make me wait—I'm fucking dying for this."

My mouth finds him again, no teasing, no delicate

touches to see what he likes, because Cooper prefers his sex on the intense side; I already know that. He goes at it hard enough to rattle pictures off the wall and test the strength of the furniture, so I try to match up my style accordingly. His hips start to jerk, shoving deeper. He tangles his fingers into my hair, and when he latches on he forgets himself entirely, lost to the experience. When I suck harder in response, do what I can to let him know how much I love the feel of him this way, it takes only a few seconds for him to find the edge, coming hard enough to lose his voice for a second.

I give a few featherlight sweeps of my tongue, until he shudders again and shifts his body back, conveying that it's too much now. Still, I just did some of my best work. Because Cooper is quite obviously sated and drained, and licked entirely clean. He swipes a hand over his face and exhales, but he doesn't open his eyes.

"If we do the whole *share what you're grateful for* thing at dinner tomorrow, you should know I'm planning to mention what just happened. I'm going to use the words *blow job* at our Thanksgiving dinner table. Just be prepared."

=18=

(Whitney)

"**W**hit! I need your hands for a second."

I dog-ear the page in my book and toss it on the coffee table with a heavy sigh. I'm happy to give Cooper my hands. Either to strangle him or to deter him away from the kitchen and steer him toward the bedroom.

I had no idea that making Thanksgiving dinner could be such a noisy affair. Especially with just two people present, secluded in a decrepit farmhouse in the middle of nowhere. But since the moment Cooper woke up this morning, it's been nothing but an ongoing racket. Apparently I've lived alone for too long, because we're closing in on four hours of this commotion and I'm nearing the limit on what I had always believed was my limitless patience.

It all started with the horrified groaning noise he made upon remembering that I don't own a television. Thanksgiving is inherently tied to football in his world, so there was no scenario in which he might let me flip on a radio as low background noise and, God forbid, not watch the game.

After he set up his laptop on the kitchen table, he proceeded to stream football coverage at what must be the max volume setting available. Then he commandeered my laptop to access the internet for all the assorted cooking quandaries that have arisen over the last few hours, most of which inspired him to curse or hum or singsong his way through the solution. All of this was after he essentially re-organized my kitchen. He asked permission, but I knew it was mostly for show. If I had said no, he would have done it surreptitiously anyway. One colander, one mixing bowl, one soupspoon at a time.

Not to mention the incessant thwack of him rough-chopping vegetables with the largest knife I own and the way he's incapable of letting a cupboard door or a kitchen drawer thud softly closed. No, he shows that cupboard door who's boss. Every time. Dishware rattles, silverware clangs.

He's cute, but barely cute enough for me to put up with much more of this. I'm comforted only by the fact that the turkey is currently roasting away in the oven alongside his spinach gratin, and the stuffing is nearly ready to go. Mashed potatoes are the last frontier. How loud can he possibly be while peeling and boiling potatoes?

When I stroll into the kitchen, Cooper has both hands deep in a large mixing bowl and is giving its contents a dirty look. I stride closer and peer in.

"Problem?"

Cooper raises his hands from the bowl of stuffing he's

trying to put together, fingers covered in gloppy masses of the bread mixture. His fingers look a bit like corn dogs that have been battered in all the wrong ways. "This doesn't look right."

The streaming football coverage blares behind us and a color commentator starts to shout. Cooper immediately cranes his neck around to see what's happening. One of his corn-dog fingers flops into the bowl.

He's so cute, I chant silently. *I have limitless patience.*

Cooper speaks again but doesn't shift his eyes from the laptop. "Brace yourself. We have to call my mom."

"Why?"

"To see if this stuffing can be saved." Still no eye contact, just a jut of his chin toward the kitchen table. "Grab my phone, will you? Put it on speaker for me."

He rattles off his pass code; I find his mom's number, press send, and hold it up for him. Two rings and—I had no idea this was possible—things get even louder.

"*Pooper!* Merry turkey day!"

Definitely not his mom. One of the brothers, I'd guess, because Cooper tries to look pissed off at what can only be a sibling-coined corruption of his name, but a grin takes over.

"Who the hell is this, Dumb or Dumber? Does Mom know you're touching her phone?"

Must be one of the twins. Cooper's family tree goes like this: Mom is Patty, Dad is Gene, oldest brother is Caleb, followed by the twins, Matthew and Michael. Then Cooper. Or, as any youngest brother with that name should be known, Pooper.

"Mom went to get Dad some more 'Stone's before the depot closed—turkey frying makes him thirsty. But this is the handsome twin. Does that help?"

Cooper tilts his head my way and speaks in my direction.

"I can't tell the difference between them on the phone. They sound exactly the same. It's creepy."

"Who's that? Mom said you were going to Aaron's. You'd better be there or she'll flip her lid. You know how she gets about you. Constantly worrying about her precious little *jujube*."

Cooper's cheeks turn one shade brighter. "Change of plans. I'm at . . ."

He pauses, and the silence on this end means I can hear all the background noise at his family's house and it's nothing but complete chaos. They must have nine televisions on. There may also be a small army of children who've stormed the castle, because it sounds like gleeful mutiny and mayhem are afoot.

Cooper's eyes flicker to mine as he continues to hesitate, his jaw flexing and working over words that don't actually come out. I raise my brows. He clenches his jaw once more.

"I'm at my girlfriend's place."

That explains the fish-hooked jaw action. *Girlfriend*. The big launch of us as a couple just happened and had I known this was coming, I would have put on a dress and done my hair.

The other side of the line stays quiet—well, sort of . . . aside from all of the *not* quietness that's transpiring somewhere in Texas. Cooper shrugs when he notes how my eyes have widened, then continues to look right at me, searching my face for a response, until a flash of unease lights in his expression.

I kiss his cheek, keeping the phone in one hand as I do. Unfortunately, leaning up to kiss him means that the phone is closer to my ear, and when his brother bellows—not an exaggeration—I flinch and immediately pull the phone away.

"*MATTY!*" A pause of three beats, maybe, then, "*CALEB!* WHERE ARE YOU GUYS?"

Cooper glares at the phone face and shouts back. "Christ, Mikey, take it down a notch! You're on speaker and Whitney's ears aren't fucking calibrated for Lowry level yet."

Oh my God. They're all *barbarians.* My head is actually ringing. I close my eyes and pray that might somehow equalize the blow to my hearing.

"Shit, sorry. But you can't just lay that kind of thing out there, that you have a *girlfriend*, and not expect everybody in this house to lose their minds. You're a goddam Sasquatch when it comes to relationships, Cooper. No one believes it's even a possibility. So they need to be made aware, stat. But I think they've taken the lead on manning the turkey fryer."

Mikey takes a deep breath and I start to cringe out of some newfound instinct, preparing for the onslaught of hollering that's bound to follow. Instead, he lets an exhale out, measuredly.

"OK, I'm good. Let me talk to this Whitney person."

I'm up, I guess. I stare at the phone for a moment. "Hi."

"I'd like to start by apologizing to your ears. Please don't leave Pooper because I hollered like that. He'd never forgive me if I ran you off and he's a crybaby when he doesn't get his way. I know, because he sniffled his way through the first ten years of his life. I was there as a witness."

Cooper gives up and goes to wash the stuffing off his hands, barking as he walks away.

"Don't tell her that. I wasn't a crybaby, I had allergies, you asshole. You try living on a cattle ranch with hay fever. I got shots for it and you know it."

"Oh, yes. I forgot. Jujube and his *hay fever*. Anyway, back to Whitney. What's your story, Whit?"

"Well, I, uh . . ."

How in the hell do I describe myself to this guy? *"I like long walks on the beach, grouchy football players, and pie? In my spare time, I try to figure out how to save my only asset from impending foreclosure?"* None of that sounds quite appropriate.

Before I can stumble my own way through an answer, Cooper interjects.

"Oh, hell, that reminds me. Mikey, would you look at Whitney's website? She owns a fruit orchard and her site sucks. Maybe you could work your web designer mojo on it, try to make something decent out of it."

I give Cooper a scowl and pinch his ass. No reaction, because he's rattling off my website address to Mikey. A minute or so passes. Mikey makes a few noises that do not sound appreciative.

"Cooper, promise me something. She's hot, right? Because this website is an atrocity. This girl had better be hot and brilliant and have a heart of gold. If you knowingly entered into a relationship with her after seeing this dreck, and she isn't all of those things, I'll disown you."

"She's all that and more. But, the website . . . seriously shitty, right? Try using it to find your way here. It's practically impossible."

Nope. No more. I elbow Cooper in the gut.

"As a reminder, I'm standing right here. Don't hate on my stuff. I couldn't pay anyone to design it, so I did the best I could. I also can't pay anyone to redesign it."

Mikey chuckles. "Whitney, sweetheart. This is fucking terrible and I can't live another day knowing it's out in the world. I can fix it, easily—with one hand tied behind my back, one of my toddlers hanging off my leg, while giving my wife a back rub and frosting a cake. And you're approved on Lowry credit, so I'll charge Cooper double, and make him pay me in beer and fishing lures. Don't sweat it."

I want to tell him not to bother. Because soon, I could be orchard-less and living somewhere else. Where? No idea. I've tried to avoid picturing what that will look like, where I'll go, or how hard it will be to start over.

Cooper takes the phone from my hand and kisses my forehead. And, now there's Cooper. My *boyfriend*.

Will he take me in? Would I go, even if he did? Because a soft place to land isn't always best for the ambitious, independent parts of your soul. Sometimes you need to fall, land squarely on your ass, and let the impact knock the wind from your lungs. Sometimes that seems like the only way to feel you paid for your failures.

The two brothers exchange a few more details and Mikey promises to turn my website into something less revolting and rudimentary. His words, not mine.

"Hey, hey, Coop. One more thing." Mikey lowers his voice. "Jana's pregnant."

Cooper's mouth drops open a little. "No shit?"

"Yeah. She's almost three months along, but they're keeping it quiet until she's a few more weeks in. Matty told me, but I figure you can keep it on the down low, too."

Cooper trains his focus on the frosted pear trees wintering in rows outside my kitchen window. He takes a labored swallow. "Tell him to keep her safe, OK?"

Mikey snorts. "Hell, he'd cover her in bubble wrap if he could. She wouldn't let him, but you know he'd do anything for her."

Cooper nods, still staring out the window. One of his arms stretches out and I find myself tugged closer, until my body presses to his side. "Be sure to hug all those little terrors for me."

Mikey promises to do exactly that, followed by the exchange of manly, and lovingly offensive, affection. After he sets his phone on the counter, Cooper moves me to stand in front of him, draping his arms over my shoulders and propping his chin on the top of my head.

"Jana is Matty's wife. They've been trying for a few years to have a kid but she's miscarried twice. Caleb and Mikey barely have to look at their wives and they're knocked up again, so being surrounded by all their healthy, happy kids has been hard on her. Matty, too."

My heart starts to knock about in my chest, a guilty

pulse that won't slow. Turns out the reason I should have sent him home for Thanksgiving had nothing to do with whether his mom could play proper nursemaid. It's because this wasn't his home. Girlfriend or not, home for Cooper was too many states away.

"Aw, shit." Cooper reaches behind me and grabs his phone off the counter. "All that, and I still didn't get to ask about saving the stuffing. Think you can handle another round?"

= **19** =

(*Whitney*)

"**C**ome on. Stop dawdling." I toss my head back and close my eyes, hoping that will prompt Cooper to get a move-on. "In. Now."

"I won't fit. You're always moaning on and talking about how big I am. Usually you're pretty enthusiastic about it, too. But this will be one of the times when my size is going to be a problem."

"The only size issue at hand is the enormity of your Texas ego. Get in the truck, Cooper, or I'm leaving without you."

Just as I don't appreciate the over-the-top bellowing persona of Cooper's truck, he apparently doesn't appreciate the subtle workhorse quality of mine. I'd consider continuing this discussion inside—where there being *so much* of him is something I never complain about; he's right about that—but the last fall farmers' market starts in two hours and we don't have time for this (or that) right now.

Cooper asked to come along, claiming he wanted to

help in whatever way he could. This, after he already spent yesterday working with me among the tree rows as we cleaned up downed limbs, leaves, and dropped fruit.

After that, I trained him on the basics of pruning. Cooper took to the task easily and even with frequent breaks to rest his knee, he still cleared more rows than I did, leaving each tree thoughtfully and symmetrically pruned. And he did it all with nothing but the sexiest sort of relaxed concentration spread across his features. The little furrows that crisscrossed his forehead as he snipped each limb and then determined his next cut ranked right up there with one of his full-on smiles.

Today, those same furrows are related to his scowl. Cooper is standing in the driveway, glaring at my truck. He draws a hand over his mouth and sighs.

"At least let me drive. Where I'm from, men don't ride shotgun. We drive."

I shoot him a withering glare. He shrugs. As much as this is an argument I *want* to have, my truck is already loaded with booth supplies and crates of apple butter . . . All we need to do is start driving.

Cooper makes his way to the driver side and opens the door for me. I give the door a tug and shut it again. He tips his head skyward, likely asking some higher power for a better solution or, if he knows what's good for him, the restraint to keep from provoking his girlfriend any further.

I count to ten, then open the truck door myself and step out, outstretching one arm to hand him the keys. He reaches for them. I yank them back.

"I'm driving us home."

"OK," he says.

The word is right, but the tone is all wrong. Mischief with a touch of sarcasm. Not nearly enough hangdog humility for my taste.

But Grand Junction is over an hour away, which leaves enough time for me to sharpen my tongue like Dorothy Parker and lecture him on suffragettes. Perhaps remind him that my father is dead, so a dowry is out of the question. And I'll spend whatever time is left over declaring exactly how much I like having the right to vote and being able to wear these here *trousers*.

———

Cooper has officially redeemed himself.

The man is a superstar. An apple butter–hawking, superstar sales machine. A *machine*, I tell you.

It's possible that his being Cooper Lowry might have something to do with all the dudes that have wandered by once, twice, even three times before finally approaching cautiously with quizzical looks on their faces. Fortunately, even when Cooper confirmed his identity, none of them asked for an autograph or insisted he pose for an awkward bro photo.

Likely because Cooper was quick to redirect the conversation to our wares. *"You like apple butter? Here, try this sample."* Then he'd nod his head, raise his brows, and grin. The guy would mirror the act, move for move, like an eight-year-old boy who just stumbled upon Santa Claus on Christmas Eve. *"We've got pints and half-pints, but we're running low. How many do you want?"*

Sales 101. Time-tested techniques currently being exploited by a man who has a real-life job that so many other guys have spent decades only dreaming about. I couldn't compete with that even if I were half-dressed and somehow incorporating body shots into my booth display.

But the women? I'm worried some of them are dangerously close to experiencing vertigo-like symptoms from circling about us. Of course, setting up next to Justin's booth did not help matters. The two of them, side by side, is too much for any mere mortal hetero woman to handle. While I can't blame the gals for wanting more than one glimpse, I'm just praying there aren't any eventual fainting spells.

"So your orchard is organic?"

The latest of the fresh-faced gawkers pulls her long fishtail braid of dark blonde hair over one shoulder and adjusts her Patagonia knit stocking hat. The three pints of apple butter she just purchased are clasped to her chest, in the crook of one arm.

"Not certified. We're working on that. But we're keeping things organic and biodynamic. Even the little stuff, like using yarrow as a cover crop to attract the good bugs and keep the bad bugs in check."

The words ring familiar in my head, as I note how effortlessly Cooper has slipped into this role. He hands her one of my brochures. She pretends to study a few lines, but her eyes return to his before it would have been possible to read a single word.

"That's *so* important. I love the premise of biodynamics. The interconnected wholeness of it all, respecting the wisdom of every living organism."

Cooper nods solemnly. She flips over the brochure to glance at the back.

"I know you said you're out of fresh apples for the year, but do you grow the SweeTango variety? My twin boys love them."

"Twins, huh? Bet that keeps you busy. Let me just confirm on that variety." He turns my way. "Hey, babe?"

I had stopped my own personal ogling of Cooper to sort all the singles and five-dollar bills he's snake-charmed out of people over the last four hours. I was now ogling all the cash in the bursting bank bag, just as affectionately.

"Babe?"

I slant my eyes in his direction. He can't be talking to me. First, there was the verbal caveman jostling of me out of the driver's seat. And now this.

Calmly, I turn his way. When my eyes meet his, I'm not sure what to think because he looks too handsome, too softhearted, and entirely at ease in my world. My little heart likes it all so much that suddenly the cutesy-pet-name thing doesn't seem quite as problematic.

"SweeTangos? Will we have those next year?"

My belly tumbles and plummets in the span of seconds. The tumble inspired by how he's phrased the question, the plummet at the prospect of there being no next year. I sweep my gaze over to the woman, if only to avoid Cooper's.

"SweeTangos are a club apple. I'm not one of their growers. Wish I were—they're great little flavor bombs."

Her face falls a little and Cooper apologizes, then sends her on her way with a thank-you that is also a subtle, but still charming, brush-off. I zip up the bank bag and toss it into the cardboard box under the table.

Cooper comes up and wraps his body around mine, his chest pressed to my back and both arms draped about my waist.

"What's a club apple?" He drops a kiss to my neck.

"They're patented and trademarked varieties with a limited numbers of growers who are licensed to grow them. You can't just go buy a SweeTango tree. You have to be selected to be in the 'club.'"

"Huh." Another kiss, this time to my temple. "I'm going to go buy another bottled water and see if that food truck is still outside. But I want to hear more about this club apple thing on the way home." He steps back. "You need anything?"

I look over one shoulder and shake my head, then off he goes. He's only steps away when Justin lopes in at his side. Turns out Justin likes football. *Justin.* The guy with the hemp necklace and the organic farm and his growlers of craft beer. *He* likes football. As they walk away, I catch the beginnings of a conversation that will either lead to the clinking of beers or a shoving match.

"'71 Cowboys up against the '85 Bears. Who wins?"

Cooper tips his head back and chuckles. "Too easy. '71 Cowboys."

Justin lets out a loud groan. "You're biased. They were mostly offense. But the '85 Bears? They had everything."

Cooper starts in on a litany of stats. Rushing yards and passing yards, total points for the year and first-down gains. Once when they're out of earshot, my heart starts to wiggle until I'm nearly convinced that one of those fainting spells I was worried about is going to land *me* on the floor.

Because how good would this feel if it were real? If the *we* part of Cooper's sales talk was more than just marketing? If we were here together—truly together?

I've always done this on my own. A sole proprietor by the very definition. So I'd long given up on the fantasy of a partner in crime, a backstop for my heart, or someone to take the lead when I'm exhausted. Then Cooper stoked that neglected ember by way of one word.

We.

=20=

(Cooper)

This morning I discovered how to tame an organic farmer's diesel truck–hating heart. Far easier than I would have thought, too. It wasn't by way of kale or tatsoi, and there wasn't any coconut oil involved. Even spending half an hour with my face between her legs hasn't elicited quite the same reaction as this newly discovered kryptonite.

All I had to do was get her in my truck and press one button.

Heated seats.

Whitney and I had another spirited debate as to what mode of transportation to use when she announced that she needed to run into town and pick up a few things at the co-op. I won in the end and now Whitney is reclined in the passenger seat, making sounds that can only be described as obscene. I'm familiar with how she sounds when I'm doing obscene things *to* her, so I know these noises pretty well. Her face is entirely relaxed but the way she's languidly squirming around on the seat, you'd think my hands were somewhere other than the steering wheel.

"God. I take back everything I've ever said about this beast. This is the best feeling. I've never felt this good. Ever."

I turn in her direction and raise my brows. She gives a coy smirk and averts her eyes.

"I can't believe you've never been in a vehicle with heated seats before. This isn't exactly new technology."

"I don't spend a lot of time with people who drive anything other than thirty-year-old pickups. But I should definitely meet new people. Based entirely on whether their vehicle has heated seats or not." She shimmies down a bit. "Can we turn it up? Does it go any higher?"

I reach over to give the dial another turn. "That's the max. Don't melt into a puddle or anything."

Whitney grabs my hand, placing it on her thigh. "Yes. It's getting even better now. Can we sleep in this thing?"

She slouches lower in the seat and the adjustment draws my hand higher on her leg. I grip the soft flesh and let my fingers trace tiny circles on the inside of her thigh. Between the feel of my pinkie finger skimming her core and the warmth radiating from that spot, I'm about one more moan of hers away from turning the truck around and going back home. The fucking co-op has to be open all day. Plenty of time to prove all the ways that what I have to offer beats the hell out of any heated seat. But when she starts to quietly give up another giggle-moan, I decide not to make this something else because she's blissed out and happy, which is good enough for me.

Just as we pull into the co-op parking lot, my phone rings with a call from Austin. I debate letting it ring over to voicemail but Whitney tells me to take it, then unbuckles her seat belt to scamper into the store. The sight of her—all of her—headed the wrong direction from my hands is motivation enough to keep the call short.

Austin's update isn't particularly surprising. My knee injury means the split clause isn't going anywhere, and Austin admits that I'm probably going to have to get used to this new reality, the one where I'm no longer a young gun or a sure thing. Instead, I'm the *veteran* player. The guy who is supposed to be a fountain of wise advice in the locker room and a steady rock of hardscrabble experience on the field.

Unfortunately, anyone who has met me would know I'm not a fountain of anything. As for hardscrabble and steady? Maybe. I'd just have preferred to wait a few more years before taking on this new role.

I shut the truck door harder than necessary and head into the store. The co-op is dusty but organized, with fluorescent lights that cast a yellow glare on the worn linoleum floor, and the entire place is practically a carbon copy of the seed store in my hometown.

With one exception.

Behind the front counter, talking a little too animatedly with my girlfriend, is a dude who doesn't look anything like the paunchy, burly old-timers who work back home. Instead, it looks a little like country music star Chase Rice stumbled into the co-op and decided to stick around. And I've met the real Chase Rice a few times, back when I played against him in college. He was a solid linebacker who probably should have ended up on somebody's pro roster, but Christ, the fucking guy *smiles* too much.

The Hotchkiss version is just as bad. A big grin and puppy-dog eyes, sporting a camo ball cap on backward, with a few hunks of light brown hair sticking out from around his ears. When he leans forward to chuckle at something Whitney says, I have to consciously breathe deeply and steadily. All to avoid going over there and doing something stupid, like pissing on Whitney's leg or knocking the big grin right off Chase's face.

"—Braden and I duck hunted in the morning, then I went to my mom's for dinner. She's over in Grand Junction, so the drive sucked, but the pie was worth it. How about you, Johnny Appleseed? Big turkey day for you?"

Whitney shimmies a little in place, claps her hands together. My eyes instinctively drop to her ass and Chase's seem to land on her tits. My hands curl into loose fists. *Deep fucking breaths. Don't be an asshole.*

"It was practically a Hallmark special. We watched football all day and ate all the traditional stuff. Except stuffing. The stuffing was problematic."

"*You* watched football? And ate a traditional dinner? High-five, sweetheart."

He raises his hand and Whitney slaps palms with him. Five seconds and I'm going over there, close enough to let my pheromones do the talking.

"I figured you were going to say you spent the day in silent protest and meditation to all that is Thanksgiving. If

I'd known you were going to act regular, I'd have invited you along to hunt ducks on the slough. Who's *we*? You invite over some Pilgrims?"

There's my opening. It takes less than five seconds and I'm behind Whitney, pressing my fly to the roundest part of her ass and slipping one arm around her waist.

Chase immediately looks confused. He darts a glance between us, then takes a better look at me, and recognition dawns as he puts the pieces together. His mouth drops open a little.

"Oh! Garrett, this is Cooper Lowry. He's the *we* part of my Thanksgiving," Whitney explains.

Garrett nods slowly, then one of those grins—and, they're nice, I'll admit that—takes over.

"Thought I was seeing things there for a second. Explains the football watching." He extends a hand my way and I latch on, finding his grip is as strong as mine. "Nice to meet you, Cooper."

Up close, I can see that he's younger than I first thought, so I'm able to dial down my initial insanity to claim Whitney with a fireman's carry out of here, while grunting the word *mine* over my shoulder. Still, he's got a good handshake, a killer grin, and puppy-dog eyes. Now I'm worried about a daughter I don't even have yet. Because this guy would be the main reason I'd keep her in the house as much as possible.

"You probably still won't get her into a duck blind. It was a ninety-minute conversation just to get her into my Dodge this morning, so there's still work to do."

Garrett laughs as Whitney takes worthless swipes at

both of us, one hand shooting out toward his bicep and the other floating back to swat ineffectively at my side. Garrett ducks her jab and shakes his head.

"Come on, you're still my favorite tree hugger. But I'm guessing if anyone can bring you over from the hippie side"—Garrett holds up his index finger and thumb, keeping them close together—"*just a little*, it's this guy."

A quick shift of his eyes to mine, and there's no ego or subtext in what he just said. I grew up with lots of guys like Garrett: honest, humble, and uncomplicated. Raised to do the right thing, always. Which means they bide their time and wait their turn—in everything. Even if it means that life sometimes leaves them behind.

He saunters into the back to grab the two jugs of dormant oil that Whitney needs to treat her trees, and when he comes back, he hefts them onto the counter and gives the tops a tap.

"Want me to carry these out for you?"

My alpha ego roars to life again, unbidden and unruly. *I* carry her stuff. *I* drive her wherever she wants to go. *I* give her orgasms. I do all of it.

Jesus Christ. Who *am* I? No other woman has ever inspired this obnoxious, over-the-top instinct to ensure that I'm the one who takes first position in everything she needs. Not that I ever considered otherwise, but polygamists are crazy, because I can't imagine loving more than one woman this way. It's fucking exhausting.

My hands thrust out and I tug the bottles forward. "No need. I'm here now."

Whitney's hands freeze as she digs deep into her wallet

for a fifty-dollar bill, turning all her suddenly peeved attention my way. Garrett smirks a little and lifts his hands away emphatically.

"Got it." A few clicks on his cash register. "You two coming to the booster party tonight?"

Whitney looks up and relaxes her posture. "Is that tonight? I totally forgot."

"Yup. Starts at six. You guys should definitely come." He thumbs in my direction. "People will swallow their tongues when they see this guy. Bonfire, deep-fried foods, all the usual stu—"

Whitney thrusts her hands up and smacks them over Garrett's mouth. "Gah! Stop. Don't say anything else!"

Garrett's brows shoot up and he immediately looks my way, his expression making it clear he wants me to see that this turn of events is not his fault. She pats his mouth with her fingers and pulls away. Garrett visibly releases an exhale through his nose while still keeping his mouth tightly shut.

Whitney shifts from foot to foot, in a playful tap-dance shuffle of sorts. "Not another word. I want it to be a surprise. Yes, yes, yes. We'll be there."

═══

Despite her excitement over the booster event, as we walk out to the truck I'm on edge, waiting for the inevitable browbeating I'm sure she'll eventually remember to give me. Whitney does not disappoint.

"Just out of curiosity, was that necessary?"

"What?"

I drop the tailgate on my truck. I know exactly what she's talking about, but this feels like the kind of moment when you play dumb for as long as you can.

She won't understand. She can't possibly understand what it feels like to be a guy, fall for a woman harder than a box of rocks off a skyscraper, and hate having any other man within a three-state radius of her. It isn't about trust or lack thereof, it isn't about thinking she isn't capable of handling herself—she can, because she's amazing. And, all her amazingness is part of the problem. Amazing women are amazing. Men like amazing.

She sighs. "The whole *I'm here now* bullshit. Garrett's a good kid. I emphasize the word *kid*. There wasn't any need to stick a flag in the ground next to my feet and proclaim my body to be a sovereign state recently claimed by you and your man-parts."

I set the dormant oil in the bed and close the gate, then gesture for her to move around the side of the truck.

"I'm sure he *is* a good kid. But he's also thought about bending you over the front counter in there and giving you his own personalized seed report, babe."

As I open the passenger-side door for her, she freezes and screws her face up. "There are so many things wrong with that statement. 'Seed report'? Gross. He hasn't ever thought about that."

"He's a guy. You're a beautiful, interesting woman who, I guarantee, is totally different from what he's used to. Different and unique fascinates us—and intrigues our dicks. So he's absolutely thought about it."

I sweep my hand toward her seat to urge her to get in

the truck. She narrows her eyes and pins her gaze on me. I sigh. "What?"

"You've been such a Neanderthal over the last few days. First, the no-riding-shotgun thing, and now this. That's also the third time you've called me *babe*. And I can't quite figure out how I feel about that." She takes a step forward, putting one foot on the running board, but doesn't climb in. "I think I should hate it, but I'm not sure. Say it again."

I lean forward. "Get your cute ass in the truck, *babe*. I'll turn your seat on."

"Shit." She climbs in and shakes her head. "I think I kind of like it. Look at me. Sitting in this ridiculous truck, just thrilled at the prospect of you turning on my heated seat, and my belly all topsy-turvy because you called me *babe*. Get me home. I feel a sudden need to burn some incense and renew my Sierra Club membership."

= 21 =

(Cooper)

Despite being in a small town in southern Colorado, the Hotchkiss booster party could have easily been held in my hometown. The night air would likely be a bit warmer there, but nearly everything else feels interchangeable. As in so many other small towns, high school football is more than just recreation here. Instead, Friday night games are a gathering place, a touchstone, and the only entertainment around.

Whitney's small hand is clasped in mine as we crest the short walkway from the parking lot, and between holding hands with my girlfriend and the nostalgia of the scene, I'm waiting for a soundtrack of radio hits from my senior year to start blaring over the PA system. When we near the field, we see Garrett and he gives us a wave. Carrying a large box in his arms, he awkwardly tries to adjust his grip on it before heading our way.

Whitney peeks in the box, then flops her hands over the top, obscuring the contents. "I'm so excited about this, Garrett. I can't even tell you."

He chuckles and nods in my direction. "I just hope you haven't set this up as some sort of a big deal to Cooper. We're just a bunch of rednecks out here, so his expectations should be in line with that."

"I've set up nothing. He's in the dark, completely."

Whitney takes a glance my way and the look on her face is nearly as giddy as when I turn on her heated seat. Behind Garrett, another guy saunters up, carrying a similar-looking box in his hands. He's wearing a State Parks and Wildlife jacket over a khaki uniform shirt, with army-green cargo pants, a wool skullcap tugged on over his dark brown hair. Broad shouldered and big, he could easily be mistaken for one of my teammates, maybe a tight end, because he's clearly stout enough to take a real hit but probably still has the agility to get the ball down the field. His scruffy beard does nothing to obscure the tight set of his jaw. He clips Garrett's shoulder with his own to get his attention.

"We've got a ton of shit left to do, Strickland. You need a hot cocoa, cupcake? If not, let's get over there."

He narrows his eyes to take me in but doesn't show any particular reaction. If he knows who I am, he doesn't care, not even a little bit. Whitney gets a quick nod in acknowledgment, but nothing else. I like this guy already.

"Relax, dude. Your face is going to freeze like that. And I already had a hot cocoa, thank you very much. I've been properly fueled by Swiss Miss." Garrett gives us a broad grin.

"Braden does not like waiting. Or people. Or fun, really. That's why he's so good at his job. He'd issue citations for too much fun if he could. But game wardens aren't exactly known for being a barrelful of giggles."

Braden mutters a few curse words and walks off. No parting words, not even a cursory chin jut in our direction. I officially decide that he's my new best friend in Hotchkiss.

Garrett heads in the same direction, walking backward. "You hunt, Cooper?" I nod. "You should jump in the blind with us some morning. You and Braden can brood silently while I try to make one of you laugh. It's probably a near impossible endeavor, but so is duck hunting sometimes."

Watching Garrett walk away, the idea of making a life here suddenly seems like a picture I could draw in my mind, without having to erase certain parts or play with the shadows.

So many years in Denver, separated from the honest life I grew up in, made my world smaller somehow. My career only did the same. Because once you drop the people you can't trust, avoid the women who only want you for your contract, and close ranks to stay focused on training, there aren't many folks left.

Whitney must have noted the change in my body language, because she gives my hand a squeeze to get my attention. When I look her way, the expression on her face is curious, and I nearly end up grasping her cheeks in my hands and telling her everything I'm thinking. Every scary, wild, crazy, confusing thought that's rattling around in my brain about my future and the two of us.

Enter Tanner Euland.

I could thank him or curse him for his timing, but when he strolls over with a gaggle of teammates in tow, he's prouder than a rooster when I greet him by name. We talk about their season a bit and before I know it, a few of the guys have whipped out their phones to show me clips of the last game, asking what I think they should work on. Because to these kids, I'm Yoda. They may also think I have the Holy Grail stuffed in my back pocket and a fucking unicorn in the truck. In reality, I'm just a guy with a bum knee who can't guide them any better than their coach already does.

One of the guys replays a clip, pushing the phone closer. I lean in to get a better look.

"You guys are spending too much time clustered up at the line after the snap. You need to work on firing out more. All that time wasted leaves the QB exposed and receivers losing potential yards."

They all nod. A few grumble in agreement, as if they knew that was the problem and I've just proven them right. Tanner starts in with another clip, but a shorter, older version of him appears at his side before he can press play.

"Tanner, go help your mom. She kicked me out for being heavy-handed with the mini marshmallows."

Whitney, the only woman in a cluster of testosterone for too long, spies an opportunity.

"And you think sending a teenage boy to assist your wife is a good solution, Kenny?"

Tanner's dad grumbles, then shoves his hands in his pockets with a huff.

"At this point, all I know is that she's in the weeds. By

way of hot cocoa and apple cider. And a booster mom losing control of the concession stand isn't a pretty sight."

Whitney tugs until I reluctantly release her hand. "Let me help. I'm sure I can handle the proper application of mini marshmallows."

She gives a little wave as she heads off toward the concession stand and my insides start to hammer and thump, watching her walk away.

OK, I need to go find Garrett and Braden so we can talk about duck hunting or debate shotgun loads. Anything that might restore my testosterone to proper levels and offset the insane urge to follow Whitney to the mini marshmallows.

On second thought, that bonfire looks a little weak. Maybe I can chop down a tree or some shit, then toss on enough fire starter to send the flames ten feet into the air. If I can just source an ax, I'm all over that.

Twenty minutes later, Kenny Euland has introduced me to the head coach of the football team, the mayor, and the Exalted Ruler of the local Elks lodge. I even meet the commander of the volunteer fire department, who happened by on his way to wrangling Garrett and Braden, two of its members. I've probably shaken more hands than I did on draft day. I'm also up to date on all the current political dramas that inevitably plague a small town.

Just as the mayor begins breaking down the details of this year's municipal budget, the PA system crackles to life with a loud pop.

"OK, folks, the concession stand closes in ten minutes—last call on apple cider from Burkeville Orchards. Our fireworks show, so kindly put on by our local volunteer firefighters and sponsored by Grand Valley Ford, starts in fifteen minutes, so find your seats and settle in."

Fireworks.

I slowly swing my gaze toward the concession stand. Whitney is standing there, looking my way and grinning with two thumbs up, her eyes wide with excitement.

She's wearing a black V-neck sweater that shows off her perfect rack and a slim little scarf around her kissable neck, she's rosy cheeked from the cold, and if I could, I'd snapshot this moment in time, just to know I'll always remember exactly what this feels like.

Because falling in love is a big fucking deal.

Right here, right now, a wonderful woman is standing there, looking at me—stubborn, stupid, demanding *me*—as if she's been charting my happiness with a deft hand and single-minded focus. Like there will never be a moment when I'll have to worry she'll do anything but take me as I am. With Whitney, it won't matter if my knee never rehabs to one hundred percent, because she wouldn't give a single fuck whether I'm playing or not. She's like a stroke-before-midnight pardon from all the pressure I've put on myself to be a pro athlete, and nothing but.

With my body not healing the way I wish it would, my being able to imagine that there's more for me beyond the game is a gift she could never understand. A few months ago, losing my career felt like the end of everything. I thought the best I could hope for was an incomplete life, one that was comfortable, but unfocused.

Now, I can actually imagine another outcome. The framework for a new life. One worth building my future on.

═══════

We make our way back to the parking lot where my truck is, and all of the crap Whitney insisted we bring along makes sense now.

Two wool blankets, a couple of pillows, and an old futon mattress she dragged out from underneath her bed. We set everything up in the truck bed, with the mattress as a base and the pillows piled up for us to lean on. I crawl in first, resting back against the pillows and keeping my knees bent while making a space for her to sit between my legs. Whitney scoots toward me, then settles in with her back against my chest.

The truck bed is facing the field, exactly where she told me to park, which at the time I thought was a little weird. But she was insistent, so I did what she said. Now I'm glad I didn't fight her on any of it, because if I had, I'd want to slap myself when I realized how much thought she put into this.

I drape the two blankets over us and wrap my arms around her shoulders.

"You're a sneaky one, aren't you? Had all of this planned out, even the blankets and pillows."

She grins. "I was totally freaking out all day; I couldn't wait to see your face. I mean, *fireworks*. The one thing that always makes Cooper Lowry happy."

I kiss her cheek, tug her body a little closer, and shift my arms so they're around her waist, leaving my mouth pressed to the side of her face. "I've got a few other things that make me happy."

"Football? Is that what you mean? I told you that doesn't count—it's too easy."

"Nope."

"Apple butter?"

I make a vaguely agreeable sound; the apple butter is damn good, but it wasn't what I had in mind. She purses her lips, feigning complete concentration.

"I know. It's rooibos tea. You love it."

Forcing a low choking sound, I shove my cold hands under her sweater, hoping to make a point that the tea is gross. She yelps at the contact of my frigid hands to her warm, soft skin.

"Hey!"

"My hands are cold."

"Clearly. You ever hear of gloves?"

Her skin pebbles up until I start to caress it, warming her with each stroke. "I like this way better. But just to clarify, you make me happy now. And touching you makes my hands happy."

My hands *are* happy now. They're up under Whitney's clothes and, aside from grasping a football, that's their happy place. I snake one hand up, closer to her breast, enough to let my thumb graze the underside. Whitney arches her back, subtly pushing the soft swell toward my touch.

"Thank you, by the way. I love that you remembered

this. The whole night makes me feel like I'm home again."

"Warm fuzzies? About your glory days?"

"Kind of." I sweep my thumb higher, taking a slow trip across her nipple. "What about *your* glory days? I'm curious what you were like in high school."

Whitney snorts. "Like I am now, but worse. I was a radical idealist. But, you know, absent of all the pesky levelheadedness that comes with adulthood. Also, I had dreads." She cranes her head to see me. "Were you a jock? Every cheerleader's dreamy fantasy?"

I give her earlobe a little nip. "Football was everything, so I didn't have time to be anybody's fantasy. If I wasn't practicing or playing, I was working on the ranch or studying."

Looking out at the football field in the distance and knowing that Whitney's never seen me play means there's something incomplete between us. Even if she isn't into the game, even if I'm on my way out, I want to know she saw me at my best, just once. Taking a deep breath, I press my lips to the crown of her head.

"Hunt thinks I might make the field in a few weeks if my knee cooperates. If I asked you to come to one of my games, would you?"

She cranes her head back to see me and her forehead tightens up. "Of course I would. Did you think I wouldn't?"

I shrug. "Just don't want you to feel like you have to."

"I wouldn't feel like that." A starter firework goes off, small and unspectacular. She nudges her shoulder back into my chest and I meet her eyes, earnest and intent on mine. "I wouldn't."

I kiss her temple and work to shake off the tightness in my chest, brought on by knowing Whitney would show up for me just because I asked. To thank her—and keep my unsteady heart in its proper place—I put my hands to work again, teasing across the silk of her bra and changing the subject along the way.

"I'm guessing the teenage Whitney only hung out with those granola crunching–type dudes, right? With a pony-tail, wearing Teva sandals. Driving around in some piece-of-shit Subaru."

She shrugs her shoulders, admitting to exactly that. I lower my voice but keep my mouth close to her ear.

"Did you let those guys touch you? Like this?"

I reach up and draw one of her tits into my hand, grip-ping hard enough to remind her I'm not like those guys she ran around with in the past. She mutters something that's probably supposed to sound like a protest, but when her head falls back to meet my chest, the look on her face says the opposite.

Her knees are slightly bent but tipped together, and when I let my other hand skim across the lowest part of her belly, just above the waist of her jeans, her legs fall open a bit.

"What about here?" My palm moves to cup her com-pletely over the denim, and she groans, reaching for my hand.

"Cooper," she whispers, a weak reprimand, countered by the desire that's impossible to ignore.

The fireworks show is in full swing, lighting up the night sky. One nip to her ear and I kiss my way down from there, across her neck and over her collarbone. She gives my hand a little swat. "Seriously, Cooper. We cannot have sex here."

I chuckle. "I know that. Don't worry, I'm planning to wait until we get home to bend you—and this dick-tease sweater of yours—over something sturdy."

Taking a quick scan of the parking lot, I decide that despite the location, the sides of the truck bed obscure enough to keep going a little. I slip my fingers to the button on her jeans and toy a bit. Her body goes taut, anxious, so I slow my movements, hoping I can convince her with my hands and an attempt at sound reasoning.

"The nearest car to ours is five spaces away and we're hunkered down in the truck bed. No one will know I'm getting you off under these blankets."

I hold my breath, waiting it out a few beats, just to see if she'll latch on to my wrist to stop me. When she doesn't, I kiss the side of her neck just as my hands make quick work of the button and zipper on her jeans. One of my hands sneaks inside her panties, middle finger moving to part her, and fuck, I can feel how much she already wants this. A strangled moan leaves my throat at the discovery, and she echoes the sound, but softer and needier.

She sucks in a breath. "You're supposed to be watching the fireworks."

I use my other hand to tug down one of her bra cups, letting her nipple graze the softness of her sweater as the weight of her breast fills my hand.

"If I do this right, I get two shows in one. Do you really want me to stop? Just say the word."

"Jesus," she mutters. "Why do you have to be so good with your damn hands?"

A huge firework goes off just as I ask if she wants to keep going. The sound drowns out her voice but she nods, and that's enough for me.

I yank on her other bra cup, then work the neck of her sweater down so that her breasts are nearly spilling out. I follow with a few slow strokes between her legs, making sure I've slicked her arousal properly across the entire span of her pussy. My dick definitely wants in, but I refuse to do so much as roll my hips to ease the ache. She gave me so much tonight—from the fireworks to the realization that I might be more than a guy on the wrong side of his career—so the least I can do is give her a fucking orgasm, just for her, without trying to steal some of the action for myself.

We've been together enough that I know exactly what she likes, the way she doesn't need too much pressure, just consistency, a steady circle of my fingers and the occasional flick of my thumb and middle finger to roll her clit.

I lean in enough to trace my lips to the shell of her ear. "Did those other guys get you wet? Or am I the only one who knows how to make you this slick?"

She doesn't respond, just bites down on her lip. I've never craved validation like this from a woman before. But looking down into Whitney's face, the need to know I'm giving her everything swells up before I can stop it.

"Whitney, I want to hear you say it. Tell me who gets you off."

She licks her lips. "You do."

"Every time?"

She smiles a little and nods. "Every time."

My entire body absorbs her answer. Contrary to what some believe, real men love giving women orgasms—we don't feel put out or obligated, we fucking live for making it happen. It plays to every boastful *hey, look what I just did* instinct we possess. Because when a woman comes apart under our stellar handiwork, we feel like a king, stronger than an ox, and a thousand feet tall.

Tonight, when it happens, she has to work hard to stifle the sound, and the only thing I regret is not getting to watch her ride it out the way she normally does. But the grand finale is in the sky, Whitney is loose and spent in my arms, and I feel a *million* feet tall.

=22=

(Whitney)

I went into the grocery store for three things. Lip balm, herbal tea, and a greeting card. The lip balm and herbal tea were for me; the greeting card was for Cooper. It has a picture of a pouty hedgehog on the front, with a silly sentiment inside about keeping your chin up, appropriately themed for a guy whose team has lost their last five games.

My plan for the drive to Denver was to craft a heart-felt, encouraging sort of note to add and make sure it ended up in his bag before the game. I would have hours to debate my closing. *XOXO, Whitney*? All *x*'s? *Love, Whitney*? Just my name? Perhaps a jaunty scrawl of my initials?

Had I stuck to the plan, exited the A&P with those three items and not been swayed by the enormous foam finger on display in the window of our local dollar store across the way, I'm positive I would be on the road by now. The foam finger is to blame. But when I spied it, I thought it would be cute, picturing Cooper's face, how he would think it was wacky and charming.

We haven't seen each other in three weeks. Three *long* weeks. Even our usual phone calls have been cut short, with Cooper either exhausted or testy from enduring day after day of rehab on his knee. But the docs finally cleared him this week and when he called to see if I was still up for coming to see him play, all I could hear was the same doubt in his voice that was there the first time he asked. I tried my best to sound *super* excited. Which I was, just not about the football part. The see-Cooper, undress-Cooper, get-in-Cooper's-bed part? Super excited.

Now my truck won't start.

I try the ignition again, my fingers literally crossed on both hands. I'd cross my toes if I could. Or my eyelashes. Anything that's remotely crossable, I'd cross it.

And yet, nothing but a weird grating noise. *Crikey.*

My head drops to the steering wheel. *Think, Whitney. Where was the last place you saw a magic carpet? Are you dressed properly to hitch a ride?* It's been years since I thumbed my way anywhere, but I'll do it.

Just as I start to consider what my cardboard sign will say—"COOPER'S BED OR BUST" seems like a winner—someone raps on the driver-door glass. My feeling so defeated means the sound doesn't surprise or startle me; in fact, I don't even raise my head.

Another quick rap. And, while a bit muffled, I'd still know Garrett's good-humored voice anywhere.

"Contemplating the wonders of the universe, Johnny Appleseed?"

I shake my head back and forth, rolling my forehead along the hard plastic of the steering wheel. Polite decency would dictate I at least roll the window down. The hand crank squeaks with every labored turn of my wrist.

When I finally look Garrett's way, he has a heavy work coat on, and he's holding a cup of cheap gas-station coffee in one hand and a roll of those atrocious powdered sugar–covered Hostess Donettes in the other. Breakfast of champions for a redneck with a miracle metabolism.

"Truck won't start. Cooper's game starts in eight hours. I'm contemplating the cost of a taxi to Denver and wondering if they'll accept my undying gratitude as payment."

Garrett sets his Styrofoam coffee cup on the roof of my truck and chuckles.

"Let's not panic, shall we? Damsels in distress are my specialty." He stuffs the donuts in a coat pocket. "Pop the hood for me."

I yank the hood release and return my head to rest on the steering wheel, hoping if I don't look, that might help. Garrett offers a few muttered and unnecessary derogatory comments on Japanese automobile design, in between asking me to give the key a turn. After a bit, he drops the hood, kicks me out of the driver seat, and takes my place for a bit of investigation. He looks silly sitting there, so tall that his head almost brushes the headliner. He doesn't bother to adjust the seat from my short-gal setting, which means his long legs end up folded awkwardly into the small space.

"I'm thinking it's the ignition switch."

I groan. "I'm thinking that sounds expensive. And involved. Why couldn't it just be something simple? Like it needs a hug or something."

Garrett raises a brow, considering my solution with a wry expression.

"Hugs might work on a Toyota, hell if I know. I'm a Ford guy. Pretty sure hugs would void the warranty on a real truck." He pulls my keys from the ignition and holds them out to me. "But the part shouldn't be too bad. Take me a couple of hours to swap it out for you. Maybe we can get you there by halftime."

I let my shoulders deflate. "Garrett, you're too nice, but I'm broke. Flat broke. Unless this part can be purchased with ten bucks and one of those hugs, I just can't afford it."

"You can't be without a vehicle, either, Whitney."

He's right. Logically, I know he is. But I'll figure out that part of the problem later. Right now, I have to call Cooper.

Garrett starts to fumble around in his back pocket and when I see that he's digging out his wallet, I start to worry he's about to do something wonderfully sweet, but entirely foolish. The kid rents what amounts to a single-wide trailer on the outskirts of town, drives the same truck he bought when he was sixteen, and works at a rural co-op, so if he thinks I'd ever consider letting him spot me some cash, he's nuts. Saving us both from that uncomfortable conversation, I hold my phone up and shake it in his direction.

"Let me just break the news to Cooper. Can you give me a ride home when I'm done?"

Garrett counts the bills in his wallet and waves me off. A text means I can avoid hearing any disappointment in Cooper's voice, so I proceed to take the coward's way out.

You want the good news or the bad news?

My phone rings fifteen seconds later. So much for taking cover behind a digital shield. One deep breath and I answer with my best attempt at an apologetic *please don't hate me, I considered hitchhiking just to get to you* kind of hello that I can manage. He must not notice the nuance because he sounds seconds away from grinding his jaw into fine bone dust.

"Now would probably be a good time for me to tell you how much I hate that phrase. The good-news-or-bad-news phrase. It's just code. There's never any good news, just varying degrees of shitty news."

Silently, I groan. Why does this have to be a situation that proves him right? I kick the toe of my boot into a small crack in the parking lot's asphalt. "I can't come to your game, Cooper."

"What's up?" His voice lowers, and the disappointment I so wanted to escape is loud and clear.

"My truck won't start. I'm so sorry, but I stopped at the grocery store on the way out of town, came out, and it wouldn't start. Garrett's here and he thinks it's an ignition switch. He said he could swap it out, but I still need to buy the part and my cash situation means I can't swing it. He's going to give me a ride home. I just wanted to tell you what's going on."

Cooper breathes steadily but noisily into the phone. "So he's still there? Garrett?"

I look up. Garrett's standing in the middle of the lot with his head craned back, gawking at a gaggle of Canada geese flying overhead as he uses one hand to nudge a miniature donut out of the sleeve and into his mouth.

"Yeah. Why? Please don't be weird about this. He's helping me."

"Let me talk to him. I won't make it weird."

Garrett looks my way as if his ears are burning. Even from here, I can see he has a spot of powdered sugar on his upper lip. I wave the phone in his direction.

He approaches, swipes a coat sleeve over his mouth, and gives me a wide-eyed look. "Am I in trouble?"

I shrug my shoulders and hand him the phone.

"Hello? . . . Hey, Cooper . . . Yeah, I'm not positive, but pretty sure."

Garrett walks away, meandering about the lot in a looping pattern as he talks. When he's done, he hands the phone back and points across the street to the auto parts store, then takes off in that direction without offering any explanation. I lift the phone and Cooper starts in.

"OK, Ms. Not-Cinderella, your Mr. Not-Prince-Charming has this under control. Garrett's going to get the parts, I'm paying for it, and you're coming to Denver when he's done."

"Dammit, Cooper—"

"Stop." He sighs. "I miss you, my body hurts like hell, and we're blowing our season to shit, game by game. I need you here, babe. Please, just work with me on this."

My heart does the strangest thing then. It somehow melts and swells all at one time. Whether it's because Cooper just said he needed me or because a part of me has missed feeling taken care of, I don't know. Since my dad died, there's been no one to do this—step in and help, even when I claim I don't need it, even when my pride gets in the way.

Cooper sighs again. "Look, there's going to be times when I have to do this kind of shit for you, Whit. You might hate it, think I'm being overbearing, or get pissed that I'm paying for things you want to handle on your own. Fine. Be pissed. Just know that underneath it all, I'm doing it for one reason. Because I'm in love with you. No other reason other than that."

My eyes start to sting. I can hear Cooper breathing, waiting for me to say something.

Just say thank you, Whitney. Thank him for handling this. For being a good man. For loving you.

I clamp my eyes shut and keep them that way. Do all I can to keep my voice steady.

"Thank you, Cooper."

=23=

(Whitney)

Because of the truck fiasco, my plan to devise that heart-felt note for the greeting card and tuck it in with Cooper's things doesn't happen, so I spend most of the drive listening to game coverage—much to my brain's exasperation. Football on the radio? Painful. Here's hoping that watching it in person is a bit less tedious.

Cooper said it would be easier to walk to the stadium from his place, so after maneuvering my truck into the parking space next to his truck, I rifle through my things and gather up what I think I'll need for the next few hours. My ID, what little cash I have, my zip-up hoodie, and that foam finger I simply couldn't resist.

The walk to the stadium takes less than ten minutes, perhaps because I'm wogging my way there, dodging around slowpoke walkers and jaywalking when necessary. When I arrive, the third quarter has just started. Cooper's only other instructions were to find the will call window, then call Tyler—who, as Cooper put it, is *"the only team minion–flunky I'd trust with you*"—and have him escort me in.

Ten minutes later, a fresh-faced college kid emerges from a side door and quick-steps my way. He's a walking advertisement for all that is our home team, dressed in team-branded gear from head to toe. When he lands in front of me, bless his loyal and devoted heart, even his shoelaces are color coordinated.

"Whitney?" He tips up his white sunglasses, perches them atop his buzz-cut blond hair, and gives me a once-over.

"That's me."

Tyler is quite likely agonizing silently over the fact that I'm *not* dressed in the appropriate colors. Except for, you know, the dumbest accessory known to man, stuck on my right hand. At least I got the color right on that.

I did peruse a little online, looking for jerseys with Cooper's number emblazoned on them, but gave up when I saw the price. Over a hundred dollars. For a *shirt*. A shirt you can't wear out to dinner anywhere that doesn't have hot wings or mozzarella sticks on the menu.

Also, I wasn't entirely sure if wearing his jersey would seem a little too high school. Can you wear your boyfriend's jersey if you're also too old to consider him as a prom date? Do real girlfriends of real football players do that? I gave up and decided to wear the long-sleeved top that Cooper refers to as my "dick-tease sweater." I kind of hate how much I don't hate that he calls it that.

Tyler continues his inspection and leans forward, closing in to see my face better.

"Nose ring. Check." He hands over a lanyard with a

laminated pass attached. "This is the first time Cooper's ever asked me to do anything, so the last thing I want to do is give this to the wrong woman."

I pull the lanyard over my head. "Would you like to ask me any wildly personal questions about him? Things only I could verify because of our intimate acquaintance?"

Tyler rears back and widens his eyes. "No. Absolutely not. We don't talk about players like that."

It seems I've officially Alice-tumbled my way into the rabbit hole of pro football. A mystical land where players are revered and respected, always. No jokes. No jests. Conversations that trend anywhere near their private lives? Certainly not. In order for me to fit in, I'm definitely going to have to adapt.

I give Tyler's shoulder a gentle tap. "I was just kidding, Tyler. Feel free to stand down."

"Yes, ma'am."

With a sigh, I wave my hand forward. Tyler takes the cue and we make our way into the stadium. A short escalator ride takes us to the upper levels and we end up in front of a suite, where the door is partially open but blocked by a security guard dressed in a neon-yellow T-shirt. Tyler points to my lanyard. I raise it up for the guard's inspection and when I do, dread and anxiety start to take over.

Despite their recent losing streak, home games remain easy sell-outs, so we're currently standing above seventy thousand screaming, bellowing, hollering, chattering people. Add in the announcers, the music, all of it, and my head is starting to swim. In my mind, I pictured myself down there, among the rest of the fans, where my foam finger might blend in. But here I am, standing in front of an executive suite, positive that nothing about me will make sense in that room.

Tyler taps my shoulder and points toward the doorway. I consider asking him if he'll come with me. But he doesn't provide a moment's chance for me to toss myself at his feet and beg, or wrap my fingers around his elbow and instruct him to pretend like we're besties. His job is done here, so he simply turns and takes off.

Time to suck it up, Whitney. You are an adaptable individual. Cooper asked you to be here, and you can handle whatever you find on the other side of that door. You can and you will.

I lock eyes with the security guard and give him a curt nod, hastening my own resolve and hoping he might return the gesture, perhaps give me a *you go, girl* kind of expression. But all he gives back is a slightly bewildered grimace.

The door sweeps open with one push and I step inside.

And, yes, I was *so* right.

Because one of these things is not like the others.

Fifteen or so women fill the room, some sitting in seats facing the field, others milling about the bar area while daintily holding a wineglass—every one of them beautiful. And tall. So tall, all long legs and lithe arms; even their hair seems exceptionally long. And shiny. And straight. Just my naturally wavy hair alone looks out of place here.

"Whitney!"

I whip my head toward the sound of my name, like a puppy desperate for attention, and find Kendra waving me over to join her, tapping the empty seat next to hers. The ten short steps feel like they take an hour to traverse, but when Kendra opens her arms for a friendly hug, I finally manage a full breath.

Then my foam finger whacks her in the side of the head.

She smooths her hair—her jet-black, glossy, long, pin-straight hair—and cocks one of her perfectly shaped brows.

"Nice foam finger."

I point the offending object toward the windows.

"I kind of thought we'd be down there." At the sound of my voice, the other women in the room zero in. "And I thought Cooper would think it's funny. Quirky."

Kendra leans back in her seat and smiles.

"I'm sure he will. You seem to have brought out an appreciation for quirky in him that we didn't even know existed."

She raises two fingers toward the back of the room, catching a bartender's attention. "If you really want to sit in the stands, I'm sure Tyler can make that happen. But we have wine up here."

A server appears over our shoulders, holding an open bottle of chardonnay in one hand and two fresh glasses in the other.

Wine. Yes. A drink will help. The server disappears after I thank him profusely and attempt to shove a wrinkled ten-dollar bill into his hands. Kendra subtly blocks the move, closing my hand into a loose fist, and shakes her head. Open bar, she tells me, and the guys always make sure the staff is taken care of.

My adoration for her only increases when she takes one of her hands and loosely rolls it through the air, silently gesturing for me to take a deep breath and relax. I take a series of calming breaths. Kendra leans toward me and lowers her voice.

"Don't let the lioness prowling get to you. You're new and you're with Cooper, so they're just preening. Half of them won't be here next year, anyway."

With my drink in hand, I take another scan of the room and the social structure becomes clear.

On the left side of the room, in the front rows, are the newbies. Most of them quite young, a few wearing jerseys—evidently I was wrong about that concept aging out after high school—accessorized with big jewelry and aloof attitudes that indicate they're balancing some pretty sizable chips on their slim shoulders. Here, on the right side, are the tenured types, wives and longtime girlfriends. Just as gorgeous and polished, but less contrived.

Finally, a few sips of wine and I'm able to focus. I lean forward and even though the suite's sight lines mean the entire field is in view, it's still hard to keep track of Cooper when he's out there. He's not only fast, but tricky. One moment he's on one side of the field and the next he's gone, only to reappear forty yards downfield. The combination of taking some time to rest in Hotchkiss and heading home for a few weeks of rehab seems to have worked.

And sixty million doesn't seem like nearly enough when he catches a pass that's almost too long and too high, then rights his body before anyone figures out he actually caught the ball, and fleet-foots into the end zone. All while dodging what seems like a hundred different guys along the way.

The sight gets me on my feet and I end up dancing around like an idiot, with my foam finger only adding more uncoolness to the spectacle. And, honestly, I do not care. Not even a little bit. Because the guy who just did *that* is with *me*. When I finally flop down, breathless but grinning, Kendra is laughing so hard she almost spills her wine.

"Did you see that? Come on! He's like a mountain goat, crossed with a gazelle, crossed with a superhero!"

She manages to stop laughing and locks her eyes on mine, but doesn't say anything. I let out a huge exhale. "What?"

She shakes her head and looks toward the field.

"I'm just so glad he found you."

———

Late in the fourth quarter, with only a few minutes left in the game, we've managed to capture a ten-point lead and our offense, Cooper included, is marching down the field yet again. Some of the women in the suite have started to gather their things, touching up their lip gloss and fluffing their hair at the roots, careful to keep the rest of their locks smooth and h so straight. Kendra leans down and puts her phone in her bag.

"You and Cooper have plans after the game? We can all go out to dinner if you want."

I give her a side-glance and consider how best to diplomatically explain that I already have plans for Cooper. Plans that don't involve other people.

She chuckles. "Right. You two haven't been in the same city for a couple of weeks. He's your dinner. I get it."

I give her a confessional grin, just as the stadium goes almost unnaturally quiet. The hair on the back of my neck prickles when I register the shift in energy. Slowly, I look toward the field, tuning out everything but the announcer's voice.

"Lowry's down. Always hate to see that, especially when it's his first game back. We'll see what happens here, but he's definitely not moving."

The suite is nearly silent, all eyes on me again, but mine are fixed on Cooper. He's on his back and his left leg is twisted in a way that it shouldn't be. Once the team trainers surround him I can't see much but his feet. Kendra puts one of her hands on my knee.

"Don't look. That makes it worse."

Her permission comes as a relief and I drop my face into my hands. Too many things are rattling around in my head and I can't decide which terrible scenario to focus on first. Another concussion? His knee again? Something entirely worse, something so bad he can't move, even if he's trying to?

Seconds tick by and if that announcer doesn't say something soon, I'm going down there to get some answers myself. Good luck to anyone who gets in my way.

Kendra shifts her hand to my back and pats gently. "OK. We're fine. Looks like it's his knee—he was just staying still so Hunt could get to him. The cart's coming. But he's moving, so we're good."

Kendra's words are meant to sound reassuring, and somewhere behind all of the rage that just roared into my consciousness, I know that. But I'm too pissed at Cooper, and this entire world, to take them as intended. I jerk my hands away from my face.

" 'We're good'? He's *moving*? Is that the fucking baseline I'm supposed to be OK with?"

Kendra answers calmly. "Yes."

I lurch out of my seat and my stupid foam finger ends up tangled between the armrests. I yank it out and thwack it against a seat back, taking out my frustration where I can.

"This barbaric sport is so stupid. Idiotic. I hate it. It's asinine that people love this shit, human beings crashing into each other like dump trucks. Crashing into *my* human being."

The room is beyond quiet now, because I just took the name of football in vain, right here in the middle of an executive suite. But the sweep of territorial, intense, anxiety-riddled emotion I'm dealing with right now is too damn much. On top of that, the bullheaded pain in the ass who inspired all that *intentionally* put himself in this position.

Kendra tugs on my arm, urging me to sit down. When I do, she forces my gaze to meet hers.

"This is who he is. For every one of those guys down there, this game is who they are." She toys with the wedding ring on her left hand, twists and turns it around her slim finger. "Good or bad, barbaric or not, this is a package deal. So, if you choose him, you choose this, too."

She takes a glance over my shoulder and points toward the door. "Tyler's here for you. Go take care of your man."

===

There's something disturbing yet comforting about the fact that I had a handler at my side before I even knew to ask for one. A player gets bulldozed to the ground? Get the trainer. Get the cart. Manage the pain. Go find the girlfriend.

Tyler leads me down a long hallway, where there are entirely too many people around—some reporters and cameramen, team staff, a few players, assorted football groupies—most of whom don't look anything but cheery. While I'm standing here on the verge of tears, these jerks are chatting away like nothing's wrong. To avoid losing my sanity entirely, I start to think about what to do when I finally get Cooper home. I yank on Tyler's shirtsleeve.

"We don't have a car here. How am I going to get him home?"

Tyler doesn't miss a beat; he doesn't even shift his gaze to mine. "Everybody knows Cooper walks to the stadium. We've got a Tahoe waiting outside."

Again, disturbing yet comforting.

Finally, a set of double doors opens and I push myself away from the hallway wall, craning my neck for a better look. Then the small crowd actually parts, Red Sea style, without even a subtle prompting from anyone in charge.

Cooper leans heavily on a pair of crutches, his eyes wary

and exhausted. When he sees me, his face shows everything I already suspected. He's done. For the season, definitely. After that, it's anyone's guess.

Stepping forward, my hands go to his face and I try to get as near to him as I can, hoping to smother out everyone else by closing ranks. My forehead meets his, the tips of our noses touch, and our mouths come so close that when he speaks, his lips brush mine.

"Whitney," he whispers.

"I'm right here."

"Take me home."

"You got it."

═══

At home, I do my best to figure out what he needs. He's hungry and dehydrated, to the point where he has a headache. Because he's the ever-organized Cooper, he already has a refrigerator full of food, sports drinks with electrolytes, and chilled jugs of filtered water. I get him settled on the couch with assorted forms of hydration and an ice pack, then work on reheating platefuls of chicken, roasted veggies, and brown rice. We eat in near silence.

After that, I persuade him to take a soak in his oversized tub. A short-lived verbal tussle ensues over whether I should join him. A naked and slippery Cooper is always appealing, which is the problem, because I know us both too well.

I draw the bath for him, adding in some Epsom salts and lemongrass oil before pointing toward the tub, wordlessly directing him with that gesture. He proceeds to stick his bottom lip out a little and, well, pout. A first from Cooper. Pouting isn't his forte; he's always more direct than that.

"Go on, get in there."

He shoves his boxers down. "I'm hurt. It's unsafe for me to be in there alone."

My eyes drift down his body and his cock actually registers my perusal, thickening at the recognition. Silly penises; they so enjoy being appreciated. Cooper notes where my attention has settled and when his hand comes forward to grasp the base, I know he's about to do that thing he knows I like so much—the thing where he touches himself, slowly and intently, with a tight grip I find fascinating.

Crap. I can't even think about it. Not now. I close my eyes but know that won't particularly help.

Frankly, I don't even need to *see* him do it. On the phone, as long as I know what he's up to, I can fill in the blanks. If he also provides me with a quality soundtrack of grunts and groans to go along? It's like someone composed a pornographic overture with my lewd weaknesses in mind, and I'm lost and done before he is.

I pointlessly slap a hand over my already closed eyes. "Don't you dare. You know what that does to me. This isn't easy for me, just for the record."

"Doesn't have to be hard." My hand drops, eyes fluttering open at the low, gravelly tone of his voice. He sticks his tongue out to brush his upper lip. "Or, it can be hard. Just a couple of tugs and I'll be there. You pick."

"How can you even consider sex right now? With your knee?"

He takes one long pull and shrugs. "Because you're *here*. I missed you so fucking much. Plus, Hunt stuck a syringe full of good shit into my knee before we left so I don't currently feel like someone just jabbed an ice pick into my leg."

I actually debate the merits of what he just said. Technically, I consider it for as long as it takes him to make another unhurried pass over his shaft. This debate of mine continues right up until he shifts his weight and winces.

I sigh. "Do you need help getting in? If not, I'm going to go clean up the dinner dishes."

He nods. "Yes. I need help. You get in first."

Turning on my heel, I make a getaway while I still can. "Nice try. Holler if you start to feel unsafe. But you'd better be near drowning when I get in here."

———

He soaks for a while, long enough for me to finish tidying up the kitchen. I find a few pillar candles stashed in a kitchen drawer and decide to bring them into the bedroom with me, thinking a little soft light can't hurt toward setting a soothing environment.

When I rifle through his dresser drawers in search of a shirt to sleep in, I find a few of his old practice jerseys, all obviously retired, since some are from his college days. The college ones are especially broken-in and soft, so I slip one on and snuggle down into his sheets. Cooper's bed, the hub of vice and sin. *Oh, how I've missed you.*

From the bathroom, I hear the tub start to drain, along with a few groans from Cooper, a little too pained-sounding to be as erotic as I'd prefer. A particularly loud curse gets all of my attention. I crane my ear toward the bathroom.

"You need help?"

"No." He curses again. "Not unless you want to come in here and really make me feel better. The *hard* way."

Cooper hop-walks his way out of the bathroom and makes it to the edge of the bed before looking at me. He tilts his head and grits his teeth.

"Do you think it's funny to torture me? Because I don't. It's cruel. I've never thought of you as cruel."

I shake my head, confused. "Huh?"

His chin juts out toward me. I look down and realize what the problem is. The jersey. Too bad; it serves him right for doing the penis-fondling thing in front of me.

"You like? I needed something to sleep in. This one is particularly soft." I draw one hand down the front to emphasize my point, leisurely enough to inspire a sharp grunt from him.

"I hate it. In fact, take it off." He drops onto the bed, working to shimmy himself back toward the headboard. "But, go stand down there, at the end of the bed—in all this goddam candlelight—while you do it. And I want you to rub on your tits through the fabric a little before you strip it off. Maybe bite your lip, too. Like some cliché jersey chaser, but one I actually *want* to fuck."

With an eye roll, I pull back the covers on the bed and he shuffles in, adjusting a few pillows behind his back. One of his arms flops out, hand flexing to encourage me into that spot. I curl onto my side and put my head on his chest, but we don't say anything for a bit.

Instead our hands trace across each other's skin, mine on his torso, one of his up under the jersey and against my lower back.

"Can I ask you a question?" Cooper says.

"Sure."

He takes a long inhale. "What would you say if I told you I was starting to think about retiring?"

My entire body turns rigid, because this question feels like the verbal equivalent of quicksand. Say the wrong thing and I might very well end up with a relationship that suffocates under the weight of that choice. Kendra's caution about what it means to choose him echoes in my mind and I try to pick my words wisely, even when all I want to do is bake him a retirement cake.

"I'd say this isn't a good day for you to ask me that."

He tilts his head down, chin bumping the top of my head. "Why?"

"Because seeing you out there today, hurt and not moving, not knowing if you were OK? I hated it. I couldn't see straight or think straight. So if I answered that question right now, it would be based on never wanting to see you that way again."

Cooper kisses the crown of my head. "Is it wrong that I love how much it got to you? Like, how good it feels knowing you were worried?"

"Yes." I flick his chest with my fingers. "It's wrong and twisted."

The room goes quiet again. The candles are scented, but with something guy-friendly, so the air is heavy with spice and musk. Cooper takes a long inhale and the sound seems to mean he wants to talk, so I move to sit in front of him, cross-legged.

"This"—he points to his knee, already swollen up to the size of a grapefruit with an ugly bruise darkening the area—"could be it for my career."

I nod. "I guessed as much."

"Why?"

"Because of Smash."

His brow furrows. "Because I smashed my knee?"

"No. Because of Smash. On *Friday Night Lights*." Cooper crooks a questioning eyebrow.

"I wanted to learn more about football. My original plan was to watch documentaries, but the kid at the old-school video store in town insisted I watch *Friday Night Lights*. When Smash hurt his knee, he was all worried about his scholarships because he was convinced he couldn't play again, at least not the way he did, that he would be too slow to compete."

Cooper stares at me for a moment, a near blank expression on his face. Great. Probably shouldn't have mentioned the whole binge-watching *Friday Night Lights* thing. I avert my eyes, taking a good, long look at the ceiling.

"I know it's a television show, but I figured that part might be pretty accurate."

Nothing. Just more of Cooper staring. Then he shakes his head slowly and pats the spot next to him. "Come here."

I crawl back to that spot and curl up under his arm. Cooper drops his head so that his lips are pressed to my hair. His next words are laced with equal parts fatigue and awe.

"I can't believe you did that. Went through all that just to understand what I do."

Shrugging, I drop my head to the space where his shoulder meets his chest. "Not a burden really—it's a good show."

"Yeah? I've never seen it."

"Two words, Cooper: Tim Riggins."

"Based on how you just said that, I'm guessing I already hate this little fucker *Tim Riggins*."

I bite a little spot on his chest and then kiss it. "So, if you retired, what would you do?"

A dark chuckle from him. "That's the problem. I've never thought about it. Always figured that if I didn't think about leaving the game, it would keep me hungry. But if I'm slow or one bad play away from IR every week, I don't want that. I won't be that guy, the one who they have to push out of the game kicking and crying. I want to leave on my own terms. And I could, you know?"

I give him an encouraging sound. He takes it. "I've done everything I set out to do. Broken a few records, gotten a ring, been to the Pro Bowl. But what the fuck am I going to do, buy a car dealership? Be a motivational speaker? I don't think so."

"What about coaching?"

He snorts. "I'd be the worst coach ever. I'm like Belichick but worse, and probably not a brilliant enough strategist to make up for being a prick. And, coaches have to talk to the media all the time. Me and Bodie Carmichael, on a regular basis? Couldn't do it. What does that leave me with? Who the hell am I without this?"

I want to tell him I get it, how much I understand the panic that comes with staring down the barrel of a new reality, one you didn't want, and not knowing who you'll be on the other side. But Cooper's done nothing to deserve this. Fate and bad luck and the fallible human body are to blame. He's done nothing but work incredibly hard and as much as it might tear me up, I'd give anything for him to be able to play as long as he wants to.

Gingerly, I straddle his lap. He tucks a few pieces of my hair behind my ear.

"I don't have an answer for you, Cooper. Here's what I do know, though. You'll be the best *whatever*, no matter what you decide."

I poke him in the chest with my index finger, right over his heart. "There's too much good stuff in here for you to be anything less than that. Sell widgets or thingamajigs. Work the concession stand at Hotchkiss High. Hell, if you became an apple farmer, you'd outpace me before I knew what to do. Doesn't matter. All the traits you brought to this career, you'll bring to the next."

His eyes go soft, tender to the point where I can see all the fear buried in there. He leans forward and presses his forehead to mine.

"What if I just decide to be in love with you for a living? You think I could be the best at that?"

I take a labored swallow. "Too easy. You're already the best at that. Challenge yourself, Lowry."

=24=

(Whitney)

"I'm not sure if waking up to you all crazy-eyed and smiling at the ceiling is a good thing or not. You look a little bit nuts." Cooper's sleepy eyes warily assess mine. "You OK?"

I nod and continue gawking at nothing with a goofy smile on my face. Spending this past week at Cooper's place while he nurses his ACL injury has been a different—but not entirely unpleasant—experience. One of the upsides? Instead of sneaking out of the sheets for a workout before I wake, he stays put. Today, on my last day in town, I end up grinning at the ceiling as soon as my eyes drift open, savoring the feel of his big arm and bum leg draped across my body.

One of Cooper's hands sneaks up under my sleep shirt, coming to rest against my belly. "It sucks that you're leaving today. I had a plan for us and we didn't get to do any of it."

"You had *a* plan? Just one? Seems odd."

Cooper's hands are big enough that he can easily pinch the flesh on the underside of my breast as a reprimand. Hard enough that I let out a little squeal, but not so much that my nipples don't also somehow appreciate his brand of punishment.

"You're hilarious." His fingertips skim the spot he just pinched, soothing the sting into another kind of ache. "I just had a bunch of ideas in my head about how it was going to be while you were here. The first time you came to visit, it was new; we didn't know what this was. This time we could have done a bunch of boyfriend-girlfriend stuff. Instead, I ended up dragging you to my orthopedic consults. Wasn't exactly what I had in mind."

By tagging along on Cooper's appointments, I learned that (a) *Friday Night Lights* isn't too far off base with their story lines, and (b) the inside of the human knee is a terribly complex world, far more than I would have guessed.

Cooper's previous MCL injury, along with the hamstring strain he's been nursing for weeks, merely set the stage for this new tear. Add in what he already asks of his body as a receiver—years of taking off downfield like a cannon-fired shot, launching sideways to elude tackles, and landing on unforgiving AstroTurf under the crushing weight of a linebacker—means those knees of his are taking the brunt. Even I could plainly see the brutal evidence of those demands on the MRIs the doctor showed us. Cooper is essentially a thirty-two-year-old guy with the knees of a decrepit, osteoarthritis-ridden senior citizen.

Given all of that, he has big decisions to make. Surgery will mean he's out next season. If he takes a wait-and-see approach, focusing on rehab, it may not work. Which means he'll still need surgery, and the delay could leave him sidelined for yet another season. Two seasons in football are like dog years. He'll be thirty-four, which is elderly by football standards.

Cooper curls his body closer to mine, moving his leg so he can trace his hand lower on my belly.

"Do you want to know what my plan was?" A kiss lands on my neck. "All the ways I intended to make this trip worth your while?"

I grin at the ceiling again. "Sure. Lay it on me."

Cooper traces his lips against my jaw, then dips his face, kissing along my clavicle.

"First, you would have gotten here in time for me to see you before the game. Early enough for me to have you before I had to get to the stadium. At least once, just to take the edge off. That way I'd know you were in the stands, properly fucked and satisfied, while I took the field loose and ready. We would have won the game—"

"You did win," I interject.

He sighs and drops his head to rest on my chest. I slip my fingers into his hair, stroking my nails gently against his scalp.

"I know, but I wanted you to see me at my best, not limping out on crutches."

"I saw you mountain-goat-slash-Spider-Man your way into the end zone. All those women in the suite thought I was certifiable, the way I was cheering. Me and my foam finger."

He lifts his head and looks me in the eye. "Yeah? You were cheering for me?"

I nod. He bites his lip for a second before letting a full smile take over. *Jesus.* That smile, the one that's sometimes so hard to drag out of him, it could be the end of me someday.

"That helps. Knowing you saw me kick some tail before this happened." His eyes track downward. Just a quick glance at his knee, then his eyes are back on mine. "After the game, I would have taken you out to dinner, somewhere nice. I wanted to show you off a little bit. You would have worn a dress, but something different from what you usually wear."

"You don't like how I dress?"

My eyes drift closed, waiting for his answer, knowing full well that I'm not exactly a walking advertisement for female fashion, while also hoping this isn't the moment he chooses to reveal how much he wishes I would wear ensembles with more sequins and rhinestones. Or shoes that don't require such sturdy laces. Like, I don't know, stilettos. Maybe he prefers his women to sport crop tops on the regular, the kind with animal patterns or fringe. If so, we're doomed.

"I didn't say that. I think you look great in everything." Cooper unbuttons my pj top, pushes the fabric aside, and gives each of my nipples a flick with the tip of his tongue. "Or nothing. But as this was *my* plan, it involved you wearing a hot dress that shows off your body. Especially these."

He takes a breast in each hand and presses them together so he can suckle the flesh of both in equal measure without leaving one unattended for too long. When he releases his hold, I realize I've been arching my back again—trying to get closer, the way it seems my body always does, consciously or not. I understand then how hard it will be to go home this time. What started out a few months ago as a pleasant distraction from my real life has become something more. A life that, while being just weeks out from losing my orchard, is somehow also richer than any version I've tried to create before. Because it includes Cooper. The wildly driven, passionate, intense man who is currently kissing his way down my body.

"I'd bring you home and that dress would mean we'd barely make it through the door before I had it shoved up around your waist. A few glasses of wine at dinner would have you climbing me like a tree, going at it like we'd never get to again. I'd give you all of that, and more, right back. Whatever you wanted, however you needed it."

My panties have disappeared, along with his boxers. No clue when that happened. Perhaps I actually tapped out for a moment, due to some sort of lusty fainting spell. Regardless, I'm bare and Cooper's rigid length is nestled against my leg, the smooth head rubbing along my outer thigh. I snake a hand between my legs, knowing what I'll find, just to see. The space there is slick, even more so than I expected. Cooper latches his hand on to mine, splaying his larger grip over my fingers to guide my movements.

"Feel good, babe?" I murmur enough of a sound to tell him it does. "Yeah? Prove it."

It's a challenge and a directive, so entirely heated that my body only turns even more eager. I draw my hand away and use those same slippery fingers to grasp Cooper's cock, circling the head, slowly. Every slip of my hand mingles my arousal with his, that bead of wetness leaking from the tip. He grunts, low and long, pumping his shaft through my grip. Once, twice, three times. Then he rolls away, coming to rest on his back.

"The only not-shitty thing about my knee being screwed up is that I love having you on top. Crawl on up here."

I scramble to my knees and throw one leg over him. Despite his ACL tear being the ever-present elephant in the room, the swelling has gone down considerably. Still, I force myself to pause, ensuring his knee is in as safe a position as possible, because I'm not feeling particularly prone to restraint at the moment. Instead, it feels like I'm a few filthy words and firm strokes away from coming unchained, and this position means Cooper will end up taking the brunt of that release.

Grasping his length again, I rub my core across the underside and lower my body until he's pressed to his abs, with me working over his length like we're a pair of teenagers who've decided to do everything *but*. Watching my hips move over him, the slick trail I leave behind, combined with the pressure in every spot I want it, is nearly enough. Every hitch of his breath, each groan and curse Cooper gives up, only drives the edge closer.

I slow my pace, one pass to tease us both. Cooper's eyes fix on the space where our bodies meet. He croaks out an encouragement, a validation, quiet enough to be nothing but a manly whisper.

"Keep doing that, Whit. So fucking hot."

I lean forward and kiss him. "Any more of these

boyfriend-girlfriend plans you wanted to share with me? Was there a hot air balloon involved? A carriage ride?"

Cooper juts his hips up, one sharp push of his body to mine, a reminder that I may have him groaning and nearly panting underneath me, but he remains just as powerful as ever.

"Nothing that cheesy. I did want to take you to the Botanic Gardens, because it's supposed to be romantic. But mostly my plan was pretty much what we're doing right now. Waking up next to you, loving up on you, just like we did this morning."

I pause my movements and focus on his face, remembering exactly how it was when we woke up.

"Would you have your leg and arm draped over me? The way you sometimes do?"

He tilts his head. "Do you like that?"

I nod, and it becomes my turn to croak out a whispered response. "It's my favorite way to wake up."

Cooper's hands draw down my back. Fingertips tracing either side of my spine, affection embedded in every inch that he covers. A sweet, sexy, entirely contented half-grin plays across his mouth.

"If it's your favorite, then that's how it would be. We'd wake up, my body covering yours, keeping you tucked in and safe, right next to me. We'd both know how right this is. How good we are together."

My eyes track over his expression, looking for anything that might convey he's reading from an invisible script of things he thinks he should say, giving me words that are less about his real feelings and more about reassuring mine.

He slips one hand up into my hair, then draws it down to rest at my neck, giving a little tug there just as he presses his hips up to meet my core. The pointed contact, flush and firm and spot-on perfect, drives a moan from my throat.

"So good together," Cooper whispers, "that you'd let me inside you without anything between us. We'd both know that no matter what happens, it's safe. That this is real."

Our eyes meet and in his gaze there's nothing but unguarded honesty. And because he's just painted the picture of a future between us I can imagine so readily it's disarming, I kiss him.

The kiss turns fevered with one nip of my teeth to his bottom lip, his hands gripping my hips so hard I can feel the dig of his nails into my skin. We keep going, until my body is grinding atop his, and we're both so ready it's painful. A grunt from him combines with his hands forcing my hips to stay put. His right arm extends toward the nightstand.

I know what would come next. And whether it's because I'm feeling too wild to think rationally or because I'm too caught up in imagining the future, either way, I drop my hand over his forearm to stop him.

"What you just said . . . about this being real? Was that true?"

Cooper moves so he can clasp his hand in mine, threading our fingers together, then does the same with our other hands. He takes a labored swallow.

"Absolutely." He releases our intertwined fingers and brings his hands to either side of my neck, pausing briefly before sliding them down the front of my body, engrossed by the path his hands take, wetting his lips as he does. His hands come to rest atop my belly. "Are you on the pill?"

"No."

The word emerges so softly, it's almost inaudible. Maybe I don't want him to hear. Maybe I hate the possibility that one of us will actually regain some sense here.

"You still want to do this? Because I do. But I don't want to pull out, either."

No hesitation, not even a slight falter in his voice. Cooper shifts my body back, leaving enough room to take himself in hand while I consider his question, weigh the risks, and do my best to think reasonably. He works the head for a bit, his big hand slipping over the crown in a steady rhythm, and somehow, he's an unexpected picture of patience. Waiting, waiting, waiting.

"If you aren't sure, Whit, that's OK. Grab a condom and I'll slide it on."

Then Cooper squeezes the head of his cock, and suddenly I want him so much it hurts. He releases that death grip and exhales, replaces it with a lazier stroke. When he uses his other hand to move between my legs, we both give up tortured groans and I'm over him a split second later. The head slips in so easily that I pause, fighting the urge to ride him hard and fierce, simply because there won't be another moment like this. Even if we last a lifetime together, *this* happens only once.

His previous demonstration of patience has evidently combusted, because he yanks down on my hips.

"Come on, don't fuck around. Take all of it."

Another tug and I yield, taking all of him. We're both breathing heavily, but I keep my hips still. He jerks my hips forward. I growl.

A low, amused chuckle from him. "That's *my* sound. If you're frustrated, there's an easy fix for that. Just use my cock the way you want to. You fucking own it anyway."

Powerful heat swims through me. How I got here, with this man beneath me, proclaiming that I own parts of his beautiful body, I could never explain. Had I never been in the position to lose my orchard, I wouldn't have met him. Had he not needed a place to escape his own drama, he wouldn't have made it to my doorstep. And yet, here we are. Fate and fear brought us together, but what we built atop those things is more.

I give in then. Cooper pulls me closer, doesn't let my body stray from his, our chests sliding over each other and our mouths doing the same. Too much foreplay turned us to tinder, so every graze of our skin is like a flint steel. Even when I try to temper the pace, Cooper won't allow it, tugging on my hair each time I try to slow and wrapping it tightly in his fist.

"Don't. Ride me hard. Do not stop."

Another sharp tug becomes all I need. I've never come so hard in my life, deep and intense, singing through to places I can't even name. Cooper curses, tightening his hand in my hair. Only when he comes does he finally release my hair, and his arm drops to the bed. My body hurts, oddly but deliciously, under the release of all that tension, the swell that comes with allowing yourself to give up the armor and make room for your every vulnerability.

Cooper remains still for a long while, eyes closed and breathing unsteadily. When he finally opens his eyes, I'm there.

Waiting and watching.

He's perfection in that moment. The rock-solid reality of a truly good man—with a very dirty mouth. I couldn't ask for more.

———

Life-changingly great sex is hell on a gal's motivation. I intended to leave Cooper's place by mid-morning, but all the postcoital snuggling derailed those plans. For hours. Then Cooper offered to make pancakes.

It would take a much stronger woman than I to turn down that offer.

Which is why a plateful of multigrain pancakes, nutty and hearty, cooked in copious amounts of butter, currently appears before me at the breakfast bar where I've been perched while Cooper does his thing. The fact that he's shirtless, wearing only a pair of low-slung pajama bottoms, only adds to the scene. He slides more butter and a small bottle of maple syrup my way, giving me a chin nudge before turning away to dish up his own plate.

"Go on, eat up."

I unscrew the cap off the maple syrup. "You don't have to ask me twice."

Cooper sets his plate next to mine but doesn't sit down. Instead, he strides toward the bedroom. "Be right back."

Around a mouthful of pancakes, I holler in his retreating direction.

"You'd better not be going to get a shirt! I was hoping you might accidentally drip syrup on your chest while you eat!"

He reappears a short minute later with his knee brace on. And wearing a shirt. Which both I and my filthy sensibilities find utterly offensive.

He places a large silver gift bag on the countertop. I pause mid-chew and give the fancy-looking bag a side-glance. Cooper takes his seat and proceeds to douse his pancakes in far more syrup than I expected he would allow himself. He gestures toward the bag with the syrup bottle, before setting it aside.

"Merry Christmas."

"What? What is this?" I use my fork to tap the bag.

He shrugs. "I won't see you at Christmas. That's for you."

Later this week, Cooper will take a hurried two-day trip home to Texas over Christmas. He extended an invitation for me to come with him, but I declined, claiming there were some orchard-oriented tasks that needed my immediate attention.

There were, I suppose. I'd heard about a community bank in Rifle that was actively investing in ag-oriented start-ups and I submitted a loan application online last week. I was holding on to whatever hope I could, willing this to be my last-ditch way out and crossing my fingers for a phone call from their office. I also wanted to call the Boulder slow money venture at least, oh, fifty-seven more times between Christmas and New Year's, to be sure they hadn't approved my application and sent the approval via the similarly *slow* postal service.

In truth, I was also petrified about meeting Cooper's family, of trying to fit in, and the possibility of losing my hearing if I was subjected to their bellowing without the cushion of a few states between us. But knowing I currently have a huge problem boiling away makes it easier to prioritize all the things that scare me to death.

I place my fork on the edge of my plate and give the bag a curious peek.

"Don't you want to open it?"

I'm not sure. The scales seem utterly imbalanced at the moment, with me staring down this innocuous bag and wondering why it didn't occur to me to bring him a thoughtful gift of some sort. Even if I didn't have the cash to buy anything, I could have made something. A macaroni necklace or a finger painting. Maybe one of those "gift certificates," the kind that entitles the recipient to a service only the gift provider can offer. *Good for one free hand wash on your beast of a truck. Good for one free hand massage. Good for one free session of me using my hands in a way of your choosing.*

I tug the bag a little closer. "I just didn't know we were exchanging gifts. I didn't bring anything for you."

"I don't need anything."

"But it feels a little weird. You got me this and I haven't given you anything. Makes me feel—"

Cooper sets his fork down and raises his hand lazily.

"Whitney, what's in that bag doesn't begin to compare with what you've given me. You, just being here, helping me work through all this shit with my knee, that's huge. Can't put that in a bag, babe. It's so much bigger than that."

He takes up his fork. "So, do me a favor and open your fucking present."

A snorting laugh escapes me, followed by a sigh, as I pull the bag into my lap and yank away the tissue paper obscuring the contents. Underneath the paper, I find clothing, in a gray fabric emblazoned with . . . squirrels.

Squirrels.

I pull them out and determine they're pajamas, a thermal-style top with bottoms to match. Once I have them in my hand, the fabric grazes my fingertips and a sudden urge to rub my face against the impossibly soft, supple material comes over me. So, I do what any classy woman would. I bury my potentially maple syrup–sticky face deeply into the softness and squirrels.

"Oh my God," I mumble through the press of the cloth.

Cooper laughs. "They're made of a cashmere blend. I thought they might keep you warmer at night than your old-man pj's. If I'm not there in bed with you, I don't want you getting cold."

I manage to extract my face from the pillowy softness and widen my eyes in his direction.

"Thank you. I'm sure I don't want to know what these cost or how many sweatshop workers were involved in their production, but I love them. And they have *squirrels* on them."

"I figured you would appreciate the squirrels. I'm glad you like them." Before I can kiss him as a thank-you, he dips his head and focuses on his plate. "Speaking of being in bed with you, I wanted to talk about my off-season."

"Talk away. I'll just continue to fondle this unicorn-

tear-and-leprechaun-giggle anointed fabric while you talk."
I give him a grin when he turns in my direction. He visibly
relaxes, shoulders loosening as he sits up straighter.

"We only have one more game, no hope for a post-
season at this point. After that I've got a few things to deal
with, but then I'll be officially off duty." His fork scrapes
across the plate as he takes a deep breath. "I'd like to come
down after that and spend the winter with you. In Hotchkiss."

My body reacts as soon as I process what he's saying,
turning tense under a rush of anxiety. Cooper notes the
change in my posture and turns his entire body so he's
facing me, head-on.

"I'm not trying to hijack your life or anything, and I can
help you while I'm there. I want to be productive. I need
to have something to focus on, otherwise I'll lose my mind
dwelling on the decision about retirement. I'm a quick
study, Whit. Teach me all about your orchard and, I swear,
I'll make myself useful."

Oh, my sweet, impossible, currently ignorant Cooper.

This is his freaking elevator pitch. Crafted to convince
me how helpful he could be. Now would be the time to
come clean. My jaw drops open, preparing to relay my
sad story, but before I can get one word out, Cooper looks
away. He's embarrassed and uncomfortable, seemingly
convinced that I don't see his value.

But the truth is just the opposite. When I confess to the
exact state of my affairs, *I'll* be the one who's embarrassed
and uncomfortable. Because it would hurt too much to see
one tiny flicker of recognition in Cooper's expression that

says he sees me as a failure. I would lose the backstop for my heart, the one he'd now become.

I can't risk it. I want to see him look at me as he did this morning, always—or, for at least as long as I can. The exact way he did when he said what we had was real.

I do the only thing I can. Sweep reality under the rug, just for now, until I have no other choice but to own up.

"Better bring your work gloves. Wouldn't want to damage those sixty-million-dollar hands of yours."

=25=

(Cooper)

We need bees. And chickens. Goats, maybe. But only if we can keep them from eating the yarrow. We'll need smart, highly trainable goats with a taste for bad weeds, but an aversion to cover crops. So, *magic* goats.

I scratch down the word *goats* in the margin of the book I'm reading, then underline it twice. Once it was settled that I would spend the winter in Hotchkiss, I decided to educate myself as much as possible on orchard management, organic practices, and biodynamics. Whitney watched *Friday Night Lights* to try to understand my world, but I've yet to find a well-crafted, heartwarming, poignant serial drama about organic apple farmers, so all I could do was order every book I could find on the topic.

The biodynamic crap will take me a bit of time. I'm from rural West Texas. Where the words *spiritual stewardship* and *holistic harvesting* aren't usually uttered, especially by farmers. Taking care of your soil? I get it. Honoring the wider cosmos? Not so much.

All my research has led to lists. Lists of things I want her to teach me more about. Lists of ideas I gleaned from my research, new endeavors she might want to consider next year. A list of supplies I suspect she hasn't been able to pay for lately, though I'm pretty sure she needs. But with one phone call, I'll be able to show up at her place bearing gifts only a girl like Whitney would appreciate. Another woman might turn up her nose at a truck bed full of surprises purchased at a co-op, but not Whitney.

I end up grinning broadly as I dial the number for the co-op, intent on giving Garrett free rein to burn up my credit card.

"Hotchkiss Co-op, Garrett speaking."

"Garrett. Cooper Lowry."

"Cooper! Good to hear from you, man. You in town? Braden and I are goose hunting this weekend—you can jump in if you want."

Christ, this kid and bird hunting. God help whatever woman manages to lure him into a love trap, because she'll have to get used to playing second chair to whatever feathered fowl is overhead.

"I'm not there yet, just trying to tie up some loose ends here in Denver. But I appreciate the offer. Next time?"

"Hell, there's always a next time. What can I do you for, then?"

I flip through my legal pad of notes and find the supply list I amassed. "I want to get some stuff for Whitney. If you don't have any of this in stock, I figured you could special-order it."

Garrett doesn't respond right away. When he does, his voice wavers a little.

"Stuff for the orchard?"

"Yeah. She uses you for most of the supplies she needs, right?"

Another pause. "Well, yeah, but . . ."

If I were there in person, I might be able to glare at him properly, because unless I'm crazy, he does work at a retail establishment where such supplies are for sale. This pussy-footing around while taking my order is weird. I flip the page on my supply list again, just to feel like I'm somehow prompting the conversation forward, even when I know the poor kid can't see what I'm doing.

"You ready? It's kind of a long list. More of that dormant oil; I'm sure we'll need to respray in the spring. Do you know anything about sweet alyssum? She's been using yarrow as a cover crop, but this other stuff seems like it might be a nice change. She can return it if she doesn't want it, right? A couple of new pairs of pruning shears, the best kind you can get. And some of the traps for codling moths. Maybe she doesn't need more, I don't know, but better to have them if she does."

"OK, um, Jesus. I don't know—"

"Dude, get a pen, write it down. You sound like you've never sold this stuff before."

I'm sure I was talking a mile a minute there. I take a calming breath and work to ratchet down my zeal a bit, before everyone in Hotchkiss decides to steer clear of the wacky football player who has decided to tackle apple farming like a defensive lineman on a stumbling quarterback.

"No, man. I just don't understand. Are you sure you want all this stuff? No need to throw good money at some other guy's setup. Let him do this stuff in the spring."

I narrow my eyes.

What. Other. Guy.

Cue the obnoxious alpha bullshit, because no other man will be in Whitney's orchard, literal or otherwise—not if I can help it.

I speak slowly, hoping he hears every word the first time so I don't have to holler. "Garrett, I'm going to need you to explain what you just said. Don't leave anything out."

"Fuck."

My thoughts exactly, kid. I grind my jaws together and try not to bark into the phone. Garrett sighs.

"Whitney's orchard is on the county foreclosure sale list that just came out. Her place is going to auction on the tenth. So unless you somehow fixed that in the last twelve hours, you're throwing money at a place where she won't be living soon."

Garrett's explanation takes a few moments for me to fully process. *Foreclosure. Auction.*

My gut starts to hurt when I finally take it all in, filter those words through what I already know and spin-dry the rest through what I *thought* I knew.

Fact: She needed a loan.

Fact: She wouldn't let me help her with that loan.

Fact: We fell in love.

Or so I thought. Maybe I was the only one who fell. Maybe I was showing her my underbelly, letting her scratch it while I nuzzled up against her, and she was just playing along. Maybe I was thinking about how to put down roots, while she was figuring out how to pull up stakes.

"Sorry." Garrett offers, likely hoping to fill the awkward silence with *something*, just so he doesn't have to listen to my unsteady breathing anymore. "I have no idea why I'm the one telling you this instead of her. But that girl's got pride, you know? Dirt-under-your-nails country pride. I'm sure this isn't easy for her to talk about."

He mutters another apology and I manage to work my way through an obligatory thank-you before hanging up. When I drop the phone onto the coffee table, it clatters loudly.

The *tenth*.

If Whitney was planning to let me in on this shit, she was taking it to the wire. Unless that wasn't the case. Maybe she had no intention at all of sharing this with me. Maybe I was going to drive down there and find that she'd bailed, no beater truck in the driveway, nothing but a swinging screen door and the faint scent of coconut in an empty house.

Anger rushes through my body before I can rationalize it away. There were a million moments when she could have told me, when Whitney could have looked me in the eye and trusted me with this—the same way I've trusted her to be my safe space. So much that she was at the front of my mind as I walked the sidelines during the last game of the season.

When the fourth-quarter clock counted down to a win, I stayed rooted in place, refusing to look away from the scene in front of me. I wanted to soak up the moment, make sure I was *right there* as it came to an end. All the noise. The scent of crisp mile-high air and success. The way the sun sets behind the upper decks of the stadium, blue and magenta, bright and beautiful.

The idea of leaving behind that part of my life? It hurt. Hurt big and deep and hard.

But I had a future. A future that was supposedly waiting for me in Hotchkiss.

―――――

Two hours later I'm at our team headquarters, reporting on time to my end-of-year assessment appointment. Inside the training room, it reeks of sweat, salt, and menthol. I drop my gym bag on the floor and swing up onto a padded table to wait for Hunt. He's still in his office, on the phone, pacing the way he does when he's trying to figure something out. A stress ball is in his left hand, at work under the flex of his fingers. He catches my eye and nods.

After another few words, he hangs up the phone and heads my way, shutting the door to his office behind him. Hunt pulls a file off the wall and flips it open, scans a sheet inside, and takes a ballpoint pen from his shirt pocket, yanking the cap off with his teeth.

"How's your hamstring?"

Fucking Hunt. No hello, no mindless small talk. Always straight to the goddam point.

"Fine."

"Any concussion-like symptoms? Headaches, nausea, vision problems, trouble sleeping, or balance issues?"

"Nope."

"The knee?"

"Still fucked up." Hunt undoes the clasps on my brace and rolls up my track pants, then proceeds to poke and prod at the remaining bruised areas on my knee.

He jots a few notes down and keeps his eyes on the file. "Have you made a decision on surgery yet?"

"No."

"Any other injuries you'd like to discuss or have noted in your exit assessment?"

"No."

Hunt lets his pen hover just above the page and I know what's coming as well as he does. Based on his hesitation, Hunt already knows that for the first time in my career, the answer won't come easy.

"Do you consider yourself fit to play football?"

Yes. I try to get the word out, force it into the universe and demand that any doubt I'm struggling with just vaporize, and recommit myself to the only life I've ever known. But doubt is all I have right now. Doubt about this job, doubt about Whitney, doubt about what's next.

I grit my teeth together and look over Hunt's shoulder. He repeats the question.

Finally, I give him the only answer I can. The one that leaves a door open to this life, the word that will give me, at the very least, options.

"Yes."

Hunt makes note of my answer and hands the form my way. I sign where I always do, but this time, with a shaky hand I've never had before.

My file flips closed and Hunt goes to place it back with the others.

"Now that we have that out of the way, how about you cut the bullshit? You still want this, Lowry?"

The sensation of crumbling inside takes over and all that doubt I've worked to keep in check begins seeping through every fissure in my body, leaving weakness in its wake. Too many places on my body are broken—from my limbs and ligaments to my heart and soul.

"I don't know."

"What about the girl? Does she have a dog in this fight? Because take it from a man who's been married for a while, they're usually right. Women analyze all the working parts of a problem before they decide what to do. If she's giving you her opinion, I'd listen to it."

I let out a snort. "I thought she did. But as of this morning, it seems she's failed to clue me in on the results of her deep fucking analysis of the problem." Hunt creases his forehead. I roll down my pant leg and reset the brace. "Are we done here?"

When he doesn't say anything, I grab my bag and head for the door, but before I clear the room, he calls out to stop me. I halt in place but don't turn his way. If I do, I'll break.

"Eight years, kid. That's how long we've known each other. And not once in those eight years have I ever seen you back down from a challenge. Not from a loss or an injury, a bad game or a tough team."

He pauses.

"Don't start now. Do what you do best, Lowry. Knuckle

down and figure out a fix. Whatever you do, don't back down, not until you're positive that this is worth walking away from."

The door to his office shuts with a click. I can't decide if I want to storm in there and tell him exactly where to shove his wise words or just clear the building before I put my fist through one of these gleaming trophy cases that line the walls.

What's worse is that he's right. I've never let a challenge stand in my way. I gave Hunt that *yes* because I wanted options. And if Whitney thinks I'm about to walk away without being damn sure I've stood up to the challenge of loving her, she's out of her beautiful, stubborn, crazy mind.

═══════

When I step outside team headquarters, my chest remains tight. Hunt may have reminded me what I'm made of, but that doesn't mean I'm any less fucked up or pissed off. My knee hurts worse than usual today and now I have a screaming headache to match. I pause under the front-door canopy and adjust the shoulder strap on my gym bag, hoping that will lessen the tension radiating from around my neck.

When I look up, my day continues to go to shit.

Bodie Carmichael and his cameraman are just feet away, scuttling in my direction with almost bloodthirsty intention. Bodie slows and lets his cameraman catch up, then they both approach in step, stopping far too close to me. He doesn't even bother to ask for permission before launching in.

"Good to see you up and around, Lowry." I nod, putting a death grip on the shoulder strap I still have clasped in one hand. Then he does his *thing*. The obnoxious hair-slicking-and-smirking thing.

"So, Coop." He pauses, tilting his head as if he knows my answer will be sound bite–worthy.

"What's next?"

=26=

(Whitney)

At home, Mother Nature turns the weather bitter cold. Frost ripples across all the branches of my trees and snow remains piled up in the aisles between rows.

It's too frigid for pruning, so I've taken up a spot on my couch for the day, reading while nestled in among a pile of blankets, praying the woodstove will do its job and warm up the house. I'm also awaiting a call from Cooper. His exit assessment with the team trainer is scheduled for today and once it's finished, he's supposed to call me with a plan. I've decided that today is the day. When he calls, I'm going to own up to everything.

The doorbell rings and a glance out my front window reveals my ever-tenacious postal carrier on the porch. He's still rocking his pith-style safari hat, despite the snow swirling around him today and the icicles hanging from my porch.

I unearth myself from the mass of blankets and make my way to the door, giving a good yank to open it.

"Whitney Reed?"

"The one and only."

He smiles and shoves forward a small clipboard. "Need you to sign for this one."

I scrawl my name where he indicates.

"Here you go." He hands an official-looking envelope my way, then slips a pile of regular mail out of his bag, wrapped up with a rubber band. He passes off the second batch. "Thanks. Stay warm."

For a man well into his sixties, the postal carrier is surprisingly lithe, skipping down my porch steps and trotting to his Jeep, before firing it up and backing down the driveway in record time.

I flop back down on the couch and open the important envelope first. Nothing but another *this is not a drill* letter to remind me that, short of a miracle, in a few days I'll be without a place to call my own. The other stack is mostly junk: a coupon book, two catalogs, and some flyers from insurance agents. But at the bottom are two letters with return addresses I recognize. The bank in Rifle and the slow money venture in Boulder. My heart starts to beat wildly.

Ripping open the first envelope, I scan the opening sentences.

> *Thank you for your application. Unfortunately, we are unable to offer financing . . .*

I drop the letter on the coffee table and lean back, trying to quell the rush of disappointment that's threatening to flood my heart—knowing a sliver of hope remains in the other envelope. With one deep breath and a prayer, I grab it and slide a finger under the flap to tear it open.

> *Thank you for the recent inquiry. Based on the information provided, we must decline your application . . .*

Defeat settles, swift and ruthless. Then a rumble of rejection follows and I'm suddenly exhausted. I held out hope for so long that knowing I've met the end of the road is enough to make my entire body weaken.

No more games. I'm out of prospects and options. Time to start figuring out what's next.

———

A day after my friendly postal carrier delivered the rejection letters, I decide to spend the morning rummaging for empty boxes behind a liquor store. Because I need boxes to pack up my things. And because this sort of thing is *always* a treat.

I spot a large box, much bigger than most of what I've found, crammed in behind the gigantic metal trash container. Why does it have to be *behind* the bin, so close to the ungodly aroma that indicates it's sorely due to be emptied? Because the universe is wholly aligned against me, I think.

I take a deep breath. Bending my knees, I slouch down to clear the large lid that's flipped back and propped against the cinder-block building, then shuffle a few steps toward my cardboard prize. Given my awkward position, the way

I'm diving straight into the smell, it's like I'm engaged in a rank round of Twister. Still, I manage to latch on to one of the box flaps and give it a yank. It tears. Doesn't move a fraction, doesn't come my way. Just rips open, right down one of the seams. Of course.

Giving up, I step back, close my eyes, and put one hand to my forehead. I try to drown out the loud rumble of a truck that sounds near enough to run me over, but when the scent of diesel replaces the garbage aroma, for the first time ever, the smell of motor oil and environmental toxins becomes a soothing salve. *Thank you, oh great American auto manufacturers, for all that you do.*

"A little early for scavenging, isn't it?"

My eyes flip open. The liquor store's neighbor happens to be the co-op. Which means the truck is Garrett's. It is definitely a diesel, and probably twenty years old, with oxidized paint so faded you'd swear you can see the bare sheet metal underneath. It's lifted and loud, personalized by a variety of hunting brand stickers on the side glasses, and has both a headache rack *and* a shotgun rack.

I came early to do my foraging, hoping to avoid a run-in with the penny-pinching guy that owns the liquor store, but neglected to factor in the possibility of crossing paths with Garrett as he arrived for work. He slams the door on his truck and sets his coffee cup on the top of the bedside.

I force a smile. "Oh, no. It's *never* too early for this kind of fun."

Garrett casts a glance toward my truck and notes the open topper, and the few boxes already tossed in the back. I don't have to explain why I need the boxes. He, along with everyone else in town, likely saw my name and property listed among all the formal sale notices in the legal section of our small local newspaper. In my youth, I always wanted to do something interesting enough to warrant my name appearing in the paper, but this is so not how I imagined it.

Garrett strides over and tosses a few boxes around, inspecting them.

"I hate the fact you won't be around here anymore, Whitney. It was nice having some new flavor in town. But Denver isn't too far. Maybe you and Cooper will come visit?"

Cooper. A wave of dizziness hits and I sway a little in place.

He never called yesterday. I also did not take the initiative and call him. I simply couldn't muster the follow-through required. Instead, I made some tea. Ate a few ginger cookies. Watched mindlessly silly cat videos on my laptop. All in all, I made an Olympic sport out of avoiding the whole damn thing.

My vertigo spell drives Garrett to place a hand under my elbow. "Crap. You look like you're about to pass out. Sorry, I take it back—you don't have to come visit. I'll just keep you as a beautiful, hippie, tree-hugging memory."

He drops the tailgate on my truck and gestures for me to come sit down. I shimmy up. "Don't apologize. It's just that Cooper doesn't exactly know about the auction sale."

Garrett runs his hand over his mouth and stares straight ahead, his jaw slack. "Fuck."

"I know, I know. I'm going to tell him."

"No. That's not what I meant." He rubs his temples with the tips of his index fingers. "He already knows. He called yesterday and wanted to buy out the co-op with supplies for your place. I know he's got more money than God, but I couldn't just let him buy all that stuff; it felt wrong. So I told him."

My eyes narrow slightly as I take in Garrett's words. *Thunk, thunk, thunk.* All the pieces start to fall into place.

Cooper knows. That explains why he didn't call yesterday, because he now knows exactly what a screw-up I am. He knows I'm about to be jobless, homeless, and aimless. Given his ever-ambitious nature, I'm sure hitching his horse to my broke-down wagon scares the hell out of him. As if all that isn't bad enough, I was too busy dodging reality and he had to hear it from someone else.

I nod slowly, and when Garrett grasps the resignation in my demeanor, he drops his head into his hands and groans. I pat his leg.

"Stop groaning, Garrett. This is my screw-up. All me."

Garrett drags his hands away from his face.

"I have no clue why I ended up in the middle of this shit with you two, because I haven't had a girlfriend since high school and I'm the last person who should give anyone advice on much of anything. But if my girlfriend kept this kind of thing from me it would cut. And cut deep. Nothing worse than feeling like the girl you love is lying to you."

"I didn't lie. I was just a little selective with the details. He has enough going on; I didn't need to dump my problems on his doorstep."

Garrett sighs loudly. "Whitney. He probably *wanted* you to dump your problems on his doorstep. Fixing shit is good for the ego."

He swings down off my tailgate and adjusts his ball cap.

"My mom watches *Dr. Phil*, like, all the fucking time. As a result, I have to listen to her recap the episodes whenever I visit. And I'm about to put verbs in my sentences, Johnny Appleseed."

Garrett tilts his chin down to lock his eyes on mine, ensuring that he has my attention. For the first time ever, the contented and happy-go-lucky Garrett I'm used to has taken leave. His usual half-grin is gone, replaced by a tight-set jaw.

"I'd bet my truck on the fact that Cooper fucking Lowry would do anything for you. Including stepping in to fix this. Because I guarantee you this . . . helping you isn't a burden. But you shutting him out? That's probably killing him."

Garrett's eyes go from hurt to hard.

"You have options, Whitney. That's huge. I'd have given anything for the same when my dad died. Don't fucking waste what you've got sitting right in front of you, because trust me, losing your land—your dirt—it's hard to take. You can't wash it off, even when it's gone."

———

With my truck bed full of empty boxes, I drive home and call Cooper. He doesn't answer. Can't exactly be surprised by that.

On his voicemail, I do my best to explain myself.

"Cooper? It's Whitney. Crap, I don't know why I just said that. You know it's me. Anyway, let me start with the obvious. I'm sorry. I'm so sorry you had to find out this way—I didn't mean for that to happen. I want to talk, but . . . let me deal with this part first, OK? After that . . . once I figure out who I am after this is over . . . we'll talk."

=27=

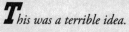

This was a terrible idea.

Why I thought it would be emotionally healthy to drive to Delta and observe the auction proceedings is beyond me. A macabre curiosity is the only reasonable explanation, and I had convinced myself that satisfying it was important if I wanted to be able to move on.

This way I would be able to see the buyer, and maybe if I was lucky, decide that they looked like a good sort of people. No matter the mechanics of how it was going down, letting go of my trees was heart wrenching and knowing they would be in capable, trustworthy hands was small solace, but one I'd gladly take. If I was brave, I might also approach the buyer and ask if I could pay a little bit of rent and stay until the end of the month.

After that? I was still considering my next move. A job with Justin in Fruita was a possibility. As was relocating to Boulder, where there were plenty of thriving organic farms that might need help. I would be closer to Cooper, but still on my own—which was important. Once all of this had played out, once the foreclosure was complete and I was set on my next move, then we would talk. But he didn't need to play rescuer and I didn't need to be saved. What I needed was to know I'd shouldered this on my own, like a grown woman. Then Cooper could decide if *that* woman—warts and fiascos and all—was who he truly wanted. It would be cleaner that way. Easier.

It's a good story anyway.

My boots squeak on the industrial linoleum floor, wet from the heavy sleet coming down outside. The weather forced today's sale indoors, into a second-floor meeting room at the Delta County Courthouse, moved from its original location outside on the courthouse steps. I clear the last flight of stairs and head down a long hallway, following the sound of voices in an otherwise quiet space. Room 210 is at the end, with the door propped open and a few people leaning against the wall just outside. I tip my head to one side and try to peek in. The room is small, and with fifteen people packed inside, it's even harder to see and hear what's going on.

An older gentleman wearing a gray Stetson, a thread-bare dress shirt, and cowboy-cut polyester pants steps back a few feet from where he was leaning with one shoulder to the wall. He points to the space where he was and gestures for me to take his place. Given that he's at least a foot taller than me, I can easily slip in there without being in his way. I whisper a thank-you as I step forward and he nods once, a faint smile on his face.

Maybe *he'll* buy my orchard. I think I might be OK with that. Sort of.

"Up next . . ." A woman's voice, clear and raised to project as best she can. The sound of shuffling papers fills the pause. "79562 County Road 56. Hotchkiss. Ten acres, one-bedroom, one-bath house, built in 1908."

My heart wants to slam through my chest. More paper shuffling. The woman calls to open the bidding.

Then there's silence. Maybe fifteen or twenty seconds, but for those moments I'm suddenly irate. As twisted as it sounds, I'm offended that there isn't a veritable bidding war going on. Do these people not understand? My place is gorgeous, from winter through fall, in the daylight and darkness. Sure, the house is a decrepit, drafty thing, but it's also a hundred-plus years old. A hundred years of life and love have taken place within those walls. Marriages and children, heartache of the best and worst kind. And the trees. For God's sake, the trees are—

"Three hundred thousand."

My internal rant screeches to a stop.

That voice. The one I know too well, not just from its pitch or tone, but from the way it *feels* when I hear it.

Before I can stop myself, I've elbowed and stomped my way into the room. Cooper has a ball cap tugged down low on his head, then a bulky hooded sweatshirt, and a pair of faded jeans that are tucked into his Danner boots. The woman running the auction sweeps her gaze to me— it would be impossible to ignore my pushy, theatrical entrance—and Cooper's body visibly stiffens.

Then he turns his head, slowly and only enough to

see me. My jaw goes slack, because he's here, he looks exhausted, and he's clearly pissed. Which makes sense, because he just paid *way* too much money for my orchard.

Cooper says my name so quietly it sounds like we're alone, in his bed or mine, and that means I feel naked and armor-less. I can't do this. Not here, not now. I'm out the door and down the steps so quickly the heavy slap of my boots to the floor echoes loudly through the building. When I shove open the front doors, the sleet immediately starts to dampen my face.

"Whitney!"

Cooper certainly isn't whispering now. Far from it, but the raw vulnerability I'm dealing with means that no matter whether he's whispering or hollering, I'm not prepared for, either.

My truck is within spitting distance, so I slow my gallop and dig into my bag for the keys, letting out a growl when they don't immediately fall into my hand. Unfortunately, even with a screwed-up knee, Cooper's long legs give him an advantage. I shake my bag from side to side and start to track the sound of jangling keys, just as he comes up behind me.

"You're going to take off? Good plan, Whit. Fucking brilliant way to deal with this shit."

Spite and anger run deep through his words. I drop my arms and let the bag swing, resigned, because whether I wanted this or not, I know he's right. If anyone is entitled to feeling a little sideswiped, it's Cooper. He mutters a few more curse words before I hear him take a long inhale. If

I could see his face, I'd guess he was working hard to keep from saying more right now.

Cooper steps around me and some of the sleet has collected on the bill of his hat. The anger in his voice isn't a part of his expression; all that's there is the strangest mix of detachment and sadness, his eyes almost emotionless. Cooper holds his own car keys up and gives a chin nudge to the parking spot only a few spaces over, where his truck sits. I should really work on sharpening my observational skills. Walked right past that beast.

He tilts his head in the direction of the truck again. "Let's talk in the truck."

I follow him the few steps required and he opens my door. I heave myself into the seat and slump down. Cooper gets in, sets the key in the ignition with a half-turn, then reaches over to turn on my heated seat.

Small gesture. Big ol' sucker punch to my heart.

Keeping my gaze trained out the windshield, I sigh. "You paid way too much. Like, twice what it's worth."

Cooper tosses a sleet-spotted manila envelope on the dash.

"That's how you want to open this conversation? No apology? No explanation? You're fucking crazy, you know that?" The rant hangs between us for a moment before Cooper lets out a defeated grunt and pinches the bridge of his nose with two fingers. "Sorry. Christ, I can't stand being pissed at you. I hate this."

"Don't apologize. I know that all of this is my fault. I'm the one who's sorry."

I let my gaze drift to Cooper, and it's clear he doesn't

know what to say next. He scrubs both hands over his face, the tips of his fingers lifting his ball cap up until he grasps the bill to adjust it lower on his forehead.

"I had a plan, Whitney."

Of course. There's the real problem. Cooper had a plan and I fucked with his precious need for control. Sarcasm creeps into my voice even when I know it shouldn't.

"Yeah? God forbid I mess with that. Please, tell me all about your plan."

His tone is flat. "Simple. You and me, a bunch of apple trees, and some magic goats. Happily ever after. Simple plan."

"Magic goats?"

"Yes. Magic fucking goats." He fixes his jaw into such a hard line that I can see his cheek flex. Probably not a good idea to ask him to explain the goats. Cooper slouches into his seat, deeply enough that his bent knees bump either side of the steering wheel.

"I need to know why, Whit. Why you kept this from me. Why I trusted you with all of my shit, but you couldn't trust me with yours."

All my sarcastic resentment washes away in an instant. He thinks this was a reflection on him, something he was lacking that compelled me to keep this quiet. Now I get to add guilt to the list of emotions I can't seem to outrun today. If only I had enough bandwidth left to properly deal with any of it.

I let my head tip to one side, far enough to rest against the door glass.

"This was never about trust or *you*, Cooper. In the beginning, it was exactly what I said—that this was my problem. And, up until a week ago, I was still deluded enough to think it would all somehow work out." I take a long inhale. "After a certain point, I couldn't tell you. You're *so* focused, *so* successful. You wouldn't be able to see me as anything but a screw-up who had her property foreclosed on."

Cooper's voice goes hoarse for a moment.

"Jesus, I don't even know where to start. I wouldn't see you that way. I don't. Because you aren't a screw-up, you're a new business owner trying to make it in an industry with long odds. I don't know why you think I wouldn't be able to understand that. And you didn't even give me the fucking opportunity to step up and prove it, show you how I feel."

I keep my mouth tightly clamped shut. Even if I tried to find some words, they wouldn't be right. Also, my eyes are busy watering and it will require all of my focus to keep the dam from breaking. Cooper slides the manila envelope off the dash and sets it on the console between us.

"Technically, I'm your landlord now. But in that envelope are draft documents my attorney put together and I want you to take a look at them. One is a business agreement that would make us partners. I'll retire and we'll start a life together, buy some more apple trees and maybe make a few babies. And I'll probably want a dog. Maybe two."

Cooper lets his head fall back to meet the headrest and closes his eyes.

"The other is a quitclaim deed. If you want, I'll just sign over the property to you, free and clear. I'll let you be, to do this on your own. No strings attached."

I try to understand what he just said, all of what he's offering me, and the possibility that he would just walk away
from the boatload of cash he just forked over. "What? Why
would you do that?"

"Because of that voicemail you left me. I know exactly
how it feels to lose what defines you. Everything I've been
feeling over the last few months? Losing my career? I heard
the same thing in your voice." Cooper pauses, then lets
out a sigh.

"That's why I did all of this, Whitney. I mean, I want
you, and I want us, but I didn't call my attorney at midnight to deal with the specifics, then drive down here in a
snowstorm, and pay double the value for your orchard, so
I could win you over like this is some stupid movie. I just
didn't want you to lose your land."

I place one of my palms to my forehead, curious if the
swell of heat and emotion I'm feeling is actually causing
my temperature to spike or if it's just a trick of the heart.
Because if I were the girl I used to be, the one who thrived
on doing what felt good in the moment, I'd have crawled
over the console at the mention of babies and a life together. My heart's decided it wants Cooper, without any
hesitation.

But I'm not that girl anymore. She would have already declared herself, loudly and joyfully, without any
thought to what it would take to make this work. The
woman I am now, the one with a few more years under
her belt and a heart that wants to take root in the right
place, under the right circumstances? She has to think
first, then leap.

Cooper clears his throat lightly, a nervous tic, before he speaks again. "I'm headed home to Texas for a couple of weeks, so take your time deciding. For the record, I want us to be partners. I never wanted anything else."

He tips his head wearily and locks his gaze on mine.

"But I need you to be sure. I've spent most of my life doing one thing, given it everything I had in me. I'm hard-wired for that kind of focus. So, whatever comes next?"

Cooper blinks once, looks over my shoulder at nothing.

"It has to be forever."

In a twist of fool's fate, it seems I got exactly what I wanted out of this trip.

I met the new owner. He was good people, no doubt.

And his hands? More than capable.

=28=

(Cooper)

Texas forever.

That was my first thought this morning as I fired up the Mule and started down a dirt road leading away from my parents' house. Essentially, I've become a walking, barely talking, breathing *Friday Night Lights* cliché.

Part Riggins (the brooding), part Smash (the knee), and just enough Saracen (the fucking *pining*) to mean that someone should just shoot me. Looking back, it was not the best choice to start streaming the series right after I arrived home from the auction sale in Delta; I was too raw for all that sentimentality. Season one and too many beers later, I was about one more emotional scene away from drunk-dialing Whitney and begging her to choose what I believed was the only viable option. Us. Together in every way imaginable.

Thankfully, I was wasted enough that finding my phone seemed like too much of a challenge. I turned the TV off and went to bed, only to start watching the damn show again in the morning, fitting in two more episodes before I loaded my truck and pointed it south on the interstate for the six-hour drive to my hometown.

Instead of a Coach Taylor, though, I have my dad. While he might not speak in motivational pull quotes, his intuition is just as rock solid. Which is why I've spent all day, miles away from the house, fixing fence and checking water gaps—by myself.

I've been back home for two weeks now and as always, my dad knows when to send me out solo with nothing but a task list and the proper tools. When I was a kid, he would sometimes set me up outside with pieces of scrap wood, some janky nails, a kid-sized hammer, and vague instructions to nail everything together. I'm sure recognizing my need for a physical distraction from whatever was going in my head is part of the psychic-radar phenomenon that comes with parenting, but his is especially fine-tuned.

I tuck the fence pliers between my upper arm and torso, then let the barbed-wire splice sleeve clenched between my teeth fall into one hand, setting it in place to secure the two ends of wire. Using the pliers, I crimp the splice into place and give it a tug, ensuring it's fastened down. I remove the fence stretcher and toss it in the rear cargo box of the UTV, then dump in the rest of my tools and supplies, drop the lid, and let the latches fall into place. Wiping my forehead with the back of one work glove, I settle my gaze on the long horizon off to the east.

My family's ranch is what most city dwellers would imagine when conjuring up a vision of Texas. Especially here, a far corner of our winter grazing pasture, where our property meets up with public lands. It's the desolate kind of landscape that appears flat but isn't, except by Colorado standards. Native short grasses dominate, with only the occasional oak motte to break up what can sometimes look overwhelmingly beige. Still, despite all that brown, it's beautiful. Not in the way that Whitney's orchard is, but in its own rugged, tumbleweed-bleak way.

I move to slip in behind the steering wheel of the UTV and fire it up, pausing when my phone chimes loudly from my back pocket.

Oh, look. Guess who it isn't? Whitney.

A round of cuss words rattles silently around in my brain, as I rake myself over the coals for indulging in that hope yet again.

Instead it's a text from Mikey.

> If you could kindly get your dumb ass back here sometime this century, the rest of us would like to eat. Mom says we have to wait for Jujube.

I let out a snort. I may be the calorie-conquering athlete of the bunch, but no Lowry appreciates having a mealtime fucked with. Especially when it comes to Sunday dinner. I shoot him a text back.

> Missing a meal wouldn't kill you. Tell Mom her favorite kid will be there in 15.

When I pull to a stop at the back of the house, all my brothers' trucks are there, and the sight of those shiny rigs means I'm thinking about Whitney again. What she would say if she were here, riding up to the house next to me, sitting shotgun while wearing a grin, and sporting the beginnings of a sunburn on her nose from helping me with the fences.

"Jesus. Did they shoot any episodes of Dallas *here? Where's J.R. Ewing? I know all of you are very busy depleting the earth of its valuable resources, but he must be here somewhere."*

I'd laugh. Maybe kiss her and pluck a stray hunk of scrub oak out of her hair, ensuring she sees when I do, just so she remembers why it's there in the first place. Because fixing fence can be boring. The best way to relieve that boredom would be to put the dusty cargo box bed to good use by persuading Whitney to lie down on her back in it. She might even blush if I cast a knowing look at her tits, then back at the scrub oak twig.

Fucking perfect, now I'm half-hard. Inconvenient time for daydreaming about a woman who hasn't yet decided what the hell she wants to do with me, or do in general. Tossing my work gloves down on the seat, I untuck my T-shirt and pray that walking into my parents' house has the same effect it routinely did back in the day, by withering an erection in record time.

Inside, the sound of fourteen voices—six of them belonging to children—fills the house. I stop in the mudroom and untie my boots, leaving them next to the others already there. The kitchen smells like every Sunday of my childhood: honey-glazed ham and scalloped potatoes, plenty of whomp biscuits, and something sweet. Cobbler or pie, maybe a poke cake, if we're lucky.

"Finally." Mikey leans back in his chair and throws his hands up, waving me into the dining room. "Hurry up and sit down before I die of starv—"

"Wash your hands first."

Mikey groans when Mom cuts him off. I give him a shit-eating grin and shrug my shoulders, meandering back toward the kitchen sink as slowly as I can. I lather my hands like I'm a cardiac surgeon scrubbing in, dry them laboriously, and then finally slip back into the dining room to take my seat between Mikey and his oldest daughter, Amelia. A crowd of faces watches my approach while still managing to carry on at least nine different conversations. I barely get a napkin into my lap before Mikey passes the platter of ham my way.

My brother Caleb's wife, Kellie, once said our family looks like what would happen if a Viking ship crash-landed ashore in the middle of a Carhartt photo shoot, which always seemed the most accurate way anyone has described our particular brand of bellowing, blue-eyed, blond, and burly. The dinner table seats ten and Kellie is the lone brunette present. Even the kids, the rest of whom are already eating while crammed in around a card table set up in the living room, are all little towheaded lovable terrors.

"Fences good?"

My dad cuts a quick look in my direction before handing a basket of biscuits off to Matty, who puts one on his plate and reaches for another. His wife, Jana, raises a brow and he yanks his hand back. Jana is four and a half months along now, which means her naturally whip-thin frame is definitely showing, but this time around, she looks healthy and strong. Matty, on the other hand, looks like he's two breaths away from letting his brawny Viking heart swell right up and out of his chest.

I put a second scoopful of potatoes on my plate—I'm off-season, considering retirement, and miserable, so my usual ultra-clean diet can just go fuck itself.

"Yeah. I didn't make it over to that far north boundary line to check water gaps, though."

"Tomorrow?"

"I'll get over there early."

Forks clink and knives drag across dinner plates as everyone starts to dig in. Caleb cracks the tab on his Keystone, taking a large swig before swallowing it down slowly.

"Christ, are you on the run from something back in Denver? Knock over a convenience store, Pooper? Because you don't act like you're going home any time soon."

The four grown women at the table sigh and groan and shush him in unison. Kellie jabs her index finger into his side. He takes another drink and surveys the female faces around him, his own becoming perplexed. "What?"

Another round of sighs. Mom redirects the conversation to the grandkids without even a hiccup, each of my sisters-in-law chiming in. Her mom-radar is even sharper than my dad's, and more attuned to the annoying, soft organs inside my chest. Despite my not sharing any details, not even so much as a passing comment about things being unsettled with Whit, my mom knows something is up. And it seems she's shared her suspicions with the rest of the henhouse. Probably during a summit meeting of sorts in the kitchen, each of the women *tsk-*

ing and clucking their tongues at my pathetic state of being.

We make it to dessert by discussing everything but me. But after inhaling a slab of poke cake, Mikey leans farther in his chair and arches his back to drop a few satisfied pats to his belly, then his eyes light up.

"Oh, hey, I almost forgot about this. Coop, I finished the mock-up for Whitney's website. Amelia, sweetheart, go grab my iPad out of the truck." Amelia is up and all the way to the door before my mom interjects.

"Michael, none of those things at the table."

"Ma, we're not screwing around—this is for his girlfriend's orchard. It's *business*."

Her gaze slants over to me, hedging to see if I'm about to crack or something. "Still, I don't like it."

I drop my napkin to the tablecloth and wave one hand in the air. All the ladies turn half-sad, half-pitying eyes my way. "It's fine."

Mikey pats his belly again. "No, it's not fine. It's *awesome*. Wait till you see it—I'm an artistic genius."

The back door slams shut and Amelia skip-jogs into the room, dropping the tablet into Mikey's waiting hands. He flips the cover open and scrolls through a few pages, then hands it my way with a grin. It doesn't take more than one glance to see that he's right. He's an artistic fucking genius.

At the top of the home page is a newly designed logo, with *Delaney Creek* in a font that mimics hand-painted brushstrokes. There's a touch of femininity in the script style, but the dark cobalt color he's chosen keeps it from looking too busy, especially with the whitewash effect he's applied to give it an antiqued feel. *Orchards* is typeset in a bold, modern font in dark chocolate brown. Hovering behind the type is the silhouette of an apple tree, so minimalist it doesn't dominate, yet somehow evokes all the tenets of biodynamics that Whitney believes in. My jaw goes slack when I realize how perfect this is and how much Whitney would love it.

Mikey leans over and clicks through another few pages, pointing out where we'll need to add text and those areas where he thinks we should add pictures from the orchard. He navigates to a page designed for Whit's bio, gleefully pointing out where he's inserted a picture of me in the spot where hers should be.

I was five years old and sitting on Santa's lap, bawling my eyes out. I'm red-faced and blubbering, with strings of spittle stretching across my wide-open wailing mouth. At the bottom of the photo, he's added a caption.

Insert photo of woman crazy enough to choose THIS GUY.

He starts to snort, laughing so loudly that Caleb and Matty launch out of their chairs and join in when they see what he's done. I force a grin, flipping them off with a strained chuckle that's the best I can manage because inside, I feel a lot like the kid in that picture.

Irony has truly made me her bitch. If they only knew. Whitney *hasn't* chosen me.

=29=

(Whitney)

At this point, I might have better luck finishing this tree pruning with a kindergartner's pair of cut-and-paste scissors. My long-handled pruning shears are officially dull.

Not unexpected since I've asked a lot of these shears over the last two weeks. I worked my way through most of the tree rows, honing each branch into a veritable work of art. But it was more than busywork: proper pruning means allowing each limb to get the right amount of sunlight, while also thinning them enough to keep the trees from overproducing fruit, which can lead to anemic product and disease. And thanks to Cooper, I now have more seasons ahead of me, so keeping my trees healthy and productive is vital.

But these shears need some love. I've attempted to sharpen them myself, but either my technique or my tools aren't up to snuff. It's time to let a professional have at it. Time for Garrett.

A quick drive into town and I find the co-op parking

lot nearly empty. Garrett and I haven't spoken since his Dr. Phil speech. Here's hoping his rural sensibilities will keep him from asking any particularly pointed questions, since I don't even have all the answers for myself yet.

He's on the phone when I step in, but he gives a wave and smile. I set my pruning shears on the counter and flip through a stray farm catalog that's tossed in a pile nearby. Garrett wraps up the call, then shoves the phone under the counter.

"Johnny, long time no see." He gives me an easy, but curious, look. "Things going OK?"

Closing the farm catalog, I set it back where it was. "Meh. OK, yes. But that's about the best of it."

Garrett picks up the shears and runs his thumb over the edge of one blade.

"Have you been pruning T-posts with these? Jesus."

"That's why I'm here. Do you think you can do anything with them?"

He squints to get a closer look. "I'll try, but these can be tricky. Give me a minute and I'll run them over the blade in back."

Garrett wanders toward the back, then disappears behind a stack of boxes towering in the storage room. I hear a machine whir to life and the sound of metal grazing over a sharpening stone. I grab another farm catalog and skim a few pages before setting it back down when nothing interests me.

A television set is mounted to the wall above the front counter, tuned to a sports station that's reporting on golf, with the volume turned down low enough that there's only the faint sound of polite clapping from people interested enough in golf that they would actually attend a tournament. Being that I've gone without a television for years, I can't imagine why I would want or need one at my place of business, but having seen Garrett's boss a time or two, perhaps it makes sense. He looks like he might spend most of his non-working hours perched in a comfortable recliner, talking about all the ways such-and-such athletes could perform their jobs better.

Coverage of the tournament cuts for a commercial break. After various spots for male demographic–targeted products, a raven-haired anchorwoman appears on the screen to report the day's sports highlights. After only a few clips of an MMA fight, I'm nearly bored enough to look away.

Then Cooper's face appears in the little box to the right of the anchor's head. It's his team head shot, the one where he looks especially unfriendly. The low volume means I can't make out what the anchorwoman is saying, so I start to shuffle through the masses of junk on the front counter, looking for a remote control. Finally, it peeks out from underneath a modern-day-useless phone book. I grab the remote and begin to jab at the button to turn up the sound, just as a clip of Cooper starts to play.

He's outside his team headquarters, glowering and grasping the strap of his gym bag like he's considering the best way to use it as a weapon. The profile of a reporter peeks into the screenshot as he makes his way over to Cooper at a dead trot.

No. Shit, shit, shit. It's Bodie Carmichael. Cooper hates

this guy—even more that he hates the rest of the media. There's an immediate instinct to swoop in on a rescue mission. I just don't know who I should save first: Cooper or the greasy reporter who's one nosy question away from a fat lip.

Bodie makes it to within a few feet of Cooper. Cooper looks up and his already stony face grows darker.

"Good to see you up and around, Lowry."

Cooper nods. Then Bodie poses a simple question, one any seasoned athlete should be able to answer while still giving up nothing.

"What's next?"

I hold my breath and wait for the screen to go black when Cooper inevitably decks anyone within swinging distance. But he doesn't do what I expect. He doesn't snarl or snap. He doesn't grab the camera or go for Bodie's neck.

It's worse.

Cooper Lowry falters. He looks straight into the camera—right at *me*, I'd swear—and hesitates. Then his expression becomes broken.

"I have no fucking idea."

The viewers hear a bleep, of course. But I hear what goes unsaid. The restless fear of a man without a plan.

Garrett comes back into the room and notes the look on my face, then swings his gaze to see what's captured my attention. His shoulders sag and he lets out a little gusting sigh.

"You know that clip's a few weeks old, right? They've been on this story for a while now. The whole retirement thing—will he or won't he?"

Somewhere along the way, in the days after it became clear I was out of options, I'd kind of forgotten about what Cooper was dealing with. The possible end of his career, the decisions he was faced with about his future. Even when we were in his truck after the auction sale and he brought it up, I was so wrapped up in my own bullshit that I didn't take it all in. Cooper was losing the only life he'd ever known. What he needed, more than anything, was to find a new home for all that determination and drive.

Then he went and gave me my world back, a second chance at everything. All he wanted in return was the same, the opportunity for a second act—with me, just so long as I was sure.

The reality was that Cooper and I needed each other as much as we wanted each other. And while I might have once thought that sounded a little too co-dependent to be sane or reasonable, I know that isn't our truth.

Our truth is bigger than self-help buzz words. Our truth is two people who met at the right time, knee-deep in their own cruddy catastrophes, who deserved the possibility of better days to come. All we had to do was take it one step at a time.

The first step? Bring Cooper home.

=30=

(Cooper)

When I near Whitney's driveway, the afternoon sun is starting to dim behind the ridge of mountains that skirt her property. I pull in slowly, doing my best not to announce my arrival by way of a Cummins motor salute, because with all that's happened since I last saw her, I need a moment to get myself together before walking in there.

She sent a text yesterday—nothing definitive, just letting me know that she had made her decision. No hints, nothing but a request to see me. I left Texas this morning and rerouted my usual way home by jumping on Highway 50 outside Pueblo, then linking up with Highway 92 to Hotchkiss. A few hours later, and here I am. Cautiously hopeful, but anxious enough to wish this were already over and that I knew whether I was about to start a new chapter or lose everything I truly wanted.

Frost covers the rows of apple trees and with the late afternoon light waning, the limbs practically glow in the haze of the setting sun. That sight reminds me of every reason I had for doing what I did. No question, Whitney deserved another chance to make this work.

I step out of the truck and give my knee a stretch, then make my way up to the porch and pause for a moment, taking a deep breath before knocking on the screen door.

"It's open! I'm in the kitchen!"

Jesus. Christ.

I close my eyes and count to ten. Storming in there and reading her the riot act is not the best greeting, but the woman refuses to follow the basic bylaws of home safety. Like locking the fucking door. Or not inviting people in without getting eyes on them first. Simple, straightforward shit.

When I shove open the door, I don't bother to stop and take my boots off—my mom would kill me, but I have bigger issues. I halt in place just beyond the threshold to the kitchen.

"How many times do I have to tell you not to do that? You don't know who's at the goddam door. I'm begging you to demonstrate some sense of self-preservation. Please."

Whitney peers out from behind a large cardboard box that's set atop her kitchen table, from which she's unpacking dinnerware. In front of the box is an old television set, and I mean *old*. We're talking 1980s at best. It has rabbit ears and dials, for Christ's sake. I point at it.

"What the fuck is that?"

Her hair is up in a messy knot on the top of her head and she's wearing my favorite sweater. The black one with the deep V-neck, and maybe it's the angle or the lighting—shit, I don't know—but I'm almost positive her tits look bigger. Maybe it's just because I haven't seen her in a couple of weeks and my hands have barely survived the deprivation of touching her. Or maybe I'm just a lovesick fool who will always see her, want her, and do my best to catalog every plentiful inch of her body.

She tilts her head and narrows her eyes. "It's your welcome-home present."

"My what?"

Whitney lets out a huff. "OK, you're ruining this. I wanted you to come in here and do your grumpy silent thing for a second. That way I could tell you I made a decision, that I love you and want to be your partner in everything. Then I would show you this symbolic gesture of my love."

She sweeps her hands open in a *ta-da* gesture at the so-called television. "That I'd wanted to make sure you'd never have to stream football on Thanksgiving again. So I drove to a biker's house in Crawford to acquire this free TV he had on craigslist."

The only thing I really hear is that my beautiful Whitney drove to some greasy guy's house, a dude who had an ad on craigslist—also known as the best way to lure unsuspecting women into your evil chamber of secrets—to acquire this . . . *thing*.

"You went to a fucking biker's house? Alone?"

She sweeps her hands wide again, all but saying *duh*, while also being adult enough to not actually say it. I raise my brows.

She lets her arms drop, props her hands on her hips, and tilts her head.

"First off, my dad was a biker, so you should tread lightly here. But we can discuss that later. Let me repeat the important part again, just in case you didn't hear me the first time around. I love you, Cooper. I choose you. I want this."

The room is so quiet I can hear every creak in the house and I'm suddenly able to process what she just said. She wants this. She wants *me*.

Whitney lays one of her hands against the amber-colored pendant she's wearing, pressing the stone to her skin. A flush rises across her chest and then it becomes hard for me to remember who I was before she shuffled her way into that drugstore, and into every part of my heart.

I clear my throat but it doesn't help. My voice still breaks. "You're sure?"

She nods once. "Yes."

I take a step closer, desperate for the feel of her. She closes the distance and puts one of her hands to my chest. Then there's nothing but the ease of my body finding hers.

"All of it? Marriage, babies, apple trees, and dogs?"

She curls up her lip. "Um, no. You didn't mention marriage before. We aren't getting married."

My lips curl up just the same. "The fuck we aren't. That's how it's done."

A scowl from her. "Marriage is just an archaic, patriarchal smokescreen. It doesn't mean anything."

My hands find her hips and I give them a rough jerk into mine. Her eyes flare.

"It's also a way for two people to show how much they love each other. How committed they are. In my case, it's also the best way to keep from breaking my mother's heart."

Whitney draws her hands down my chest and works them between us, teasing across the fly of my jeans. The move means my heart starts to thump wildly and my dick starts to wake up from his depressed slumber of the last few weeks. She brings her voice down a notch and slows the delivery of her words, because she can feel it all.

"I'm on board with everything else. The orchard, the dogs, the kids. Even though your high-handed genetics probably mean I'll eventually end up trying to corral a passel of boys who are into rolling coal in their big, obnoxious trucks or mudding in some farmer's field while listening to terrible bro-country songs. Plus, they'll be all brawny and stubborn—"

I step forward and take her face in my hands. I kiss her. Hard and fierce, long and heated, the way we both need and deserve. When I pull back, her eyes stay closed. I brush a few tendrils of hair off her forehead and kiss a spot there.

"Our kids will be awesome. Rolling coal or mudding, playing ball or trying to save the world one tree at a time, they'll be perfect. Don't worry about that."

I kiss her again, softer this time. Once we both retreat, I take another glance around the kitchen. I need a notepad. So many things to do.

Whitney pinches my side. "Hey, don't do that right now—disappear on me and into your head. Speak, Cooper."

"I'm thinking about all the things we need to do. I mean, we can't raise kids in this house—it's too small. We have to remodel. Or, shit, we'll build another house, one for us to live in, and keep this as base for the orchard. Maybe we can set up a retail store here and really focus on agritourism endeavors. Tours, a gift shop, a farm stand—"

Before I can catch her, Whitney is slumping out of my arms and landing softly, cross-legged on the kitchen floor. I panic, thinking she just executed the world's most graceful fainting episode, but when she lazily drops her head into her palms, I realize she came to sit on the floor on purpose. I do my best to find the floor right in front of her, albeit less gracefully.

My hands come to her shoulders and I give them the gentlest shake I can offer. "Babe, what's wrong?"

Her head rocks back and forth in her upturned palms. Finally, Whitney lifts her head to face me and her eyes are worried.

"This is enough for you, right? I don't want you to leave football unless *you're* sure. Don't do it for me, or this place. All of it will be here when the time is right. Do it when you're ready."

My fucking amazing Whitney. Checking in to be sure I've made my own decision the right way. If I'd had any reservations, this would have sealed the deal. She's the best person I could hope to share a life with because she understands why I am the way I am—the traits that I built my success on are the same traits that make moving on so hard. But Whitney is generous and funny, full of fire and heart—and she's made me want to find the same in myself, here, with her.

"I'm ready. This is the right time; I'm sure of it."

I urge her closer, and Whitney crawls into my lap, straddling her legs around my waist and wrapping her arms around my shoulders. My dick immediately registers the position of our bodies, and he's quickly able to deduce how easily we could make this scene less about emotion and more about some serious makeup fucking. The front of her body presses to mine and my hands itch to perform a complete inspection of her tits, of size and weight and softness, but I force myself to keep them around her waist. She draws back and taps her index finger gently to the center of my forehead.

"You're doing it again. Disappearing into your head."

I blink. "I was thinking about your tits."

Her mouth drops open slightly, her face blank for a moment. Then she laughs, sounding light but exasperated. Maybe I should apologize for objectifying her. Gently, I press my lips to her temple.

"I was also thinking about how from damn near day one, I think you got what makes me tick. And you never asked me to be something else; you just loved me anyway. I just want to make you feel the same way."

Whitney puts a soft kiss to each of my now-closed eyelids. Voice lowered, she nearly whispers. "You do."

Another kiss, this time to my forehead.

"But I don't love you *anyway*. I love you *because*. Because you're a grouch, because you're determined, because you're a good man. Because, Cooper."

I stifle the contented sigh that wants to escape. I am not an adolescent girl. I do not swoon or sigh, unless that sigh is to express my exasperation or irritation. But on the inside? I'm an almost-retired pro football player who's doodling hearts and kittens in my Trapper Keeper.

Whitney shifts her weight and my dick gets us back on track. I use one of my hands to trace the V-neck of her sweater, then tug the neckline down far enough that the lace of her bra comes into view. She takes a slow, deep breath in.

"You do realize I can't actually watch a game on that TV, right?"

Whitney makes a half-hearted questioning sound and arches her back, moving all of her softness closer to my hands. Screw it. I think she missed this part almost as much as I did. I tug the sweater and the lace cup down until she's on display. She releases a soft moan as her head drops back. I haven't even really touched her yet, so now's probably the time to let her in on what needs to happen. Pretty sure if I do this right, I'll get my way.

"I'll need a big screen. Like a seventy-five-incher. With 4K." She groans. "Ultra HD."

I let my palm hover just over her flesh. Whitney lets her head drop forward enough to lock her eyes on mine.

"I don't know anything about what you just said, but I love you *because,* Cooper. That includes the big screen and the video games."

I grin, cup her flesh, and she rewards my touch with an impatient twist of her hips. Maybe now's the time to push my luck just a tiny bit more.

"Marry me."

"No." Her voice is light and breathy, but her tone is decisive.

Huh. I'll have to keep working on that one. No worries; I have plenty of time. Whitney knows exactly what she's getting into with me and I have every day of forever to work on convincing her—and all those nights to go along with them.

If it takes a hundred years, no matter. I'll keep asking. Keep proving myself to her and to what we are together.

Until I've given her every reason to say yes.

Acknowledgments

First and foremost, thank you to Elana Cohen for offering a second (and third) opportunity for me to move forward as a published author. I'm tremendously grateful for your support of the stories I want to tell—and the way I want to tell them.

Another big thank-you to my agent Victoria Lowes, for your dedication and persistence. Thank you for doing what you do with endless grace.

Thank you to Lori M. for beta reading *First Step Forward* and providing sharp, insightful feedback that was essential in making this book stronger. To Carly Bornstein of CB Editing, thank you for providing a manuscript review that was both comprehensive *and* workable—your notes helped better define these characters and their story.

To the entire Pocket Books team, thank you for making these books sparkle and shine, from beginning to end. A special thank-you to Marla Daniels for stepping in to steer the ship on this one for a bit.

Thank you to every reader who picked up the *True* titles

and by doing so, helped make this new series a reality—
I hope you come to love the Grand Valley stories. Your
continued support is what makes all of this possible.

And to Warren . . . thank you for making it easy to
write about good guys with great hearts—who say what
they mean, mean what they say, and stay true to what matters most.

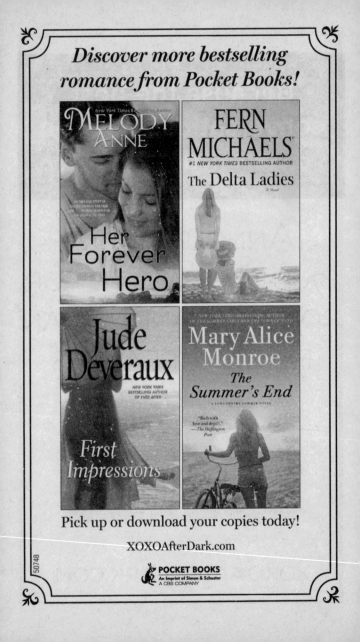